“Is Kheldrin to b[illegible] freedom and the price of my crown?”

At this, ai’Jihaar squeezed Anghara’s hand lightly in support, and then let go, stepping away. But it was al’Tamar who spoke first, his eyes blazing.

“No hostage,” he said proudly, his head high. “Sif Kir Hama will find out the hard way. This prize is beyond him.”

“He has an army . . . an army willing to die for him,” Anghara whispered.

“They may well be called upon to do that,” ai’Jihaar said. “We have been invaded before . . . and none have stayed long enough to leave more than a few lines in the Records. Sif knows nothing about Kheldrin. He may not yet realize he has a foe in this land which could well prove too large a bite even for him to swallow.”

“What foe?” said Anghara, her voice still soft—but her eyes had kindled quietly, and now glowed almost silver in the firelight.

“The desert,” ai’Jihaar said, then laughed unexpectedly, laughter which fell into the expectant silence like shards of glass. “The desert fights for us.”

BOOKS BY
Alma Alexander

THE SECRETS OF JIN-SHEI
CHANGER OF DAYS
THE HIDDEN QUEEN

CHANGER OF DAYS

ALMA ALEXANDER

An Imprint of HarperCollins*Publishers*

This is a work of fiction. Names, characters, places, and incidents are products of the author's imagination or are used fictitiously and are not to be construed as real. Any resemblance to actual events, locales, organizations, or persons, living or dead, is entirely coincidental.

EOS
An Imprint of HarperCollins*Publishers*
10 East 53rd Street
New York, New York 10022-5299

ISBN: 0-06-076575-5
www.eosbooks.com

First Eos paperback printing: June 2005

First published in New Zealand by Voyager, an imprint of HarperCollins*Publishers*

Printed in the U.S.A.

10 9 8 7 6 5 4 3 2 1

To that great Once and Future Fellowship of Writers—
from the legends to those with names as yet unknown, who
inspired me, entertained me, encouraged me and finally
made me one of them.

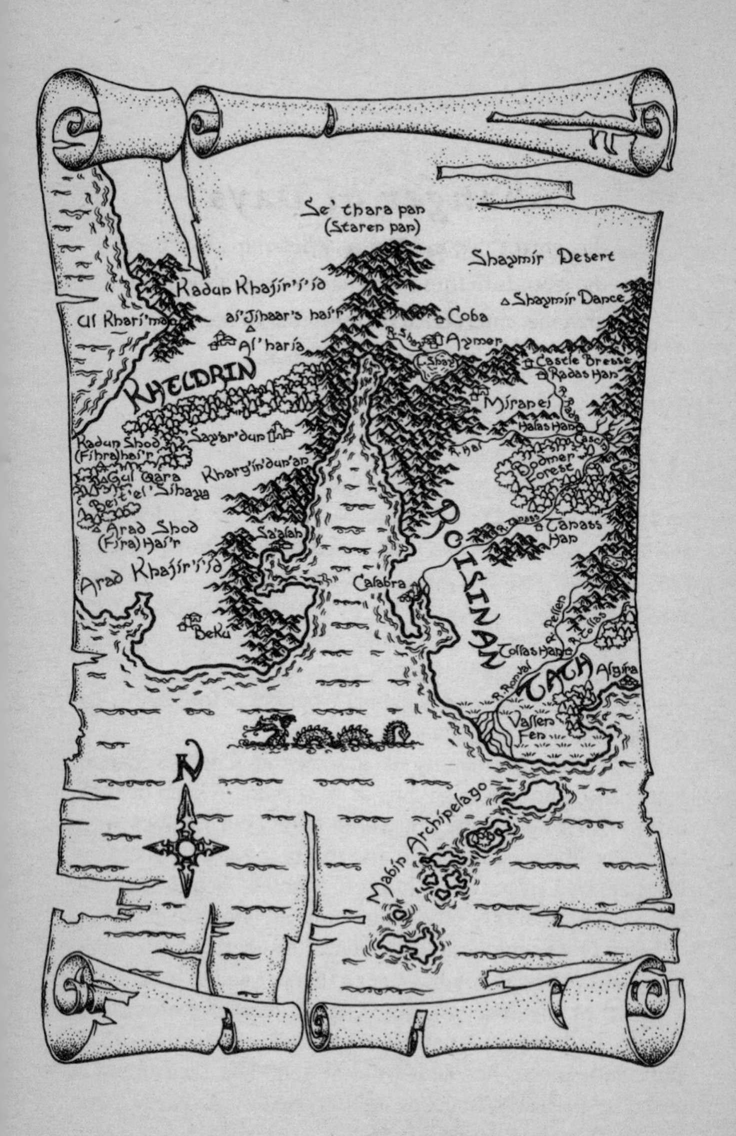

Se' thara pan
(Staren pan)
Shaymir Desert
Shaymir Dance
Kadun Khajir'i'id
al'Jihaar's hai'r
Ul Khari'ma
Al'haria
Coba
R. Shay
Aymer
L. Shay
Castle Bresse
Radas Han
R. Radas
Miranei
Halas Han
R. Hal
Casch
Bodmer Forest
KHELDRIN
Say'ar'dun
Kadun Shod
(Fihra) hai'r
Gul Qara
Beit'el'Sihaya
Kharg'in'dun'an
Arad Shod
(Fira) Hai'r
Sa'alah
R. Canass
Canass Han
ROISINAN
Arad Khajir'i'id
Calabra
Beku
R. Pellen
R. Tollas
Tollas Han
R. Ronval
TACH
Algira
Vallen Fen
Mabin Archipelago
N

Changer of Days

The story so far

When Red Dynan, King of Roisinan, dies in battle, his illegitimate son, Sif, is offered command of the army and the crown by Dynan's general, Fodrun. As Sif leads his troops to victory, Dynan's widowed queen, Rima, realizes her nine-year-old daughter, Princess Anghara, is in mortal danger. The Queen spirits the girl away to Cascin, to the household of her sister, Chella, while she tries to ensure Anghara's succession. Rima's fears are justified, and she dies in Sif's conquest of Roisinan—but not before laying the groundwork for Anghara's succession.

Anghara's real identity is a secret at Chella's manor, where she is known as Brynna in an attempt to keep her safe from Sif. However, the household tutor Feor realizes Anghara bears the seeds of Sight, the ability to see events hidden from normal eyes. Feor, himself Sighted, begins training her, as well as subtly preparing her to reclaim her throne.

But it proves impossible to conceal Anghara. Untrained in Sight, she poses no small danger to herself and to others, and a wretched incident involves Kieran, another fosterling at Cascin, with whom Anghara establishes a special relationship, and Ansen, her aunt's oldest son. The confrontation costs Ansen dearly; he loses sight in one eye. Anghara's true identity is revealed, and Ansen, bitter and angry, stores the knowledge silently against payment of the blood debt. Chella sends the girl to Castle Bresse, a place of safety where she can be fully trained in the use of her gift.

Bresse provides sanctuary for less than three years before Ansen betrays Anghara. She is far from trained, but the sisters manage to spirit her out of the castle before an enraged Sif turns his fury against anyone with Sight. He proclaims there is no place for witchery in his realm and burns Bresse to the ground. All the sisters die in the flames.

Travelling alone, Anghara meets a blind beggar woman, who turns out to be a Kheldrini *an'sen'thar,* a priestess from a strange land. The people of Kheldrin are far from human and their powers prove to be old and vast. The priestess, who perceives an extraordinary potential in the young girl, breaks with centuries-old tradition and asks Anghara to return with her to Kheldrin. The priestess assumes the role of teacher, and Anghara spends the next two years adapting the techniques of the Kheldrini *sen'en'thari* to her Sight.

After receiving the last prophecy of a dying and venerated oracle deep in the Kheldrini desert, Anghara finds in herself the power to defy al'Khur, the Kheldrini Lord of Death himself, demanding back a life he has taken. He bows to her will, calling her "Changer." He reveals to her that she has a great destiny but must forget their encounter until she is ready to claim it. Anghara is then instrumental in raising another oracle to replace the one which offered her its last words—and the new oracle's first prophecy is a call to return to her kingdom.

The Prophecy of Gul Khaima

"Reaching from the dark, the bleeding land waits.
A friend and a foe await at return;
love shall be given to him who hates.

In fires lit long ago the blameless burn;
a broken spirit shall opened lie,
a bitter secret to learn.

Beneath an ancient crown the unborn die;
the hunter is snared by the prey he baits;
sight shall be returned to the blind eye."

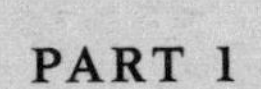

PART 1

Kieran

It was raining in Roisinan.

The Kheldrini ship glided into the harbor of Calabra at twilight, with the first torches already guttering under sheltering roofs streaming with water. The air was rich, damp, cool, filled with the sharp, brittle smell of autumn which opened the floodgates of memory and released a torrent of small, exquisitely painful recollections into Anghara's mind. As she had found it difficult to believe that anything other than the yellow sand of Arad Khajir'i'id lay beyond the mountains that sundered the desert from the sea, so now she found it equally hard to think that there was anything else in the world except this wet autumn evening on the shores of Roisinan. There was a lump in her throat which she couldn't quite seem to swallow as she stepped off the ship, dressed decorously Roisinan-fashion and wrapped in what had once been Kieran's cloak, the same one she had taken from Cascin and treasured carefully throughout her years in Bresse and the Twilight Country—her Kheldrini finery she carried bundled up in a parcel in her hand. Home. She was home. Everything about this place she knew, she remembered, it was all stamped soul-deep into her; she forgot for the moment, lost in the sheer joy of it, why she had fled Roisinan, and the cage she had once seen hanging in a street of this very town.

She stood motionless for an instant, lifting her face into

the drizzling rain much as Kieran had been wont to do back in Cascin, and for the same reason—in the past two years Anghara had not seen water often, rain least of all. The few violent desert storms that had come her way had been a far cry from what she revelled in now—and she had all but forgotten the feel of raindrops on her skin. Her eyes were closed in a kind of rapture, and her face, if she had only stopped to think about it, was full in the light of a nearby torch, underneath a half-drawn hood that offered little concealment. A man standing a few paces away, talking to the captain of another ship which had come into harbor almost at the same time as Anghara's and had berthed alongside, glanced casually at the passenger who had just come off the Kheldrini vessel, and then looked again, narrowing his eyes in sudden interest. Before Anghara had opened her eyes and moved away from the quayside, the man had abruptly excused himself from his friend and stood waiting in the shadows. When Anghara walked away from her ship and into Calabra to look for food and shelter, he followed her at a judicious distance.

She did not choose the hostelry where ai'Jihaar had taken her on her last sojourn in this place. That held too many memories, even for her; and it was a place where the Kheldrini traders often stayed when in Roisinan. Anghara wanted to reconnect to Roisinan, not wallow in memories of Kheldrin; she picked a sturdy Roisinani inn just off the quay. She even had plans of joining the common room crowd for a while, listening to the sound of her own tongue, not heard since she left Calabra two years before—if one didn't count ai'Jihaar in the beginning, or al'Jezraal's own surprising, Shaymir-gleaned prowess. But once the landlord's buxom wife showed her into her room, the lure of the narrow bed proved too strong. Anghara hadn't realized how tired she was, how much emotion could drain one's strength, and she had been living on little else but emotion, culminating with tonight, ever since she had sailed from Sa'alah. There would be time—there would be time for everything. For now, a jaw-cracking yawn reminded her that the best thing to start with would be a good night's sleep; she yielded with good grace, leaving the common room for another time.

Her dreams were strange, laced with odd premonitions of which she could only recall the sense but not the substance when she woke the following morning. She brooded on them for as long as it took her to dress and get ready to step outside and begin reclaiming Roisinan, only to dismiss them as she closed the door of her room behind her. A pale sun was shining from a washed-out sky, the air crisp and cool from last night's rain; the day was full of promise. Anghara breathed deeply of it, touching again the edges of last night's joy, tasting it as though it was sweet wine—and then, gray eyes determined, she set her mind sternly on what lay ahead.

The first order of business was the purchase of a horse. Anghara spared a swift, regretful thought for the gray dun she had ridden into Sa'alah—his owner, the yellow-eyed young man from Kharg'in'dun'an, had said that nothing she would ever ride afterward would match that mount. She set out in the direction where, according to the landlord, lay a posting stables which might offer a far more ordinary beast for sale.

She had left her premonitions behind in her room, but on this bright, innocent morning she could not get rid of a prickling between her shoulder blades. Several times she turned sharply, but never saw anything untoward behind her, and hated herself for waking this suspicion so soon.

What if someone recognized her?

Fool, she chided herself, after yet another glance behind. *The years in Kheldrin, and before that the years in Bresse . . . Who is likely to recognize you after all this time?*

But the feeling persisted. Perhaps because of it, she was far too eager to conclude the deal for the horse—to be out of this place, with its invisible eyes. The stable owner sensed her urgency, and got away with far more than he would if Anghara's full attention had been on the bargaining. Nevertheless, she walked out of the stables as the owner of a quiet bay mare; the mare had cast a shoe the previous day, however, and it was agreed she would be delivered to Anghara's inn after she'd received the required attention from the smith.

Outside, the inexplicable menace had thickened. Anghara shivered as she stood for a moment at the stable's door, raking the street with anxious eyes. Still nothing, still nobody.

"I can leave as soon as I get the mare," she murmured to herself, more to reassure herself by the sound of her voice than anything else. "In the meantime . . . it's probably best to go back to the inn . . . and wait."

She stepped off the threshold into the street, and a few quick, cautious steps took her around the corner. The apprehension which beat in her had put a furtiveness in her step which she had to consciously quash, if she didn't want to find herself thought of as guilty by suspicion. Every so often she caught herself looking like an escaping thief, anxious to avoid detection. "There's nobody out there," she told herself firmly. "Nobody."

But there was.

Not behind her, but ahead. Even as she lifted her eyes, she recognized the youth who had paused to glance at her on the other side of the street with a sudden pang of knowledge which made her heart miss a beat.

Adamo! Or was it Charo . . . She never had been able to tell them apart at first sight . . .

But even as she straightened, her eyes wide, her hand half raised in a motion of greeting, it was too late. A quiet step behind her was her only warning; even as she began to turn, an arm slid around her waist and yanked her into an archway that opened into the street. Another hand, bearing a rag drenched with something pungent, clapped over her mouth and nose. It all happened too fast—she didn't have a chance to reach for the power that could have saved her. Before she lost consciousness she was dimly aware of the hand holding the rag none too gently pinching shut her nose while someone held a vial of some noxious-tasting liquid to her lips. She swallowed convulsively, gasping for air, before her conscious mind had a chance to refuse. The drug, for some kind of a drug it had to be, was potent and took effect almost immediately, spreading in a slow liquid fire into her bloodstream.

Somewhere deep inside her something was laughing hysterically. *Hama dan ar'i'id,* a small voice chanted; you are never alone in the desert. And she had behaved in the streets of Calabra with that dictum in mind. But she was no longer in the desert, and she had paid for her carelessness. She thought she shaped a few syllables in a dying voice—*Adamo . . . Charo . . . help me*—but the cry remained in her mind, and she finally went limp, collapsing into the arms of her captors as she slid into unconsciousness.

They had been quiet and professional, and they had not drawn any attention to themselves—it had almost looked as though Anghara had stepped backward into the archway herself. But there had been six of them; Adamo saw them all, and he was alone. It would have been foolhardy to attempt a rescue, especially here in the streets of Sif's harbor city against soldiers wearing Sif's colors beneath their concealing cloaks. But without a doubt it was Anghara. The relentless search for his foster sister had been the kernel around which Kieran's small band of rebels had formed. These were proving a hard nut for Sif to crack, simply because he could never find them. There was a danger, simply by standing on the street and showing he had seen what had happened, that Adamo might well draw unwelcome attention onto himself, and by inference onto Kieran's group—

Anghara's only chance of rescue. So he hunched his shoulders, lowered his eyes and hurried on. He didn't need to follow the men who had seized Anghara. There could be only one place they meant to take her.

The posting stables around the corner seemed the most obvious place for her to have been coming from, and Adamo, after a small hesitation, ducked inside. "Anyone here?"

The stable owner peered out of a stall, wiping his hands on already filthy breeches. "Can I help you, young sir?"

"My master has need of a horse," said Adamo, adopting all the swaggering arrogance of a young squire. "A quiet beast; it's for his lady. Hers was lamed the other day, and it is urgent that they leave for home at once. Have you any for loan or sale?"

"Well, now, I don't really keep ladies' mounts," said the stable owner, scratching his head. "Perhaps the gray over there?"

Adamo gazed at the indicated gelding with a jaundiced eye. "He's swaybacked, and looks as if he would shake my lady's bones apart," he complained. He looked around. There could have been only one reason Anghara had been in here, to obtain a mount. Now which . . . "How about the bay, there?"

"She's just been sold, not minutes ago," said the stable owner, not without regret. He could probably have gotten an even better price off this green young retainer than he had from the preoccupied girl who had just left.

"The young lady I saw a moment ago coming out of your establishment?"

"That's the one," the stable owner nodded. "The mare's to go to her at the King's Inn just as soon as I can get the smith to look to the shoe she's cast."

Adamo clicked his tongue impatiently. "But nothing else that I see here will really do . . . the King's Inn, you say? My master's need is urgent; perhaps if I could speak to the young lady . . ."

"That's nothing to do with me," the stable owner shrugged. "The horse is to go to her, she's paid me fair and square, and if you want the beast you must talk to her. But she seemed quite set on the animal. I doubt that she'll sell . . ."

"Are there any other stables nearby?" Adamo asked for form's sake, and listened with some impatience to the litany of instructions the query brought forth. As soon as he could make his escape, he hurried back the way he had come, peering cautiously into the niche where the two men who had attacked Anghara had pulled her, and into which Adamo had seen their four henchmen follow. It was a gateway, leading into a cobbled courtyard, but both the gateway and the courtyard were empty. Adamo raked the place with his eyes but there was no further sign of them. Sif's men and their prey must have slipped behind one of the closed doors. Swearing softly, he turned and hastened down the street, toward the harbor and the King's Inn. What possessed her, he thought violently and irrationally, to choose an inn with such an ill-omened name? And where had she been all this time? It was partly the shock of seeing that familiar face so unexpectedly, when he, one of many, had almost given up hope of ever finding Anghara again, that had paralyzed him for one precious instant, which Sif's men had seized to good advantage. He should have . . . He should have . . .

The possibilities of what he should have done buzzed round in his head like angry bees. Even as he was racing to the King's Inn, he was berating himself for not following the abductors. Perhaps they would stay in the city another day in some lair, and a rescue could have been tried with the handful of Kieran's men who were in Calabra. But it would be difficult to catch Sif's soldiers by surprise, and if there had been six on this detail it stood to reason there were more where these had come from, and possibly still more within earshot. And, counting Adamo himself, there were only five all told in his own small group. They had not been sent here as a fighting unit. And Kieran . . . Kieran would have to be told . . .

Wishing all the while that Charo, who was much better suited for this kind of intrigue, was in his shoes, Adamo managed to charm the landlord's wife at the King's Inn into believing he was her newest lodger's half-brother, who should have been here to meet her yesterday but was delayed on the road. After one or two lukewarm refusals, she eventually agreed to let him wait for Anghara's return in her room.

A swift search gave him nothing but more mystery. The package containing Anghara's Kheldrini regalia baffled him; if the landlady had been one whit less sure of herself, Adamo would have been quite prepared to believe she had let him into the wrong room. Knowing with bitter certainty that Anghara would not be back to claim any belongings she had left behind, Adamo packed the intriguing paraphernalia and, giving the landlady a wide and cautious berth, took his leave.

Only one of his men was at their lodgings. He'd been laying out a solitaire with a battered pack of cards when Adamo arrived, and looked up with an expression of patient boredom at the sound of the opening door. One glimpse of Adamo's face and that expression fled; the man leapt to his feet with a haste that overturned the small table before him, sending cards flying everywhere. "What in the world has happened?" he demanded. "You look as though you just saw a ghost."

"I have, and she's very much alive . . . and in trouble," Adamo said, tossing Anghara's package onto his bed. "Where are the others? We move out today. Kieran spoke about pulling out from the base shortly; if he's not there he might take some finding, and this can't wait."

The other man had turned pale, knowing instantly the identity of Adamo's "ghost." "Are you sure?" he gasped.

"There is no doubt," Adamo said grimly. "Come on, Javor, move. They will also move today; with that prey they will not wait. Our only chance lies in getting to Kieran in time, and cutting them off before they reach Miranei."

But it took over an hour for the other three in their company to be rounded up, and by then Adamo had changed his mind, concocting a different plan.

"Javor, you, Helm and Merric cut across to the fords of the Hal; make sure you are there before this group. It shouldn't be difficult, there's three of you and the Gods only know how many of them, with a prisoner to slow them down. If you can, harry them—but don't do anything foolish. Stay at the fords; I'll go with Ward to find Kieran, or if nothing else to get some reinforcements. We'll meet you at the fords; if we get there in time, we can be waiting for them. If not . . . we'll have to trust to speed and providence."

Kieran had put Adamo in charge of this group, and the men scattered according to his orders. He and Ward, the grizzled, taciturn old veteran, left their three companions at Calabra's northern gates and cut east toward the river, riding hell for leather toward the Tanassa Hills and their ruined Dance—closing, had they but known it, one of the circles in Anghara's life. One of Kieran's secret bases lay in a cave a bare stone's throw from the Dance where, once already, Anghara had found a friend.

They rode their beasts almost into the ground, and made Tanassa Hills on their third day out of Calabra. Adamo flung himself off his trembling horse almost at the cave's mouth and staggered inside, his vision blurring from fatigue. "Kieran? Is Kieran here?"

"He should be back before dark," said somebody whose face kept sliding out of focus. "Hey! Cair! Some wine! What happened to you up in the city? Faith, but you look spent! It must be serious news!"

Before dark were the only words Adamo heard. He glanced out through the cave mouth at the dim autumn day. "What is the hour now?"

"Almost noon," came the mystified reply.

Before dark. That was too long. Adamo straggled onto his feet again. "Where did Kieran go?" he asked huskily. "Can anyone help me find him?"

Glances were exchanged over his head. "Wouldn't you rather wait? You might miss him altogether, him coming in, you going out after him . . ."

"There's no time," Adamo said. *Every hour I wait is wasted, every hour gives them the edge . . .*

"I'll go with you," a young man said, already fastening a cloak over his shoulders. "Can your mount manage? It looks done in. Take a rested horse."

Even Kieran wasn't sure how he had become the acknowledged leader of a dedicated group of rebels who had achieved the dubious distinction of being an avowed thorn in Sif's side. It had all started with Feor sending him out after Anghara—and then Sif had started his systematic annihilation of the Sighted. Kieran had needed to be in the right place at the right time only a few times before the dispossessed, those bereft of land or spouses or children, began to form the nucleus of his following. Whole villages were pledged to him now, less than two years after he'd started protecting the helpless and the vulnerable against Sif's scourge—and it was as well, for Sif knew his name, and would have given much to smash him. But for Kieran Cullen of Shaymir there were more boltholes in Roisinan than even Sif could easily cover. Sif could only hope that one day soon the youth would bite off too large a morsel, engage in a conflict too big for him to finish, and be finished by it in his turn. Either that, or some traitor be found to sell the secret of Kieran's bases, so they could be found and destroyed, smoking him out into the open where Sif could hunt him at his leisure. In the meantime, Kieran found his band swiftly growing—where Sif was still capable of winning his men, heart and soul, and knowing that those men would go through any Hell at his word, what ai'Jihaar had foretold had also come to pass. Too many in his land now hated him for what he had unleashed upon his people. And Kieran, aside from providing the leadership to do something about that, had also never stopped believing Anghara Kir Hama was alive—and if the hope of her name had taken root in her people, that could only be laid at the door of Kieran's own unswerving faith.

He had gone to meet one of his informants on the day Adamo had arrived with the news, at the edge of a village in a valley fold on the outskirts of Bodmer Forest. There were plenty of villages where he could have ridden in openly and been welcomed with open arms. This village was not one of them, which was why he waited instead under the eaves of the forest for the man to come to him.

This was where Adamo and his companion found him. Kieran had been standing a little apart from the rest, his deep green cloak pushed back over his shoulders to reveal dully gleaming mail and allow easy access to the sword which hung at his waist. He'd turned with a half smile at the sound of approaching horses and footsteps, expecting the man from the village below, but it vanished almost instantly as he realized who his visitors were.

"Adamo!" he said, taking a swift step forward to lay one hand on the trailing rein of Adamo's horse and steady his foster brother in the saddle with the other. "What are you doing here?"

Adamo slipped out of the saddle and gripped Kieran's arm with the strength of the demented, not to be expected from a man so obviously on the edge of exhaustion. "Anghara, Kieran. I saw her in Calabra."

Kieran went white at the name, and clutched at Adamo's shoulder with an equally rigid grasp. "Where is she?"

Adamo's knees finally buckled underneath him. "They got her. Sif's men. I saw it, but could do nothing . . . they were six, and I was alone . . ."

"They'll be halfway to Miranei by now," said Kieran, through bloodless lips.

"I sent Javor with the other two . . . to head them off at the fords if they can . . ." said Adamo, and pitched forward into Kieran's arms in a dead faint.

Kieran stood still for a moment, holding Adamo very gently. *Dear Gods,* he thought desperately, *was it for this that she survived . . . that I searched for her for all those hopeless months, and was not there when she needed me the most . . .*

But that one moment of regret was all he allowed himself. He turned, blue eyes splinters of hard steel, his voice terse. "Kel, you stay here . . . when our fellow arrives, make my apologies, tell him I was called . . ."

"Tell him the truth, Kieran," Kel said, eyes flashing with both dismay and exhilaration.

Kieran clenched his fist. "Yes," he said fiercely, "tell him the truth, damn it; he will understand what this means. Tell him to proclaim this on the village common if he has to; the more persistent the rumor that Anghara is alive and Sif has her prisoner, the more damage it will cause him. I must go. If they left at the same time as Adamo and rode at some speed, there is very little likelihood we can still cut them off at the fords, but I'm going to try. Once he has her inside the keep . . ."

"Gods' speed, Kieran," Kel said. He had been with Kieran from the beginning, and knew that Anghara was more to him than the lost Queen of Roisinan, who would replace Sif and bring peace and mercy to the realm. She was all that—but above everything else she was a small girl who had once wept in Kieran's arms, who had been ready to lash out, at the risk of her own existence, at anyone who raised an arm against him.

The two men clasped each other's arm for a moment, holding one another's gaze, and then Kieran turned away. Adamo had regained a woozy kind of consciousness, and someone had helped him mount. He sat weaving in the saddle. "Go without me," he said, and it was torn from his throat. "I couldn't keep up. I'll come after you . . . as soon as I can."

"Detouring back to the cave would take too much time," said Kieran. "Go back and rouse the men. Bid them follow at once; we'll meet on the plains."

"It is done," Adamo whispered, turning his horse with a weary pressure of his knees.

"Make sure he stays in the saddle," Kieran said to the man who had ridden with Adamo.

"I'll get him there safely, and deliver the message," the other said. "Then look for me on the plains."

And they were gone, riding away through the trees. Kieran vaulted onto his own horse. "Will one of you bear another message?" he asked the rest of the men who had been with him, all mounted and waiting.

"I will," said one, after an almost imperceptible hesitation. They'd all known what the request meant—a wild ride in the opposite direction, away from the confrontation to come. But Charo was at another secret base near Cascin, and he was also Anghara's cousin and foster brother, who had been no less zealous in the search. He'd want to know; he'd want to ride to them, even though he would be far too late for either victory or defeat.

"Tell him what we know," said Kieran, without repeating unnecessary details he knew the messenger was well aware of. "Tell him we will leave a message at the fords if he misses us there . . ."

"It is done," the man said. He dug his heels into his horse's flanks, turning the beast almost in a pirouette, and took off at a gallop toward a road that would lead him through Bodmer Forest.

Kieran gazed after him for a moment, where the undergrowth he'd barrelled through still swayed, and then drew at his own reins. "The rest of you . . . follow me."

They flew across the plains like eagles, but they were riding after a foe who had a head start and who would have reason to move fast. Kieran's heart was a stone in his breast; if he failed here, then it would be all but impossible to do anything for Anghara. Not even he had challenged Sif in the shadow of Miranei Keep. No one had.

It said much for the power of Kieran's vision, which had taken deep roots in his men, that the bulk of his force joined his handful on the plains within two days. They all pushed on, grimly intent, although Kieran, who did not want to reach the fords just in time to see Sif's contingent slaughter his exhausted men, kept the pace just short of headlong. The plains of Roisinan vanished beneath the flying horses of Kieran's band; they grudged the hours of darkness when they had to stop and allow the animals a few hours' breathing space.

It was a gallant chase, but it had always been just a hope, and it proved vain. When, close to their goal, they spotted the thin column of smoke, Kieran sent a pair of scouts to investigate. One soon returned, his face gray and grim.

"It's Adamo's man, Javor," he reported, reining in his horse next to Kieran.

"Just Javor?" Kieran asked sharply.

"The others are dead." It was a blunt statement of fact, but these were seasoned men. This was not the first time death had stalked them.

"What happened?"

"There were only three of them," the other said ominously. "Perhaps you'd better hear it from Javor."

When Kieran reached the camp, Javor was having a none-too-clean bandage removed from a deep gash in his shoulder. The second scout, who had stayed behind to do the duties of a healer as best he might, looked up as the troop arrived.

"This looks nasty," he said. "Where's Madec? It ought to be cleaned, and bandaged properly, and I think he's got a fever."

Kieran slid off his horse and came to kneel beside Javor. "What happened?" he repeated quietly.

"Adamo told us to harry them," Javor said, through teeth chattering from the ague shaking him. "But there is only so much three men can do . . . We got here ahead of them . . . but they were over fifty strong, and we could see her, she was in their midst . . ."

Kieran bit his lip. "What did you do?"

"If only there had been more of us . . ." said Javor.

Madec, Kieran's healer, had arrived by this stage and was kneeling at Javor's other side, laying him gently on his back onto a clean cloak spread on the ground.

"He's almost delirious, Kieran," Madec said.

"You can dose him in a minute. I need to know . . ."

Javor tried to raise himself on one elbow, but he chose the wounded arm, and simply buckled again. Madec bent over him, frowning, but Javor stretched out his good hand to clutch at Kieran's sleeve.

"We tried to hold them . . . but they were too strong . . . They were here . . . only yesterday . . . yesterday morning . . ."

He sucked in his breath sharply as Madec's probing fingers moved over the wound, and then his eyes rolled back in his head, his hand failing from Kieran's arm.

"Sorry," Madec said. "He's fainted. You'll have to wait for the rest; I'll need time to get the fever down."

"Yesterday!" Kieran said, getting up in one swift, savage movement.

"We can still catch them," someone said. Someone who hadn't dismounted.

"We cannot give battle to more than fifty men, not now," said Kieran violently. "We would waste our strength, and achieve nothing. But yesterday! Dear Gods . . ."

"They are obviously riding as fast as they can," said one of Kieran's lieutenants, a man called Rochen. "They've got to be just as tired as we are. While they did not shy at riding down three men, they might balk at offering a fight to a group as large as us."

"Especially if they know what they have with them, and it seems as though they do," added another man.

"Kieran, we have a chance of catching them," said Rochen. "I say we try."

A fervent murmur ran through the men. The one who had spoken earlier had not been the only one still mounted. Kieran's gaze swept over his men with a hot pride in his eyes, and he reached for his own reins. "Six of you, stay here with Madec and Javor," he said. "Madec, you pick them." Asking for volunteers would seem to be like asking if anyone wanted a tooth pulled. "The rest of you, follow me. We'll give them a run for it."

A ragged cheer went up; weariness seemed to fall from them like a discarded mantle. Even the horses pricked up their ears; one or two even found energy for a spirited, defiant neigh. Men laughed.

Madec, who looked dangerously as if he would pick six volunteers to stay behind and then take off with Kieran himself, made his choice almost apologetically, and the named men dropped away from the main body with muttered oaths.

"Yesterday," Kieran murmured, still aghast at the smallness of the margin which had cost two men their lives. Then he urged his black mount forward. "We can get them," he said, willing himself to believe it so that the rest of his men might. "Let's go!"

They whooped and followed him, Rochen at his elbow, an incongruous grin splitting the young lieutenant's broad face. But their enthusiasm was checked abruptly with a simple and effective ruse not much further on. No other group had passed the fords of the Hal since the previous day; the swathe that had been left by the skirmish was still clearly visible, as were the tracks on the other side of the ford. What brought the pursuers up short was the sudden division of the main body of the tracks into several different trails. The group had fragmented into at least four or five smaller companies. At least one of these seemed to have taken off ahead of the others at a faster gallop; another had veered off toward the nearest foothills to the left of the plain, the first harbingers of the great mountain range that had given the throne in Miranei its ancient name. A third group had ridden eastward, back toward the forest. Kieran reined in, dismayed.

Rochen had also stopped, and leaned forward to study the place where the tracks diverged. "They seem to have had their own wounded," he said. "Look, over there—traces of blood. They may have stopped to take care of their men. Helm and Merric did not sell their lives cheaply."

"But which group has the queen?" asked Cair, slipping off his horse and squatting down for a closer look.

"The fastest, probably," Rochen said, straightening. "They'd make straight for home."

"Maybe that's exactly what they want us to think," said Kieran. "Perhaps they just sent two people on ahead to warn someone what is on its way, and the others took her . . ."

"We split up?" Cair suggested, getting up.

"We can't," said Rochen soberly, glancing at Kieran.

"We split up, we run the same risk Javor and the others fell foul of," said Kieran. "There is a strong possibility, for example, that those of us chasing the group headed into the hills might well find more than we bargained for."

"Ambush?" queried Cair. "For whom? They don't know they're being chased!"

"Don't they?" said Kieran, rubbing a weary hand over his temple. "Whose did they think the three men at the ford were?"

"They shouldn't have shown their hand," murmured Rochen regretfully.

"Adamo as good as told them not to. But that would have meant simply standing by and letting them take her through at their leisure."

"Which just isn't in any of us," said Rochen, with a sudden, surprising smile. "The Gods rest Helm and Merric, but they were brave, foolhardy men. Kieran . . ."

"Forget the rest," said Kieran, after a moment's thought. "Let's ride after the van. There is a good chance she is with them. If not, then they will bring her in through some postern gate . . . and I haven't the men or the knowledge to besiege every gate in Miranei. Let's try and get this lot. If Anghara isn't with them, they will know where she is, and we won't waste time chasing shadows. Let's move!"

But in the thunder of galloping hooves Kieran was still hearing only one word. *Yesterday.* Sif's men passed here yesterday. Anghara was here yesterday. Yesterday had been the window of opportunity to halt Anghara's captors in their wild ride to Miranei. Kieran had a despairing, sinking feeling that today was already too late.

For Anghara, the hours and days which followed her abduction in Calabra ran together into a bland, homogeneous grayness—her captors had the dosage of the drug nicely gauged, and another dose would materialize just as she was beginning to recover from the one before. Her head ached, and if left to herself she would have wanted nothing else but to be left in peace, to curl up in a small dark place and sleep. But sleep would not come to her, and left in peace she definitely was not. Instead, she registered dimly the commotion around her—milling, man-like shadowy forms; large, looming quadruped shapes. She was hoisted up into the arms of a mounted rider, and the horse was flying through the blur that was Calabra's street, out through the city's gate, and onto the open road. *This is not the horse I bought,* she thought blearily, still clinging to enough conscious awareness to realize the heavy, military gray horse she was on bore no resemblance to her newly acquired bay mare. But there was no strength in her to wonder at this. She drifted in and out of consciousness, staying in the saddle only through the strong arm of the rider holding her there. Once or twice she tried reaching for the power of Sight, but the experience was so unpleasant, her head splitting with a fiery stab of agony every time she tried, that she abandoned her attempts. It was easier to simply lie back against the soldier who carried her, and empty her mind of everything.

Her escort rode as though furies were after them; rests were few, and short. Fatigue exacerbated Anghara's symptoms even further. Lashed securely to the rider who carried her, she spent most of the journey in a kind of grayed-out doze, far enough from true sleep to deny her its rest yet close enough to ensure an almost complete divorce from awareness and reality. Occasional exchanges, when the old drug was just wearing off and the new dose had not yet been administered, caught at her mind; some were curiously triumphant, others merely flat and grumbling. The odd thing was that the triumph was muted, usually spoken in softer voices, apart from the main body of men; the complaints were loud and vociferous.

". . . the king will surely reward us . . ."

". . . until I tell Leil at the barracks, he'll kick himself . . ."

". . . Gods' sake, isn't it someone else's turn? My horse is nearly . . ."

". . . stupid; if she were in a litter, we'd still be three days back on the trail . . ."

". . . just who is the chit anyway? We're breaking our necks for someone we don't even know . . ."

". . . you don't think someone will try to spring her . . ."

". . . she's coming round. Who's got the *tamman*?"

And then the drug . . . *tamman?* . . . would be forced down her throat again, and she would slip away into her gray haze.

She would remember later—much later—that there had been a skirmish along the way somewhere; would recall yells, and screams, and blood, and hearing one man call her name in the melee. It would be a dim and fuzzy memory, but she thought she had lifted her head at the sound of her name—and been pushed, none too gently, into the folds of her escort's cloak, down into the dust and the grime and the sweat-smell of hard riding. She had not had the strength to try and lift it again; and had blacked out for a while. When she came back to some sort of lucidity, it was to the sensation of lying on the ground upon the same cloak, or a similar one, impregnated with the same smells and textures. She sensed movement around her: moving shadows, an occasional groan of what might have been pain.

". . . I tell you, definitely being followed . . ."

". . . split up, and leave them chasing ghosts . . ."

". . . with the fastest one? They would expect that she . . ."

". . . really think that there's only three of them . . ."

". . . a back door. They cannot guard every postern gate at Miranei . . ."

". . . time we were moving. Look to her, someone. Where's the *tamman?*"

Hills . . . steep slopes full of sweet mountain grass . . . hooves on rock . . . once, a meadow sprinkled with bright flowers which nodded at Anghara as she tried to focus her bleary vision on them. Another day, and then yet another . . . another night . . . a golden sunset . . . and then, abruptly, high walls where there had been wide-open spaces; flickering torches instead of daylight; the still, stale fug of a place which had not seen the sun since the day it had been wrought, instead of crisp, cool mountain air.

This time there was nothing fuzzy about the memory when it came—this was the place she had seen when al'Jezraal had invoked dungeons in the Catacombs of Al'haria. This was the real thing; the knowledge cut at her, sharper than any thought since she had left the stables in Calabra. Her escort left her, alone at last, and somewhere above in the quiet darkness of the dungeons of Miranei, Anghara distinctly heard, as she had in her vision, the dull, ominous thud of a distant door closing with a finality that was absolute. They were gone, and she was in darkness, alone.

The *tamman* had brought Anghara to the point where this realization meant nothing more than that they were leaving her in the blessed dark, to curl up without being bounced on the back of a galloping horse, to finally try to sleep. It didn't matter that her bed would be a hank of filthy straw on the flagged stone floor, or that the air in her tiny cell entered through an open grille in the stout oak door—a grille that looked as though it could easily be shut. She craved sleep—a long, wholesome sleep lacking the pain, the numbness, the gray fuzziness and the constant nausea that had been her companions for long days and nights on the road. And, without *tamman,* she did finally sleep—the last innocent sleep she would have for a long time, had she but known it, untainted with the horror of knowing what she would wake to in the morning.

When she did wake, it was to a weakness which made it next to impossible to perform the simple act of sitting up, and unabated nausea which was, if anything, worse than before. But queasy and shaken as she was, she was lucid, for the first time in days, perhaps weeks—she suddenly realized she had no idea how much time had passed since she had paid for the bay mare in the Calabra stable. She moaned, pressing her fingers to her temples; her head felt like a wayside smithy where a battalion's horses were being shod. She tried to get up and take the few steps toward the hole in the floor that served as a latrine. Her legs wouldn't hold her; eventually she crawled there on hands and knees, and was violently sick.

She seemed to feel better, as though she had thrown up some poison which had been slowly killing her. There was a half-full pottery jug of water on the floor by her bed; she reached for it, rinsed her mouth, and then swallowed a few gulps. It was stale, with an odd taste, as though things she would be better off not knowing about had leached into it during its long standing—but it was clean. Anghara wiped her mouth with the back of her hand and only now turned to make a closer inspection of her surroundings.

She was in a solitary cell, only just long enough for her to stretch out on the straw that was her bed and no wider than perhaps five short paces from wall to wall. There was an old, rusted fitting on the wall just above the straw. Anghara had to stare at it for a while before it occurred to her that it was a flange for fastening a chain. There had been a mate—once she knew what to look for, Anghara could see the hole in the wall where it should have been attached, but it had either been removed a long time ago or simply rotted away. They were just the right distance apart to spreadeagle a prisoner against the wall.

"I should be grateful," Anghara murmured to herself, shuddering, "that they didn't see fit to put me up in those."

Aside from these grisly furnishings, the straw pallet, the jug of water and the latrine hole, the place was empty, the walls blank, the ceiling low and louring. The cell wasn't quite dark—faint light from a torch outside in the corridor filtered through the open grille, and it was this that had allowed Anghara her scrutiny. Her mouth curled into a tight, bitter little smile.

"But the Gods always give what you ask for," she whispered softly, remembering her wishes on the journey to this place—a small, dark place to sleep, and to be left alone. She had been given it all. "How long, I wonder? How long before you forget all about me, Sif . . . or before you send a loyal sword to end everything?"

It wasn't clean. She would never have done it like this. The drugs . . . the dungeons . . . it wasn't clean. It stained the name of Kir Hama, the proud lineage of ancient royal blood.

Kieran's voice suddenly came to her, from years ago—that day on the banks of a Cascin well, on which he had first found out who she was. *Sif is your brother . . .*

And then her mother's, from before even that, from the mists of memory that clung to the mind of a child, perhaps only three or four years old: *He looks like you,* Rima had said, standing at a window and watching the young Sif in a courtyard below. Behind her, the shadowy figure of her husband had smiled. He had chosen never to hear the bitterness that edged Rima's voice every time the subject of his son came up between them.

Her brother. Her own father's son.

None of it mattered. He was king in a land he had wrested from the hand of a little girl. That she had been born to the crown, that she had worn it before him—all this was irrelevant. Dynan was dead, Sif was king, and there was space on the Throne Under the Mountain for only one monarch to reign over Roisinan. And it was his land as well as her own.

She could have witched the door of that dungeon open quite easily with what ai'Jihaar had taught her over the years—if only she could have touched the power without seeming to tear at her mind with poisoned talons. Maybe it was the drug—perhaps, Anghara thought hopefully, now they had her safely in here they would forget about the *tamman,* giving her a chance to recover. Perhaps. There was nothing for it but to wait—for what, she was not quite sure, but wait she must.

They hadn't quite forgotten about her yet, at any rate, because she was shaken from a light doze by the rattle of a small trapdoor she hadn't noticed before. It opened near the bottom of the cell door, only just wide enough to admit a battered tin plate.

"Supper," a gruff voice announced, "and if you want fresh water pass the jug out with the plate when you're done."

Anghara had surged from her place on the pallet—but her head still swam when she moved too fast, and the few precious moments it took her to gasp herself back into a semblance of steadiness were all it took for her efforts to be in vain. She stood on tiptoe next to the door, trying to peer out into the corridor.

"Wait!" she called. "Come back!" But her only reply was silence.

Defeated, she sank down on her knees beside the plate of food. It looked greasily congealed, and, worse, cold; but she was starving. Her mind recoiled but her stomach accepted—it was food, and after the first instant, when she had to taste the foul mush, it didn't matter what her mind thought of the meal. She finished, and banged on the door with the empty container, hoping to attract the guard back again. Nobody came. Anghara pushed the empty plate and the water jug against the little trapdoor, and stood waiting by the door in expectation, determined not to be caught napping again.

When she woke, she was cold and stiff from the position she had collapsed into, on the cold stone floor at the foot of the cell door. The headache was back, and the nausea. They must have slipped more *tamman* into the food. The plate was gone, and the re-filled water jug stood by the trapdoor; Anghara was alone once more.

They'll never let me talk to anyone again, she thought bitterly, leaning her forehead against the cold stone wall, fighting the urge to start beating her head against it. She tried once more to reach for Sight, and paid for it by being sick all over again, only just making the latrine hole in time; she leaned over the edge of the noisome pit, continuing to retch even when there was nothing left to bring up. Now that she thought about it, there had been a ghost of a taste of the drug in the food, but she had thought it only a lingering memory of what had gone before—and even if she had known beyond a doubt, what could she do? The only options open to her were to suffer the *tamman* and stay alive as long as she could, or stop eating and save Sif the trouble of killing her by starving herself to death.

"I will live," she muttered, but her voice was wretched even as she uttered the brave words. It was not life she was choosing—not this, not in here. For one whose every waking moment for years had been spent in the company of a powerful gift, the lack of it was an exquisite torture she was only just beginning to comprehend. She wasn't even sure if it was a deliberate cruelty, or something careless and inadvertent, a simple side-effect of keeping her from using Sight to escape. And how did they even know she was Sighted?

The answer came easily enough. Bresse, where they searched for her and where she would not have been if not for Sight. And Ansen, who had, almost inadvertently, led her there—who had, perhaps, brought Sif there, too, and paid a high price.

She soon lost count of the days, and ceased to speculate about why it was taking Sif so long to get round to killing her. She didn't know autumn had flowed into winter and the first light snow fallen already on the mountain, or that blizzards piled it man-deep around Miranei. Neither did she know that, on the morning of her seventeenth birthday, Sif himself stood and watched as she slept, her bright hair tangled and matted, the bones of her delicate wrist standing out like a fledgling bird's.

"What are your orders, my lord?" the guard had asked deferentially.

"I will decide, in due course," Sif had said, taking a last look and turning away. He knew he should have had her killed weeks ago, but he was finding it curiously difficult to sublimate that knowledge into action. Nothing had changed in his feelings for Anghara Kir Hama—she still stood in his way, and would for as long as she breathed, but her ghost seemed easier to bear if it was still housed in a living body he could keep under observation. Killing her would set that spirit free. The dictum would be the same as at Bresse—*I did what had to be done*—but Bresse had not vanished from his mind just because he had managed to rationalize its destruction, and he knew Anghara would be a far tougher ghost to lay. Even watching her now—thin, grubby, unkempt—there was still something in her that was royal, and the line of her jaw, while undoubtedly more feminine and delicate, reminded Sif forcefully of the man who had fathered them both. *I could have loved her,* Sif thought, surprising even himself with the idea. *A younger sister . . . but no, she is not my sister. She could still snatch the throne from me . . .*

The words had trembled on his lips then, closer than ever before to being said, but he didn't say them. He walked away abruptly, the jewelled pommel of his sword winking and flashing in the dim torchlight. "Just keep her safe," he said tersely to the guard.

"Aye, my lord."

And Sif climbed the stairs out of that place, and put it from his mind, inasmuch as he could ever keep the refrain of Anghara's name from rolling around within his thoughts like a lost glass marble.

That had not been the first time he had gone to see his prisoner—nor the last. Anghara never knew, but she drew him, as a wound under bandages and out of reach advertises itself by incessant itching. He'd gone down on his way back from Kerun's Temple at Chanoch, the Festival of New Fire. Perhaps if he had gone before, when the old fires were being extinguished and everything stood in the shadow of death, perhaps he could have willed her doom. Instead he felt a superstitious dread at doing it after the new fires, those of the resurrection, had just been brought in from the Temple.

At Winter Court, he'd thought. I'll do something at Winter Court. But that year's Winter Court proved particularly fractious, and Favrin Rashin had chosen the winter to launch a new offensive in the south. Distracted, preoccupied, Sif had other things to think about. Anghara had somehow been reprieved again.

In late-night meetings beside a roaring fire with a guard at the chamber door to ensure privacy, Sif had discussed the subject with the only man in his entourage who knew everything—Fodrun, the general who had given him Miranei.

"If I gave you the power," Sif had said bleakly, one night,

toward the end of winter, sitting wrapped in a royal gown of gray wolf fur, with his long legs stretched out toward the fire, "would you issue the orders to kill her?"

Fodrun sucked in his breath, waiting for the strength to refuse this man whom he had raised to be king, but Sif lifted his eyes from the fire and rested them on his Chancellor. They were glittering with a sort of savage amusement. "No, you don't have to worry, old friend. I do this myself, or it is not done at all. Yet . . . I was ready to do it at Bresse, so ready that the entire community died in her stead. And now, now that I have her in my hand, I take it a day at a time, and wait."

"My lord . . ." Fodrun began carefully. Sif waved him into silence.

"I know it all," he said, "every argument, and everything I know tells me I am a fool. There is no fear that she will ever be rescued; one day she will die in that dungeon, and that too will be a death by my hand. But at least her blood will not be on me. And yet . . ."

"Your own father had prisoners who died in the dungeons," Fodrun said pointedly. "And your great-grandfather . . ."

"King Garen of hallowed memory had traitors enough to fill more dungeons than even another keep of Miranei could hold," said Sif. "And my father—my father's traitors were few. There had to have been more than I knew of, back then when I was at the court by the king's sufferance, a bastard-born, would-be prince not privy to the secrets of the council chamber. But I can remember only four men whose crimes were heinous enough for them to be condemned to the living death."

"And no women," said Fodrun thoughtlessly.

Sif threw him an angry glance. "Can I help it if my nemesis is a woman?" he demanded.

"Sif," said Fodrun, throwing caution and the trappings of royalty to the winds, "my lord, if you are seeking my advice, it is simply this: do not poison your life and the rest of your reign by forever keeping your father's daughter between you and what you hold. Make an end to it. Somehow. And then leave it behind, and go on."

"If I had been in Miranei when they brought her in," said Sif thoughtfully, "I would probably not have hesitated. But the closer I came to Miranei after the message of her capture reached me in Shaymir, the less clear things became. For example, where is Dynan's seal?"

"Do you know for sure it was with her?"

"This keep was taken apart," said Sif. "It was not with my father when he was buried and I can swear to you it was not in the keep he left to go to war. And when they caught her, she did not have it."

"How did they know it was Anghara?" asked Fodrun with some curiosity. "Surely it would have been difficult for anyone from Miranei to recognize her—the last time she was seen here she was but nine years old, and what is she now . . . sixteen?"

"Seventeen," said Sif tersely, not elaborating. A vision of Anghara as she had looked on her birthday arose unbidden in his mind, and he pressed his lips together into a thin line of irritation. Then he took a quick swallow from the wine goblet he held, his eyes staring unfocused into the fire. "And you are right—it was no man from Miranei who recognized her—the squad that captured her is captained by one who used to work for Lyme of Cascin, before Lyme abandoned the manor. This man had been at Cascin while Anghara was there also—and hers is a face you do not forget easily. It was he who recognized her. And there are a few others from Cascin in that squad—I do not throw away resources, and when they came to me, I took them. Of those fifty-odd men, Fodrun, only about five knew what it was they had in their hands; the others had no idea why the great haste to get this girl to Miranei was necessary." He grinned, a wolfish grin.

"I was fortunate it had been the captain himself who knew her at the quays. But then . . . I always knew he had potential."

"At the quays? What was she doing there?"

"They made enquiries—three ships had docked that day, two quite late. One was Khelsie."

"And the other two?"

"Routine," Sif said, "and both swear they had no passengers. My men tried to get something out of the Khelsies, but they couldn't find anyone who spoke anything but that cursed tongue of theirs."

"But surely there must have been a trader of some sort on board," said Fodrun, "and surely that trader needs to speak a little Roisinani if he expects to trade in Calabra?"

"If so," Sif shrugged, "he could not be found." He paused, glancing at Fodrun sharply. "You don't think . . ."

The thought gave them both pause for a moment, but then Sif shook his head. "Never. She must have escaped Bresse with almost nothing. How could she have survived there—no money, no way to communicate? Besides, the Khelsies . . . no. It had to have been one of the other ships."

"Perhaps she was trying to find a way out of Calabra, and not back in," said Fodrun speculatively.

"Perhaps," said Sif, who had forgotten his captain had also told him that the thing which had drawn his attention to Anghara was the glowing look of joy on her face—the joy of return.

They sat in silence for a moment, but then Sif laughed—a brittle, hoarse laugh with little mirth in it. "We seem to have moved off the subject," he remarked conversationally. "What to do with Anghara Kir Hama."

But Fodrun had regained his composure on that score. "My lord," he said, "there is no escaping it: if you will not give the word to kill her, there is no alternative but to leave her in the dungeon."

Sif mastered a flash of temper and managed a grin. "I guess you already gave your counsel," he said. "Winter Court is long gone; but I don't need a ceremonial occasion for this, do I? It would be just as easy to do it on the quiet, now . . . There's Senena's babe—it's due before too long. I will need my mind clear for other things . . . and the throne truly free of Anghara's shadow . . . for my heir." He frowned at the leaping tongues of flame in the hearth for a moment, marshalling his thoughts, then he shook his head, tossing back the remains of the wine in his goblet. "Leave me," he said. "I need to think upon it."

"My lord," said Fodrun, rising to his feet and bowing before he withdrew from the room. It was doubtful if Sif had even heard him. He had leaned his head against the high back of his chair, closing his eyes. "Whatever I do, you are waiting for me, Anghara Kir Hama, Queen of the Dungeons," Sif muttered softly, wearily, into the empty chamber. "I would give my promise of Glas Coil and the hereafter if I could only change things so that you never existed . . ."

Sitting in moody silence before the flames leaping in the hearth, he psyched himself up to make an end. Before he fell into a fitful doze, he made up his mind to issue quiet orders concerning Anghara before he broke his fast the next morning.

But once again circumstances brought an eleventh-hour reprieve. Before Sif had time to summon those who would need to know that his hospitality to the Kir Hama Princess would be extended no longer, another messenger came galloping into Miranei on a lathered horse, and such was his message that everything else was driven from Sif's mind.

"How could they get through? I left half my army there to protect her!" he raged, as the exhausted messenger poured out news of Favrin Rashin's daring raid on Torial, the southern manor Sif had recently ceded to his mother, the Lady Clera.

"My lord . . . there were only a handful of them . . . they slipped in wearing our uniforms . . ."

"Dear Gods . . ." Sif moaned, covering his face with his hand.

"They took very little . . . it was as though they simply wished to show us they could . . . but your lady mother insisted on coming out on the battlements . . . it was an accident, my lord, a stray arrow . . ."

"Saddle my horse; I will ride at once," said Sif grimly, straightening. "Get any unassigned men north of the Hal to be ready to follow as soon as they may. This insult cannot go unpunished."

It was Fodrun himself who brought his horse into the Royal Courtyard and stood waiting, holding its reins, until Sif emerged from the tower. "My lord," he began, "winter campaigns . . ."

"Winter is over, Fodrun. Look out from the battlements—the snow is almost gone from the moors. It's spring; and Kir Hama luck rides high in spring."

"And the babe . . . and . . . the other thing . . ."

"I plan to be back for Senena's confinement," said Sif with a savage smile. "Just as soon as I've taught young Favrin a long-overdue lesson. As for the other . . . There'll be time enough when I return. Nothing could possibly change in the space of the few weeks I'll need to clear up this campaign once and for all."

Sif rode from his keep believing those words. But even as he and his entourage rode away south, things were already changing in the keep he was leaving behind.

The first seed of change had been planted as close to home as Sif's own bedchamber. On the night he and Fodrun had spoken freely about Anghara, they believed themselves alone. They were mistaken. And that of which they had spoken was no longer a secret buried between the two men in that room and the five who had snatched her in Calabra.

Because he never bothered to use it, Sif hardly ever remembered the small minstrel's gallery tucked into an alcove high under the rafters of the royal bedchamber. Dynan had often had musicians there, discreetly secluded from the king's bedchamber by a carved and fretted wooden screen; Rima had loved going to sleep to the quiet strains of a solitary lute or harp, relaxed in the aftermath of her husband's caresses. But neither of Sif's marriages had been a love match, and he never thought in terms of courtship or loving seduction. There was only one access point into the gallery—a low, insignificant door leading off a seldom frequented corridor on the floor above the royal bedchamber, where the musicians could come and go without disturbing the king. That door had been locked, the key was in the possession of his chamberlain, and Sif had wiped its existence from his mind.

But Senena, his child-queen, had frequently found herself in need of a quiet, private place where she could hide from an intrusive and inquisitive court and the pretense that was her life.

Few in Sif's court had frequented his father's Miranei—some had discreetly retired into the country, and others Sif himself had removed for reasons of his own. What remained was a court with more than its fair share of sycophants who tried to cultivate Senena in hopes of obtaining Sif's ear, and who had done exactly the same thing to Colwen, his first queen. Given this company, Senena chose instead to befriend the chamberlain, who had also served Dynan—a kind and gentle man with no expectations from her. He had daughters her age, and was not fooled by the act she put on for Sif's nobles. It was he who offered her the sanctuary of the minstrel's gallery, and armed her with the key to its door.

In recent months, as she grew large with child, Senena came to greatly appreciate this refuge. Colwen, who had left the court after her repudiation to accept a convenient marriage proposal from a border Duke, had returned to Miranei, apparently for no other reason than to flaunt her own swelling belly. It seemed her Duke had succeeded where Sif had failed, and had got her with child; and although Senena would deliver her child before Colwen, the spurned queen wanted to be in attendance when Senena went into labor—just in case Senena offered Sif a girl. Colwen did not omit to tell anyone the midwives had said that her own child was bound to be a boy. Sif ignored both the gibes and the woman; Senena was possessed of a thinner hide. Her gallery was a lifesaver.

She had been there when Sif had brought Fodrun in. She had not meant to eavesdrop; but she had fallen asleep in the comfortable armchair her friend the chamberlain had procured for her, and by the time she'd woken the conversation below was in full swing. Moving would mean the risk of an inadvertent sound, putting both her own head and the chamberlain's into the noose; she sat in silence, hoping they would finish their business soon and leave. But she could not help hearing what they spoke about. When she finally grasped that Anghara Kir Hama had not lain buried in the family vault these eight years as everyone had blithely supposed, but was instead a living prisoner in the Miranei dungeons, the shock was so great that even the baby within her turned and kicked violently.

Anghara . . . alive . . . that meant Sif's claim to the throne could only have been treachery . . .

The next morning had been pandemonium, with the arrival of the messenger from Torial and Sif's almost instant departure. Senena welcomed the distance between them, at least until she had a chance to come to terms with her new knowledge. But once Sif had left and Fodrun, whom he had left to be his lieutenant and her shadow, had been detained elsewhere, she donned a voluminous cloak and made her way to the great doors in the bowels of the keep. They stood banded and barred with iron, and blackened with centuries of smoke from the torches which always burned in two sconces, one on either side of the gate. Two soldiers stood guard before the gate to this underworld, their swords naked in their hands.

"Hold," one of them said, his voice low and somehow fittingly sepulchral in this place. "Who comes?"

Senena had counted on surprise, and was amply rewarded by the sight of their faces as she pushed back the cowl of her cloak. "The queen," she said. Her voice rang with confidence and authority she had never had, never even felt, as Sif's wife; but these men weren't to know. "Let me pass."

"Lady," began one, dropping creakily on one knee, "it is not meet for a woman that you go down there . . ."

"It is for a woman that I go," said Senena. "I will not need to descend to her if you have her brought here to me. I wish to speak with her. Is there a place where I could do so in private?"

The two had exchanged glances. "A woman, my lady?"

"Lady, we cannot . . . your husband the lord king . . ."

"The king is not here," Senena said. "I sit beside him on the Throne Under the Mountain. Do as I say."

Still they hesitated, and something kindled in Senena's pale eyes that was steely and implacable. A part of this came from imitating Sif's own regal attitude, but another part was entirely her own. She may have been young, she may have been timid and sensitive, but she had a core of strength and nobility which would have set her apart even without a crown on her head. Sif had chosen his queen all too well.

"Do as I say," she repeated to the two guards, and in that moment the swift and imminent retribution they read in her face overruled the nebulous possibilities of what Sif might do when he returned to Miranei.

"This way, my lady," one of the two said, handing her through the grim gate and into a guardroom where a fire burned brightly on the smoke-blackened hearth. Two more men had been lounging there, but they leapt to their feet when Senena entered. Her escort barked at them to get out, sending one of them down to the lower levels to get the prisoner.

They ran into unexpected trouble when the gaoler Sif had placed to watch over Anghara refused to hand her over without specific orders from Sif. But when the messenger they sent came panting back with this refusal, Senena calmly slipped off the wedding ring Sif had given her, with its miniature Roisinani crest worked in jewels.

"Give him that for a token," she said, "and ask if he will rather face his lord's wrath when he learns I have had to climb down into the vaults myself?"

It wasn't Sif's own ring, but even the jailer had to bow to the fact it was a royal token, and, not without grumbling, hunted out the key for Anghara's cell from the bunch hanging at his waist.

Anghara had long ceased to believe the door of her cell ever opened—even she must have been introduced through the trapdoor at the bottom, which yielded everything from food and water to fresh straw every now and again. She sat curled up on her pile of straw, staring owlishly at the widening crack of light which entered through the opening door.

"Come on," said her jailer gruffly, "ye're wanted."

Another first; nobody had spoken to her directly for months. She sat frozen; she had to be manhandled to her feet when she showed no signs of moving.

It was a long journey to the top; there were steep stairs, and Anghara hadn't walked more than five steps for a long time. Whatever Senena had expected, it was not the pale, wide-eyed wraith of a girl, wearing a filthy dress which was only a memory of its former self, with whom she was confronted in the guardroom. The dress hung off the frail prisoner—the delicate bones in her narrow hands and fragile wrists were almost visible through the skin.

The two girls' eyes met, held.

"Senena . . ." whispered Anghara through cracked lips, not seeming aware she had spoken.

"Put her down in that chair," Senena commanded, "and then leave us." Somehow it did not seem strange that this girl, whom she had never set eyes on before in her life, should know her on sight.

The soldiers obeyed, and Senena knelt at the foot of Anghara's chair, taking the thin, cold hands into her own and trying to rub warmth into them. Her eyes were wide and haunted. "Oh, Gods . . ." she murmured, staring into the hollow-eyed face beneath the matted red-gold hair. "Sif, what have you done?"

Anghara didn't know whether to bless Senena or curse her.

Their first meeting had not been scintillating—after uttering Senena's name Anghara couldn't seem to gather her wits about her to say any more, simply staring at the young queen's flushed face. Senena did not stay for long on that first visit, but she left specific orders—and in her wake the grumbling soldiers provided a lukewarm bath, the first Anghara had had since she had left the Kheldrini ship in Calabra, and a change of clothing. It was nothing grand, but anything would have been better than the rags to which her dress had been reduced over the long months of her captivity. She had clean hair, clean clothes—even her food had climbed a notch or two in quality, and, best of all, since Senena had begun showing an interest, there had been precious little *tamman* in it. In their second meeting, and those that followed, Anghara began to remember how to relate to another human being. At first it was no more than a few words, but then, as Senena persisted, Anghara slowly started to cross a wide and trackless ocean back to the shores she once knew.

The upside of all this was that she was beginning to regain a sense of her own humanity; the downside was, of course, that she felt her captivity all the more keenly every time one of her meetings with Senena came to an end. And she knew with bitter certainty that it would all cease, one way or another, as soon as Sif returned to Miranei. When he found out what Senena had been up to in his absence—and he could hardly fail to—Sif had it in his power to take his revenge on Senena in terms that could be just as gruesome as those that applied to Anghara herself. It was entirely possible that the little queen would only be kept alive long enough to deliver Sif's heir.

And nothing had prepared Anghara for the fact that she and the girl who carried the living seal to Sif's reign could be friends. Senena herself initially seemed oddly confused as far as her own motives were concerned—she was, after all, befriending a ghost whom the king had successfully "buried," and whose resurrection could mean only disaster for her husband. But she seemed to put the more complex issues from her mind—perhaps her first impulse had simply been to see for herself, to check the truth of the wild story she had overheard from the minstrel's gallery, but this rapidly passed into something like affection. She met with Anghara almost daily, knowing, as Anghara did, that their time together was running out fast.

It was from Senena that Anghara learned how much time had passed in the world outside; on finding out that Anghara's birthday had been spent alone in the dungeon, Senena took an almost child-like pleasure in organizing a belated birthday feast, which they shared in the guardroom. Anghara could not bring herself to eat much—her spartan diet and something about the *tamman* seemed to have affected her appetite—but she tried not to wreck Senena's festive spirit by appearing gloomy and ungrateful.

"What would you have liked for a birthday present?" Senena asked, sitting on the edge of the hearth like a hoyden, her brocade skirts almost dragging in the ashes.

There might have been a time when Anghara could have named a great many things, but her world had shrunk to the dungeons of Miranei, with no prospect but death waiting for her—death swiftly, or slowly by starvation, at Sif's whim. The greatest, most burning wish of her heart was to once again touch that part of her which was power—to know the breath of Sight again. But that was beyond Senena. Anghara glanced upward, her eyes filling with unexpected tears, only to meet more unforgiving stone above her. And at that, it was easy—even Sight shrank from the weight of that stone.

"To see the sky," Anghara whispered, "to feel the wind upon my face once again. It's been so long since I have walked in the sunlight . . ."

"It's a small enough thing to ask," said Senena slowly.

Anghara looked down, her lips curving up into a ghost of a smile. "No, not even you, Senena. They might have turned a blind eye to all this, but only because I have not passed those doors . . . and nor will I. Someone might see me up there, and afterward . . . there will be no holding it in. Death waits for me up there."

"No more so than in here," said Senena stubbornly, and then bit her lip as she realized what she had said. She reached out to lay an apologetic hand on Anghara's arm. "I'm sorry . . . not today of all days . . . I shouldn't have said that . . . But there has to be a way—you're not asking for a guide into the mountains, surely taking you up on the battlements for a few minutes could hurt nobody."

Anghara's eyes were sad. "Don't get my hopes up, Senena. I have learned to hope for nothing, it is less painful."

This, it seemed, had been entirely the wrong thing to say. Senena's eyes glittered, and she lifted her chin with a grim sort of determination. "I will see it done," she vowed.

Just as Senena had once sat listening to a conversation thought to be private between a king and his counsellor, this exchange in the guardroom in its turn was overheard by a pair of ears not meant to be privy to it. Even as Anghara was being escorted back to her cell and Senena left the guardroom to begin a determined attempt to accede to Anghara's wish, a message was already making its way down the corridors of the keep, out across snow-piled courtyards, into the cold, empty white streets of the city, to a shabby hostelry just inside the city gates. The boy who carried it, a wiry waif of some eight years or so, looked around the inn's common room with a swift glance, and crossed unerringly to where two young men sat in desultory silence by the fireside. He pulled at his forelock in an age-old gesture of respect, but what was in his eyes was closer to adoration as he lifted them to the face of the older of the two, a dark-haired youth with piercing blue eyes. The boy handed over a much-folded scrap of parchment, tugged his forelock again, and left without uttering a word. The youth opened the parchment, and sat staring at it in silence for a long while; then he rose to his feet, crumpling the message almost heedlessly as his hands closed into fists at his sides.

"This is it," said Kieran, and his voice was flat and cold, a steel blade leaving its sheath. "Sif is coming back within days, and we will not get another chance. We go in tomorrow."

Kieran's men had caught up with the splinter group they had been chasing, but they hadn't found Anghara; worse, the group contained none of the five men whom Sif had spoken about, the men who knew who Anghara was. Those whom he had caught could tell Kieran very little except to gloat over the fact he had run after the wrong bait and the prize he had been after was that much closer to the point of no return. Perhaps he could have taken a lucid decision if any of those men had had the barest inkling of what they had done. But instead they crowed over an achievement that was meaningless to them, except perhaps inasmuch as they had figured out who was chasing them and they had managed to comprehensively hoodwink someone with Kieran's reputation. When one of Kieran's men lost his patience and floored a grinning soldier with a violent blow, Kieran had not intervened, and neither had Rochen; after that, killing was but a step away. Kieran had long since gotten over his sensibilities where enemy lives were concerned, but these were revenge killings, done in cold blood. He was not proud of them, or of himself for standing back and abrogating the responsibility. The truth was, he had been furious, sick with anger and helplessness. That didn't excuse what he had done, but at least it made it easier to cope with—it was as though naming his sin drew some of its sting.

"I'm not giving up," he had said, driven into a dangerous, almost fey mood. If Anghara was really immured in Miranei, his actions would be as insignificant as a mosquito trying to bite a knight through armor. He knew it. The knowledge was a poisoned arrow in his heart.

By this time both Adamo and Charo were with him, and the brothers, who keenly remembered the Cascin to which a waif they'd known as Brynna Kelen had arrived so many years ago, seconded him fiercely in his hunger to free their royal cousin.

"Let us go into Miranei," Charo had advised wildly, "there are ways of finding out the exact numbers of guards, and we can take twice our number, we have proved that many times already . . ."

"Yes," Adamo had said, no less implacable but still a voice for calm reason in an ocean of turbulent emotion. "We have proved it . . . but always with a clear line of retreat, and the possibility of returning to fight another day. I have never seen the dungeons of Miranei, but I doubt we can take them without trouble—and even if we managed, the gates of the keep can be shut against us, and we can be hunted down and spitted like rabbits. No army has taken Miranei. Ever. And we . . . we aren't even an army."

"Are you suggesting we just go away?"

"No," said Adamo, "but neither am I suggesting we throw

our own lives away on something that is clearly impossible. We will go into Miranei—but we will wait. And I will try and make a friend or two amongst the guards."

Kieran had shaken his lethargy off then, and taken charge. "Yes. We will wait. As long as we know she lives I will give up neither the hope nor the chance of saving her. But a large group will only attract attention."

"A handful will not be able to do anything when the time comes," Rochen had pointed out.

"We will stay in touch," said Kieran. "I was not suggesting we sever all ties." A round of ragged laughter went up at this; Kieran looked up at a circle of bright eyes. "Ten," he decided. "No more than ten."

"I," said Charo flatly. Not asking, stating. Adamo did not even need to speak; his eyes spoke for him. Kieran nodded.

"Adamo, Charo, myself . . . seven others. I will not choose. We leave camp tomorrow at dawn—I will take the seven who wait for me." He caught another eye, bright, determined, and shook his head imperceptibly. *Not you, Rochen. I need someone to lead those who stay outside.*

Rochen looked very young all of a sudden, his face slipping into a black, sullen scowl; but his brow cleared, and he lifted his head, looked straight at Kieran, nodded. And then, because it was still stronger than him, turned away.

The seven were waiting with their saddled horses when the three foster brothers emerged from the camp the next morning. Kieran, already mounted, reined in lightly, sweeping his company with hard blue eyes. "It's the most bitter duty of all you have chosen," he said softly. "The waiting may be long . . . and we may be waiting for disaster."

"And maybe also for a miracle," one of the men murmured.

"They pulled straws," said Adamo, his voice deceptively gentle. "Every one of those men staying behind is wide awake, listening to us go, and cursing the long straws they pulled last night."

"For Anghara," said Charo, "and for you. You kept the dream alive. If anyone can snatch her from the dreaded dungeons of Miranei, it's you."

"And I need to be unlucky only once," said Kieran. "Then it will all have been for nothing. Perhaps Sif has already given the word . . ."

"Sif is not at Miranei," said Adamo. "And many things can happen before he returns."

He had been both right, and wrong. Sif had been in Shaymir; but nothing happened where Anghara herself was concerned, not while Sif was away, not when he came back. Chanoch, Anghara's birthday, Winter Court came and went. Kieran's handful mingled with the guard, and they knew that Anghara still lived. And then winter was almost over—and came the morning Sif rode away from Miranei like a whirlwind to wreak his revenge for his wounded mother. And then, on the heels of that . . . Senena.

Unknown to Sif, one of the guards who had stayed behind on duty in Miranei was far more than a simple soldier. It was he who had sought out Kieran in his hostelry, a gray-eyed man with ash-brown hair with the build and cast of the man who had once been Red Dynan's First General.

"I know who you are," he had said simply, coming to stand beside the bench in the inn's common room where Kieran had been sitting with Charo. Kieran heard the double hiss beside him—Charo's quick indrawn breath and the loosening of the blade in his scabbard—and raised a swift hand to forestall murder.

"Sit," Kieran had invited. His eyes were hooded; his voice guarded.

The young man slid into the seat opposite Kieran's, avoiding Charos eyes. "You need have no fear," he said, his voice low. "I have known for some time. I will not betray you. I . . . know why you are here."

Outside it was snowing; perhaps it had just been a quick gust of cold air that swirled inside as someone opened the inn door that made Kieran shiver where he sat—but there was something deeper. A touch of prescience, perhaps. "Who are you?" Kieran asked.

"Melsyr, son of Kalas, who was King Dynan's general."

"I thought he died, in the same battle that claimed the king," muttered Charo, dimly recalling a few remembered phrases heard from Feor in happier times.

"Almost," said Melsyr. "He survived long enough to curse Fodrun, whom he had himself picked and brought to the king to be made Second General. He never believed Anghara was really dead. To him, Sif was a usurper who seized the throne when he saw the chance, and Fodrun nothing more than a traitor."

"Yet you serve in the usurper's guard," Kieran said blandly.

"I was in the guard when Dynan was king," said Melsyr hotly. "To leave when Sif came . . . it would have signed my father's death sentence."

"But he died," said Charo.

"Yes. Bitter, angry . . . yet unmolested. And on his death . . . yes, I stayed. I have a young wife, a small son. And I know naught but soldiering."

"And now?" Kieran said. "What changed, that you should come to me?"

"My father's queen, and my own, is in Sif's dungeons," Melsyr said tersely.

"I am listening," said Kieran, and his voice had changed, very subtly. Melsyr had dropped his gaze to the scrubbed deal table between them, but he lifted his head at this, and met eyes that were no longer chips of blue steel.

They were still too few, but Melsyr was a source of information that had eluded them until now. Kieran learned details of Anghara's captivity; Charo, who had rapidly changed tack and taken Melsyr as a messenger of the Gods, had more than a few illusions shattered as he proposed one or two wild plans, now that they had a man on the inside.

"Suicide," Melsyr had said flatly. "There might be one or two guards who could be turned—especially now that Sif himself is not here. When he is . . . I do not know what it is in him, but men follow him unto death. If he were here . . . I do not know if even I would have found it in myself to go against him . . . even now . . . knowing that time is against us, and that you are her only chance."

"But we could overpower the guards at the gate, and then we could . . ." Charo persisted stubbornly.

"I do not doubt your courage," said Melsyr. "But the guards at the gate are the least of your problems. They are changed every hour; you would need a guide down into the fourth level of the maze of catacombs that are the dungeons of Miranei. All he would have to do is delay you . . . just a little. The next detachment of guards would come, and find the bodies you will have left at the gates. Then even if you freed the young queen you would find the gates barred and held against you on your return. They would have you precisely where they wanted you—in the dungeons. And you would all die, one way or another."

Charo had been convinced, eventually, but such was the pitch to which he had worked himself, he had to get up and stamp out into the snow to cool his frustrations. Adamo had come to take his place, and the cooler heads arranged with Melsyr that he would be their eyes and ears in the keep, and send a message as soon as anything changed . . . if it did.

And now it had. Senena had sworn to it. Impossibly, incredibly, they would have a chance. Kieran stood rapt in the common room of the inn where he had waited for so long, with tears in his eyes. He was remembering a rainy day now many years in the past, shaking off the wet in Cascin's hall with Feor while other arms bore Anghara away into some women's fastness to be dosed against catching a chill.

She will need a friend.

"So be it," he breathed, as he had done then, repeating the vow. *I will take you from here, or I will perish in the attempt. Without you . . . nothing I have done during these long empty years has any meaning.*

Kieran's men slipped into the keep in inconspicuous ones and twos, himself following with Charo at his heels. They came together unobtrusively at the back of a barrack stables, mostly empty now that its inhabitants were away bearing their owners to Sif's war, and settled down to wait for Melsyr's signal.

"Who's to guarantee she'll be able to do it?" murmured one of the men, wrapped in his cloak and sprawled over a pile of loose straw. "Fodrun is hardly likely to give his approval. And keeping this from him . . . I wonder if the little queen's got it in her."

"She'll do it," said Kieran. He spoke as though he had knowledge of it, as though it had never been in any doubt.

"Do you have the Sight?" mumbled a skeptic from the dark.

Melsyr's son turned up in the morning, moving like a shadow, with a basket of victuals and a message that nothing was known yet. None of them could eat much, but Kieran insisted—this was the worst waiting yet, with the imminence of something immense hanging over them, and used as these men were to being in tight spots together, stretched nerves made for uneasy companionship. Eating would give them something to do. Besides, they had learned the hard way never to scorn offered food—they never knew what lay around the next corner.

Melsyr himself, still in uniform, came at dusk, but even in the dim cobwebs of twilight shadows hanging from the rafters his face seemed to glow. Kieran's hackles rose.

"She's done it," Melsyr whispered. "Tomorrow. It will only be for half an hour, up on the northern battlements—up where the mountains crowd up to the keep, it's the most isolated place. There will be ten guards with her, four more at the foot of the stair, and Fodrun himself will be in charge."

For a moment none of them could speak over the violent thudding of their hearts. And then Kieran did, his voice low and steady although his eyes were twin blue flames. "And you?"

"I am to be with the four guarding the rear," said Melsyr. His teeth flashed white in the gloom, a promise of intent. Kieran recognized it for what it was, and reached to lay a hand on the other man's shoulder.

"The Gods alone know if or when we might need you again," he said, and it was a warning. "Do not let yourself be suspected. Above all, do not help us. It would be best if you could manage not to be there."

They could barely distinguish one another's features in the dimness, but that which passed between them needed no light. It was gratitude, and pride; it was a fierce joy, and a love born of what could become a great friendship. It was Melsyr who broke away first, briefly covering Kieran's hand with his own and then stepping away into a bow.

"As you will, lord," he said. "I will switch duty with someone tomorrow . . . much as it galls me not to be there to see you take the Princess from this place, perhaps it would be more useful if I were on guard at a back door." He grinned again. "But have no fear; if we do meet at some gate, I'll ease your passage as much as I am able, and you have my full permission to deal with me as best you deem suitable at the time. Something tells me you will return; I will be here for you when you do. There will be," he added, unconsciously echoing Sif's words, "time enough."

And then he was gone. Kieran stood very still for a moment, his hand dropping to his side; then his fingers closed into a white-knuckled grip on the haft of his dagger. When he turned to face the expectant men waiting in the darkness behind, the power of his resolve was about him like a bright cloak, and they had to choke down the impulse to raise what would, for all of Kieran's determination and courage, be a decidedly premature cheer.

"We'll wait for moonrise," Kieran said tightly. "Then we go. We must be in place when they come."

More waiting; but this time they were coiled springs, waiting only for the hour of their release. When the hour Kieran had appointed came, they filed out of the stables, ten shadows, ten intruders trespassing uninvited into the heart of Sif Kir Hama's realm, waiting to snatch the greatest treasure in his keep. Stepping softly across the cobbles of inner courtyards, keeping to the edges where the shadows were deepest and snow still lingered in dirty gray piles against damp stone walls, Kieran stole a moment to wonder with grim amusement if Sif, tossing restlessly in the grip of his dreams somewhere in the South, knew just what would be happening in his castle the next morning.

They found their way to the northern battlements without meeting another living soul, the castle sleeping quietly around them, sunk in the innocent dreams that come in the darkness before dawn. The ten men waited wakeful, stoically enduring the bitter cold of the mountain night, which proved winter was with them still and spring only a promise of dimly remembered warmth. It wasn't the first time they had waited in cold darkness for the dawn. They had learned to bring themselves into a state of almost suspended animation, keeping themselves alert in anticipation of what was to come, ready for action at a whispered word, yet able to stand like a statue carved of stone until that whisper came. And it came not long after dawn broke and the pale morning sun touched the mountains beyond the battlements with a rim of luminous gold.

They walked warily when they appeared, the ten guards Melsyr had promised: three in the van, naked swords at the ready, eyes hooded and watchful; two on either side, in single file, forming two sides of a square which was completed by the three bringing up the rear. Inside this living square walked . . . but there were two cloaked figures, hoods pulled forward to hide their features.

It took Kieran a precious second to realize who the second figure must be. *Dear Gods. It's Senena.*

But it was all set, and his arm had dropped in the prearranged signal before the thought had a chance to properly cross his mind. And then there was no more time to think, only to call out a swift warning to Adamo, who waited just behind him with his sword naked in his hand. "The other is Sif's queen! Beware!"

But Charo had already taken out one of the rear guards, soundlessly, and pirouetted with a kind of deadly grace to spit another on the point of his blade even as the man turned, startled, to face him. The four on the sides had a man each to take care of them, but Charo had broken an instant too soon. The guards didn't have the time to yell for reinforcements, but the ring of steel on steel in the silence of the mountain dawn as Sif's men turned to defend themselves was clarion enough.

Sloppy, thought Kieran grimly, even as he beat aside the blade of his own opponent and left his dagger in the man's exposed throat. *We had all the advantages. It should have been over quietly, quickly.* He lifted his eyes and his blood ran cold.

Fodrun had taken the stairs two at a time, leading not only the four remaining guards Melsyr had promised but another ten. Three or four showed signs of being summoned hastily, protected with leather vests instead of light guardsman's armor and armed with sturdy quarterstaffs rather than steel, but the rest were grimly businesslike. It was obvious they would kill where they had to but their first priority was to snatch the cowled woman in the midst of the shattered guard square and spirit her away back to the darkness of her captivity. And Kieran was too far away, even as the knowledge hit him and he recognized her by her bound hands. Anghara tossed back her hood, somehow managing to unerringly meet his eyes across the battle taking place between them. Recognizing him. Saying goodbye.

Something gave him strength. He leapt over his fallen foe, leaving Adamo to battle it out alone with the two guardsmen who had accosted him—one from the original guard square and a member of the reinforcements who had leapfrogged across to offer his support. Charo had realized what was happening and was hastening Fodrun's way, but was stopped by one of the quarterstaff wielders. Fodrun reached Anghara a split second before Kieran, and gathered her to his side with his left arm, his sword gleaming wickedly in his other hand.

"Would you believe me if I told you I never wanted her death?" he said. "But now . . . it is too late."

"It is never," said Kieran through clenched teeth, "too late."

"I must have been mad," said Fodrun, more to himself than to the foe who faced him, "to have ever sanctioned this."

Kieran had enough presence of mind to offer a grim smile at this admission; Fodrun's eyes darkened, his own lips thinning into an almost invisible line as he shifted his grip on his sword in anticipation of Kieran's challenge.

But then Senena screamed, and things became a blur.

Kieran was aware, as though watching things which were both ludicrously speeded up and enacted in grisly slow motion, of an expression of pure agony that washed across Anghara's features even as she sagged into a dead faint in Fodrun's arms. Fodrun, to whom she had become a sudden encumbrance, let her slip down at his feet and turned back to face him. At the same time, Kieran was aware of Charo's exultant shout as he made his opponent stumble on the edge of the stairs, lose his balance, turn on his heel with the quarterstaff flailing out of control in his hand, and tumble backward head over heels down the steps. The end of the man's quarterstaff caught Senena a glancing blow across the abdomen, making her double over in pain. She lost her footing, stumbling over the edge of the first stair, falling awkwardly while trying to protect her swollen belly to slam side on into the battlement wall, then sliding down it into a graceless sprawl. Kieran's sword seemed to have moved of its own accord; when he looked at his weapon again, he found it streaming with blood. He blinked, looking around for the victim—and saw Fodrun lying face down at his feet, the general's blade flung an arm's reach away, balancing precariously on the top stair. The blood pooling beneath him was beginning to ooze out, reaching for the edges of the soft dark cloak they had given Anghara.

Who lay motionless a few steps away, her eyes closed, pain still etched into a deep line on her brow.

Kieran dropped his sword, heedless of his surroundings, and knelt beside her. Her head lolled almost lifelessly on his shoulder as he lifted and cradled her against him, smoothing away strands of bright hair that had fallen across her face. The moment had him by the throat—after all this time, all these years, here she was in his arms—had it all been for nothing?

But no—she breathed. Kieran closed his eyes briefly, sending every prayer of gratitude he ever knew to whatever Gods cared to receive them. His own dagger was lost; Fodrun's, bound at his waist, was close enough to snatch. Kieran reached for it, too dazed by the moment to appreciate the irony of Fodrun's dagger being the instrument of Anghara's release as he cut away the rope that bound her hands.

"Anghara?" he said softly. Now that he was looking upon her again, he was unprepared for how strange the name still seemed when applied to his little foster sister from Cascin. But this gaunt, pale young woman was no longer the little girl he had left behind. It was Anghara Kir Hama he held this day, not the child he knew as Brynna. "Can you hear me?"

She opened her eyes even as a finger of sunlight found its way around the towers and poured itself onto the battlements where so many lay dead or dying. The pain was still there, the pain he had seen touch her not a few moments ago, but receding. She stared at him for a long moment, and then the gray eyes filled with tears. "Kieran . . ."

He had to swallow twice before he could speak. "Can you walk? It's time we were away from here . . . before they send what's left of the entire garrison."

"Help me up." Her voice was faint, cracked, faded. *Gods,* thought Kieran, shocked despite himself as his arm went around her thin waist while he helped her to her feet. *What has he done to you?*

But the physical punishment had been nothing, he could tell, compared to the specter of pain that haunted her eyes. Inside, there was something broken—something that would take a great deal more healing than simply reversing the effects of solitary confinement and starvation.

Charo was beside them, his wild warrior's eyes unexpectedly brimming with tears. Anghara saw him, held out a hand; he took it, clasped it with both of his, for once completely bereft of words. It was, uncharacteristically, left to the usually mute Adamo to break the cocoon of silence being woven around Anghara—but only because, as usual, he said everything important with his eyes, pools of remembered love and affection as he gazed at Anghara. The words he found to say were sensibly practical. "It's time we were leaving," he commented, and at that Kieran took charge again.

Looking around, he saw his men mopping up the remainder of the guard. The rest of the keep still was—still seemed—deceptively quiet. Whatever chance they had of carrying this off was here, right now. The keep could rouse at any second.

"Adamo, round them up," he said, his voice swift, quiet. "Twos and threes, as before. There's still a chance they will open the keep gates before all this is discovered, there will be people crossing into the city—slip into the crowd. If you have to, leave your weapons—we won't be tagged immediately as intruders, not if we leave quietly. Charo, help me; you and I will stay with Anghara. I can carry you," he said, turning to the girl whom he still supported in an upright position with an arm around her waist, "but it might look a little bit less conspicuous if you walked. Are you able?"

Anghara began to nod; then her eyes slid past his shoulder and onto the stairwell littered with corpses, and lighted on the ungainly bundle of wheaten hair, sprawled limbs and great belly that was Senena. Her breath caught. Kieran turned, saw what she was looking at. His arm tightened a little, in support.

"I must go to her . . ." Anghara breathed, retrieving her hand from Charo's grasp. Her frail form was imbued with surprising strength as she stepped away from Kieran, stumbling toward the stairs and the still form lying there. Kieran exchanged a glance with the others; at a nod, Adamo peeled away and began collecting the rest of the men together. Kieran and Charo followed Anghara.

The little queen's gown was soaked with blood, and her hands were clenched into tight fists of agony; Anghara covered her legs with her own cloak, folding the child-queen's small hands into her own. Tears were running freely down her cheeks. "She was kind to me," Anghara said, very softly.

Kieran came down on one knee beside her, a hand on her shoulder; Charo bent to touch Senena's brow.

"It's the babe," Charo murmured softly. "She would have had it hard anyway—she was so small and frail. She's still alive, but barely; and death will be a mercy . . ."

But Senena, slowly and in infinite pain, opened her eyes and stared into Anghara's face. "To walk . . . in the sunlight," she whispered. "To see . . . the sky."

"Senena . . ."

But Senena's eyes were lucid, and oddly triumphant. "I am not his," she said, finally seeming to understand the motives which had led her to befriend Anghara. "He will not raise a dynasty out of a son of my body . . . Come back to Miranei, Anghara . . . Reign for me in Roisinan . . ."

Her eyes remained open, but her spirit was suddenly gone—they were empty, windows of pale glass. And Anghara reached again, for something she remembered—something she had once done as if by right—the presence of a God, and the glory of his gifts. But there was nothing there, nothing but emptiness and white pain which bent her double once again over Senena's body.

Come to me now, al'Khur! I am an'sen'thar . . . I wear your gold . . .

But through a veil of pain his voice came back to her: *Another whom you might have wished to save will come to me before we meet again . . . I see suffering . . .*

And another voice, from years later, the voice of the oracle which had given her a cryptic rhyme at Gul Khaima: *Beneath an ancient crown the unborn die.* The Crown Under the Mountain. Senena's unborn son. And Anghara's own helplessness.

"I am blind," she whispered, finding in the hour of Senena's death the courage to name something she had known for a long time but avoided facing. "He has taken the Sight from me. I am blind."

Anghara wept as though her heart would break, as though all the world's sorrows were contained in the still body which lay before her—broken promises, divided loyalties, shattered lives. When Kieran slipped an arm around her shoulders, the slight pressure of his hand an invitation to rise, Anghara lifted a tear-streaked face up to him and shook her head violently.

"We can't just leave her!" she said, and her voice was hoarse from crying.

"Let them find us here, and we all join her in Glas Coil before this day's noon," said Kieran. "We will burn a wand of incense for her soul in a temple as soon as we may, for she was a friend to you, and a great lady . . . but for now, Anghara, come, it is past time we left this place. Or it will all have been for nothing. And Senena herself would have wanted you to win free. Come."

He thought she might resist still as he helped her rise, for her shoulders were rigid beneath his hands, but she had bitten down on her sorrow and held it all ruthlessly in check as he bent to gently close Senena's eyes. Charo had already arranged the little queen's limbs in a more seemly fashion underneath the merciful concealment of the enveloping cloak, and now Kieran, murmuring a prayer of passage, reached to pull the cloak up to cover her face. Anghara had shut her own eyes, and tears welled unchecked from underneath her closed eyelids, spilling through the long eyelashes and down her cheeks. When Charo came round to take her arm, and the gentle pressure of Kieran's hand guided her to take a first step down the staircase awash with the blood of dead men, Anghara went where they led her, submissive to their will.

They had done the impossible—and it had all seemed, in retrospect, to have taken a ridiculously short time. Luck was still with them as they left the scene of the carnage; there was a sense of violation in the courtyards of the keep as Kieran and Charo, supporting Anghara between them, slipped through—but the keep still knew nothing of the vile deed, or who had done it. However, there were more than the usual number of the guards at the open gate, and they seemed uneasy about something. Kieran had stopped just out of sight, behind a jutting corner still deep in morning shadow; he and Charo watched grimly as two of the guards stopped a handful of servants on their way to the city marketplaces and rummaged through their bags.

"They'll never let us through," said Charo.

But Kieran was remembering something—throwaway words, quickly forgotten in the gathering power of the night before, uttered back in the stables. Melsyr's quick grin in the darkness . . . a flash of white teeth . . . *I'll swop duties with someone; it might be more useful if I'm guarding a back gate . . .*

"The postern," said Kieran brusquely. "It's our only chance. Come on."

They wheeled and stumbled back the way they had come. Kieran hesitated at the next corner, and Charo leaned closer. "Do you know where we're going?" he hissed.

"I know where Miranei's postern is from the outside," Kieran hissed back. "I could hardly ask directions for it in here. Adamo found out from one of his friends, and he said . . . give me a moment . . ."

"Go left," said a faint, unexpected voice. "There's a passage from this courtyard."

Kieran glanced down at Anghara with a sense of surprise. He should have remembered this was her childhood home. He nodded. "Come on, Charo."

He saw the archway leading into the passage she had mentioned, and then had to flatten the three of them against the wall as five soldiers emerged, moving fast. Their faces were set into expressions ranging from unease to what was almost panic in the case of the youngest. They passed without turning their heads; Kieran waited for a tense moment to see if any more were likely to emerge before drawing his blade with a soft hiss. "I'll go first," he said softly. "You follow, Charo, help Anghara. Be careful."

Charo nodded, wasting no words, loosening his own weapon. Kieran moved forward with wary caution. The narrow arched gate widened into a broad walkway—initially a tunnel, torches guttering in sconces on either side, abruptly metamorphosing into a cloister surrounding a grassy square with a fountain set into the central sward.

"Keep to the left," Anghara's voice came from behind, pitched only just loud enough for Kieran to hear. "There's another arch straight ahead."

There was; Kieran slipped inside. A sudden noise made him lift his hand, stilling the other two into silence, but the sound of footsteps faded into the distance and Kieran crept forward cautiously once again.

"Turn right at the end of this corridor," came the instruction, just as a blank wall seemed to cut off all forward passage. A narrow lane branched right and left at the T-junction, and Kieran, peering both ways, stepped into the right passage.

"At the end of this corridor," whispered Anghara, "there's a door; the latch is on this side, but there might be a guard on the other. We'll come out at the foot of the West Tower; the postern is set into the base of the tower itself."

"Wait a minute," said Kieran softly. "The West Tower? This isn't the postern I know. That lets into the city. This one . . ."

"This one leads into the foothills," said Charo, a touch of quickening excitement in his voice. "Well done, cousin. If the unease spreads out into the city, at least we'll be well out of it . . ."

"In the mountains, on foot, with no supplies at the tail end of winter," said Kieran. "Still, the idea has merit. If we are seen to enter Miranei for the first time only after this whole mess, it might be easier to get out again quietly, as opposed to us trying to sneak out of the city once what happened this morning becomes known."

There was no man at the latch-gate at the end of the corridor, but there were three at a small sturdy door set into the Western Tower. One of them, wearing the insignia of a commander of some rank, was leaning casually on the ill-tempered face of a gargoyle made of tarnished metal and wearing a black iron ring through its broad nostrils, set into the door.

"That's the postern?"

"Yes," Anghara said, and her voice was barely louder than breath. "The door is stone. From the outside, you can't see it. It looks as though it is a part of the wall . . ."

There was a sudden silence, and even as Kieran turned his head he saw Anghara crumple soundlessly and Charo's arms go around her as she fell. "Out," Charo said, "like a candle. It's all been too much."

Kieran paused for another moment, turning back to the conversation at the gate, and then his lips tightened. "Set her down just inside the door," he said, "and we can only pray that nobody comes this way until we're done. Make it fast, Charo; if we make any more noise in Miranei today, we will never get out of here. I'll take the captain."

Charo nodded. "The other two are mine."

The surprise was total, and that instant in which the soldiers could do nothing but gape open-mouthed at the two apparitions who issued forth from the maw of the keep was all Kieran and Charo needed. The captain had time to pull his jewelled dagger out of its sheath, but looked unsure as to what to do with it; all too obviously a lordling of some description. Few men in Sif's army had leadership positions through court connections rather than merit, but there were some; the captain on postern duty this morning was one of them. Kieran felt no compunction in despatching him, thinking even as he straightened that he had probably done Sif a favor. When he turned, it was to see Charo bending over the second man he had just bested. Kieran could see the guardsman's chest moving in short, shallow breaths.

Charo seemed curiously reluctant to finish him off.

"What is it?" Kieran said, taking a step closer.

"The other one's dead, but this is Melsyr," said Charo. "I only skewered him through the shoulder; it should bleed enough to convince them he put up a fight, but not so much that his life is in danger." Charo grinned, the dangerous, wolfish grin of a man who had just killed—a man who scented victory. "This is a great heart," he said. "If I ever meet him again, I swear I'll bow before him."

"Get Anghara," said Kieran, wiping his blade on a corner of the dead guardsman's cloak and sheathing it. Charo bounded away toward the gate, and returned bearing his foster sister's limp form in his arms.

"She weighs no more than a Cascin goose," he said, the indignity of the remark almost an antidote to the anxiety in his voice. "She's still out; I don't like the look of it."

"She'll be all right," said Kieran, very gently. "It's a pity you had to knock Melsyr out . . . he said he'd give much for a chance to see us take Anghara out of here."

But when he looked down on Melsyr's prone form, he saw an echo of Charo's grin on Melsyr's face, his eyes open and blazing. "Go," he said. "I have seen. The Gods bless you."

Kieran dropped onto one knee beside him, pressing his good shoulder in a gesture of gratitude which spoke louder than any words.

"There is a horse and some blankets in a copse just off the path," Melsyr said, grimacing with pain. "I made them ready, on the chance you might pass this way. I could not do more."

"You did enough," Kieran told him. "More than enough. Will you be all right?"

"They won't suspect me," said Melsyr. "Go."

Kieran rose to his feet. "We'll meet again," he said. "Stay well."

He pulled at the ring threaded through the gargoyle's nose, and with a groan of protesting hinges the postern, a part of Miranei's battlements, swung slowly open. When the thick stone door was open enough for him to see a glimpse of trees and mountains, Kieran dropped the ring and glanced about. "We can't close this from the outside," he said. "As soon as they get here they'll know exactly where we went. Come on, we need a head start; they'll be after us before we know it."

Charo slipped out first, Anghara still in his arms; Kieran followed. They found the copse easily, and the things Melsyr had left there. He'd chosen a good horse—perhaps it was his own.

"When they discover where we came out, they'll look for us in the hills," said Kieran thoughtfully, rubbing the horses soft nose in an overture of friendship. "We ought to be far from here by then."

"The others don't know where we are," said Charo, "and we can't go far on our own with one horse, two blankets, and a saddlebag of food."

"You'll have to go back to the inn," said Kieran. "That's

where the rest will come, if they manage to get out of the keep. At the very least leave a message that we'll try to cut across the moors and link with Rochen."

"We might all stay in the city longer than we wish," said Charo grimly. "And if they dig into our stories too deeply . . . none of us will see Rochen again." And then his eyes cleared again, glowing with a fierce exhilaration. "But we did it!" he crowed, hitting his thigh with a closed fist. "We did it, Kieran! And now . . . now the real work begins."

"Yes, and now Sif will scour the country for us with even greater zeal. I don't know why he held back for so long, but when he finds out what his hesitation has wrought in Miranei, he won't make the same mistake again. We've shown our hand; he knows the only thing we might want with Anghara is to raise her up in his place. And he won't sit back and let that happen."

Anghara moaned softly, turning her head. Both youths turned sharply at the sound, in time to see her eyes flicker open.

"Rochen will be at Lucher?" Charo said tersely, without taking his eyes off Anghara. She was very pale, and her skin was drawn tightly across cheekbones which seemed to be made of glass.

Kieran nodded mutely. Charo raised a hand to adjust his cloak's fastening at his throat. "Get her there," he said. "I don't know what that devil did to her while she was in his clutches, but this is a score I'm taking on. Look at her."

Kieran hadn't taken his eyes off her since he had first seen her upon the battlements at dawn, unless it was to find a path in Miranei's labyrinthine courtyards, or raise a sword to clear it before him. Charo's words had already been written in his own heart.

"She looks too frail to be real," said Charo.

"We'll meet you in Lucher," said Kieran. "Get going."

Without another word Charo turned and melted into the dappled shadows of the wood.

Anghara still looked impossibly fragile, but her eyes had regained the steadiness he remembered from years before; it was this that gave Kieran the first intimation that the words he had been repeating ever since they had snatched her—*she'll be all right*—might have some truth. He had not quite wholly believed them himself.

"We still have a moment or two," he said. "Do you want to rest a while longer? I think Melsyr left a wineskin . . ."

She nodded; taking the gesture as an assent both to a few more minutes' rest and a sip of wine, he rummaged for the wineskin and passed it over, dropping to one knee beside her. She lifted the skin to her lips, took a few swallows, her eyes closed; and then she laid it on her lap and met his gaze, her own eyes once again brimming with tears. "I missed you," she said, very quietly.

"I promised Feor I would find you," Kieran said. "I must have scoured all of Roisinan seven times over; we buried Feor last summer, and he went to his grave thinking you lost forever. Where were you, Anghara?"

"Kheldrin," she said softly, dropping her gaze.

The bluntness of it took him by surprise.

"Kheldrin?" he echoed, when he'd got his breath back. She could almost read his mind—the shock, the doubt, the sense of violation; he was from Shaymir, after all, and, as al'Tamar had admitted, occasional Kheldrini traders had long been finding their way into Shaymir from the northern fringes of the Kadun Khajir'i'id. The Shaymir folk had seen more of "Khelsies" than the average Roisinani. But even in Shaymir, Kheldrini, when their hosts weren't bargaining for their silk or amber, were avoided, suspected and feared. Perhaps it wasn't entirely surprising, the Shaymiri, if anyone, would have glimpsed some of the more arcane aspects of

Kheldrini culture. Kieran hadn't been back to his native land for any length of time since he had been sent to foster at Cascin, but he was a son of Shaymir for all that. And now Anghara, whom he had steadfastly sought over long years throughout what he thought of as the civilized lands, named as her sanctuary what had always been drilled into him as a dark and dangerous country.

"Why Kheldrin, for all the Gods' sake?" he demanded. "You could have come to us—to me; you must have known we would shelter you. I could have protected you . . ."

"I was a child, and you were young; you had no base to fight from, as you do today—not then. And remember where I ran from—remember what happened to the last place which gave me sanctuary . . ."

"How did you survive Bresse?" he asked, his voice husky. "Feor went to seek you, and found only a message: *The young queen lives.* It was then he sent me after you. I traced you to the river . . . and the river seemed to have swallowed you. And yet . . . I was sure you were alive, and waiting somewhere . . ."

"I was safe, Kieran," she said, reaching for his hand. "I was safe, and . . . there were times when . . . I was even happy. And I learned . . . so much."

"Khelsie magic," he said, too quickly, his reaction a recoil born of pure instinct.

A shadow of pain crossed her face. "We are not so very different from one another," she murmured. "But Bresse, Kheldrin . . . it doesn't matter. It's all gone, Kieran. There's a great empty place inside of me where Sif ripped something away; I cannot even reach for Sight any more. I tried, at the battlements, to help you . . . it would have been easier, less bloody, less violent . . . but you saw what happened."

"Does Sif know?"

"I think . . . Senena knew." There was a catch in her voice, and Kieran, seeking to distract her from this line of thought, raised her to her feet.

"Come on. It's time we were moving. They must have organized themselves by now. I'd rather not be here when they discover the open postern."

She let him hoist her onto the horse and then he vaulted up into the saddle behind her, holding her against him with his left arm. They rode in silence, with Kieran choosing to skirt the edges of the concealing foothills for as long as he could, until the bulk of the castle was almost out of sight. His silence was composed of the peace of finally holding the foster sister lost so long ago, whom he had sworn to find and protect; of calculations as to how best to get Anghara to Lucher, the loyal village; and of contemplating how many of the men he had led into Miranei would walk outside its walls again. He also kept an ear cocked to their rear, waiting for sounds of pursuit. It was Anghara, therefore, who watched the gray expanse of moorland which stretched out at their left; and Anghara who roused in the circle of Kierah's arm to point at a distant smudge on the horizon.

"Over there," she said quietly. "What's that?"

Kieran reined in the horse, narrowing his eyes against a sun which had already leapt almost into the noon zenith, and then drew his right hand over his face in a gesture of unutterable weariness. "Sif," he said. "It has to be Sif. He's too early, damn him. We're too close to Miranei. It is not over yet."

"Perhaps we should have stayed in the keep," said Anghara faintly. "And just barred it against him."

"You do not have the men or the arms to hold it," said Kieran. "Yet. Your name has been kept alive in Roisinan, but it will still take more to convince them its bearer is likewise. And only then . . . Right now, there are too many with their loyalties still divided, and their knowledge of the keep is more than enough to hand it to Sif in a siege. Remember, that's how he achieved Miranei in the first place."

Anghara looked down onto her folded hands for a moment and bit her lip. But when she glanced up at Kieran, her gray eyes were steady. "And now?" she asked.

"I hope Rochen wasn't in his path," said Kieran. "We might be on our own. But I still mean to try and get you to Lucher. At least there they will shelter . . ."

"No," she said. "If there is any chance of Sif taking it out on the innocent . . . no. Where would you look for Rochen and the rest of the men?"

"There should have been a base camp . . ."

"Is that where the rest of them will make for . . . if they get out of the city?"

"Yes, but . . ."

"Let's find that first. And then we shall see."

"But we'll have to ride almost at the army's heels, across open moors," said Kieran helplessly.

"Until they get to Miranei and learn what happened there," said Anghara, "they will not be looking back."

Kieran said nothing more, but when the smudge on the horizon drew level with them and resolved into Sif's returning army he urged the horse into a cautious canter, angling into the moors and to the rear of what he thought Sif's main body of men might be.

The luck held for a span longer; Kieran led them into a shallow curve which skirted Sif's rearguard, and they flanked the army unobserved. But then it seemed as though their good fortune had come to an abrupt end.

A ring of cold ashes. A broken knife half buried in the turf. Trampled ground. A torn piece of cloth, dark with what looked like blood.

"Yours?" Anghara asked quietly after a moment's stunned silence in which Kieran had simply sat his horse motionlessly and stared at the evidence before him.

"If any escaped," he said after another moment, his voice sounding tired and much older than his years, "I will find them; I know where they will have gone."

He slipped off the horse and crouched closer to what had been the campfire, peering at it.

Anghara, wincing, let herself down as well, rubbing a cramped leg; she let him have his silence. The horse nosed rather hopelessly at the bitter moor grasses at its feet.

The sun slipped slowly across the sky; days were still winter-short, and there wasn't much daylight left. Anghara walked about for a few minutes to stretch her legs, then returned to lean gratefully against the horse's warm, hospitable flank. She still felt weaker than a new-hatched chick, and was contemplating calling to Kieran, a few paces away and engrossed in his investigations, to leave off and try instead to find a place where they could stop for the night. But then the silence of the moors was broken by . . . something. The horse lifted its head, with a snort; Anghara reached instinctively for its nostrils.

"Kieran," she said sharply, a fraction of a second before his own head came up, and he sprang to his feet, loosening the sword in his scabbard. Horses.

"Take the beast and get back," he said levelly.

She would have demurred but a look at his face stopped her; she did as she was told. From behind the shelter of the horse's body, she stared across its back as the thunder of approaching hoof beats metamorphosed into four riders. Four riders wearing the livery of the keep guard.

She heard Kieran's sword sing free of its sheath, and in the next moment she heard her own voice shouting, "Kieran! Put up! It's the twins!"

Charo, in the lead, stood up in his stirrups and waved, as though to confirm her words; Kieran's sword sank down until its point rested on the spongy sward. "Four?" he said softly, sick at heart.

"Kieran!" Charo called out. "Wait!"

Now they could see the newcomers were leading two empty horses, one saddled, the other free, led only by a rope halter.

It wasn't until they came to an untidy stop almost at Kieran's feet that the significance of the deserted campsite occurred to them. Adamo swallowed convulsively. But it was left up to Charo to ask, "Are they all dead?"

"Not all," said Kieran. "Or there would be bodies."

Anghara hadn't thought of that. Of course; there would have had to have been bodies if Sif's soldiers had simply overrun the camp. Sif's army wouldn't have waited to bury the dead. There had to have been survivors.

Adamo straightened in the saddle, casting his eyes around the moors. Shadows were lengthening. "Perhaps we'd better find a place to lie up tonight," he said. "And I'd rather it wasn't here. I wouldn't like to light that cold fire."

"We brought your Sarevan, Kieran," said Charo proudly, glancing in the direction of the bare-backed horse he himself had on a lead rein. "We didn't have time for such niceties as saddling a riderless horse. Sorry."

"Whose was the other?" Kieran said.

"It's Daevar's," said Adamo quietly. "We lost him to an arrow; we couldn't tarry to pick him up when he fell."

"And the others?" said Kieran bleakly.

"They didn't make it."

"You were shot at?" Anghara asked him abruptly. "Were you followed?"

They hesitated. It was Charo who answered at last. "The main gates were still closed when we turned to look for the last time."

"I think they have their hands full tonight at the keep," said Kieran grimly. "If anyone could organize a posse at this short notice out of the chaos we left behind, it's probably

Sif—but he's got important deaths to deal with tonight. We may have a few hours."

"He might think it better to chase after us while we're still close enough not to tax his men," said Charo.

"He's just come back from a campaign," said Kieran. "All he may know is that five men were seen fleeing the city, one of whom was accounted for by a lucky shot; the escaped prisoner wasn't with them. Four men aren't worth the trouble, and he won't want to lose the important trail in the dark. He'll come for us tomorrow. We'd better put as many miles between us as we can before then."

Their choices were few—north through Brandar Pass into Shaymir, back into the western hills, or down across the open moors, south or east, and in either direction there was a river barring their way. But beyond the southern river lay Bodmer Forest, and that was Kieran's country. They would find shelter, and allies. If only they could outrun Sif's army to get there.

They snatched perhaps an hour or two of sleep, long after midnight; Anghara had found it hard to rouse from an exhausted slumber when Kieran gently shook her awake in the dark hour before dawn so they could ride on. But she insisted on Kieran riding his own horse; riding double would only wear out the horses and slow them down.

The moors around Miranei itself were an extension of the mountains at its back—mostly high, flat country. But the land folded itself into gently rolling fells as the small company rode south and east. They drove the horses hard, but they'd had to slow down a little once they gained the fells; they could ill afford an accidental toss or a lame horse. They paused for a moment at what felt close to midday, to give the animals a brief respite; the sun was warm upon their upturned faces, and the horses were already lathered with effort. The ground rose before them, first gently, then increasingly steeply; they were in the lee of the bare slope of a hill, not very high in its own right but looking as though it might command an unimpeded view of the surrounding moors. And there was an illusion of greater height, imparted by the presence of a tumble of huge granite boulders crowning the hill. At least one of these, too obviously shaped to be natural, looked as if it had once been a Standing Stone. Anghara's eyes were full of this. What Kieran saw was different. A vantage point.

"From up there," Kieran said abruptly, "we would know."

"Yes," Anghara agreed. "We would know."

There was something still of power on the hill's broken crown, something which clung to the hill like a barely visible mantle. Perhaps it was this that held Kieran back, despite his earlier comment. His companions sat their mounts in morose silence, one or two casting their eyes back the way they had come. They knew without doubt they were being followed—having Anghara with them, how could they not be—but they didn't know by whom, or how many. The hill could tell them. But the hill first had to be climbed; and none of them seemed to have the inclination to do it.

In the end it was Anghara herself who swung down from her mount with a decisive motion. She staggered and almost fell as aching legs, weakened by the punishment of this hard ride so soon after her long incarceration, set up a clamor of protest. She caught herself on the pommel of her saddle and stood with her head bowed for a moment, gathering strength; then she let go, tossing the reins of Melsyr's horse to Adamo, who caught them more or less automatically.

"We have to know," she said, turning to Kieran, her eyes defensive. "And I am blind. I may as well look with other sight."

"And if anyone's watching, they'll know exactly where we are," said one of the men.

Kieran reached a decision and swung off his own horse. "We'll both go," he said.

"Madness," said Adamo. "Now if we lose you, we lose you both."

"For the sake of all the Gods, then, hurry! My bones tell me they can't be far behind," said Charo, chewing his lip.

Anghara was still weak, looking more frail and transparent than ever, her eyes bruised with great dark circles which bit into the pallor of her cheeks. Something gave her strength, though; she turned and strode up the incline without looking back, leaving Kieran to scramble after her. He reached her in two or three long steps and frowned.

"You've changed," he said. "In Feor's classroom you were always the cautious, careful one. I don't remember you being this impatient, this rash. First bearding Sif's army on the open moor, now this. What are you trying to prove?"

"It is Sight that drives me," she said, "the Sight that is gone from me. You, who have never had to live with it, cannot know what it's like to lose it. It's like I'm missing half my soul." She shivered. "This place is . . . there's something about this hill. Even blind, it touches me. It is a dark feeling . . . as though something . . . died . . . and yet, I welcome it. Even that. It heals me while it wounds me." Her eyes glittered strangely as she stared up at the tumbled stones. "I have talked with the Old Gods, Kieran. There is real power in Kheldrin."

"I cannot understand you when you talk of those things," said Kieran. It had taken severe self-control not to snap again at the mention of that alien land.

"No," she said, not looking at him, smiling into the distance. "You're human."

"So are you, damn it!" he said, goaded to anger.

"No," said Anghara, softly but emphatically, remembering an echo of a God's voice—al'Khur had called her something . . . what was it? A name of power. Inhuman power, great enough to have shackled a God's will. And he had said . . . he had said she would claim it. "Once, perhaps, I was. No longer. Even blind, no longer."

Their last few steps to the hill's summit were taken in silence. Snow still lay in the crevices of the huge boulders. Anghara's foot sank ankle-deep into a pile hidden in the cool shadows underneath the stones as she scrambled onto one of the lowest and crouched there, slowly sweeping the horizon with eyes shaded under her hand against the bright midday sunlight. Suddenly her hand dropped from her face into a pointing arrow in one graceful motion.

"There. Look," she said, keeping her voice low although there was nobody to hear her except Kieran. "They are too far to see what standard they bear. But it is Sif. Only he could lead so many, so soon. They've sent out an army, Kieran. If we cannot outrun them, we are lost."

Kieran swept his eyes from the distant cohorts of men who hunted him, staring at the empty, winter-gray moors with something like despair. "Back," he said at last, but his voice was flat, and there was no hope in it. "Back to the horses. I don't know where we can run that he can't follow, but I will not wait for Sif to simply pluck me like a trapped pheasant. I plan to give him as much trouble as I can."

But Anghara sat back on her heels and turned steady gray eyes on him. "Take the others, and go for the forest," she said, very quietly.

He whipped around to face her, not knowing whether to be angry or simply baffled. "And you? What of you? You don't think I'd just leave you for him, do you? I didn't snatch you from Sif's dungeons to hand you back to him on a silver platter!"

"I'll make for the coast," said Anghara, with only the briefest of hesitations. "There will be a ship at Calabra that will bear me."

"You would never make it," began Kieran, and then the import of her words struck him. "Calabra? Where would you go? Kheldrin?"

"Would you set me on the throne in Sif's place, Kieran?"

"I wanted to find you, to make sure you were safe," said Kieran, after a slight hesitation. "I did not think beyond that, not in detail, but yes, that is what I would do." His eyes blazed with love and loyalty. For the men he led, Anghara's name had been a symbol, a word to conjure light with when Sif's darkness became too great to bear. For Kieran, a part of her had always been, would always be, the little foster sister to whom he had once given his cloak in the rain. If she were a queen, that was something over and above this—but when Kieran had ridden the length and breadth of Roisinan, keeping Anghara's name alive, it had not been Anghara Kir Hama he sought. It had been a little girl he had once loved.

"I came back to claim Miranei," Anghara said, with a brittle laugh. "It was time, the Gods said. But it isn't time, Kieran. Not yet, not now. Would you let a cripple rule Roisinan?" Something swirled in her eyes for a moment—pain, wrath, madness—then it was gone, but Kieran knew what he had seen. He shivered suddenly, not from the cold, from a prescience that was bone-deep: she was wounded, and Kheldrin was the only place that could heal her.

He fought the knowledge; it went against everything he had always believed, but he knew it for truth, and at last he squared his jaw and met her eyes. "You'll never make it," he repeated. "Calabra of all places will be watched. But there is always Shaymir."

"Shaymir?" Anghara repeated, genuinely puzzled for a moment, and then her face cleared with comprehension. "You mean the mountains?"

"The Khelsies come. Somehow," Kieran said, shrugging his shoulders.

"But I don't know the mountains," Anghara said slowly. "I don't know the way."

"If there is one, it can be found," he said steadily. It struck a chord with her, as though she had heard the words before; and then she remembered. It already seemed like centuries ago, but al'Tamar had said it to her beside the ocean at the foot of Gul Khaima. *Paths can be found.*

"As for the mountains . . . you won't be alone." Kieran reached up to the boulder on which she was still perched, and swung her down to the ground beside him. "I will be with you."

5

In retrospect, Kieran almost wished Anghara had argued harder. Or that he had listened. The trek to Kheldrin had always sat ill with him; but the closer they came to their goal, the worse he felt about the whole thing, even given that strange, soul-deep knowledge which kept telling him Kheldrin was the one place she would find healing. Yet even so . . . the closer they drew, the stranger Anghara became. Kieran glanced across the campfire where she lay sleeping restlessly, her bandaged arm folded across her belly, and frowned, crushing between suddenly savage fingers a sprig of Shaymir desert sage he had been rubbing against his palm. The sweet scent of the herb lanced him, as always; it acted like a drug, cracking open sealed memories with the ease of magic. This time, with Anghara lying there before him, the memories were recent.

Sif. Miranei. The army on the moors.

Once Anghara had made up her mind, back by the hill crowned with the Standing Stones, there had been no real discussion. Adamo had taken her decision better than Kieran had expected.

"Kheldrin?" he asked quiedy. "Was that where you'd been hiding all this time?" He rooted in his horse's saddlebags, digging for something which had migrated to the bottom, and hauled out the small package of Anghara's *an'sen'thar* finery he had rescued from the inn in Calabra. "Is that where these came from?"

Anghara received the bundle and sat staring at it for a long moment before lifting her eyes to meet Adamo's. "Yes," she said, and her voice was oddly emotionless, flat. "That's where these came from." *I wonder if I will ever have the right to wear them again* . . . an uneasy thought, brushing the surface of her mind. Unspoken.

Charo had had to be almost forcibly restrained from adding himself to the party which was to go on to Kheldrin, but eventually it was Anghara's word that held him. "Stay," she'd said. "Raise me an army for you to lead."

After that, it was only a question of trying to figure out a way to make Sif abandon the chase long enough for them to slip away. As usual, it was Adamo who thought up the means, and Kieran who pieced together the plan.

"Isn't Ram's Island close hereabouts?" Adamo had asked speculatively.

It had taken Kieran less than a second. He clicked his fingers. "The boat."

"What boat?" Anghara asked. She had yet to mount Melsyr's horse again after coming down from the hill. She stood leaning against it, her eyes half closed.

"There's always a boat hidden there. The island's midstream, too small and overgrown to be of any interest to anyone but a bunch of brigands like ourselves," said Charo with a limpid grin. "It comes in useful in emergencies."

"Let's go," said Kieran. "It's only for a little while longer, Anghara. Can you manage?"

"I'll have to," she said; but she spoke through clenched teeth and it took her three tries before she could regain her saddle. After long months in a tiny airless cell she was exhausted. Kieran and Adamo exchanged worried looks behind her back—but that back, once she'd managed to remount, was straight. She was asking no favors.

They rode like the wind, aware they were leaving a broad trail for Sif to follow—but the subterfuge Kieran had in mind would start later, and Kieran had nothing against Sif's knowing his quarry had made for the river. There was little chitchat as they pushed forward. Night caught up to them, and, like the night before, they paused for only a few hours before moving on. They rode most of the next day, until the exhausted horses began to flag, keeping just a step ahead of Sif's army, with only the low hills denying the hunters a clear sight of their quarry. Twice Charo and another man circled back; twice they returned with splashes of fresh blood on their clothes, and riding fresh horses. Anghara had taken one look, and forbore to ask for the details; of course Sif would send out scouts, fast riders who would be able to shake free of the bulk of the army and chase after the fugitives on swift steeds. It seemed few of these men would live long enough to return to report to Sif.

But the dispatching of a few scouts was not enough.

"We'll never make it," one of the men muttered, as the sun began to sink on their second day out. "We'll kill the horses first."

For answer, Adamo pointed ahead, where sunlight glanced off something bright and lanced into the eye. "Water," he said economically.

Here the River Hal made a shallow loop northward, wending its way through the hills, and it was this loop they finally gained in the dying hours of their second day as fugitives. The horses snorted and pricked up their ears, scenting water.

"Don't let them drink too much," Kieran said, easing his own horse close to the bank and slipping off its back, glancing swiftly up- and downstream. "Where is the island?"

Charo gauged the lay of the land with a quick, experienced eye. "It's upstream," he said. "Not too far away. Which horse is the least winded? I'll go for the boat."

"He'll have to swim out for it," said Adamo, before Anghara could ask.

If she could have asked. By now she was drooping like a scythed flower; it was doubtful she could have lasted much longer on horseback. In Adamo's opinion, it was already miracle enough she had managed to stay with them thus far.

"Perhaps it's just as well you'll be taking to the water," Adamo said to Kieran in a low voice. "She'll need a rest before she will be able to ride again. Given a choice, she should have been taken from that thrice-damned dungeon straight into some goodwife's feather bed, and fed herb infusions and chicken broth until she got her strength back."

"Instead she gets this crazy escape, a wild ride across the fells, and is dropped from the spit into the fire," said Kieran with a grimace. "If only Sif had got back a day later . . . we wouldn't have had to run like this. There would have been time." He stirred, glancing back over his shoulder uneasily to where two of his entourage had gone to keep an eye out for Sif's forerunners, then threw a restless glance in the direction Charo had vanished. "Come on. If the horses have had enough, let's follow Charo."

They found him sitting beside a small coracle drawn up on the shore, his sword naked on the ground beside him, pulling his boots on. Hearing their approach he'd reached for the blade and then relaxed as he realized who they were. Beyond him, some distance away, a dark blot in midstream, bathed in dark shadows; it was already twilight, with a pale moon riding a sky still bright with traces of sunset.

He'd glanced up with a smile, some crack at the ready, but before he had a chance to speak one of the rearguard came galloping back on his exhausted gray. "It's too close, Kieran," the man said as he came to a shuddering halt a handspan away from Kieran's own horse.

"Where's Keval?"

"Dead," came the shocking response. Only now did they register the dark stain on his tunic, the way he sat with an arm folded painfully against his ribs. "There were six this time. We did for four, and I think we wounded number five, but Keval paid for that—and number six is on his way back to Sif even now. I hadn't a hope of catching him, not even if I'd taken one of his friends' horses. Whatever you're planning Kieran, do it now. My guess is that you have perhaps an hour before Sif falls upon us."

Kieran slid off his horse, tossing the reins to Adamo. "You take care of him for me," he said. "Come, Anghara. It's time we were away."

It looked as though he'd simply gone over to help her down from her own beast, but it was painfully obvious to Adamo, who was watching closely, that he lifted her bodily off the horse, and that if he had not she would have fallen. Kieran supported her firmly but unobtrusively the few paces to the boat, and lifted her inside.

"I'll be right back," he said.

"Kieran . . ." She'd reached out and caught the edge of his sleeve, eyes wide and ringed with bruised purple circles, shocking against the pallor of her face.

"What is it?" he asked, turning back.

She'd glanced back past him at the three who waited beyond, her gray eyes filled with tears. "Kieran . . . don't let anything happen to them . . ."

She might have turned seventeen, but Kieran suddenly, heartbreakingly, saw the nine-year-old Brynna Kelen in her face, and something in him rose now, as then, to stand over her and shield her from harm. Unexpectedly, surprising even himself, he bent forward to kiss her lightly on the brow. "It will be all right. Wait for me here."

Charo had pulled on his boots and gone to stand with the other two waiting in the moonlit twilight. Three of them. Not enough—surely not enough . . . Sif could reach out and crush them without trying. But then Kieran squared his jaw and strode across to the waiting men.

"I want him to think we've all crossed the river," he said quietly. "Once across . . . there's three of you, seven horses. Split up three different ways—Adamo, you take care of Sarevan for me, the rest of the horses go with only one of you—perhaps Sif will think that the biggest group . . . We'll see. Ditch the uniforms, for all the Gods' sakes, as soon as you have a chance. Rendezvous at the forest base, but only once you're sure you've shaken them. Go to ground somewhere first, if you have to. Those who lived through the obliteration of Rochen's camp are bound to do the same. Link up with whomever you can—and then go, spread the word. We will return. And when we do, we'd better have an army at our back."

"We'll have one waiting," Charo promised. And then, the clown in him unquenchable, he glanced down at his boots with comic consternation. "You mean I'll have to get these wretched things off again? The dainty lad whom I took them off had feet three sizes too small—that's punishment enough, but pulling them off and on like this is torture. It's a good thing I won't have to walk . . ."

"Shut up, Charo," Kieran said affectionately. "Get going. Tell Rochen . . ." he stopped, swallowing a sudden lump. Rochen had been a good friend, a marvellous lieutenant, but there was no guarantee he would be amongst the survivors of that fateful camp, no guarantee he would be receive any message Kieran might think to send him. Anyway, the important things . . . he'd know without being told. "Go," he said instead, reaching out to clap Adamo on the shoulder. "The Gods go with you."

"And my blessing. And my gratitude. And my love."

Anghara. Somehow she'd clambered out of the coracle and approached unheard; now she stood a pace beyond Kieran, swaying but straight. It had been another abrupt metamorphosis; there was nothing about this figure of moonlight and shadow that recalled a little girl called Brynna. This was all queen, the Kir Hama name mantling her like a cloak. Adamo was the first to move—to take the few steps that separated them, and fall to one knee before her, taking her hand in both of his.

"My queen," he said, but his head was not bowed, and in his eyes was all the love given to a sister. "We will be here when you return."

Charo came next, bending over the same hand with the gallant grace that was the essence of him. And then, equally characteristically, he ruined it all with a fierce grin that lit the twilight like a beacon. "Yes! When you come back . . . it will be to ride into Miranei and claim more than just a dungeon for your own! And I'll be there to open the gates for you!"

The last man, Bron, had been bound to her through the rescue from Sif's dungeon, and, before that, through Kieran's tireless, faithful search. But he didn't have the bonds the others shared with the young queen. Not for him these intimate farewells. All he could do was kneel before her, as Adamo had done, and reiterate Adamo's promise—but Anghara raised him, gently, and her smile for him had no less warmth than she had bestowed upon the others. Taking him in; his had been a mad adventure, and he was part of the family now, tied with blood. His own, shed in Anghara's cause, even now stained his tunic—a blood brother, then, where the rest shared closer ties. But there was always a blood price; the old Gods of Kheldrin had taught her to accept the gift this one had bought.

And then it was over, and Adamo, with a last glance at Anghara, was on his horse, the reins of two of the empty-saddled beasts tied securely to his saddle. The other man, Bron, had the other two. Charo had paused to haul off his stolen boots once again and bundle them up in his cloak, high up on his back, before mounting his own horse, wincing as bare feet slid into cold iron stirrups.

"No point in getting one's shoes wet when one doesn't have to," he offered by way of explanation as he urged his horse past.

Adamo's mount was already fetlock deep into the river. Bron's followed. Charo urged his in at a canter, and plunged into the water with a yell only partly muted by his recollection that there might be an army close enough to hear. And then they were all no more than bobbing dark shapes in the moonlit river.

"Come," Kieran said. "It's time we were moving."

The boat was conspicuous on the pale water, but Kieran couldn't help that—he could only hope Sif's men weren't watching their silent progress upstream. Anghara's farewell seemed to have taken the last of her strength; she lay huddled in the prow of the coracle—asleep or unconscious—while Kieran rowed them up the Hal, toward the forest.

It was full light when Anghara woke, to find the small boat pulled into a stagnant rush-filled pool at the river's edge. Kieran, stretched out on a piece of dry, sandy ground nearby, was dozing, but sat up as her eyes opened as though pricked by some sixth sense.

"Morning," he said, smiling warmly. "So far, so good. How are you feeling?"

"Like all my bones have been broken, and reset in the wrong places," Anghara answered truthfully.

He gazed at her for a long moment, his eyes thoughtful. "It won't do," he said at last. "You won't last a week. You need some place to lie low for a few days, sleep safe, eat properly."

She roused. "Kieran, I told you, I don't want to put anyone in any danger . . ."

"Even Sif," said Kieran stubbornly, "is hardly likely to go bothering every woodcutter for news of you just yet. And we'll have to leave the river before we get to Tanass Han anyway. There's an old man who lives at the edge of the forest; his wife bandaged a festering arm for me once. They'll take you in." And, when she looked as though she would protest again, he raised a peremptory arm to forestall her. "No arguments," he said. "Anghara, don't you understand? You're riding the ragged edges, even now . . . Sif is quite possibly only hours behind us, and there is no way we can outrun him, not with you as weak as a day-old kitten. You'll be safe with old Miro and his wife. It's just for a few days; you need to get your strength back, and this is a start."

But Anghara had latched onto something else. "You sound as though you mean to leave me there."

"I do," he said, and then had to smile at the expression on her face. "Not to abandon you. But I do need to get us some horses, if we plan on getting any further. The way we are . . . This bedraggled crew, in this kind of craft, would cause a definite stir in Tanass Han—and you can be sure Sif will hear of that. Our paths now lie on the back roads."

And so it proved. Miro and Ani, his wife, took in Anghara without demur; Ani had her tucked up in bed within an hour of her arrival, and Anghara, despite her protests, surprised herself by waking almost six hours later, rested and ravenous. There was no sign of Kieran.

He was gone for six days, returning on the seventh with three mismatched horses. Anghara fairly flew at him. "Where have you been? Don't you know I've been out of my mind with worry?"

"Didn't Miro tell you? Sif hasn't been seen in this part of the world of late." Kieran asked, dismounting from the tall bay gelding he rode.

His tone was lightly teasing, and she turned away with a growl of frustration. He was at her side in two long strides. "Hey," he said, "I didn't mean to distress you. It's just that I didn't want to be seen bargaining for all our horses at any one place . . . and besides, you look a lot better. The week has done you good."

She'd glanced up at him, and then down again; there was once again a swirl of what was almost madness in her eyes. But he couldn't be sure he'd seen it—it was gone when next she met his gaze.

He'd wanted to make her stay another few days, at least—Ani was something of a wise-woman, and her herbs and potions seemed to have done Anghara the world of good. Her face had lost that taut, stretched look, and she had a bit of color in her cheeks; she was still painfully thin, but that would take time to remedy. Still, all of this was only physical; there was a restlessness in her which no herb of Ani's could heal. And that, in the end, could eventually undo all the good. Anghara was fretting to be on her way, and Kieran finally agreed.

The journey proved even more complicated than Kieran had originally thought. There were more patrols on the roads than ever before, and keeping clear of them was almost impossible; every now and again some path would be blocked and they would have to go around. They doglegged their way northeast, where the mountains which separated Shaymir from Roisinan faded into a broad saddle of low hills, tough to guard and easily accessible on horseback. But Sif kept pushing them further west, keeping them on track for the one place Kieran had hoped to avoid.

Bresse.

It was almost inevitable, in the end, that a last detour brought them within sight of the foothills where Castle Bresse used to stand. Anghara reined in and sat very still, her eyes on the remembered vistas. Kieran, a pace further, stopped his own horse.

"Anghara . . ."

She turned those luminous eyes on him—no madness there now, only a quiet, ineffable sorrow. "But I must," she said. "Perhaps, if we'd passed a day's ride away from here . . . but, now, I must. I cannot ride past this place without seeing what Sif has made of it."

"I'm not sure that's such a good idea," he muttered, but she had already nudged her horse's head around, and he could only follow.

The years had been kind. Not much was left of the White Tower; but the harshness of the ruin had been softened by ivy, and tiny white mountain flowers had woken to spring and peered shyly through the tall grass. White, like the robes the Sisters of Bresse had worn.

Anghara slipped off her horse and walked stiffly toward what had been the base of the tower. The earth had fallen in over what had to have been the stairway to the tunnel by which she had escaped. The whole layout was irreparably changed, but she went unerringly to stand at what had been the base of the tower's stairwell and raised her eyes up imaginary stairs into the corridors where she had first learned to ride her wild gifts.

"Ah, Morgan . . ." she whispered. "Where are you now . . ."

Feor had said there'd been a message left at Bresse for those who had the senses to hear it. A message which spoke of what had been done here, and in whose name; and a final testament: *The young queen lives.* Anghara strained with every fiber, every nerve taut with effort, but she could hear nothing except the sighing of the breeze in the tall grass and the occasional thrush among the trees. Perhaps, after all these years, it had faded away . . .

But even while not hearing Morgan's voice, Morgan's words, something deeper in her knew they were still here, they haunted this place and would do so while the world endured. And the pain of being deaf to them tore at her until she sank to her knees amongst the ruins with a cry of utter anguish.

Kieran, who had left her alone with her ghosts, came up at this and knelt beside her. "This was exactly why I didn't want to pass this way," he said, his voice filled with compassion, as he readied to lay a gentle hand on her shoulder.

Anghara turned and buried her face in his shoulder, sobbing; she had so much to say she could say nothing at all. Kieran respected the silence, holding her, offering the solace of his presence because he didn't know how to give her anything else.

"Do you think I'll ever be able to hear them again?" she asked plaintively after a while, rubbing at her tear-spiked eyelashes.

"I don't see why not," Kieran said sturdily, although he had no clue what she was talking about. But it seemed to do the trick. Anghara scrambled to her feet, flicking clinging bits of brush off her knees.

"Come on," she said, suddenly anxious to leave. "I can't . . . I can't bear this place. There is too much here . . . that I remember . . . too much I cannot reach . . ."

"I agree," said Kieran, with some alacrity. He didn't like the look of her. The madness had swirled back into her eyes, gray-blue, as she stared at the ruin of the White Tower, and he hated it when she started sounding fey. It separated them, an almost physical barrier he had no hope of ever scaling or even understanding. He wouldn't be sorry if the Khelsies told her the damage was permanent and she had to learn to live without the dangerous, fiery gift of her Sight . . . and then he caught himself with a gasp. These were Sif's thoughts, Sif's rationalization for the destruction he had let loose amongst his people—the destruction Kieran had spent the last four or five years fighting against. *What am I thinking?* he asked himself, aghast. *Would I really throw away something that someone I love treasures simply because I cannot understand it?*

In one thing, at least, Anghara was right. They would do

well to leave this place as soon as they might. It was doing neither of them any good.

There were also patrols in the foothills, but it was too broad a frontier to guard with a soldier on every knoll. They slipped through unobserved, and crossed into Shaymir on Kieran's birthday, a fact he found oddly symbolic.

Beyond the foothills, the land sloped away into moors not so much different from the one they had left behind in Roisinan.

"I thought this was a desert country," commented Anghara, who had never been to Shaymir.

"You'll see plenty of desert soon enough," Kieran said. The words were vaguely familiar; Anghara groped for them through a fog of confused memories, then recalled ai'Jihaar—ai'Jihaar on the ship. The same words had been said at the beginning of her last exile.

"There's no need to try and tangle ourselves into the real desert country before we have to," Kieran said. "You've no idea how difficult . . ." He caught her looking at him with a wry smile. "All right," he said, with a self-deprecating grin of his own, "so you do have an idea. Still . . . Let's stick to the plain while we can; and then I'd like to get us fresh horses for the next stretch, or perhaps even camels . . . but that depends on how rough the mountain passes might be—"

"*Ki'thar'en* are very adaptable," Anghara said.

"What are?"

"I mean . . . camels. We took them from the coastal plain into the Arad . . . and then into Khar'i'id . . ."

She got a blank stare in reply, and decided to leave it. Time enough for geography lessons, if they got through into Kheldrin. And, please the Gods, Kieran would never have to learn what Khar'i'id was . . .

The Shaymir plains soon petered out into what was only technically not desert—they became dry and dusty, the only grass intermittent hummocks of tall, dry, whispering blades.

Squat, spiny cactus-like plants began appearing, and after them it wasn't long before the harbinger of the real desert, the spicy, sweet fragrance of the tiny desert sage, reached out for them.

Kieran had become increasingly uneasy about Anghara. She wrapped herself in long, brooding silences which would last for hours, riding in a cocoon of solitude which was almost frightening. Once he caught her almost sleepwalking, wandering away from a campfire while his back was turned and stepping into a desert night without any idea as to where she was. That night they'd heard the distant baying of the colhots, desert predators who lived on carrion when they could find it, nevertheless fearless and inventive hunters who never avoided easy prey when it crossed their path. Another time she had sat beside a different campfire—and silent tears ran unheeded down her cheeks as her hand closed on a fistful of dusty sand, letting it trickle out between her fingers.

And tonight, here on the edge of the desert, he'd started awake to a breath of sudden wind which rushed through the still night like a sigh, and what had sounded like a strangled cry. The fire had died to glowing embers and the occasional faint flicker of flame; it was too dark initially to see anything, and Kieran narrowed his eyes to sharpen his night vision. Anghara's nest of blankets on the other side of the fire was empty.

He scrambled to his feet, groping for his sword. "Anghara! Anghara, where are you?"

Again, a sound; a sob, it sounded like. A sob of pain.

"Anghara!"

He took a few steps away from the fire and all but tripped over Anghara who lay prone on the sand. She clutched a narrow-bladed, black-hafted stiletto in her right hand—for a moment it was unfamiliar, but then memory returned and

Kieran recalled seeing it in the package Adamo had rescued from the Calabra inn. A Khelsie dagger.

A long gash on her left forearm oozed blood into the desert sand. Kieran's heart sank. "What in the name of all the Gods are you doing?" he whispered. "What heathen magic is this?"

She'd opened her eyes and they were twin gleams in the darkness. "It was in the name of the Gods that I did it," she whispered despondently. "There was a time . . . but now . . . look . . . there's blood on my sleeve . . ."

"Of course there's blood on your sleeve," he said uncomprehendingly, sheathing his sword and bending down to drape her good arm around his shoulders. "You've just laid your arm open. Come on, we'd better clean that up, its full of sand, and I wouldn't know what to do if it gets inflamed or infected."

"There was a time," she said, suddenly and strangely calm, "when there would have been no blood at all. But they didn't come . . . *al'Zaan, Sa'id-ma'sihai, qa'rum mali hariah?"*

And she'd fainted, gone slack in his arms, still clutching the black dagger in a death-grip he couldn't loosen. He'd left it, then, turning his attention to the wound it had inflicted. It wasn't deep, but it was long, running from the inside of her elbow to the wrist. She didn't seem to have sliced any major blood vessels, but there was a significant amount of bleeding nonetheless and much of it had clotted already, forming a crust around which blood still oozed. Kieran cleaned it up as best he could—twice he restarted the bleeding he'd staunched, and eventually had to resort to the emergency pressure points he'd learned from Madec, the healer who rode with his own band. Battle-spawned knowledge he had never thought he might have to use with Anghara Kir Hama, Queen of the Royal Line of Roisinan. He'd used a clean piece of linen to bandage the gash securely. During his ministrations Anghara had not stirred, nor let go of the black dagger. She seemed to be lost in some unpleasant dream of her own, tossing her head from side to side in the uneasy swoon she had fallen into—or was it sleep? Her brow was filmed with a thin sheen of sweat.

They were still far from Kheldrin.

Seated by the fire, staring at Anghara's restless slumber, Kieran found a small sprig of desert sage beneath his hand and pulled it out of the ground, almost unthinking, rolling the leaves between fingers and palm, releasing the scent into the clean desert night, remembering . . . and deeply afraid.

Anghara had been wrong. The Gods had come, the old Gods whom Kieran did not know. He had felt their breath on his face when he'd started from sleep. She had called them, and they had come, wild, loose, dangerous—Gods who had not walked on the eastern side of the Kheldrini mountains for more generations than anyone could remember. But they were here now, and she who had summoned them had no strength left to control them. Kieran's soul was cold as he sensed eager, inhuman eyes on the girl who writhed in the grip of violent nightmare in the pitifully small, safe circle of a dying campfire.

Kieran had been dreading the morning, but Anghara woke to lucidity—not that she could fail to wake to full knowledge of the events of the previous night, with a black dagger dark with dried blood clutched in one hand and a tight bandage on her other arm. Having inspected these, in silence, she raised her eyes to meet Kieran's rather wary blue gaze and, somewhat unexpectedly, laughed.

"It's all right, I'm not dangerous," Anghara said with a wry smile still playing around her mouth. She'd run an experimental hand over the ground at her heels, but it was too hard to scour her dagger clean desert-fashion, by simply plunging it into the sand. "Can I have something to clean this with?"

Kieran passed a rag. "I don't really want to ask this," he said carefully, "but what were you trying to do last night?"

She answered without looking at him, bent industriously over her blade. "Trying to prove something," she said, very quietly. He couldn't see her grimace but he could hear it in her voice as she said, "Although why I picked last night to try, I can't tell you. All I did was prove . . . that it still makes me ill . . ."

"What does?" He was on his feet. "Are you all right?"

She looked up at that, with another smile. "No, Kieran." There was pain in her eyes; her voice, infinitely gentle, was raw with it. "I wonder," she said, her eyes wide, focused somewhere beyond the horizon, "if he knew how deeply he wounded me . . ."

He. Sif. The specter who had ridden into Shaymir with them. Kieran's eyes darkened. "But you did . . ."

She focused her gaze back on him, after a beat of silence. "Did what?"

But Kieran had already thought better of it. Now was probably not the time to tell her about what he had felt last night. "No, it's not important. Do you feel like some breakfast?"

"I couldn't eat a thing," she said wanly.

"We've a long day ahead," he said, sounding like a mother scolding a recalcitrant child. "You need to keep your strength up."

"Very well," she said, after a small hesitation. "I'll try."

She didn't eat much, but Kieran didn't press the point. Anghara always seemed at her weakest in the morning, oddly enough—just after she had supposedly spent a good few hours resting during the night; it was as though she drew whatever strength was hers to muster from the effort of the day. This morning, more than ever, she seemed edgy and restless and frail—as though she smelled something in the wind.

"I feel . . . as though we're not alone," she said at length, pausing to look around as she was about to mount her horse.

Kieran felt an icy shiver down his spine. "What do you mean?" Could she sense them after all, those whom she had called here?

"I don't know," she said. "It's as though . . . Ah, but I'm dreaming. Oh, my head! I'm dizzy with headache. Kieran, what happened last night?"

"I only . . . woke when I heard you cry out," he said carefully, avoiding her eye.

She'd mounted by now, and seemed absorbed by the dried blood on her sleeve. But she roused after a moment and gave him a brave smile. "All right, I'm ready. Where to from here?"

"I think it's safe to start edging a little to the north now," said Kieran. "We should be past the Dance . . ."

"The Dance?" Her horse shifted nervously under sudden conflicting commands from heel and bit. "The Shaymir Dance . . . Perhaps that was what triggered . . . Is it close by? Can we . . ."

She had been luminous, transformed; a sudden light had flashed in the wide gray eyes. But then she reached for Sight—out of instinct, from the plinth of power—and Kieran could see the instant of breaking. She crumpled in pain, the light fading; there had been something in her face at that moment that had been almost old.

A weird gust of wind chose that moment to explode out of nowhere, blowing dust and sand into a small twister at the horses' feet; it faded almost as soon as it came, leaving the debris it had picked up to fall where it would. In its wake the air grew solid, still, as though Kieran was breathing honey. But as he drew his first shallow, ragged breath of it, even that was gone, leaving nothing but a sense of a vast and brooding power. Still struggling to get his breath back, Kieran became aware that Anghara was speaking.

". . . sorry. I swear, I felt it less keenly when I was shut up in Sif's dungeons—now that my body is free it's harder for the soul to accept it's still in chains . . . Are you all right, Kieran? You look as though you've seen . . . a ghost . . ."

That too he saw breaking on her face—the realization of who his ghosts were. There was a blank look in her eyes which frightened him, a white shadow around her mouth. "They did come," she whispered, her voice hoarse with emotion. "I called them, and they did come . . . and I can't even sense their presence . . ."

This time there was no conflict; the horse reacted to a

sharp stab of its rider's heels and set its ears back, breaking into an explosive gallop. But not before Kieran, in the instant she turned away, saw the flash of tears in Anghara's eyes.

Kieran swore softly. He was hampered by the packhorse tied to the back of his own saddle, and Anghara was rapidly opening up a distance between them. "Anghara! Wait!" he yelled, urging his own mount into a gallop in her wake. "Wait!" *I didn't ask your damned Gods to come to me!*

It was debatable if Anghara was still in control of her plunging animal by this time. She seemed to have given the beast its head, merely hanging onto the reins as best she could. When the horse stumbled over some small hollow in the ground, the lurch was enough to throw her clear; she landed well, but hard enough to make Kieran wince. Her horse came to an uncertain stop a few paces later, snorting, aware of a sudden lifting of weight and peering back to see what had become of its rider, before turning its attention to what sparse grazing grew in that place. Short of a desultory flick of its ears, it paid no attention to the approaching thunder of the other horses. Kieran rode up, sliding off his own mount almost before it had come to a full stop, and raced to where Anghara lay.

She was dusty, and the fall seemed to have wrenched open the cut on her arm, where the linen bandage was seeping red. But it didn't look as though there were any bones broken, although she would probably be black and blue for days.

"I'm sorry," she whispered, even as he dropped to one knee beside her and reached out a hand to her face. A tear squeezed its way past her closed eyelashes and left a wet trail down her dusty cheek. "Kieran . . . what if I'm never myself again?"

The gray eyes had opened at that last question and there was such unbearable pain in them that all Kieran could do, in the grip of a wave of inexpressible tenderness, was to reach out and take her into his arms. She clung to him, driftwood to a rock.

"Can you get up?" he asked, after a moment of silence. She sniffed loudly and nodded, letting go of him and grimacing as the pain from her wounded arm finally made itself known. Kieran also glanced at it. "We'd better sort that out before we go any further."

She sat quiescent while he was bent over that task, but as he straightened she said, very calmly, "Tell me, Kieran. What did you see?"

He met her eyes candidly. "Nothing, and that's the truth. But I felt . . . the night you cut your . . . you called them, I woke and felt the wind on my face like a breath—and afterward, while you slept, there were eyes in the night. And now, now there was a whirlwind at my feet, and then the air became . . . like no air I have ever breathed."

The God-presence. She knew that well. Her eyes were wide, as though with shock. "I can't sense them . . . I can't feel anything . . ."

Kieran reached out and shook her shoulder. "Don't," he said, aware she had been about to try and channel Sight again, seeking for that which eluded her. "Don't torment yourself. They came when you called them. Isn't that enough?"

She laughed, a bitter little laugh which broke on a sob. "Never. It will never be enough." She recalled with a sudden clarity the touch of unearthly wings, the immortal eyes set into the great vulture head; the creature who had spoken with her, who had given her the gift of resurrection—al'Khur. Was he beside her now, waiting to take it back? "It will never be enough." She got up, dusting herself down as best she could with her good hand. "Can we go?" she asked, and her voice was plaintive, nothing left in it of command.

"I'll get your horse," said Kieran after a pause, squeezing her shoulder in encouragement.

The horse was lame, which was not entirely surprising; Kieran transferred the packhorse's load onto Anghara's beast and her own saddle onto the erstwhile beast of burden. They would be slowed down, but they wouldn't have kept the horses for much longer anyway; Kieran planned to trade them for camels as soon as they came upon some decent specimens.

They rode off again, north by northeast. And all the time Kieran had the uneasy feeling of someone's eyes on his back; had he known any Kheldrini, he would have smiled at their adage that one is never alone in the desert. In this moment, he would have known exactly what they meant. But Anghara showed no awareness, and Kieran didn't bring the matter up. They passed too far from the Shaymir Dance to see it.

That night, deep in the shadow of Kheldrin, Anghara spoke, somewhat unexpectedly, of Roisinan.

"An army," she said, her knees drawn up into the circle of her arms, staring into the small campfire. "I told Charo to raise me an army. Where is he to get an army to match Sif's, the army which was my father's? And if he does, and if I by some miracle hold Sif at bay, what is to stop the Rashin clan from taking advantage and taking Roisinan from both of us? It is my land, my inheritance—but am I throwing it to the wolves just so I can call it my own?"

"It was always yours. As for the army . . . yes, Sif's is trained, and it has been devoted to him, but if they learned you were alive and . . ."

"They knew I was alive when they helped him take Miranei after my father's death. The knowledge didn't stop them."

"I wonder if Fodrun ever regretted his decision?" Kieran said thoughtfully.

Anghara turned to look at him, her eyes twin mirrors reflecting leaping flames. "What do you mean?"

"They won the second battle at Ronval, and won it well. But part of the reason Fodrun supported Sif was that he believed Sif could deal with Tath. But in the years since—well, with half-competent generals, you could have done as well as Sif."

"He couldn't be king until he knew no other could claim his throne."

"And yet—when he had you, he held you . . . why didn't he kill you the minute he heard you were in his hands?"

A memory surfaced, old, faded—a little girl crossing a cobbled courtyard, one hand firmly held in the hand of a nurse, the other clutching a small doll. An uneven cobble, a trip, a stumble; the doll went flying. By the time the little girl had straightened herself up and looked around it was already back—in the slim brown hand of a boy with pale blue eyes and hair very like her own. She had politely offered a thank-you, as she had been taught; he smiled—a little tightly, but he smiled. Had that been their first meeting? Anghara couldn't remember; but she could clearly recall her feelings. It had been only a stirring, but it had been there—a dim potential for affection which had never flowered.

Perhaps Gul Khaima had known all along. A line of its odd prophecy came floating back now: *love given to him who hates.* Could Anghara have loved her brother? What was it that had stayed his hand?

But Gul Khaima was part of Sight; already she could sense clouds gathering in the back of her mind even as she skated on the edges, with ominous rumblings of thunder warning her of what would follow if she went too far along that path.

She rubbed her temples with her fingers, closing her eyes. "Kieran . . . if they can't heal me . . . if they can't help me in Kheldrin . . . I don't know if I can come back. I can't claim Roisinan when I am not mistress of my own soul."

"They will," said Kieran, with more confidence than he

felt—or wanted to feel, given his own glimpses of knowledge of Kheldrini methods, reinforced now by Anghara's own actions, which he had witnessed firsthand. "But even if they can't . . . don't throw Roisinan away lightly. Sif has reigned for years without Sight. It can be done. And there are many who would give much to see you sit once again on the Throne Under the Mountain. It is yours."

"For years," Anghara said, "I lived with that. It is mine. I just wonder, should that time ever come, if I love it enough to renounce it."

"But if not Sif, and not you . . . who else is there? Tath? Would you allow your father's slayer to sit on his throne?"

"That isn't fair," she said, wincing.

"I rescued you from Sif's dungeons. Now it seems I must try to lead you out of another of your own forging."

They were nearing the outcrop of low, copper-bearing hills lying behind Kieran's native Coba and many small settlements just like it. The hills divided the settled and fertile basin of Lake Shay from the vast sandy desert stretching away to the north—a spur of the great mountain range which swept south to embrace Miranei and give it its ancient name. As the sun was setting behind the hills on the second day, Kieran shaded his eyes against the low golden rays and pointed to the shallow slopes of the foothills.

"There's a village," he said. "We can make it there before it's completely dark; rest for a day or so. Perhaps they'll have camels for sale."

But there had been a strange hesitation in his voice, and Anghara had noticed him cast an uneasy glance behind them. "Are you afraid they'll follow you in?" she asked steadily enough; obviously the Kheldrini Gods were still Kieran's companions, if not her own. "Don't worry, al'Zaan will not enter a place where there are walls; ai'Lan is never strong without sunlight. You're left with only ai'Dhya, and al'Khur."

"The Lord of Death?" Kieran said, shivering slightly. Anghara had spoken a little of her Kheldrini sojourn on their journey; Kieran knew, at the very least, the identities of the Old Gods in their Kheldrini incarnations. "That's quite enough for me."

But he spurred his horse on with his heel, and before long they had reached the first houses in the village. Most were dark; one or two showed soft yellow lights through small, slit-like windows. One, a large, low building, poured a whole ribbon of light through an open doorway.

"That would be the tavern," Kieran said. "Most of them offer a bed or two for the occasional traveller—although Shaymir doesn't see many of those. Come on, we'll try our luck."

There was a room, with a single bed; if they were willing to share, the landlord was happy enough to provide an extra pallet if it was required—at a price. "I usually keep two rooms for hire," the thin, stooped man told them, standing in the doorway with his long arms crossed across a concave chest, "but there's a husband and wife in the other one, visiting singers. They arrived yesterday, and they've got next door . . . This room's all that's going."

"We'll take it," Kieran said. "One more thing. Do you know of anyone who might have camels for sale?"

The landlord's eyebrow rose a notch. "Bound for the desert, are you?" he inquired conversationally. "Well, I don't know . . . old Borre might have one or two he might part with. But I'd be careful there if I was you. He's a good trader, but I'm not sure if an entirely honest one."

"Thanks for the warning," Kieran said. "Where might I find the man?"

"Borre? In my common room right now, like as not," said the landlord laconically, turning away. "I'll get you the pallet. Anything else you need?"

Kieran shook his head, and the landlord went out, closing the door behind him.

"You're different down here," Anghara said.

Kieran turned his head toward her. "How?"

"I'm not sure . . . but you seem . . . a part of this place, somehow. Even your accent changes. I've never heard you speak in quite this voice before."

"Just coming home," said Kieran succinctly.

Quite suddenly she seemed to withdraw from him a little, her eyes veiled with memory. Stepping off the Kheldrini ship in the harbor . . . Roisinan in the rain . . . *I never had a chance to come home . . .*

"I'll have them bring up something to eat," Kieran said, noticing the sudden weariness which cloaked her. "You take the bed; try and sleep, you look tired. I won't be long."

"Where are you going?"

"Just downstairs, to the common room," he said. "I want to try and find this Borre."

She was on the point of insisting that she go with him, but she was tired. More than physically weary—soul-tired, exhausted from trying to keep at bay something she had once so wholeheartedly embraced. The bed seemed like an excellent alternative to spending a night in a loud tavern common room redolent with ale fumes and the violent reek of coarse Shaymir tobacco, for which the Shay valley was well known. In the end she said nothing, letting him go. Alone in the small room, she gave herself to the embrace of a mattress softer by far than the ground which had been her bed these many weeks, and slept dreamlessly until the sun crept through the shuttered window.

The room was empty as she opened her eyes, but the door was opening even as she blinked to admit Kieran, with a freshly washed face and a striped cotton towel around his neck like some strange ornament.

"Good morning," he said cheerfully. "I'm not sure he'll remember after all the ale he put away last night, but I'm supposed to meet our friend Borre this morning and pick out three camels in exchange for the horses, if he liked what he saw—he was meant to inspect them this morning. Want to come?"

Anghara, after a quiet and peaceful night, felt fresh and rested, sharp, quickened. More alive, somehow, than she had felt for . . . for almost as long as she could remember. "I won't be a minute," she said. "Is there anything for breakfast?"

Kieran couldn't hide his surprise, but it lasted only a split second, to be replaced by a smile of real pleasure. "I'll have them prepare something downstairs," he said, tossing his damp towel over the back of a fragile-looking chair which stood in the corner of their room. "I'll meet you down there."

Anghara combed out the tangled chaos of her bright hair with the comb a Kheldrini woman had given her, a long time ago, when she had woken to vision on a cool desert night. That, too, had been saved for her, tucked securely into the package Adamo had rescued from the wreckage of Calabra and her homecoming. Perhaps it was asking for trouble, using something so fraught with memories, but Anghara resolutely closed her mind to all but the most prosaic of the comb's attributes. She washed her face, pulled her travelling dress straight at her waist, and went downstairs.

The common room was largely empty. Kieran was waiting with a dish piled with hot food, and she stopped in the doorway, laughing. "I couldn't eat all of that even in the days when I could swallow a proper breakfast!"

"You mightn't want it, but I do," he said. "It's for both of us. There's hard bargaining ahead."

Anghara giggled. She felt strange, light, as though she had shed years and was a little girl again. "What's he like, our friend Borre?" she asked, mimicking Kieran's own voice of earlier that morning.

Kieran thought for a moment. "A trader," he said at last,

lowering his voice, "to his marrow. I would not be in the least surprised if he hasn't sealed a bargain or two with Khelsies in his time although I'm far from sure on which side of the mountains that was, and he'd die rather than admit to anything. Still, he seems to know something about a passage—it seems there's a singing rock not too far north of here, and that's where the pass starts . . ."

"A singing rock?" echoed Anghara blankly.

Kieran shrugged. "That's what he said last night. He was quite drunk at the time, but he seemed to be making a bizarre sort of sense."

"Do you trust him?"

"Not as far as I could smell him, although that's probably quite a distance. But an old trader doesn't offer his secrets on a platter. Still—it's a beginning."

They finished their breakfast and walked out into the morning; for all that it was still the dawn of spring, here on the edge of the Shaymir desert the trembling heat of summer already shimmered in the air. There was a corral at the far end of the village, partly shaded against the sun by a raised roof of thatch. Borre was bent over a camel's foot, scowling furiously as he looked up at the sound of footsteps. The old trader schooled his face into what passed for a smile at his customers' approach. This was a frightening sight; what teeth remained in his mouth, where they weren't black with decay, were stained a poisonous yellow by a lengthy and intimate relationship with the strong Shaymir tobacco.

"Well, if it isn't my young friend from last night," he said, his accent the flattest Anghara had yet heard, leaving her on the edge of comprehension.

"Have you checked the horses?" Kieran asked, leaning casually on the corral fence.

"Aye, my man looked them over this morning," Borre said. "Two are sound enough, but the third seems lame . . . it might have a bearing on the price . . ."

"It's nothing a few days' rest wont cure, and you know it. What have you to offer us?"

Borre glanced toward a knock-kneed beast drooping disconsolately in the shade of the corral's thatched roof, but changed his mind abruptly as he noticed a sardonic expression cross Kieran's face. The old trader cleared his throat. "The two yonder might do you," he said, indicating a pair of animals standing together close to the bar of the corral fence, chewing placidly at a mouthful of fodder.

Kieran slipped underneath the fence pole and into the corral, and Anghara walked round on the outside until they were on a level. The camels watched Kieran's approach with lofty disdain. "I haven't had that much to do with bargaining for camels lately," Kieran said in a low voice as he stopped before the two beasts. "I've long forgotten what I used to know about them."

"The one on the left looks old," Anghara said softly. "Look at their teeth . . . and be careful, some of them have a nasty habit of trying to take a piece out of you if you give them a chance."

"This one has teeth as bad as yours," Kieran called back to Borre after he had obeyed these instructions. "How long do you think he'd survive if you put a load on his back?"

"Oh, they're hardy beasts . . ." Borre began.

"I don't doubt it," said Kieran. "Have you any others?"

It took a while, but eventually Kieran found himself the owner of three reasonably sound camels for the price of three horses and a further handful of Roisinani coppers. Borre wasn't entirely happy, but he was content—he planned to go south soon, and he could unload the horses there for more than he could hope to gain on the handful of camels he had in hand.

"Where might you be going with these, then?" he asked after they had shaken hands on the bargain. "What might you be looking for in the desert with the summer coming on?"

"Nothing you could make a profit on, friend," Kieran said with a laugh. He deliberately refrained from mentioning his conversation with the old trader in the common room the night before, waiting to see if Borre would bring it up.

"If you're planning on running as far north as the Staren Pan, you'd best be warned—the wells are low this year," Borre offered, his face studiously blank.

"There's always water in the mountains," said Kieran, countering this chess move with one of his own.

Borre nodded sagely, as though he understood everything. "Rock and stone," he murmured, "rock and stone." He patted the neck of one of his camels proprietorially. "They'll be all right, as long as there's sweet red sand waiting for them in the end."

Anghara's eyes flashed at this, and then she hooded them again, veiling them with her eyelashes. She had never seen the Shaymir desert, but to her red sand meant only one place, what al'Tamar had lovingly called Harim Khajir'i'id, the red desert of north Kheldrin. Once it would have been easy to hide her feelings, pulling a concealing cloak of Sight around her; now she had to fight her beating heart and will the color from her cheeks without the help of her gifts.

She turned away, hearing Kieran's voice as if from a great distance as he made the arrangements for the camels to be delivered to the tavern when Borre's man came to collect the horses and their tack. The joy of that morning had somehow gone out of her, replaced with . . . she couldn't put a name to it, a sense of expectation, of dread, even fear. Without in any way being of it, it felt like . . . Sight.

"They'll bring us saddles and bridles when they bring the camels, a straight exchange for our own tackle." Kieran slipped out of the corral again beside her. "What is it? You're so white . . ."

She took his arm. "I don't know," she said slowly, her

eyes wide. "I can't help feeling that something's about to . . ."

"Kieran!"

". . . happen!" Anghara finished, whirling in the direction from which the soft female voice had come.

Kieran had done the same, even more quickly, hand already on the pommel of his sword. But even as he turned there had been an incredulous recognition on his face. He knew that voice, although he hadn't heard it for years . . .

"Keda?"

"Kieran . . . *Anghara* . . . I thought you were dead . . ."

Anghara's eyes were wide and staring, but it was she who made the first connection. What was it the landlord had said . . . visiting singers in his other room . . . husband and wife . . . "The singers in the other guestroom in the tavern," she gasped.

"You're married?" Kieran asked softly, sadly, making the leap himself. "I didn't know . . ."

"Oh, Kieran . . ." Keda's eyes filled with tears. "I wanted to tell you . . . I wanted you at my wedding . . . having a brother for an outlaw isn't easy. I know you vanish to make it difficult for Sif to trace you, but I lose you as well. There have been times I haven't known if you were alive or dead . . ." She stepped up to her brother and folded him into a fierce embrace; Kieran buried his face in her hair, closing his eyes, and brother and sister stood for a moment in silence. Then Keda disentangled herself, keeping hold of one of his hands and tugging at him like a child. "Come on," she said, and her voice was pure joy, "I want you to meet Shev . . . and you must tell me what you are doing here . . ." She turned and smiled at Anghara, reaching out with her other hand. "You've grown . . . but you're so thin, so pale . . . When word came of what happened to Bresse, I mourned you, and the Lady Morgan . . . did she escape?"

"No," said Anghara, dropping her eyes.

She heard Keda suck in her breath in sudden comprehension, in compassion, in pity. "Did you ever . . . go home?" she asked.

Kieran laughed, a short, harsh laugh. "Oh yes," he said. "We found it rather hard to escape the hospitality of Miranei at the last."

There was something deep here, and Keda sensed it, threw up her own guard. "Not here," she said, squeezing the two hands she held, one in each of her own. "Come, let's go back to the tavern. Shev will be waiting for me. It's all right, you can trust him," she added swiftly, noticing Anghara's eyes quickly seek Kieran's face. "Oh, come—we have to sing in the tavern tonight, it's part of the bargain with the landlord—and there's so much . . . How long are you staying?"

"We were hoping to leave within two days," Kieran said, falling into step beside her.

"So soon . . ."

The next questions were obvious—what were the two of them, deposed queen and Roisinani outlaw, doing together here in Shaymir, and where were they headed? But Keda had already schooled herself against asking anything more here in the street. And Anghara, who had been desperately fighting to keep at bay a flood of old memories, finally failed. Her vision faded into a buzzing whiteout; she stumbled at her next step and would have fallen had Kieran, with some strange sixth sense, not reached out with a supporting hand. Here were the last three survivors of Anghara's first wild brush with her power; there was a link somewhere, a link she could not deny, but one which carried oblivion in its wake—an oblivion rooted deep in Sight, whose touch was now so dangerous to her. She couldn't seem to make her legs obey; walking was completely beyond her. Kieran lifted her up without another word and carried her back to the tavern.

Keda, Kieran's true sister, flinched when Kieran mentioned their destination—was there nothing on this side of the mountains that could help Anghara? Were they sure? But, again like Kieran, once she accepted the necessity she did so in a deeply practical way. Her husband Shev hailed from the deep desert; Keda pumped him for any information which could help the two voyagers.

"I've never been to Kheldrin," he said, holding up both hands in mock self-defense, "but I know a song about a Khelsie caravan and a singing rock . . ."

"Singing rock?" said Kieran sharply, turning his head. "Borre mentioned something about a singing rock last night. What is this place?"

"I passed it once, on my way south," said Shev. "It isn't a place I'd have wanted a closer look at. Nobody has said anything definite about it in terms of a passage to anywhere—but there is a song about it . . . and singers often cast into song truths they don't wish to discuss out loud." He rubbed the bridge of his nose nervously with his hand. "I've seen Khelsies but once," he said slowly, "a handful who seemed to have done the impossible—they emerged from the Staren Pan in broad daylight, and were alive to tell about it. They spoke our language—after a fashion. But I dreamed of them after, and they were not pleasant dreams. There is something truly . . . alien . . . about that folk."

"No more than we seem alien to them," said Anghara, who had recovered enough to join the conversation.

Shev gazed at her with something like awe. "To live with them for two years . . . I don't think I could have done it."

"Are you sure . . ." began Keda again, twisting her fingers together.

"There is no other way," said Anghara quietly, but with an iron conviction.

Shev took a deep breath. "Then," he said levelly, "I will show you the way."

It had taken many words—some harsh, at the last, spoken in private between husband and wife—but in the end it was arranged. Keda would stay behind in the tavern, discharging their responsibility to the landlord until Shev returned . . . and Shev would ride with Kieran and Anghara, guiding them to the singing rock.

They reached the landmark in three days. The wind and the sand had sculpted a stone obelisk with a narrow oval eye at the top, an opening which drew a constant sighing wail from the wind threading through. That sound, the otherworldly lament of the wind, had been a travelling companion for some time before they sighted the rock itself, and Anghara had hated it. Kieran could see her shuddering every so often in the high saddle on her camel. Now he could see the imprint of Kheldrin on her, the easy balance of a rider used to the jolting rhythm of the desert beasts—and wondered at it. But Anghara, whom the sound took inexorably back to Khar'i'id and the memory of Gul Qara, didn't trust herself to tell him the story. Not here. Not yet. Not after every promise of Gul Qara seemed to have been buried in the dungeons of Miranei.

She was doing very little to guide her mount, and when Shev's and Kieran's stopped, next to the eye-stone, Anghara's lurched to a standstill beside them with a disgruntled comment. Anghara looked up briefly. "Here?"

"So the song says," Shev said. Despite the levity of his tone, his face was drawn and serious. For him, the shadows in the gray rocks beyond were full of staring golden eyes.

Kieran hesitated; this was the point beyond which mistakes became deadly, and he knew very little about what lay ahead. He had to take too many things on trust—on trust, or not at all. But after that brief hesitation he lifted his head and his eyes sparkled with determination. This, upon reflection, seemed as good a place as any to plunge into the unknown. "Well, here goes," he muttered, casting a yearning glance toward the familiar land they were leaving, whose chief attraction quite possibly lay in the fact it was not Kheldrin.

Shev leaned over to lay a hand on Kieran's arm. "Be careful, your sister could not bear to lose you again."

Kieran grimaced. He planned to be as careful as he could, under the circumstances. He wished he had more idea of what he had to be careful about. "We will," he said aloud, choosing not to bring up his misgivings with Shev. "Take care of Keda."

"You sound as though you don't mean to come back."

"Oh, I do," said Kieran, quite adamantly. "Just as soon as I can."

"Well, then, good luck," said Shev after a short, awkward pause. "May the Gods be with you."

He'd looked away to Anghara, and didn't see Kieran glance back over his shoulder, and shiver. There would indeed be Gods with them in the mountains, but they were hardly the tame, benign Gods whose protection Shev had been invoking.

Shev didn't wait to see them go, nor even turn to watch them take the first step into the mountains. He'd wheeled his own camel and urged it into a ponderous run, turning his back resolutely on the two by the singing rock. There were some things a man would rather not set eyes on. He didn't have the Sight, didn't even come from a family in which it ran, but sometimes it was given even to ordinary mortals to sense something of that other world in which the Sighted moved. And there was something about the young pair setting off on this journey that raised Shev's hackles. It might have just been the distant memory of half-forgotten Kheldrini traders, alien and golden-eyed, who had made such an impression on a little boy long ago—but even had Shev never set eyes on a Kheldrini he would have sensed something about Anghara's going. Roisinan-born, Kheldrin-fostered, she had become the link binding together the shattered shards of a world, a world whose fate turned on that first step she took into the shadows of the mountain.

There was a path, but not for long. As he saw it vanishing onto bare rocks, Kieran's heart sank. Had the old songs been no more than a trap, set to lure the unwary and the reckless to their death? But then Anghara peered ahead and pointed, "There is a ledge," she said. "Look."

It was steep and worn, but it was the only way they had. They forged ahead, single file, Kieran in the lead followed by Anghara and the pack camel. The ledge twisted and turned, following the cliff face, until it presented them, some hours later, with a triple fork. From this point one path ran level, straight ahead of them, until it folded out of sight behind an outcrop of rocky shale; one climbed steeply upward, even more tortuous than the one they had been following; the third, deceptively gentle, dipped subtly downward and vanished into the shadow of a gigantic overhanging rock. Kieran stopped, peering down the alternatives.

"I wish I could trust this level one," he muttered darkly. But he trusted nothing in these mountains, and an easy path laid out at his feet was instant cause for suspicion. "The one going down . . . it's too early to start descending. So it's this, or uphill. What do you think?"

Anghara's eyes, when she looked up, were oddly muddy,

and her face was flushed as though with fever. "Left," she said, speaking as if it took a great effort to do so. "Up."

Kieran turned his camel in that direction, ignoring the snort of disgust the animal offered when presented with its rider's choice.

They were lucky that time. Not only did the path straighten out on a high shoulder after a while, but they also discovered a shallow cave which housed a coy spring, well hidden in the darkness deep inside the cavern's maw. It slopped over the edge of a shallow rock basin and quickly vanished into a crack in the stone. There wasn't much of it, but it was fresh and clean, and Kieran camped by this place, taking the time to refill all of their water bags. There was no guarantee anything like this would offer itself again once they crested the mountain and began descending the parched slopes on the Kheldrini side.

The decision at the fork seemed to be the last rational one Anghara made. The next time she told Kieran to choose one fork over another, they lost two days while they extricated themselves from a pathless stony wilderness; and the time after that, she chose a trail which led them to an unequivocal dead end, where a massive cliff face stared them down. After that, she left it to Kieran; and even if she did offer an opinion Kieran took it reservedly, going with his own judgment. He was worried—he had believed, somehow, that her mind would begin clearing as they drew closer to Kheldrin. Not that he was a competent judge, but it seemed to him that, if anything, she was getting worse. Her arm wasn't healing; and, driven by something stronger than herself, she had tried again to commune with her Gods through a blood offering. This time Kieran had been on his guard, and prevented her from doing major damage, but he had felt the agitation in the air around him even as he pulled the black dagger from her hand. Suddenly afraid at what Gods cheated of a sacrifice could do to them, so vulnerable and exposed on the mountain, he had pricked his own thumb with the tip of the dagger and offered the blood welling up from the puncture into the swirling wind. *Take it . . . take it . . . but let her be . . . she is not strong enough to stand against you . . .*

He'd had to turn back and calm a distraught Anghara, and in the chaos he had forgotten his action. Later, remembering what he had done and curious as to the total absence of any pain or discomfort, he'd looked for the small self-inflicted wound—and was thoroughly terrified to discover no trace of it. Just to be on the safe side, he packed the black dagger away amongst his own things, keeping it out of Anghara's hands. The next time he might not be watching; she could kill herself. Still, an odd uneasiness persisted at the back of his mind. He wished he didn't feel as though he had just burned Kerun's holy incense in a profane place.

But all this Kieran could rationalize on some level, and accept—it was devotion due to different Gods. The first real shock, the first sense of how deeply Anghara had been changed by her Kheldrini years, came when she rose one morning and donned the golden robe and the two *say'yin'en.* For a moment, Kieran could only stare. He was well aware of what Khelsies looked like, and there was nothing in Anghara of that narrow face and golden eyes—and yet, and yet . . . The soul that looked out of Anghara's familiar wide gray eyes belonged to a stranger. She said something, her tone imperial, her language the harsh guttural syllables of an alien land.

"Come back," Kieran said simply, and, for a wonder, it seemed to work. She blinked, lifted an arm as though suddenly curious about the golden silk of the sleeve in which it was encased. When she looked his way again she was Anghara again—his Anghara, her eyes soft and troubled. "I don't remember . . ." she began, and then her voice petered out into silence.

"It's all right," he said gently. Coming closer, he peered curiously at the great globes of yellow amber around her neck. "What do these mean?"

He seemed to have grasped intuitively that they meant something—he had never even considered the possibility they were mere ornaments. Anghara, with a pensive half-smile, stroked the massive old *say'yin* al'Jezraal had given her during the Confirmation Ceremony, and told Kieran of Al'haria, its *Sa'id,* and the Hariff clan which had taken her as one of its own. This went on, in fits and starts, during the entire day; Anghara would begin something, lapse into silence, and finish that story (or, as like as not, begin another) at some later stage. All kinds of things Kieran hadn't known about emerged during these confused tales, even that which she thought she could never tell him—the black desert called Khar'i'id, known as the Empty Quarter, and the oracle which lived there; the death of Gul Qara, and its testament; the raising of a new oracle by the sea. Even, finally, about the touch of a God's wing, and the gift al'Khur had given her. The gift of resurrection. Much of this came out in tangled and convoluted ways, leaving Kieran to piece it together as best he could—but one thing was immediately obvious. Kheldrin had been far from a simple sanctuary for a deposed queen. It was built into Anghara now, a part of her. Kieran began to understand how her inability to sense those whom she had, in spite of herself, called to her, would wound her bright spirit. Rendered powerless through ignorance and lack of skill when it came to Sight, he was unable to do anything except stand back and watch it bleed.

The mountains were bleak and harsh. Little grew there, other than a few hardy lichens, the same lifeless gray as the stone on which they were anchored. There was the occasional brave attempt of a tree to gain a foothold, but all were twisted and stunted and if they had ever been green, it was only a memory. And it all seemed to go on forever; once, on a pinnacle from which he had a clear view to all sides, Kieran felt his heart sink when he could see nothing but more broken, empty gray ridges unfolding in any direction he looked. He hadn't wanted Anghara to see, and he hurried them from that place—but she knew, somehow. It was one of her good days, lucid and clear, and she smiled at him from her camel with the sweetness he remembered of old.

"Are you sure that anything exists beyond these mountains?" he asked, offering a tired, slow smile in return.

"We'll make it," she said, gazing at him with steadfast trust. "And the Kadun . . . is beautiful."

Their mounts were also beginning to suffer. They were vociferous in their complaints, and one of them, although Kieran could discover no physical reason, began to limp badly—it seemed, out of protest. Their pace slowed to a crawl. Their water supplies dwindled, and they came across no more friendly springs hidden in the shadows—only, once, a weeping cliff with a thin film of moisture upon the bare stone. The camels discovered that, and stood licking at the cliff face; Kieran called a halt, and spent a few frustrating hours trying to rig a way to collect enough of the precious fluid to fill at least one of their empty water bags. That he succeeded was a tribute to ingenuity and perseverance, and Anghara had been herself for long enough to tell him so. But the next morning she seemed to have forgotten, withdrawing from him, muttering incomprehensible invocations to alien Gods in a language Kieran didn't understand.

As they drew closer to their destination, Anghara was plagued with odd hallucinations—visions conjured up before her by her churning mind. Once she stopped Kieran and pointed with a shaking hand to a bare rock peak, wailing that she could see the towers of Miranei and they must have gone around in a huge circle. Another time she stared into the distance, speaking softly of sea-sculpted red rock, a fishing village nestled against the cliffs, and a great Standing Stone upon a tall pillar above the ocean. All she could see in reality was more tumbled and broken lifeless gray stone; but such were the words she chose, even Kieran thought he could smell distant salt in the air and hear the sound of breakers upon the foot of the oracle's pillar. And it seemed as though there had been a touch of Sight in that particular instance, because by evening Anghara was racked with pain and fever, incoherent, completely unable to continue her journey the following morning. Kieran could do little other than make her comfortable and wait it out.

By this stage they were already descending, their path following a decided downward slope. Kieran expected no miracles from the Kheldrini desert when they reached it—at least not until they found someone qualified to deal with Anghara's plight—but at least they would be out of these bare, soul-numbing mountains, and in the land of country Anghara, at least, knew tolerably well. It would make the burden lighter if they could find someone with the knowledge to help. His very helplessness drove Kieran, even if he was heading for the one place he would never have wished to see under ordinary circumstances. But he could see Anghara was suffering, and he could feel that pain in himself. By now he would have done almost anything if he knew it would help.

The end came unexpectedly, and Kieran, who was so used to seeing gray rock on every side, was slow to realize what his eyes were showing him. They emerged from under a huge overhanging rock and found themselves on a narrow plateau, whose horizon was a distant line where sky met smooth coral dunes, with the occasional wind-sculpted spire of red stone.

The hesitation was all Anghara needed. She urged her camel forward with a glad cry, seemingly completely unaware of the hundred-foot sheer drop separating her from her beloved desert. Kieran shouted an incoherent wanting and leapt from his saddle; he landed with all his weight on one ankle and felt it buckle as he rolled with the fall, staggering to his feet with a grimace of pain to throw himself after her camel's dangling rein.

The space before the edge of the plateau was narrow; ordinarily, Kieran would have stood no chance. It was something superhuman that drove him, a sense of outrage. *Was it for this that we struggled and suffered through these wretched mountain passes?* But even that would hardly have been enough. As his fingers closed hard on the rein he was aware that something else had halted the beast, moments before he had reached it. And, gazing with a shiver down the precipice into which Anghara would have tumbled, he could see what it had been.

Or, rather, who.

At this distance the figure was tiny, but there was no mistaking the bronze gleam of the skin, the bright copper hair revealed by a thrown-back cowl . . . burnouse, Anghara had called them. The stray fact swam into Kieran's mind as he stood transfixed and staring down at the Khelsie who had, somehow, stopped Anghara from hurling herself into oblivion in her joy at seeing the red desert again.

The distance separating them was too great for any communication Kieran understood, but still he received the clear impression that a path to the right of the plateau would lead him to the desert . . . and that his unexpected ally would wait below while Kieran and Anghara descended. Kieran glanced at Anghara, who sat very still on her quivering animal—he couldn't tell if she had felt anything, but she didn't react at all when he softly called her name. Some force had certainly touched the camel; the animal stood in uncharacteristic silence, showing the whites of its eyes. At last Kieran fastened the rein of his animal to the back of Anghara's saddle, took her own beast's reins, and began leading the small cavalcade down the desert path on foot.

It was a hot and uncomfortable journey, made in silence—here, about to come face to face with something he didn't know and still mistrusted, Kieran was alone. But he set his jaw in a determined line, his blue eyes hard. This was what they had come for. There was never any guarantee Anghara would reach this place—she had come for help, and, glancing back at her rigid figure and wide, staring eyes, it was more obvious than ever that she needed any help these people could give her.

The desert met them slowly, subtly, drifts of red sand piling up against the mountain buttresses. At the bottom the path began to twist and meander, doubling back on itself, at least once leading Kieran into a blind alley out of which, backed as he was by three camels, he had the greatest difficulty in extricating himself. Seriously considering the possibility that now, here, at the end of the line, he could become completely lost in the maze into which the path had unexpectedly turned, Kieran stopped for a breather and to take his bearings. He could smell the desert, a sharper, hotter scent in the air brought to him by the occasional gust of a warm breeze, but it was hidden from him by what seemed to be a continuous wall of rock. Did the Khelsie lure him here for a slow death? Kieran cursed under his breath, rubbing his sleeve against a forehead damp with sweat. When he looked up again, it was with a start that he saw the Khelsie's slight figure standing before him, as though Kieran had conjured him up with the ignoble thought. His hand jerked instinctively toward his blade, and the other put up both of his own, palms toward Kieran.

"Peace! I am unarmed."

He had spoken in Roisinani; accented and colored by the Shaymir dialect, but it had unmistakably been Kieran's own language. Kieran dropped his hand, torn between feelings of resentment toward this creature speaking his tongue and immense relief. With Anghara incapacitated, the problem of communicating with anyone they met in this alien desert had loomed large in his mind.

"I am al'Tamar ma'Hariff," the man continued. "In this country, she whom you accompany is of my family and my clan. Although . . . she looks little like the Anghara Kir Hama who accepted the name of Hariff . . ." He had glanced at Anghara while he spoke, but she was still wrapped in her silence and solitude. The man's golden eyes came back to Kieran's face. They were deeply concerned. "Something is wrong," he said, very quietly. "Something is deeply wrong."

Kieran swallowed. "She is . . . ill. I don't understand what the matter is . . . I don't have Sight. But she was captured by Sif Kir Hama, who rules in Roisinan, and something done to her in captivity has affected her mind . . . her Sight. She believes somebody here in Kheldrin can help her."

"What happened?" al'Tamar asked. He took a step closer, and suddenly swayed. *"Hai!"* he whispered, closing his eyes. "Was it she that called al'Khur to ride at her back?"

Kieran felt his hackles rise. "She did. She doesn't know how well she succeeded, though. She can't sense them."

Again the piercing golden gaze. "And you could." It was not a question; it was a statement of certain knowledge. The eyes, however, were troubled. "And yet you are right, you do not carry what they call Sight in Sheriha'drin. How, then, is it possible that you can sense the presence of the God when an *an'sen'thar* cannot?"

"Can you help her?" Kieran asked, steadying himself against the neck of the nearest camel against a wave of sudden and absolute fatigue, as al'Tamar watched him intently.

"He is gone," al Tamar said unexpectedly, "back into the desert from which he had been summoned. It was al'Khur's strength that sustained you. You felt him go?"

Kieran, whose head was spinning with exhaustion and strain, could only nod soundlessly.

"No," al'Tamar said, in answer to an earlier question, "I

cannot help her. But she was right—there are those who may be able to. Her old teacher—ai'Jihaar—has a tent in a hai'r south of here. That is where I think we should take her. Can you ride?"

"Yes," Kieran said through clenched teeth.

"I have one or two spare burnouses back on my ki'thar," al'Tamar said, tugging out a piece of material tucked into his waistband, "but until we get there, use this. She can have mine."

"What about you?" Kieran asked, accepting the strip of cloth automatically.

"I was born here," said the other. "And it is not far." With a soft word he made Anghara's camel kneel, and came up to wrap the desert veil about the girl's head and face with deft fingers. Kieran stared at the bronze hands, so gentle, so loving; a profound, powerful reeling stirred somewhere in the depths of him at the sight, something that should have been familiar, easily identifiable, if only he wasn't so desperately tired . . .

When he had finished, al'Tamar stepped back—and then looked Kieran's way, aware of his scrutiny. There was an odd expression on his face. Bare now of its cowl, he looked strangely young and vulnerable underneath copper hair drawn back from his high forehead. The two pairs of eyes, blue and gold, locked together for a long moment across the bowed and hooded head of the girl between them. And then al'Tamar dropped his gaze. "Are you . . . her *qu'mar*?" he asked softly.

Kieran, about to answer that he didn't know what that meant, caught himself—he did. Of course he did. Even if the word was unfamiliar, the tone in which the question was asked left no room for doubt—al'Tamar wanted to know if he was Anghara's husband, her mate, and Kieran was stunned at the strength of a sudden, desperate wish to be able to say yes.

Just when had his protective love for a young and vulnerable little foster sister turned into the passion of a man for a woman? Kieran couldn't say. All he knew was that in the space of an instant he was gazing at Anghara with different eyes, suddenly able to understand with blinding clarity exactly why he had never been able to stop searching for her. Why he had been desperate enough to snatch her from Miranei to gamble the lives of men who trusted him; why, on this last journey, he had suffered when he had seen her pain. And why, lacking Sight, he had been able to sense the Gods she had called. Something tied them together, something with roots deep in the past—even Feor had known, choosing Kieran to seek Anghara when she vanished during the dark years of Sif's purges—but it had flowered only now, and Kieran was suddenly struck by the power and beauty of the flower.

And knew he might have realized everything too late.

"No," he said in answer to al'Tamar's question. His voice was very soft, but raw with so many things that al'Tamar flinched. After a beat of silence he clucked at Anghara's camel, which rose with a creaky complaint.

"You ride the other," he said to Kieran, his level voice giving no indication of what had been revealed.

"And you?"

"I will lead, to my ki'thar. We can rest in my camp; I have lais tea, and at least she will sleep. Tomorrow, we go to ai'Jihaar—she will know what to do."

It would have been false heroics to insist on walking—Kieran's ankle throbbed savagely, but even if he had been fit he knew he could not measure himself in these deserts with one who had walked them since childhood. He wearily mounted his camel, head drooping, and surrendered the rein to al'Tamar, who paused briefly at the camel's head, gathering the reins in his hand—as though waiting for something.

And that, too, Kieran felt without the need for words, as though the thought had been inserted in his mind. He straightened for a moment, groping for dignity. "I don't think I returned the courtesy of introducing myself," he said. "I am Kieran Cullen of Shaymir."

"I might have known," al'Tamar said, nodding to himself, a slight movement, almost imperceptible. "She often spoke of you."

"I think . . . I remember your name, from when she spoke of Kheldrin on this journey," Kieran said.

"She is my friend," al'Tamar said, "and I honor her for the things she has done. It grieves me to see her like this. Tell me . . . how did it happen that she fell into her brother's hands so soon after she left us?"

"Bad luck," Kieran said, "and bad timing."

"Then I do not understand why ai'Dhya would have stopped us coming this way. Surely if trouble lay ahead for her in your harbor city . . ."

"The Goddess?" Kieran was slower than usual, blunted by his fatigue. "What has ai'Dhya to do with this?"

"Anghara and I came this way when she set out for her country. We wanted to find a way through the mountains and save her the long journey south—and ai'Dhya sent storms to head us off. Anghara said the Goddess told her there was nothing but useless death waiting for her on this path. But if the south was just as dangerous . . ."

"But someone was there to see," Kieran said slowly, fighting to understand. "To see, and to know she had been taken. And Sif was away from Miranei. Her life was bought by circumstances. Taken in Shaymir, under Sif's hand, she would have died and nobody would have been any the wiser. This way there were friends ready to try anything to save her . . . who knew she was immured in Miranei . . ."

"The oracle," murmured al'Tamar.

Kieran raised an unsteady hand to rub his eyes. "What oracle?"

"I remember to this day what Gul Khaima told her on the

morning she raised the Stone," al'Tamar said. "*A friend and a foe await at return.* So it proved. *Hai!* The Gods are great!"

They lapsed into silence, gaining al'Tamar's camp half an hour later, where his ki'thar stood tethered in the shadow of an outcrop of red rock. Kieran found he wasn't too tired to help Anghara from her camel, and to carry her into the small black tent al'Tamar had pitched. But once he had laid her gently on the nest of blankets and tried to straighten up, the world twisted into a sudden whirlpool of heat and color; he swayed, and sank beside her on the red sand.

He didn't know how long he slept, but when he woke it was dark and cool, and a light coverlet had been spread over him. Anghara was still where he had laid her, her breathing deep and even with sleep, a long strand of red-gold hair curled across her cheek and under her chin. Kieran stared at it for a long moment, as if hypnotized; his fingers, of their own volition, reached to smooth away the errant curl.

A sound at the tent flap made him snatch his hand back as though her bright hair had burned him. Turning, he saw al'-Tamar silhouetted against what looked like firelight.

"I thought I heard you rouse," al'Tamar said equably. "Would you like something to eat?" He intercepted Kieran's instinctive glance back at Anghara, and Kieran could see a sudden flash of teeth as the young Kheldrini man smiled in the half-light. "She will not wake soon," he said. "That is good; she needs to heal, and sleep heals better than anything. You . . . the God has ridden you hard. Come, eat."

Kieran obeyed, flinging back the coverlet and emerging from the low tent in a half-crouch. The stars were bright and low, almost close enough to touch; for a moment he allowed himself to stand and simply gaze at them, enchanted by this vivid night sky. After a while he sensed al'Tamar coming to stand beside him.

"You said you came from Shaymir," al'Tamar said. "Do

they not have stars in your desert?" It was a laconic question, full of an odd humor. Kieran realized his feelings must have been written plainly on his face.

"I have not been in Shaymir—the true desert—since I was a child," he said, tearing his eyes from the sparkling sky with an effort, aware of a strange feeling of kinship for this young man. "In Roisinan, unless you are high up on a mountain top or, sometimes, upon the seashore . . . the stars are higher, further away. The only thing you can touch is their reflection in the water."

Kieran saw a curious yearning pass briefly through al'Tamar's eyes before he cast them down to the red sand at his feet. "You delight in our sky," he said. "And I . . . I would give much to touch the reflection of a star in the water."

It was a moment of deep sharing—but then it was gone, and al'Tamar gestured toward the fire. "Supper," he said. "Come."

Kieran followed obediently, and sat cross-legged beside the fire. And then, as his host bent to retrieve the flat unleavened bread he'd left to bake in the embers, something slipped from inside his robe and hung swaying over the fire. A *say'yin,* much like the ones Anghara had worn. But this one was massive, heavy amber globes interspersed with solid silver spheres etched with spiral patterns. And at the end of it . . .

Kieran blinked, sure the firelight was playing tricks on his eyes; but when he looked again it was still there. "Where did you get this?" he demanded, uncoiling his body to reach for the Royal Seal of Roisinan, which hung from a Kheldrini chain.

As he straightened, al'Tamar's eyes were calm. "When she left for Sheriha'drin," he said steadily, "she left me this, to work into the *say'yin* I promised to make for her. Even then, she knew. She said she would be back for it . . . and I have worn her *say'yin* since the day I wrought it, so it will not be seen by unfit eyes until the day she chooses to reveal it. And perhaps it was this . . ." The golden eyes were mirrors, reflecting the flickering of the small fire. "I knew you were coming . . . although not why," and he glanced back at the tent with sorrow eloquent in every line of his body, "I did not know she would need me . . . and yet I have been at the cliff since dawn, waiting for the traveller I knew must come."

They spoke no more of it, al'Tamar simply tucking away the *say'yin* with the Royal Seal. Kieran didn't press the point. If half of what the young Khelsie—damn, but he could not cure himself of thinking of them in those terms—said was true, the Seal had in itself been a talisman, a little miracle; al'Tamar had shown himself a worthy guardian.

In some ways, the Kheldrini desert itself brought about a miracle of a different kind. Anghara was still not herself, not by a long way—there were hours, once an entire day, in which she seemed to dwell on some plane far removed from that of her companions. But here, in the red sand of the Kadun Khajir'i'id, she also spent far more time lucid and self-aware. How much of a blessing that was Kieran wasn't altogether sure, because it was here in the desert that the memories of her greatest achievements rooted in Sight were closer and more able to torment her. But the desert itself seemed to offer her healing, as though it was something in the very air she breathed. With a dose of lais tea every night, even her sleep was more restful and restoring, untroubled by disturbing dreams. But that was al'Tamar's responsibility, and Kieran, who after bringing Anghara to this place could do little more for her, felt increasingly superfluous. To his credit, al'Tamar tried to keep him involved—but when Anghara lapsed into some distant memory and began speaking in Kheldrini, there was little al'Tamar could do except offer apologetic looks to the burnouse-swathed outlaw from Roisinan, who was beginning to feel severely out of his depth.

Other than this, their journey across the desert was uneventful. When, finally, al'Tamar pointed at the palm shapes silhouetted against the desert sky and identified the hai'r as ai'Jihaar's home, Kieran was assailed by conflicting feelings—relief, anticipation, apprehension, anxiety, even fear. This was the reason they had come, the guiding light which had pointed the way for so long; for Anghara's sake, Kieran prayed her faith had been justified. The alternative didn't bear thinking about.

But even here, at the harbor where Anghara could have expected her journey to end, it was not given to her to have smooth sailing. The small caravan was greeted by an old servant, who stood fierce guard at the firmly closed entrance to ai'Jihaar's tent and refused to let them approach. There was a guttural exchange between her and al'Tamar. Kieran understood nothing, but there was palpable frustration in al'-Tamar's voice and from the way the old woman stood with her arms crossed across her chest and her feet planted sturdily apart it was apparently a stern denial of ai'Jihaar's presence.

"What is it?" Kieran demanded at last during a lull in the conversation, when he could stand it no longer.

Unfastening his burnouse with an agitation Kieran had never yet seen in the self-possessed young man, al'Tamar turned toward him. "She says that ai'Jihaar has been very ill, she is finally resting . . . and this spavined daughter of a she-*afrit* will not allow her mistress to be disturbed before sunset. If at all."

He probably hadn't meant to be humorous, but Kieran's mouth quirked at al'Tamar's trenchant characterization. But when Kieran met the implacable golden gaze of the old woman his amusement melted away as he mentally seconded al'Tamar's description. He favored the old servant with a sour stare. "So what now?"

For a moment al'Tamar hesitated. "Al'haria," he began, "is only a day or so from here . . ."

Kieran glanced at Anghara, who swayed unsteadily on her camel's back, her eyes closed. He felt a wash of bitter disappointment. "Another day?" he demanded harshly. "Look at her! And what's in Al'haria?"

"A *sen'thar* tower," al'Tamar said. "One of the biggest. And there is . . ." His head suddenly came up and his face was a picture of an almost comical distress. *"Hai!"* he muttered, "ai'Farra is in Say'ar'dun . . . who is there to look to Anghara?"

He must have been broadcasting his frustration on a broad mental band; two things occurred simultaneously, almost before Anghara's name faded from his lips. One was that Anghara herself sat up, her eyes flying open, and looked around in confusion as though reacting to an urgent summons; the other, that a weak voice which still somehow managed to remain peremptory called from inside the red tent. The old servant's arms dropped to her side and her face set into a sort of sullen mask, but at this direct command she nevertheless stepped aside. In an instant al'Tamar was off his ki'thar and halfway to the tent. Even as Kieran made as if to follow the young Kheldrini paused at the tent-flap, turning his head.

"Wait," he said, his eyes pleading but his voice nonetheless firm. "Wait here with her."

This was not Kieran's territory; already he was being excluded, gently but firmly. He had brought Anghara where she had needed to be, but in order for anything to come of this journey Kieran now had to hand her over to this land and its customs. Now, at the cusp, he was finding this harder than ever to accept. His jaw set, he slipped off his camel, helped Anghara off hers, and led her into the shadow of the palms beside the small pool of brown water. She went without demur, allowing herself to be led, like a child.

Like a child . . .

Ambushed once again by his own conflicting emotions Kieran sat her down in the shade and stood over her, staring down at her aristocratic profile, guarding her from dangers only vaguely grasped, far from sure he would be of use if anything assailed her. That which threatened her now, here, could probably not be turned aside by a well-wielded blade.

She had thrust back the burnouse and the dappled sunlight beneath the palm trees teased out bright gleams from her red-gold hair. It was in tangled disarray, and Kieran vividly remembered a time when he'd helped her comb out her damp mane when she was a little girl back in Cascin. He would have smiled had he known the same memory had caressed her on her first night in the desert all those years ago—had been, perhaps, the trigger which allowed her to become all that she was. But at this moment, gazing down at the girl who could not have looked less like a queen if she tried, his fingers itched for a comb he had once plied upon a little girl. He dropped into a crouch beside her, and she turned questioning wide gray eyes on him.

"Anghara . . ."

But al'Tamar, with an impeccable sense of timing, chose this moment to thrust open the tent flap and urgently beckon them into the tent. Kieran sighed resignedly and helped Anghara to her feet.

It was cool inside, and smelled not unpleasantly of incense and herbs—Kieran's nose twitched at the familiar aroma of lais, combined with something different, a herb he didn't know. Probably medicinal. The woman lying propped up on her bed of cushions and woven coverlets looked as if she needed all the help she could get, every bit as ill and drawn as her servant had intimated. She was shrunken, old, her arms thin and stick-like beneath their load of silver bracelets. Her blind eyes were filmed with white, but she seemed to focus unerringly at the spot where Anghara stood and held out her arms toward her.

"Oh, child . . ." The old woman's voice was rich and tender, brimming with love and compassion. "What have they done to you?"

Kieran's hand had still been cupped lightly around Anghara's elbow, holding her arm as he had escorted her to the tent; she had accepted this passively, going where he led her as though she had been no more than a walking doll. Now, suddenly, she seemed to come to herself and tore away to fling herself into the old woman's arms with a glad cry.

Kieran bit back a cry of his own, which was her name, and let her go.

He was still watching this reunion, feeling oddly bereft, when he felt a gentle tug at his own sleeve. "Come, let us leave them," al'Tamar said. "If they should need us, they will call."

"Will she be able . . ."

"I do not know," said al'Tamar softly. "But let her try."

Outside, golden eyes hooded against the bright sunlight, al'Tamar crouched in the shade to wait with all the patience native to his race. Kieran seemed to have lost every ounce of patience he had ever possessed. He restlessly paced the edge of the pool, repeatedly ran anxious fingers across the knots on the camels' tethers, as if they were about to fall apart at his touch; then stood staring at the image of the sun in the still waters of the pool. The sun itself hung unmoving in the sky, as though time had stopped, and yet it seemed as though it was hours later that al'Tamar's head suddenly came up, as though he had caught a scent in the wind. He hesitated, and then rose in one fluid motion. "I think we are wanted," he said.

Kieran glanced between al'Tamar and the red tent, a little wildly. "How do you know?"

With maddening calmness, al'Tamar shrugged and said, "ai'Jihaar can be very imperious."

Anghara was Kieran's first thought; as the two young men ducked into the tent it was her that Kieran's eyes sought. He saw her lying curled up amongst the jin'aaz silk cushions at ai'Jihaar's feet, so still that for one terrifying moment he thought she was dead. But then he saw the rise and fall of her breast, the slight smile on her face that belied what looked like tear trails on her cheeks, and realized she was sleeping. More deeply than she had been able to do since her journey began, even counting the lais-induced slumbers here in the desert. This was healing sleep; flooded with feelings of relief and gratitude Kieran's eyes left Anghara, after a last lingering caress, and sought the healer.

The old teacher, ai'Jihaar, looked more frail and exhausted than ever—and yet, at the same time, utterly implacable. Old steel, well forged. Kieran bowed to her with respect, even though she couldn't see him.

"There is too much broken here. I am too weak to do alone what must be done," ai'Jihaar said, one of her hands resting lovingly on Anghara's bright head. "There are things in the tower I do not have here. And yet . . . I am loath to let her go into Al'haria alone, and I cannot travel with her . . ." She clicked her tongue against her teeth. "Well. They will just have to come to me. But after what little I have done I am so weak I cannot even call them . . . You will have to go to the tower, al'Tamar. Tell them . . . do not tell them too much. But tell them to get together the things that would be needed for a *mar ha'dayan.* There should be a pair of silk-seekers, with matching hurts. Bring a handful of *sen'en'thari.* No whites, this is far beyond them. Grays; strong grays. And . . . ai'Farra."

"She is not there," said al'Tamar, with the careful patience of one who has already apprised a forgetful convalescent of the facts and is resigned at having to repeat everything. "She has been in Say'ar'dun for the last month."

"So you said. Forgive me," ai'Jihaar's lips thinned in self-reproach. "Tell my brother to send me the one who is in charge of the tower in her absence. I need the strongest the tower has. This is an emergency. You can tell al'Jezraal I said so; tell him I will not deprive Al'haria's tower of its *sen'en'thari* for too long."

After casting a long glance at Anghara, al'Tamar rose to his feet. "I go at once," he said quietly.

Then ai'Jihaar seemed to recall something else, lifting her chin, she focused on al'Tamar's face with filmed, blind eyes with an uncanny ability that made Kieran's hackles rise. "Should you be here at all, al'Tamar?" she inquired with deceptive mildness.

Kieran had not thought that the bronze skins of Kheldrin would show a blush, but now he saw they did; al'Tamar's cheeks glowed as though burnished as he hung his head. "Rami understands."

"Does she, now? I hope so; I went to a lot of trouble to arrange that match," ai'Jihaar said, and it was immediately obvious that she and the young man she was dressing down were related, even if it was only through the dry sense of humor they shared. "Give my greetings to ai'Ramia and her family . . . and, if it is necessary, you have my full permission to shift any guilt concerning your sudden absence from your own betrothal celebrations onto my shoulders."

"That has already been done," said al'Tamar, in all seriousness, "but yours were not the shoulders. Rami knows my allegiance is to al'Jezraal, that I go where he sends me."

"And he sent you on a wild *shevah* chase into the Kadun, did he?" said ai'Jihaar, a shade maliciously.

"Not *shevah,*" al'Tamar countered steadily, lifting his head. "A queen *haval'la,* perhaps."

Her blind eyes still focused precisely on his face, ai'Jihaar tilted her head thoughtfully. Then she lifted her hand, in blessing as much as farewell. "So," she said, very softly, "Go to al'Jezraal, then; tell him you caught your queen, and she is sorely wounded. And then go back to Rami, al'Tamar. Find room in your heart for a *qu'mar'a* of this world."

After a moment's hesitation, as al'Tamar contented himself with a final long and painful look at Anghara's face, he turned abruptly and ducked out of the tent.

Kieran followed him. The old servant was nowhere in sight. On his way to where his ki'thar stood tethered in the shade, al'Tamar paused by the edge of ai'Jihaar's well to draw a gourd of water, offering it first to Kieran, a wordless acknowledgment of his presence; Kieran accepted it, took a sip, and passed it back.

"Who is she?" Kieran asked, his eyes drawn back to the tent as though magnetized. "She looks impossibly old . . . as if she's well past her ninetieth year . . ."

For a brief moment al'Tamar permitted a smile to dance in his golden eyes. "We are a long-lived race. *An'sen'thar* ai'Jihaar has seen almost two hundred summers."

Kieran, who had received the water gourd back for another sip, choked and went into a paroxysm of coughing. Quickly rescuing the gourd from spilling its contents onto the hungry sands, al'Tamar thumped Kieran on the back.

"She was Anghara's teacher," al'Tamar said. "She is the oldest of the *an'sen'en'thari,* and very wise. Anghara knew well where to seek for help. Only . . ." al'Tamar's own glance kept sliding back to the tent. "I mislike this illness of ai'Jihaar's. It would have been better if this matter had been kept from the tower—especially with ai'Farra not . . ." He paused, and his face twisted into an eloquent grimace. "There are . . . always politics," he added.

"Do you think someone might wish to harm her?" Kieran asked quickly, and the pronoun had shifted; he was no longer talking of ai'Jihaar. This was more in his own sphere; if there was anyone who wished Anghara harm, they'd have to go through him first—and he was more than willing to lay down his life for her. He had been willing in Roisinan; and he was even more so here, in this place, where everything was unknown and all seemed strange and treacherous.

"Not in that way," al'Tamar said, having noticed Kieran's hand come to rest on the hilt of his blade. "And should anyone try to do her physical harm, it is to my uncle the *Sa'id* they would have to answer. And Anghara is dear to the *Sa'id*. She healed his son of a careless wound in the desert; she raised him an oracle; and she bought his sister back from al'Khur . . . with what price, we do not know."

Kieran's head spun. "Then that . . . was true?" he whispered. "Back there in the mountains . . . she spoke of meeting al'Khur . . . of wresting . . ." He hadn't believed Anghara, had thought her story of resurrection in the Black Desert no more than a dream, just as her seeing the towers of Miranei in the shape of the mountain peaks had been. But now he was hearing it from a different quarter, and it gave the story the solidity of truth. Anghara had met and bargained with a God—the same God whose strength, if al'Tamar was to be believed, had sustained Kieran and Anghara on their journey through the mountains between worlds.

"True," al'Tamar agreed. "Now go back; ai'Jihaar had not dismissed you. I am the one with an errand and a duty."

He was about to mount his ki'thar when Kieran's hand on his arm stopped him. Again, as once before, the eyes locked for a moment, blue and gold; Kieran's face was oddly gentle.

A duty. The betrothal ceremonies that waited for al'Tamar; the girl called Rami who "understood." "Do you love her?" Kieran asked, aware he was crossing a boundary into something deeper than a casual companionship, knowing he would not be rebuffed. It was a double-edged question, leaving itself open for al'Tamar to answer as he chose.

The narrow, bronze-skinned face of his betrothed swam vividly into al'Tamar's consciousness for a moment; then faded, transmuting into a white, alien countenance with a pair of wide-set gray eyes. "Rami is a good girl," he said carefully, deliberately sidestepping and closing his eyes for a moment to chase the vision away. "I will learn to."

There was an unspoken "but" which hung in the air between them, and it was Kieran, at the last, who gave it voice.

"But your queen *haval'la* will always come first with you," he said, the phraseology of the desert coming more easily to his lips than he would have believed.

At his words al'Tamar's head came up sharply, as though a dagger had been thrust into his side. His nostrils flared, and then he laughed, a sharp, brittle laugh. "And you said you did not have the Sight of Sheriha'drin. For one who is blind, you are far too at home in other people's minds." He drew a ragged breath, looking away at the horizon, then climbed into his ki'thar's saddle, clucking for it to rise. From the height of this perch he looked down, and his soul was in his golden eyes. "Take care of her," he said; there was iron control in his voice, and still Kieran heard it tremble as it put this renunciation into the spoken word, made it real. With a slow movement carved from dignity and pain he laid the reins of the ki'thar across the saddle and reached up with both hands to remove the *say'yin* he had made for Anghara and carried faithfully for so long. With a last look, he held it out to Kieran. "This passes on," he said. "When the *sen'en'thari* come . . . the Gods alone know where I will be. And this is hers. Will you give it to her for me?"

There was much that Kieran could have said, but there was something in the clear air of the desert that made platitudes hard to utter. Truths were harsh out here, but truth was all there was. Kieran accepted the gift, because there was nothing else he could have done. "I will," he said.

With a high and almost royal pride, al'Tamar bowed to

him from the saddle, giving the graceful desert salute. Then he dropped his gaze down to the ki'thar's reins. *"Akka!"* he cried softly; the lumbering beast rolled its long-lashed eyes in disdain and broke into a shambling trot as its rider wheeled it about.

Kieran watched him until he was only a mirage, a shimmering speck on the heat-trembling horizon. Then he turned abruptly, slipping the *say'yin* around his own neck and tucking it away out of sight, before ducking back inside the tent.

"So," ai'Jihaar said softly, even as he let the flap fall. "You are her Kieran." Hers was a disembodied voice in that first instant in which his sun-dazzled eyes adjusted once again to the cool dimness of the tent. When he could see again, it was to find the white-filmed eyes now focused on him, just as disconcertingly as they had been on al'Tamar moments ago. "Come closer."

Kieran did, for the simple words had the force of a command; ai'Jihaar reached out one frail hand and ran her thin fingers over his face as gently as a butterfly's touch.

"You have a strong face," she said. "And the strength to stand against unknown Gods. Yes, al'Tamar has told me," she said, feeling him flinch beneath her hand. "You do not know it, but there are few who could have done what you did. Her contact with the Gods has been severed . . . and yet a bridge has been cast between them over the chasm. You. You took a live diamondskin in your hand for the sake of one whom you loved . . . and its poison could not touch you." She paused, her hand lingering on his cheek in an oddly maternal manner, and then she allowed it to drop back into her lap, leaning back against her cushions. "There are things I need to know from you. Anghara's mind is a cauldron of confusion and pain. You must tell me."

"Tell you what, lady?" Kieran asked, confused by the breadth of the command.

"Everything," ai'Jihaar said, refusing to help him. "Start

from the beginning, from the moment she returned to Sheriha'drin and her path crossed with yours."

Kieran ran a tired hand through his hair. "That will take forever," he said.

"We have two days," said ai'Jihaar. "On what you say her healing may depend. Omit nothing; let me be the judge of what is important. Begin."

There was a gift in this, too. The images which flowed into Kieran's mind as he started talking were too vivid to be mere memories; it was as though ai'Jihaar was listening to him with only a small part of her concentration. With the rest, she was reaching out and taking the story he was telling straight from his mind. There was a part of Kieran which knew that, only a short while ago, he would have gibbered at this flagrant invasion of his thoughts. But now he accepted without demur; there was another part which was aghast at the ease with which he accepted this alien touch. Kheldrin was working its insidious magic.

Except for one instance when she bade him pause and called for the old servant to bring food and refreshments, ai'Jihaar did not interrupt. After he had eaten she nodded wordlessly at Kieran to continue. Finally, exhausted and surprised to find lamps lit around him and the tent full of dancing shadows, he allowed his voice to fade into silence, having reached the point in his tale where he'd helped Anghara off her camel. Only then did ai'Jihaar draw a deep sigh.

She asked for his hand, the one which had given the blood sacrifice in the pathless mountains, and fingered his smooth, unmarked skin. "It is as I thought," she said pensively. "You are a channel . . . and because what you give is her offering, it is accepted. The Gods took your sacrifice, from one who was never marked as their own. Perhaps it is as well that you do not know what dangers you courted there. But perhaps it is best if you let me hold the dagger for her now."

"I will bring it to you," Kieran said, not without some relief.

"It was well done," ai'Jihaar said, her voice a vindication of the action he had taken out of desperation. She had asked him for the black dagger where she could have commanded; this was kindness, and trust. "I will guard it for her; she shall have it back from your hand if you so wish, if . . . when . . . she is restored to her power. But that dagger is not a thing to be left alone too long; it needs close contact with life. What you do not give freely, it might well choose to take by itself."

That he already knew. There had been a dark dream or two since he rode with the dagger in his baggage; dark dreams, tinged with the blood for which the knife of sacrifice was asking.

Kieran emerged into the coolness of the desert night. He didn't need light—the contents of his packs had been lived with for so long now he could have found his way through them blindfolded. He found the black dagger more by touch and a sense of velvet darkness than by sight, his hands oddly twitchy as his fingers closed around it as though the blade was eager to be let loose to do its work.

"This place is getting to me," Kieran muttered, wrapping the black handle with a handful of his cloak to break the contact between the dagger and his bare skin.

Anghara stirred as he returned to the tent, but ai'Jihaar quelled her with a touch and reached out a hand for that which Kieran carried. "Quickly," she said, and Kieran let go, not unwillingly. The blade changed hands; ai'Jihaar frowned down at it. "I am not sure," she said slowly, "what could happen when we try to break this bond of yours. Anghara knew when you held her blade. I hope you are not already in too deep . . ."

Kieran had a dull feeling that those words ought to have conveyed a sense of dire peril, but the immense fatigue he had felt at the foot of the sundering mountains had returned a hundredfold. He surprised himself with a jaw-cracking yawn and ai'Jihaar raised her head swiftly from contemplating the black dagger. "Forgive me," she said. Her soft voice had lost all harshness and command. "I have been selfish. I have asked much, and offered little in return—but I am grateful beyond words that you found yourself at Anghara's side when she needed someone. My servant has prepared your bed; if there is anything you find you still require, you have but to ask."

"A bed will be welcome," Kieran said slowly. "I can't seem to recall when last I had the luxury of one."

"It has been a long while," she agreed. "Perhaps it is even longer than you realize. Do you have any idea what day it is?"

"I knew when we left Shaymir," Kieran said after a short pause in which he tried fruitlessly to calculate the time gone by since they left Keda's husband at the singing stone. "After that . . . things blur a little. I had no real way of keeping track."

"The day after tomorrow," ai'Jihaar said, "is celebrated as the eve of the festival of Cerdiad in Sheriha'drin. It is almost midsummer."

"That is impossible!" Kieran gasped, caught thoroughly off guard. "We couldn't have spent a month . . . more than a month . . . in those mountains. We would never have survived! It's not possible . . ."

"You forget," ai'Jihaar said, "you had a God who walked at your back."

"But al'Tamar said al'Khur helped us," said Kieran helplessly. "A month . . ."

"He helped you," ai'Jihaar said. "You would not be here if he had not. But helping you does not mean he let you lightly into his realm."

"Others crossed those mountains before us," Kieran said stubbornly.

"That is true. But consider—more have tried than have succeeded, a great many more; and those who did succeed almost always fared badly here. There are people in Kheldrin who consider the mere presence of *fram'man'en* sacrilege, and are ready to act in accordance with this belief. And while there are a few of our folk who have been across those mountains and returned, even they prefer to keep their own counsel, and they are the Gods' own children." Her thin hands closed over the black dagger, hiding it from Kieran's sight under a fold of the coverlet and a welter of silver bracelets. It seemed to restore him to himself; he blinked, looked away, down at Anghara.

"Worry no longer about her," said ai'Jihaar in her unusual syntax, guessing his thoughts with an uncanny ability. "Everything that can be done, I will do. She was right in one thing—in no other place could she begin to be healed. But whether we prove able to fulfill our charge remains to be seen. Her brother may well have done worse than kill her."

"Can you heal her?" Kieran asked huskily.

"She once healed, without knowing how, or why," ai'Jihaar said softly, and her gaze was brooding, turned inward. It was an old memory she was dusting off and holding to the light. "More than that—she conquered death itself. For such a one . . . we will dare much."

Kieran bowed to her in silence and left her.

After, he was never able to tell if it had been real or a dream; but he remembered, much later, looking outside into the dark, moonless night and seeing ai'Jihaar standing by the pool before her tent. But it was none of the ai'Jihaars of that day's audience—not the old woman weakened by her illness, nor the imperious *an'sen'thar,* nor the gentle teacher, nor the teasing, bantering aunt sending her truant nephew back to his betrothal celebrations. This was a creature of power, wreathed in a column of white fire, her arms out to the dark sky full of those huge, impossible desert stars. *Give me the strength,* she seemed to be saying. *Whatever her bargain with you, Sa'id al'Khur, surely it was for this that she took me from you—whatever her bargain, I will fulfill it. Only give me strength. She asked you once for my life; I ask for hers.*

The bargain we made between us is almost complete, a'sen'thar, a disembodied voice from the stars seemed to reply. *She has forgotten, as I bid her; in one day she will remember it all. And when she does . . . her life is no longer in my hands.*

There should have been little in that first encounter with ai'Jihaar to reassure Kieran on anything at all—yet he slept the sleep of the innocent, and the trusting. When he woke the next morning, left undisturbed in the curtained corner of the tent which had been given over to his use, it was closer to lunch than breakfast, and Kieran's stomach soon reminded him that the previous night's supper was hours away. He was ravenous.

He was also alone. He had always had the facility of knowing when he was sharing air with someone, and when at last he made himself presentable and peered into the tent from his enclosure, it didn't surprise him to find it empty.

Anghara . . . What had they done with Anghara . . .

Even as trust began to flee and all his apprehensions come flying to his shoulders like waiting vultures, Anghara pushed open the tent flap and ducked inside. Her cheeks were rosy, her eyes bright.

"Well! So you're awake at last! I was about to defy ai'Jihaar and come and roust you out. The day is half done already."

"You look well," Kieran said, leaving a hundred things he might have wished to tell her unsaid. It was all there in his silence, had Anghara wanted or been able to read between his words.

But she chose not to look past the obvious. "I feel much

better," she said, "although ai'Jihaar tells me I'm nowhere near mended." She managed to make it sound facetious; Kieran didn't know whether to thank ai'Jihaar, or to rail at her for playing with Anghara's feelings.

"Where is she . . . ai'Jihaar?" he asked instead.

Anghara giggled like a young girl, which, after all, she still was. "Much against ai'Fatmah's sensibilities, ai'Jihaar decided to perform her daily ablutions at the well instead of having water brought in to her. She's almost done; and then she's asked ai'Fatmah to put together a midday snack. And after that," she laughed again, "you might as well go straight back to bed, because it will be time for the afternoon rest."

"And you?"

"Oh, ai'Jihaar might want to grill me again—she has been asking an unconscionable amount of questions since I got here."

"Don't I know," Kieran said, unable to keep it back.

"You, too?" Anghara said, eyes twinkling. "It might be your turn, then. I'll find ways to amuse myself. Besides, we're to have company before long. If ai'Jihaar knows her brother and her fellow *sen'en'thari* at the Al'haria tower, those whom she has sent al'Tamar to summon should be here tomorrow, if not even late tonight."

"You know about all that?" Kieran said abruptly. "You were fast asleep when it was being discussed."

"No *sen'thar* is ever truly asleep, I think I heard much of it myself, although ai'Jihaar also told me."

"But you said you were blind . . ."

The smile slipped a little. "So I am. But here in the Kadun . . . I don't know. Things seep through. Here, and . . . well . . . it's like when I felt the Standing Stones on the moor when we were running from Sif."

He'd destroyed her mood, and was sorry for it. But she was none the less luminous for having her spark quenched, merely banking to the glow of yellow embers. Yes, she was blind, but ai'Jihaar had held out a ray of hope, and Anghara was clinging to it like a drowning man might cling to a spar. There would be a chance for her. She waited for it with a hunger that yawned visible in her gray eyes in unguarded moments. A hunger in which there was no room for anything else—not for Roisinan that was her inheritance, and certainly not for . . . how had ai'Jihaar put it to al'Tamar just before he left? For a *qu'mar* of this world, still less one who had not, in so many words, declared himself and of whose true feelings, hidden beneath so many layers laid down over the passing years, he could hardly expect her to be aware.

These thoughts were less than helpful. Kieran smothered them, ruthlessly, and offered a sharp, deliberate smile, part of whose dazzle was pure pain. "So you expect them tonight?"

"It's possible," Anghara said, responding, once again, only to the obvious, as if to a few dry autumn leaves upon the mirrored surface of a black, cold depth of water below.

"I wonder what they will make of me?" he said with a grimace, raking his dark hair back from his brow with long fingers.

"They . . ." Anghara stopped abruptly, frowning delicately as if she had just allowed a stray thought to trickle away irretrievably, like sand through fingers. But when Kieran lifted a quizzical eyebrow she made a self-conscious wave of her hand. "I forget what I wanted to say." She glanced back over her shoulder as the tent flap lifted again to reveal ai'Fatmah with a laden tray, closely followed by her mistress. Today ai'Jihaar was clad in her gold robes, with the full *say'yin'en* due her rank; once again Kieran bowed before the subtle power which coursed through this small, frail woman, disregarding the inescapable fact that his gesture would go entirely unnoticed.

As it would have done, if ai'Jihaar had been anyone other than who she was. The old *an'sen'thar,* however, smiled eerily at something she couldn't possibly have seen and met it with a studied and appropriate response.

"I am friend to you, as I have ever been friend and teacher to Anghara," ai'Jihaar said. "There is nothing which requires obeisance between us. Come, sit by me; we have so very little time before the others arrive and we must be about doing . . . what must be done. But while we are still alone, come, and tell one who loves your land about green Sheriha'drin."

"Alas, it has not been a pleasant country these last few years," Kieran said.

"The bleeding land," ai'Jihaar said, nodding.

"The oracle," Anghara offered, at Kieran's slight frown. "*Reaching from the dark, the bleeding land waits.* That's what Gul Khaima told me when I left her."

"The bleeding land," echoed Kieran. "Yes." He glanced at Anghara out of smoldering eyes. "I have always believed," he said softly, "that you . . ."

"Not yet, Kieran," Anghara said, raising a hand to forestall him. "Not yet. Perhaps not ever. So much depends on what . . . happens in this place."

"But you are ours whatever the outcome. You have always been that. And we, yours. That was all written long before Sif snatched the Book of Hours to write his bloody reign into it."

"Your feelings do you credit," said ai'Jihaar. "Without you Anghara would never have been in a position to choose. And yet it is still she in whose hands the choice remains . . . as the power to grant lies in the hands of the Gods. Remember that."

"Nothing changes for me, whether she is Sighted or blind," said Kieran desperately, turning to face ai'Jihaar. "I don't understand the first and cannot pity the second; for me she remains Anghara, once foster sister, now my rightful queen."

"Peace, Kieran," Anghara said, reaching out to lay a small cool hand on his arm. It was all he could do not to snatch it up and kiss it, but with a great shuddering sigh he controlled himself and once again let much of what he would have blurted out remain unsaid. Now was not the time, if the right time could ever exist for all that was buried within him to be brought into the light of day. Restive fingers fluttered up; touched the hard curved surface of a *say'yin* made with love he now wore hidden against an auspicious hour. And it was al'Tamar's peace that welled up through his hot palm, giving strength to his silence. He bowed his head.

"Tomorrow," Anghara said, giving his arm a gentle squeeze. "Tomorrow we will know everything."

They were expected in the morning of the following day, but it was late afternoon when emissaries from the *sen'thar* tower of Al'haria arrived—seven women wearing gray beneath cowled black djellabas and blue burnouses, and one, riding a magnificent blond-maned dark dun, whose robe gleamed gold. Behind them plodded a pair of ki'thar'en bearing a clutch of sleepy-looking servants, and another who carried a load carefully bundled and muffled in corded layers of padded woollen wrappings with the occasional gleam of rich jin'aaz silk.

Feeling unwell that morning, ai'Jihaar had not emerged to greet her guests. It made little difference, for her they were as visible from the inside of her tent as if she had risen to wait for them outside.

"A gold," she murmured. "But not ai'Farra . . . *Chud,* now that we need her, now she visits her mother in Say'ar'-dun . . ."

Anghara, too, had chosen not to emerge from the tent, but, lacking ai'Jihaar's unearthly senses, she was reduced to peering through a slit in the entrance flaps. "There is just the one gold," Anghara said. "She's veiled, but I don't think I know her."

"Hai!" breathed ai'Jihaar. "She has a cold soul fire, that one—the color of shadows in the hollow eye sockets of a desert-bleached skull. Her name is ai'Daileh; she was raised to the gold after you left, in the Beku tower, down in the Arad, and ai'Farra had her brought to Al'haria. She is strong, this young one, but hard, too hard . . . She kills cleanly, but I wonder if she has it in her to heal?"

"You say ai'Farra brought her? But aren't you also . . ."

"It is not for such as I to question the Keeper of the Records' choice of successor. And ai'Farra is . . . ai'Farra. When you forced her hand by choosing Hariff, she declared herself in other ways. I suspect one of the greatest seals on ai'Daileh's suitability had roots in the fact that she, too, is Sayyed. It changes the balance of power in Al'haria. And ai'Farra was never one to allow the chance of power to slip through her fingers."

"Should I disappear?" Kieran asked. He had been standing back, arms crossed almost defensively across his chest. Whether from the old, ingrained wariness of "Khelsies" or from something newer, deeper, to do with Anghara and her own gifts, Kieran's scalp was crawling; never before had he been prey to a premonition this strong. Trouble was brewing, that much was certain.

"No," said ai'Jihaar. "It's not as though they don't know you are here. But leave the talking to me."

Kieran was more than happy to oblige. He merely withdrew a step or two, deeper into the filtered reddish half-light which pervaded the tent and from which his eyes glittered like sapphires.

At the entrance, Anghara's narrow, silk-sheathed back suddenly stiffened, and her hands dropped from the tent flaps to fly to the sides of her head.

"Are you all right?" ai'Jihaar said instantly, even as Kieran's own arms uncrossed, his right hand seeking its instinctive position on the pommel of his sword.

"The pain . . ." Anghara moaned, backing away from the tent entrance.

"Stay," ai'Jihaar said to Kieran, who had already tensed to leap forward, without turning her head. "This is not something where you can be of help. Come, Anghara."

Even as Anghara staggered toward the pile of silk cushions where ai'Jihaar reclined, the hail came from outside. *"Sa'hari, an'sen'thar?"*

"Iman'et?" ai'Jihaar said, and then glanced down at the tight mask of pain which still rode the features of the girl who had collapsed at her feet. *"Dan'ah,"* she added. Inadvertently al'Tamar had extended Kieran's Kheldrini vocabulary during the journey from the mountains—Kieran knew what *sa'hari* meant. And the response—*iman'et,* enter. The third word he hadn't come across, but its import was obvious as the tent flaps lifted to divulge a single representative of the small caravan which had just arrived. *Dan'ah.* Alone.

The voice asking admission had been cool, assured, and the imperiously gold-robed figure which ducked into ai'Jihaar's tent suited it well. Now free of its burnouse, ai'-Daileh's face was chiselled rather than sculpted—all sharp angles and no curves. The line of her jaw could cut, and her eyes were golden ice. They flicked to Kieran briefly, taking his measure, then turned away as though he had been no more than an interesting and mildly distasteful piece of furniture. Kieran was dismissed, left to smolder in silence while the two gold-robed Kheldrini priestesses, who held Anghara's future in their hands, proceeded to have a conversation of which he understood not a word.

"You sent for us, *an'sen'thar?*" said ai'Daileh ma'Sayyed. The tone was formal, correct, polite; no less deference than required between a senior *an'sen'thar* and a junior sister who, nonetheless, herself wore gold—and not a grain of sand more. All too aware of death and of mortality, ai'Daileh's approach was that of coiled power, content to wait a little—for it would not be long—before ai'Jihaar's world passed into the keeping of hands such as her own, younger, stronger, chosen by ai'Jihaar's own Gods. "I am here, together with seven gray sisters. They wait without for your word, as you commanded. *Sa'id* al'Jezraal was not completely forthcoming; he merely said you would tell us why we were required."

"She is the reason," ai'Jihaar said, very softly.

At last ai'Daileh's eyes slid down to Anghara. Her lip curled—a little. It might have been the beginning of a smile. "The *fram'man an'sen'thar.* I have read of this one, in the records ai'Farra has made of the raising of Gul Khaima. She has returned from Sheriha'drin?"

Beneath ai'Jihaar's soothing touch Anghara's face had cleared a little, but her cheeks were scarlet, and her eyes . . . Kieran had seen those haunted eyes before, back on the bare gray slopes of the mountain across which they had struggled to gain this land. Anghara was back in a place he thought they had long since left behind. His heart sank; there was a twinge, almost instantly gone, in the hand which had tasted the black dagger on her behalf.

"She is back," ai'Jihaar said, "and she needs our help." She had to stop, draw breath. She suddenly looked all of her age and more, beside this dangerous young priestess she had invited into her home. But it was for Anghara she was fighting, child of her heart, and so she gathered her strength and power and straightened. "I have been ill," ai'Jihaar said stiffly, as though making the admission galled her. "And that which ails our sister is beyond the strength of one, were I ten times younger and my health as sound as it was when I was your age." It was a subtle reminder, and ai'Daileh did not miss it. The golden eyes swept down briefly, veiled by spiky copper eyelashes. "Therefore I have summoned you, and those whom you bring. She has returned from the brink in the day or so she has been here with me, but now, when you arrived . . . I did not think that all this power in one place might well prove to be too much for her."

"What is the trouble?" ai'Daileh asked delicately.

"You have read of the *an'sen'thar* who raised an oracle," ai'Jihaar said. "Look, and tell me if you sense her here with us today!"

It shook the self-possessed young priestess to find the wreckage that she did—shook her to such a degree that her face actually softened for a moment as she gazed at the silent, motionless Anghara. But it was gone by the time she lifted her head to look at ai'Jihaar again. "There is something odd here," she murmured.

"The first thing we need to do is to forge again the bridges that were broken," ai'Jihaar said, choosing to ignore her remark, not wishing to take the first bite out of the subject of Kieran just yet.

"Is that possible?" ai'Daileh said thoughtfully.

"We will find out. Have you come prepared?"

The younger woman nodded. "A white ki'thar lamb, not yet four full moons old. Two of the wounded silkseekers brought in to us . . . although I still cannot understand how you knew we had two with the precise hurts you wanted."

"I do not have to be at the tower to know what passes there," said ai'Jihaar calmly, folding her hands serenely in her lap. "You have the silkseekers. The rest?"

"I have brought the *Rab'bat Rah'honim.*"

"It is well."

After a moment of silence, while she regarded Anghara with curious eyes, ai'Daileh said, "Perhaps there is after all little we can do."

In response ai'Jihaar raised an eloquent eyebrow and ai'-Daileh crossed her arms, a little defensively, but ai'Jihaar could not see this, and ai'Daileh's voice, when she spoke, was cool and distant. "Perhaps this is no more than the price she pays for taking the Way—she, *fram'man,* to whom the desert should have been forbidden . . ."

Tension crackled in the air; Kieran didn't have to understand the words to gather a sense of looming danger. There was something in ai'Daileh's face and in the way she looked on Anghara that outraged him, a dismissiveness, a speculation . . . He stiffened in the shadows; keeping his peace seemed for a moment to be beyond his powers. Who did she think she was, this gold-robed . . . Khelsie? To slight thus one who had, *fram'man* or no, spoken face to face with ai'-Daileh's own Gods? The words formed in his mind, incandescent, ready to burst forth—*have you ever looked al'Khur in the face and lived, desert priestess*—but ai'Jihaar was a quiet flame in the darkness, a still white light which reached out and quenched Kieran's anger, delicately, gently.

"I was afraid of this," ai'Jihaar said out loud, as though her mind had not, for an instant, been focused elsewhere.

The voice was flawlessly controlled—a little resigned, a little regretful, yet shot through with a solid resolve which found its mark. Even Kieran caught the tone of those words; ai'Daileh herself jumped as though the words had been a dagger pointing at her throat.

"Even ai'Farra has grown past this," said ai'Jihaar. "You . . . you have never known Anghara of Sheriha'drin, or what she did, apart from that which you have read and which has been relegated for all eternity to the dust of the catacombs. There, perhaps, she was as great as her achievements. Here, all you see is a helpless *fram'man* girl-child with a wounded soul. Tell me now, ai'Daileh: are you able to rise above what you see and reach for what you know? If not . . . I will not allow you near enough to do her harm unless I have your sworn word that you came here to heal, not sacrifice."

No, her eyes were not ice. They smoldered now in the angled, chiselled face; ai'Daileh's hands were balled into tight fists at her side. Kieran wished passionately that he could understand what was transpiring here—he had been holding his breath, watching the face ai'Jihaar couldn't see. He exhaled in a long, quiet sigh even as ai'Daileh lifted her chin in what was part pride, part defiance.

"I would not harm one who has been confirmed to gold as I have," she said slowly. "I may not have liked to see it done—but it was done, and it stands. She is *an'sen'thar,* the same as I."

"Your sworn word," said ai'Jihaar, implacable.

"If you believe it necessary, you have it. I am here; I will do what I can to heal a sister in the Way. I will work no harm upon her. May I have leave to withdraw, *an'sen'thar?* I assume you would want us to begin as soon as everything has been made ready."

"You may leave."

With that ai'Daileh bowed lightly and turned to leave. She paused at the entrance, glancing back, taking in Anghara's wide and unseeing gray eyes, Kieran standing tense and ready in the shadows, ai'Jihaar bent over Anghara's bright head—and Kieran reeled as he heard unspoken words echo distinctly inside his head: *You are getting old, venerable one. There was a time you would not have needed an oath to know a sister's heart.* A little regret, perhaps; but more of triumph, of satisfaction, perhaps even a little malice.

Then ai'Daileh was gone; and, shock on shock, ai'Jihaar's own voice, quite physical and substantial, but frailer by far than the chance thought he had just caught. "That one," ai'Jihaar said in Roisinani, almost in a whisper, "she would have taxed me even were I not as weak as this . . . Curse this affliction! Where is ai'Fatmah?"

"Shall I look for her?" Kieran said, coming closer.

"No time . . . There is a vial in the chest there at the back, blue glass . . ."

Kieran was already there, throwing open the lid, searching with frantic hands. There were two blue vials, damn it. He hesitated, and his eye was caught by a glint of metal. The edge of a blade—Anghara's dagger. A memory of honey-thick air . . . eyes in the desert . . . blood . . .

"Kieran . . ."

He snapped out of it with a start, aware he had been sitting entranced for some minutes, while ai'Jihaar's voice behind him was softer still, fading . . . He snatched at a blue vial at random. Where ai'Jihaar had seemed to be bending anxiously over Anghara, it was now all too obvious that Anghara was the support ai'Jihaar slumped against.

Kieran thumped down on his knees on the cushions beside ai'Jihaar, lifting the lid of the vial as he did so. "Here it is," he said, lifting one of her hands and folding it around the blue glass. Unstoppered, it smelled familiar, oddly familiar in a land where everything was strange to him, but he had no time to wonder, and ai'Jihaar had taken a swallow or two before either of them gathered their thoughts.

It hit them both at once.

"Lais," Kieran whispered, staring at the vial in horror. "That's lais . . ."

"Concentrated essence," ai'Jihaar said, allowing her hand to fall to her lap. "Kieran, what have you done? It is in the hands of the Gods, perhaps, even now . . . bring me the other vial. Perhaps there is time."

Kieran flew to the open chest, keeping his eyes averted from the fatal dagger gleaming within and retrieved the second vial, which ai'Jihaar received from his shaking fingers. She opened it herself and tasted a few drops.

"See if they are ready outside," ai'Jihaar commanded softly, her eyes closed. Kieran left her reluctantly to peer through the tent flaps. Already the little hai'r looked different—ai'Daileh had taken charge.

One of the servants who had arrived with the small caravan was reverently unwrapping the great black drums, the

Rab'bat Rah'honim. One was already free, standing upright in the sand, polished black wood drinking in the clear golden light of a desert afternoon and wrapping it in the mystery of impending darkness. The smooth, tanned skin stretched taut upon it had once been a white ki'thar. The great drum's mate, still only half divested of its wrappings of soft wool and red and gold jin'aaz silks, showed black where the other showed white. Black ki'thar'en were even rarer than white; this second skin had been a gift from the Gods. Beside the drums, each almost the height of the *sen'en'thari* who were to play them, stood one of the gray sisters, her small hands dwarfed by two massive drumsticks made of the same black wood as the drums.

Two more of the grays were busy with what looked like housekeeping duties around three black desert tents which had mushroomed on the other side of ai'Jihaar's pool. A third, at the doorway of one of the tents, was folding up a large piece of scarlet silk while keeping up a soft conversation with somebody within.

And ai'Daileh herself presided over the preparation of a crude altar within the shelter of the palm trees. It was still early for the ceremony. She was explaining something to a companion out of Kieran's line of vision, and stood with her arms raised, the sleeves of her golden robe baring her arms almost to the elbow in what looked too much like an invocation for Kieran's taste. He drew back.

"I don't think they're ready," he said, glancing back to answer ai'Jihaar's question. The old *an'sen'thar's* eyes were drooping. "Soon though," he hastened to add, "ai'Daileh looks as if she is almost done. The drums are still . . ."

But even as he spoke a deep, reverberating boom echoed through the hai'r. Kieran's head snapped around. The two drums were both standing free, the servant scurrying away with the neatly folded cloths, silk and wools that had been their travel garb. There was something elemental about the black drums, a feeling enhanced by the two gray sisters who stood behind them, each armed with a single great drumstick. It was the one at the white drum who had struck first; even as Kieran watched, the other brought her stick down on the black ki'thar skin. The drum responded, its tone a shade deeper and darker than its twin. The white drumstick descended again; the black; the white; the black . . . the rhythm was almost too slow to bear, slumberous, lulling.

"She won't start till nightfall now," said ai'Jihaar distantly, startling Kieran into remembering she was there. "Call ai'Fatmah; I need her to brew me something potent . . . *khaf,* black, sweet, strong. I have to stay awake until the ceremony begins."

Obeying her meant leaving the tent, going out into the full sight of those strangers who had yet to see him. Kieran gave himself no time to think about it. He pushed the flap and stepped outside.

He was the immediate focus of at least three pairs of eyes. Four. He turned at the doorway of the smaller tent which ai'Jihaar's servant occupied to meet again the smoldering golden gaze of ai'Daileh, watchful, calculating. Kieran held it for a moment, and then slowly and deliberately offered her a courtly bow springing from the centuries of tradition that were part of old Roisinan, before turning his back on her and slipping inside ai'Fatmah's tent. He could sense a ripple of the golden priestess's amusement follow him inside. The black drums were still beating slow time.

The hours are slow to pass when watched. The minutes of those still to elapse before nightfall dripped with agonizing deliberation; each one might have been a perfect replica of the hour of which it was a part, carved in miniature by a master craftsman. Drinking *khaf* in quantities that would have kept a ki'thar awake for a month, ai'Jihaar waited, hoping the lais she had swallowed wouldn't slow her too much, that the *khaf* would neutralize it quickly enough for her to be able to watch over ai'Daileh's ritual. Anghara seemed to have been pushed deeper than ever into a trance by the relentless boom of the black drums, and sat dreaming. Kieran simply waited. For nightfall. For truth. For salvation.

It was fully dark when ai'Daileh finally came for them, but three great fires had been lit and the hai'r glowed with ruddy light. It pushed past ai'Daileh into the tent, making of her a dark silhouette, the night lurid behind her.

"We are ready to begin, *an'sen'thar.* Come. Bring the daughter of Sheriha'drin."

"She is Anghara ma'Hariff in this land," ai'Jihaar said as Kieran helped her rise to her feet. Her voice was steadier, more absolute, than her physical body. Kieran could feel her sway as she leaned on his arm.

"Of course. May I be of assistance?"

"Thank you. There is no need." Kieran had raised Anghara also to her feet and now stood between them, ai'Jihaar on one arm, Anghara on the other, as if in some bizarre courtly dance, waiting for instructions. Now ai'Jihaar turned her head in his direction and smiled, dropping into Roisinani. "If you will conduct us to the altar . . ."

"Wait," said ai'Daileh quickly. "For her who chose the Hariff and who raised the oracle in Kheldrin . . . but to allow a true *fram'man* to witness *sen'en'thari* ceremonies . . ."

All Kieran understood was an implacable challenge to his presence; his hands tightened involuntarily on both Anghara's arm and ai'Jihaar's. The old *an'sen'thar* had turned away from him to gaze steadily on ai'Daileh's face; reassurance came only in a gentle return of pressure. As the drums beat inexorably outside, ai'Jihaar did not flinch. "Perhaps, afterward," she said to ai'Daileh as she urged Kieran forward, "I will tell you just how much this particular *fram'man* already knows. Lead the way, ai'Daileh."

The younger priestess hesitated for a long moment, eyes on Kieran, and then whirled, a quick, almost angry motion.

Kieran, leading the two remaining gold-robed women, followed in silence, far from certain if ai'Jihaar had successfully defended his right to stand with Anghara, or signed his death warrant.

The drums seemed to speed up as they emerged and followed ai'Daileh along the edge of the hai'r's small pool toward an altar raised amongst the palm trees. Kieran saw the remaining five grays ranged around this; one held a plaited leather leash, on the other end of which stood a quiescent white ki'thar lamb. At the feet of another rested a small cage with two white and gold birds, both of whom seemed to have one broken wing.

"Take us to the altar," ai'Jihaar said softly, "and then step back beyond the palms."

"Are you all right?" Kieran asked—ai'Jihaar felt curiously insubstantial underneath his supporting arm, as though she was no more than an illusion, or a spirit.

"I will be," the old *an'sen'thar* said.

Kieran halted a bare pace away from the stone plinth ai'-Daileh had raised for an altar and pressed ai'Jihaar's fingers again. "We're there," he said.

"Give me Anghara's hand," ai'Jihaar said. Kieran relinquished it, with sudden misgivings; ai'Jihaar felt his fingers tremble and sensed his hesitation. She spared a final smile for him. "It will be all right. Go."

Suddenly ai'Daileh's strong voice rose in a strange chant, and Kieran retreated hastily until he felt the rough bole of one of the palm trees behind his back. He saw the young priestess raise a black dagger, eerily similar to the one he had himself held in his hands; so many things were coming clear now, as he watched for the first time the ritual in which the blade belonged. He watched the young gray lift the white lamb onto the altar; he saw ai'Daileh's grimly gleaming blade descend, and rise gory from the sacrificial altar, the priestess's golden robe bearing no mark from the Gods' blood.

There is blood on my sleeve . . .

He saw Anghara flinch, heard her cry out something, stretch out a hand toward the altar, and then stagger, almost fall; it was all ai'Jihaar could do to keep her standing. There was no letup in the drums and ai'Daileh went across to Anghara, lifted her head and stared intently into her eyes—what she saw didn't appear to please her. She went into a huddle with ai'Jihaar, bracing Anghara upright between them. Kieran's head ached fiercely; the drums throbbed in a cloud of pungent, muddled scents of *khaf,* lais and exotic incense they had begun burning. The resulting ferment found a dark and quiet place just behind his temples and hissed there like a nest of adders. His eyes had begun to water; he closed them for a moment, drawing deep breaths, leaning the back of his head against the rough bark.

When he looked again, Anghara had been passed to two of the grays to support her, and both the golds, the old and the young, had gone to the altar. The gray with the birdcage had gone with them. The birds within were oddly quiet, sitting still, as though understanding their fate and resigned to it. They made no protest as each *an'sen'thar* reached out and chose one to hold between her hands.

Kieran didn't understand the words being spoken. He didn't have to. All around him the air was growing still and solid, much as he remembered it from the Shaymir desert. There was power here—but it was dark, and none of it belonged to Anghara, who stood swaying imperceptibly to the beat of the black drums, oblivious . . . except inasmuch as she appeared to have shaken off the support of the gray sisters and stood unaided beside the altar stone.

Was it working, then? Was her strength beginning to be restored to her?

At the altar, the two broken-winged birds were brought together upon the stone, breast to breast. First ai'Daileh spoke over them, voice low and smoky, then ai'Jihaar responded, slowly, softly; holding their birds with one hand, both lifted a black dagger high in the other, and then both daggers came flashing down in concert, piercing both birds. Blood, looking black and viscous in the firelight, welled out through the white and gold feathers; the daggers pinned the two birds together, touching at the place where the blade entered the hilt, like a cross.

The fires exploded into sparks. A smile crept onto Anghara's face, but her eyes were still empty, glassy, and the smile was unpleasant. The air thickened unbearably; Kieran thought he could see it coalescing into long white streamers before his eyes, like mist, or the ragged remnants of ghosts. He was breathing in gasps; something heavy crushed down on his shoulders, bowing them, buckling his knees. He resisted, clenching his fists, lifting his head defiantly to stare up at the star-strewn sky. *You are not my Gods. I do not bend my knees to you.*

But others had. One of the grays was down; another buckled to one knee even as Kieran's eyes swept past her; and then, very slowly, ai'Jihaar seemed to crumple into herself as though her robe was suddenly hanging on empty air. She folded soundlessly, like a wraith; Kieran heard someone cry out in anguish, and was dimly aware that it had been himself. Anghara did not react.

But ai'Daileh did. She knelt beside the old *sen'thar,* a slim, long-fingered hand coming to rest upon ai'Jihaar's closed eyes. Then she rose. A step across to Anghara, who seemed to turn and laugh; and then, slow motion, in time to the driving beat of the drums and through the slow, thick air, came the sound of ai'Daileh's voice.

Once again Kieran couldn't understand her words, but the darkness of her voice woke the knowledge of death that slept within him and he felt the coldness of it freeze his bones. He could read it in ai'Daileh's eyes, across the space which divided them, as she turned to face him. She had offered sacrifice to the Kheldrini Gods, but it was death itself she had called into this circle, not al'Khur, its Lord.

Kieran's death.

"She means to kill you."

The words were so precisely an echo of Kieran's own thought he believed for a moment he had himself uttered aloud what was in his mind. But then the real identity of the soft, urgent voice was gradually borne in upon him—al'Tamar. He had the presence of mind not to turn. He remained still, eyes locked with the Kheldrini priestess; only his lips moved, all the shock of the moment in his voice.

"What are you doing here?"

"I came when I saw who was to lead the caravan," said the other swiftly from the deeper shadow of the lais bushes just beyond the palm trees. "Kieran . . ."

"I won't lie down and die," Kieran whispered fiercely. "Not easily. Kerun and Avanna! I am no ki'thar lamb to feed the Kheldrini Gods' bloodlust!"

A stray thought returned to taunt him—he remembered vowing to himself, not so long ago, that he would be willing to lay down his life for Anghara, who was his queen, whom he loved. Was this not, in fact, what ai'Daileh would ask from him?

No. Not like this. Fighting for her, yes, gladly, offering his strength and power, all that he was, to what she could become. Not this. Not this useless spending of a life not yet done, a meaningless spilling of blood into an empty wilderness. There was still so much to do . . .

And yet . . . if he could be sure her life would be bought back for Roisinan . . .

No.

It had all taken a fraction of a second, all the arguments, counter-arguments, justification, denial—it all streamed through his mind, fell into place, and was locked in. No.

A fraction of a second was all ai'Daileh needed. When Kieran looked toward the altar again, it was to see two of the remaining gray sisters, attended by two of the servants who had accompanied the caravan, making their way steadily toward him. He straightened, loosening his blade.

Am I to fight women? he thought, appalled at the prospect.

"I will stand with you," came the desperate, whispered voice of al'Tamar.

"No," Kieran said quickly. "Don't throw your own life away here tonight. What of your Rami?"

And there was no time for more, for they were upon him, and he saw that one of the two women carried, rather gingerly, a large pottery jar and the other bore a thin, night-colored net. The servants came empty-handed, and were somehow all the more menacing for that.

"Beware of the pot!" hissed the disembodied voice from behind Kieran, and then it was too late for anything except fighting for his life. The one with the pot had opened it and hurled its contents in Kieran's direction even as al'Tamar had uttered his warning. The two large yellow scorpions that had been inside, each almost the length of Kieran's forearm, were not pleased; their temper was dangerous, and they were poised to strike at the first thing that stood in their path.

Kieran twisted out of the way. One of the scorpions landed softly beside his foot. It righted itself quickly, planting all its feet squarely in the sand, and paused for a moment, its venomous tail lifted and waving slowly over its back as it waited to get its bearings. The gray *sen'thar* with the net was flanking Kieran dangerously, with the servant at her heels, but even as he turned to glance around, the scuffle of his foot on the sand decided the scorpion and it lunged in his direction.

Kieran had his dagger out, stalking the killer who was stalking him. As the scorpion moved so did he, leaping aside and turning to stab the dagger, with a wet sucking noise, into the sand at his feet squarely through the scorpion's broad yellow back, snatching his hand away as the poisonous tail whipped back and forth in its frenzied death throes.

He felt the net fall about him like a whisper of night even as he straightened, looking around frantically for the second scorpion.

The net was thin, but inhumanly strong, made of material which looked uncannily like jin'aaz silk. If this was so, then this was the stuff of a spider's web, turned back to serve its original function—catching prey. His hands were tangled in it, and it twisted around him even as he struggled to free himself, biting into his skin with unexpected viciousness. But it seemed to be a weapon of capture, not captivity; having served its purpose, it was removed once the servant had pinioned Kieran's arms behind his back with a more conventional cord. There were plenty of hands lent to this work; if some of them were soft and female that didn't mean they lacked strength or power, and Kieran's struggles went for naught. Someone had also removed his sword-belt; he felt curiously naked without it. He had been quite successfully distracted; now, the struggle done, Kieran took a moment to wonder dispassionately what had become of the second scorpion.

Now that her prey was safely confined, ai'Daileh, who had taken no part in his capture, approached him, a sardonic smile on her face.

"You gave your word to ai'Jihaar," Kieran muttered in his own tongue, not expecting her to understand, but it was not in him to go in acquiescent silence into the darkness.

"I swore not to harm her," said ai'Daileh softly and quickly, in Roisinani. She nodded her head in Anghara's direction, without allowing her eyes to leave Kieran's face. "I also swore to do my utmost to help restore a lost sister to the Way from which she had strayed—or been pushed. So far, the Gods have not responded to our offerings. We need more."

For a moment Kieran was too stunned to reply, and then recovered with a sense of bleak inevitability. "I am not," he said, "o serpent of the desert, a wandering interloper who is fitting fodder for your Gods. I came with a queen who is also of your *an'sen'en'thari,* to seek help in your land. I am friend and servant to the very one in whose name you would kill me. And while I would willingly give my life for her, I will not let you spend it like this. Anghara would not will it and ai'Jihaar would not have permitted what you intend."

"She is an empty vessel waiting for the Gods to fill her," said ai'Daileh, her voice dark and mystic.

"And I am what is left of her power!" Kieran said.

"You do not know of what you speak," she said loftily, from the full height of the pride and the arrogance of her lineage and calling.

"Are you so sure that you do?" Kieran asked bitterly.

If only his head wasn't aching . . . half the thoughts that filled his mind were hardly his own, full as he was of Anghara's pain and confusion, and he had to concentrate. There was no knowing what had hit ai'Jihaar, a simple surfeit of lais which had finally caught up with her or some backlash of the power which surrounded them, or how long she would remain out of this game—ai'Daileh's senior, Kieran's ally. In the meantime, he was on his own—and if ai'Daileh succeeded in destroying him, anything might still happen. Even with al'Tamar in the shadows, waiting to see if he needed to show, at the bitter end, his own hand, and perhaps throw into dust and ashes the carefully cultivated illusions with which he had so far been protected from ai'Daileh's ilk.

Despite her command of his language, ai'Daileh had neither the patience nor the inclination to converse with an eastern barbarian she would rather see under her knife. She turned her back, imperious as any queen, not even deigning to answer.

"Bring him," she said briefly.

And then there was no hope. Kieran lifted his eyes to Anghara's face, still flushed with fever; she was standing alone, swaying gently to the rhythm of the *Rab'bat Rah'honim,* the black drums which had kept up their inexorable beat. He remembered her laughter; the bright spark of life and the deep pools of gentleness within her gray eyes, legacy of Rima, the girl from Cascin who had married the King Under the Mountain. And later, the gray-blue madness Sif had put into those same eyes, the madness which was there now—laughing, yes, but laughing as Anghara Kir Hama had never laughed. With gloating, not joy; with fury, not passion. Destructively.

"Anghara," he said, his voice low.

It was as though she couldn't hear him, as though he didn't exist.

Her sharp white teeth bared in a feral smile, ai'Daileh turned. "Do you begin to see at last?" she said. "You are nothing, until you are the sacrifice."

"I am what was in her," he said, suddenly utterly certain of the truth of ai'Jihaar's interpretation—which she had not conveyed, had not had the time to convey, to ai'Daileh.

Because now, in this moment of truth, he remembered the instant in which it had happened.

On the walls of Miranei at dawn, when Kieran had faced Sif's Chancellor, Fodrun, once Dynan's Second General whom now many knew by the whispered title of Kingmaker. Fodrun, Anghara's jailor in Sif's name, had taken her and held her as a hostage and a shield against the naked sword of his enemy. Kieran now recalled the scene with a preternatural clarity. Pain had washed across Anghara's face as she had tried to reach for Sight, pain which had stabbed his own soul. He had raised his sword and brought it down upon Fodrun, cleaving through the older man's defenses as though they had been made by a greenstick boy, not a master of the blade. A blow of pure power, owing nothing to training or prowess gained through practice—and the power had not been his. It had poured into him from without, from that place which Anghara had tried to touch in her blindness and could not, and which he, because of his love for her, could. Did.

He remembered coming to himself afterward, almost dazed, gazing at Fodrun's corpse as though unsure who had killed the man at his feet. He remembered this was the hour in which Anghara had finally admitted she was blind, neither realizing that she had found another set of eyes through which she could See.

He looked upon her again, this girl whom he loved, who now looked so little like the captive who had walked the battlements of Miranei.

It was Midsummer's Eve back in Roisinan, the festivities of Cerdiad probably well into their swing. On another night like this, years ago, a little girl had broken the spell which had guarded her own existence because a bright blade had been raised over one whom she loved. That little girl filled Kieran's eyes, his heart.

"Anghara," he said again, meeting with little response. And then, desperately, forced to bend over the altarstone under the pressure of many hands and seeing the shadow of the black dagger rise above him, unable to fend this knife off as he had once tried to do with another lifted against him by Ansen of Cascin, he put his heart and soul into a final cry. A name, long forgotten. "Brynna. *Brynna!*"

The effect, although totally unexpected, was all Kieran could have hoped for. A sibilant sigh swept through his captors; hands dropped off him, *sen'en'thari* backed away. The drums faltered in their beating, stopped. And in the silence, three things. A whisper, whirling from mouth to mouth like an invocation—*ai'Bre'hinnah, ai'Bre'hinnah.* The God-thick atmosphere in the hai'r breaking with a sound like a bell, the air within cold and sharp with something like pain, sorrow, or regret at inevitable partings. Anghara, her head coming round with an audible snap, staring at him for a long moment—a long, completely lucid moment—before lifting her hands to her suddenly bloodless cheeks and uttering "I remember!" before her knees buckled underneath her. For a brief instant Kieran thought he could see someone—something—else like an after-image in the bright air above her: a creature of golden light spreading enormous white wings, and her face was Anghara's.

An unseen hand—it might well have been al'Tamar's, because the rest seemed paralyzed by the name of a girl who had never really existed, except as a mask for an imperilled young queen—sliced through Kieran's bonds. He took a moment to glance at the round-mouthed faces surrounding him. He didn't understand what had just happened, but knew he had been handed a chance which would not be repeated. He might have been costing Anghara her immortal soul, but she was in far more peril with ai'Daileh and her treacherous oaths. Without hesitating for longer than it took for a moment of regret, and another of violent self-blame (without his ministrations ai'Jihaar might have been better able to withstand the rigors of this night), Kieran scooped Anghara into his arms and raced toward the ki'thar pen.

The gate was open—ai'Tamar, again—but none of the ki'thar'en were saddled. Perhaps they could be ridden thus by someone who knew how. Kieran had neither the skill nor the time to look for ki'thar tackle, but ai'Daileh's dun was another matter.

"I'm sorry," Kieran murmured as he reached to rub the

soft nose before rigging a makeshift rein from the animal's halter and somehow clambering, with Anghara still in his arms, upon the dun's bare back. He wasn't sure to whom he was apologizing—to Anghara, for taking her from what was perhaps her only chance of salvation; to the dun, for the inevitability of a slow death in the open desert; perhaps, even to ai'Daileh herself, whose treasure he was stealing. The dun snorted, wary of the sudden double weight on its back and the strange riders it was being asked to bear. But Kieran had always had a way with horses and these exotic Kheldrini dun'en were no different from the animals he had ridden in Roisinan in one respect—ai'Daileh's dun trusted the gentle hands which guided it, and obeyed. The animal and its two riders passed silently through the gate of the ki'thar pen and vanished into the desert night, the dun's blond mane gleaming in the bright starlight.

Kieran was bitterly aware he might very well have killed them both. Unless Anghara, who knew more about this desert than he, came to herself properly—and soon—they were in desperate trouble. It was unlikely that passing nomads would be as proficient in Roisinani as the *sen'en'thari*, even if they could be persuaded to listen to *fram'man* without bolting; and if they were unable to ask for help, they were truly on their own. Kieran didn't know where to look for water. He would only have been digging them deeper if by some chance he did stumble upon it, for he was blissfully unaware of the guiding principle that here in the desert water always belonged to someone and permission to use it had to be asked and paid for. Even if he had thought to try and make it back to the mountains, there was no al'Khur to ride at their back. They had no supplies, nothing except a dun whose strength would give out before they were halfway and a girl still weak in the eddies of power woven around her. Even Kieran's sword belt was still in the camp—their only weapon was the small dagger he carried concealed in his boot, and without burnouses they would be easy prey for the desert sun.

"I'll have to go back," Kieran murmured, even as ai'Jihaar's hai'r sank out of sight behind its sheltering red rock.

But first, they needed a place to hole up in. And quickly, before dawn, before the sun came out to weigh them down with inexorable desert heat. But the Gods, it seemed, had not entirely left them—or else blind luck rode at their heels. In the hour when the sky began to lighten, Kieran saw a narrow black slit yawn in a pillar of red stone. Hardly able to believe the possibility of a reprieve when he had already begun to despair, Kieran urged the dun closer and found the slit led to a cool, shallow hollow in the rock. It was just broad enough at the base for the dun to squeeze past; the animal wasn't happy but entered nonetheless, although not without a couple of protesting snorts.

"You learn that from the ki'thar'en?" Kieran asked the dun lightly, rubbing its nose with an affectionate hand once it had entered the cavern. The dun lipped at him hopefully, and Kieran smiled sadly. "Sorry, friend. Nothing. I'd share if we had anything at all. We'll go back later, you and I, and then, maybe, if we're lucky, we can both get what we need."

The one thing Kieran had managed to appropriate in his haste to escape was a horse-blanket which had been flung across the fence of the ki'thar pen. Now he laid this down on the cool sand for Anghara. Watching her shiver uncontrollably in the grip of whatever had claimed her in those last few minutes of the aborted ritual, Kieran tasted defeat, the bitter pill of utter helplessness. The choices, ai'Jihaar had said, all lay with Anghara, or with the Gods to whom the appeal had been made; but it had been ai'Daileh who had made the choices in the end, not Anghara. And in the aftermath, for one who had once sensed those same Gods riding the winds at his back, the Kheidrini desert was ominously empty. Kieran felt as though all the Kheidrini Gods had simply been wiped out last night, as though they had never been; there had been an instant during the ceremony when he was sure he had sensed a cool and immortal farewell, and he wondered at it. But that was a question for the scholars and desert philosophers to ponder in years to come; what was important now was Anghara, and survival.

Her hands were icy when he took them into his own to chafe some life into them, her nails blue with cold, all the more frightening when Kieran could feel the solid, almost palpable heat beginning to beat through the crack and into the cavern. Anghara kept muttering things under her breath but she used Kheidrini and her own language arbitrarily—Kieran was unable to make sense of it. He heard, "No blood, not up here, not ever; but he hadn't been to Gul Khaima and didn't know of Anghara's edict. Later, she would murmur, "I remember . . . I remember it all . . ." and then she would go into what sounded like a long, broken dialogue in Kheidrini from which Kieran was able to glean only ai'Jihaar's name.

One thing was constant. "Cold," she moaned, returning to this again and again in between long dark silences and all the other things she had been saying, "so cold . . ." But the brightly woven horse blanket was all they had. When not even wrapping Anghara into a cocoon seemed to help Kieran stretched out beside her and took her in his arms, sharing the warmth of his own body.

And because he was Kieran, and she was Anghara, and this was the first time he had held her in his arms since that day in the mountains on which he had learned from his deepest soul that he loved her, he embraced her gently. He stroked the bright hair away from her flushed face and murmured soft words of love and encouragement. "It's all right," he whispered, willing himself to believe it, trying not to think of possible pursuit searching for them even now, of the dun tracks in the sand which could lead pursuers straight to this sanctuary. "It will be all right." And it seemed to work, because she quietened down and settled first into a doze and then into a deeper sleep. And Kieran, on whose heart her small hand rested, lay very still and wondered that she didn't wake at the hammering of it beneath her fingers.

He couldn't rest for watching her sleep in his arms; his head still ached impossibly, and a day without water didn't help matters any. He had ample time to think, though, and the one conundrum he was unable to solve was how to halve himself when night fell. He knew he had to ride back to the hai'r but that would force him to leave Anghara alone. Taking her back with him was unthinkable, and not going himself for at least some necessities of survival, if not to seek out ai'Jihaar or al'Tamar and ask for help, would be suicide.

His arm soon went numb, where Anghara's weight rested on it, but he wouldn't move, and perhaps wake her, for the world; eventually he drifted off into a shallow doze. When he "woke," it was hours later, the light filtering in through the crack much more golden, shading already into the ruddiness of a desert sunset. He was hungry, and his mouth was furry from lack of moisture. The dun seemed to have the same problem; it was the animal which had woken him, crossing over to push at him with a long aristocratic snout, managing to look at the same time both imperiously demanding and somehow pathetic. Glancing down at Anghara Kieran saw she was awake, and watching him in much the same way.

"Are you all right?" he asked, instinctively drawing her closer, reaching out to touch a cheek of waxy pallor.

"I will be," she said, "I think." The weakness of her voice smote him to the heart; she gave him a smile. "I couldn't bring myself to wake you, but I've been lying here watching you for some time. My poor Kieran, what I've put you through . . ."

"I won't say it's been easy," he said, his mouth quirking at the corners; now, in retrospect, some of their troubles had been leavened with lighter moments which made the memories bearable. "And it just got harder. I have to go back, Anghara—for something. For *anything*! When I ran from that place I ran with you alone; they had stripped me of my blade, and even that is still in the hai'r. We need waterskins; we desperately need water. I don't know if they've been looking for us, but if they have it's only a matter of time before they find us . . ."

"And you escaped sacrifice, a dedicated offering—ai'Daileh will not let it go at that."

"I have to go back," he repeated. "You . . . I hate leaving you . . ."

"Go, do what you must. I shall be here."

They had to wait until the very threshold of the twilight before Kieran would ride out; the night would, in any case, be lighter, tonight there would be a sliver of moon gleaming amongst the stars, and Anghara, at least, knew how the clear desert air could amplify moonlight. It would make Kieran's task both easier and much harder—easier to find the hai'r in the wide country empty of familiar landmarks, but also easier for him to be observed by anyone who might be looking. Anghara worried about it; if she had possessed her full faculties she would have been able to blur Kieran so that he would be harder to see. But she could not, and Kieran, whose constant and nagging headache was a legacy of the power she had poured into him, didn't know how to tap into it.

Anghara felt strong enough to walk with him when he roused himself to leave. She looked so much like a wraith in the wash of moonlight, still pale with a residue of day which lingered in the air, that Kieran was almost moved not to go, he was far from certain he could count on finding her waiting when he returned. Almost. But he knew he had no choice, none at all—unless it were to stay here and die with her.

"I'll leave you the dagger . . ."

"Take it," she said, closing his fingers around the weapon he held out to her. "If anyone finds me—I wouldn't have the strength to wield it. And it would make me feel better to know you had it. You might need it more. And I . . . I am in the hand of the Gods."

"I'm not sure . . ." Kieran began, frowning, after a beat of silence.

She understood his unfinished sentence instantly. Her fingers, surprisingly strong for their transparent appearance, closed on his hand. "What?" she demanded. "I felt something, also . . . I thought I heard . . . you called me Brynna last night . . ."

"Yes . . . and the *sen'en'thari* seemed to know more about the name than I realized. That was what gave me a chance to run. But you—you looked at me as I said it, you said you remembered . . . what did you remember, Anghara?"

"Everything," she said, and tears welled into her eyes. "The name . . . al'Khur gave it to me, a long time ago."

"How could he? It was your name in Cascin, long before you knew what Gods walked these sands . . ."

"But he did. My mother chose my identity for Cascin; I don't know what made her choose that name, but I think hers was the Sight of prophecy and power. All I know is, al'Khur knew the meaning of that name when our paths crossed in the Khar'i'id. He then put a geas on me that I should forget it until the time came for me to claim it. And last night . . . last night I remembered everything that passed between us when I faced al'Khur for ai'Jihaar's life. Do you know what he called me then, Kieran? *Little Sister.* The Lord of Death called me his little sister."

"He called you Brynna?" Kieran said, still bewildered by this new piece of the puzzle.

"Not quite," said Anghara. "It was a far older name."

"What name?"

"Changer," said Anghara. "That is what *bre'hin* means.

Change. And at the end of every Age a Changer of Days comes to Kheldrin, and the land is broken, and made anew. And the old Gods are broken also, and put aside, and the Changer is the harbinger of those who are to rule thereafter." She smiled, and the smile this time was distant, remote, oddly alien. "Do you remember how I told you, back on the moors, that I was not quite human any more?"

"I remember," Kieran said. "And I remember telling you that you were. You *are.* Whatever else you might be."

"I don't deserve you," she said after a pause, her voice changed again—lighter, full of a gentle teasing, yet brimful of gratitude and appreciation.

Kieran, halfway through reaching his hand to touch her cheek and offer a response to that last remark, froze suddenly and the caress turned into a warning brush of his fingers on her shoulder.

"What is it?" she asked, picking up his unease.

"I thought I heard . . . it's almost like a song."

She relaxed. A little. *"El'lah afrit,"* she said. "The sand sings. It sometimes happens in the evenings; perhaps the weather is due to change."

He was almost ready to accept this, but then stiffened again, peering out across the sand. "No. Wait. Listen."

A tense moment passed; and in the silence which followed they both heard clearly the sound which had warned Kieran—a soft disgruntled grumble which could only have come from a ki'thar. It was close. Too close. Kieran's right hand flew to where his sword customarily hung, and found empty air; it clenched into a fist, and then dropped helplessly to his side.

"Kerun!" he whispered, invoking the God who presided over disasters in Roisinan. "Too late . . ."

The dagger was in his hand, at the ready, but it was pitifully inadequate as a weapon and Kieran knew it. And if they managed to entangle him in their accursed spider web again . . .

But the voice which came floating out just before its owner emerged from behind the red mesa which held Kieran's little cavern was familiar; and so were its words. "Peace," it said. "I am unarmed."

Kieran's arm dropped; he observed distantly that his hand was shaking. "Are you a *jinn* of the desert, al'Tamar ma'Hariff, that you come bringing salvation every time I believe there is nothing beyond the next moment but death?"

"I go where the Gods send me," al'Tamar said, smiling.

"And where I lead him," said another familiar but thoroughly unexpected voice.

"You shouldn't be riding," Anghara said gently, coming forward to help ai'Jihaar off the ki'thar whom the old *an'sen'thar* had just made to kneel.

"I am the best judge of that," ai'Jihaar said haughtily. "While ai'Daileh has gone, she has left one of the gray sisters in the hai'r. I knew one or both of you would have to return sooner or later but I needed to see you at once, and it was hardly practicable to bring you and Kieran back to the hai'r while ai'Daileh's minion remains."

"We brought water," said al'Tamar more practically, approaching with a waterskin. Kieran was the closer, but he indicated Anghara with an almost imperceptible nod of his head and al'Tamar passed the waterskin to her first.

"We need to talk," said ai'Jihaar as Anghara tilted the waterskin and took a deep draft.

Kieran's head came round as though ai'Jihaar had slapped a lead rein on him. She had, in a way. Even as he fled from the stone altar, the guilt of having caused the failure of Anghara's healing had quietly begun gnawing at him. But ai'Jihaar knew this, of course. She knew everything. Even now, as Kieran turned to look at her, she reached for a muffled package hanging from the saddle of her ki'thar. "I believe you left this behind, Kieran," she said, passing the long, slim shape to him with a sure hand.

He accepted the parcel and unwrapped it to discover he

was holding his own sword. It was set, however, into a new belt, one made from soft but strong ki'thar skin. A gift from the desert; a subtle way of telling him no blame attached to him, at least not from this quarter. And ai'Jihaar was still a powerful friend in this hostile land.

His hand closed over the gift. "I cheated your Gods," he said evenly.

"Have you?" ai'Jihaar asked. "There was a time you used to be able to sense their presence. Can you now?"

"Not for some time," Kieran said, his voice low. "But I am no measure of . . ."

"I sensed them," al'Tamar said. "I sensed them for the last time when you called Anghara . . . by that other name. After that . . . the desert has been empty; except for a faint and distant echo of al'Zaan who is Lord of the Desert and remains so for as long as it endures, whatever comes to pass. But the rest . . . they are gone."

"He is right," said Anghara, who had drunk her fill and now handed the waterskin to Kieran. He accepted it mechanically with one hand, the other still occupied by the ki'thar belt and his sword. "They are gone. There are too many things I haven't been able to see or feel of late—but I felt that. I felt the instant of their going."

"Yes, ai'Bre'hinnah," said ai'Jihaar. "Now you are the only God of the Twilight Country . . . until you raise others for us."

"The Changer is not a God," Anghara said quickly, turning her head to stare out into the desert. "You always told me the Changer is more like ai'Shahn, a spirit, a messenger . . ."

"Yes. But God, also, because in the void of the Changer's coming, until new Gods are born, there are no other. It is of you and al'Zaan that the new Kheldrini Gods will be made; it has always been so when a Changer comes. But because you are who you are . . . I think you are also Changer for your own land, Anghara of Roisinan. You may well find that the Gods you raise here will supplant your Kerun and Avanna. There will be many things transfigured when you return to your land."

Kieran suddenly remembered a disembodied voice he thought he had dreamed in the palm-fringed hai'r only a few nights ago—the distant cold voice of the stars, al'Khur's reply to ai'Jihaar's prayer. *She has forgotten, as I bid her; in one day she will remember it all,* the disembodied voice had answered. *And when she does . . . her life is no longer in my hands.*

It had been the truth. It had not been Anghara's existence which had been at stake here, after all; it had been al'Khur's own.

"But if they are gone," Ahghara said slowly, turning back, with tears sparkling in her eyes, "does that mean I have forfeited every chance of gaining back that which I lost?"

"No," said ai'Jihaar gently. "Just the opposite. It would have taken strength I did not have to reach out to the Gods and demand your healing from them. Now, now that I know what you are . . . *hai,* but you never mentioned that name to me, in our years together! But I should have known it was no accident, that meeting in the Dance . . . Now that I know what you truly are, there is no need to go further than yourself for help. You are all that is left."

It was Kieran who reacted first. "Wait," he said quickly. "She cannot. There is little left in her but heart. What do you mean to do?"

"You are right," said ai'Jihaar. "It is to ai'Bre'hinnah to whom the appeal will be made. It is you who will be called upon to pay the price—to give back all you have been carrying for her for so long."

So. It was to be no different from before—sacrifice, and to alien Gods. But this time Kieran saw his path clear, and there were no shadows upon it. He bowed his head in the moonlight before the old desert priestess, submitting. "I'm ready," he said.

He had been standing very close to the *an'sen'thar;* quite unexpectedly, ai'Jihaar reached out and traced his jaw with a delicate, blue-veined hand. "Yes," she murmured, her voice thoughtful. "I think you are. Come, let us go inside."

No one questioned how she knew of the cave behind them as she led the way in, leaving al'Tamar to hobble the ki'thar'en and follow her and the two young Roisinani inside. Her nephew seemed to have been briefed in advance, because he entered the small cave in silence and immediately began a series of preparations. The only time he spoke was when Kieran would have risen to help him as he began to kindle a small fire in the center of the cave; al'Tamar's voice had been no more than a whisper, but it was enough to send the other back to his place. "It is not your turn yet. Wait."

When his fire was ready, they sat down in a circle, leaving a space for al'Tamar to claim when he was done, as if this had been rehearsed many times. A sweet incense stick was lit, and Kieran's eyes stung with unexpected tears as he was reminded of the pungent perfume of desert sage, a scent with special meaning for him. It had never failed to prod memories into wakefulness, sharp as a dagger, bright as a flame. He would have asked, but already there was a tension in the air, a sense of ritual, something too vast and brooding to be disturbed with insignificant questions.

Her voice quite changed from her usual cadences ai'Jihaar said, "ai'Bre'hinnah, Changer of Days who walks Kheldrin again, woken by Khar'i'id, blessed by al'Khur, we come to you to ask your aid. Grant us the gift of your power."

And Kieran, in whose hand Anghara's own cold, small hand rested, felt its skin grow warm. The flickering shadows in the cave parted, as if a curtain had been drawn from the face of a sun; and in the midst of this flamed the creature Kieran thought he had seen when he first uttered the fateful name in ai'Jihaar's hai'r. Bright and golden, cool fire flowing over great white wings, shining from painfully familiar soft gray eyes which were looking directly at him, with compassion, with understanding. Bereft of words, sharply aware that somehow, in an earthly plane, he was holding this winged goddess's hand in his own, Kieran could only gaze mutely at the apparition.

It, too, was silent for the space of a few heartbeats—and then it spoke. Its voice was high and distant, Anghara's, and yet not. A voice which only al'Khur had heard until this moment—heard, and recognized, and bowed to its right to demand back a life already taken.

"I must first accept it back from the place where it has been given for safekeeping," the goddess said. "Will its keeper return it?"

Kieran found his voice, "Willingly."

"That promise may mean more than you can know in the hour in which you give it. I ask you again, will you give up the power?"

"It was never mine, to claim or not," said Kieran. "If I carried something, for a while, which another found too great a burden, I am content. Ask what you will of me, for it has always been yours."

"So be it," said the goddess, echoing his own words of long ago.

Kieran had been linked to al'Tamar on his other side, as Anghara had been to ai'Jihaar in her turn, and the two Kheldrini to one another, completing the circle. Now he found the circle broken without being able to remember how it had happened. Both his hands were held fast in small fingers, as a pair of great white wings whispered down through the air and folded around him, cutting out the play of shadows on the cavern walls, the leaping flames, the sight of al'-Tamar to his left. What came was darkness, darkness studded with a million points of bright golden light, like an expanse of desert sky. It was a painful beauty, and it fell upon him like a cloak, settled on his shoulders, into him, through him. Something that had been within him surged to meet it, feeding the golden lights, pouring light like lava into the darkness and obliterating it until everything blazed white and gold, lancing Kieran's eyes with physical pain even through closed eyelids. And the light was like a knife. Yes, there was sacrifice, because it came cutting down upon him, piercing him, cleaving him apart and prising him open, carving channels down which the golden glory that was power ran like water and collected in great deep pools in the heart of him. And in the shelter of the vast white wings Anghara drank back what had been taken from her, and Kieran could feel the light leaving him as though it had been lifeblood, draining away, fading. It was an exquisite pain—a white agony delicately balanced with the joy of watching Anghara's eyes grow brighter until there was nothing in the world except the light of her power—a white and golden face framed with a cloud of burnished hair, and a gentle touch of immense white wings.

At one point he felt a sharp pain in his hand where once he had laid it open with a slim black dagger, asking the now vanished Gods not to claim their sacrifice from one who was not strong enough to give it. He felt something warm and liquid run down his fingers. Without looking down he knew the old Kheldrini Gods were claiming one last sacrifice—and this, after all, was blood which had already been freely offered. But Anghara had tightened her hands around his, and the light blazed more golden than ever. *No. No blood. Not ever again. Not for death.*

It was hers to demand, now. Hers to state what sacrifices would be accepted. Hers, finally, to honor the conviction on the basis of which she had once, years ago, refused to become *an'sen'thar.* The same basis on which she had given Kheldrin its second oracle, forbidding the ancient Gods to approach without also surrendering the very rites and rituals which made them what they were. And here in the desert cavern ai'Bre'hinnah chose to heal as Anghara Kir Hama had once healed in a hai'r on the edge of Beit el'Sihaya—cleanly, instinctively, thinking the hurt whole and making it so through force of will. Of power. The pain disappeared; even the trickle of blood on Kieran's fingers was gone in the time it took for him to draw a breath. And then, without warning, he was adrift, released; the white wings were lifted, the golden light drained from him. For a moment he was blind, seeing nothing but darkness, much as he might have done had he walked into a dark room after staring directly into the sun; he was aware of a supporting hand, and that it was far too delicate and fine-boned to belong to Anghara.

"I'm all right," he whispered, and his voice sounded strange even to his own ears. With a gentle pressure of his hand, al'Tamar signalled he had heard and understood, but showed no signs of moving away. Kieran's assurances were obviously not enough to disprove the physical evidence.

As his sight came blurring back Kieran could see that the Goddess they called ai'Bre'hinnah was still with them—but now she was a discrete entity in her own right, far more solid than a beautiful vision, her hands held out over her earthly twin. Anghara, looking small and curiously crippled beside this vast winged incarnation of herself, raised her own hands to meet the palms of the Goddess. They touched; Anghara cried out, whether in pain or in joy it was hard to tell. The air outside trembled with pearly light, rang with an echo of distant bells, a memory of a land far from these red sands. And then it was over—the fire guttering, the incense stick burned down to a smoldering nub, a thin wash of moonlight pencilled on the floor of the cavern, sharp and slender like a silver *tei'han.* She whom they called the Changer was gone; there was only Anghara, kneeling beside the remnants of the fire. Just for a moment Kieran glimpsed the nimbus of gold, which wreathed her head—a final, parting gift from the goddess—then he was back into his own body, his own senses, and the auras that were the soul fire of the Sighted were once again hidden from his dull human sight.

He had been strong for so long, when Anghara could not be; now, it seemed, the situation was reversed. It took a major effort of will for Kieran to straighten up and sit back, with every bone, nerve and sinew in his body screaming protest. Anghara, on the other hand, was transformed. She sat with her head high, her shoulders back; this was the first time Kieran had seen the queen for whom he had dared so much in the full glory of her power. In this moment, she was Kir Hama, and royal. And then, as she turned, she reached out to him, and the wave of sudden weakness in his bones had little to with the ordeal he had just been through and everything to do with the blaze of love and concern in her eyes. She looked at him for a moment, mutely—just looked at him, for some things are best said with silence. And then he smiled, and held out his hand, and she took it, and laid it against her cheek.

It could have been a moment for many truths to be revealed, for they had been alone within it, oblivious of their companions; but ai'Jihaar, with unaccustomed bad timing, shattered it with an artlessness which, in her, seemed coldly deliberate. Because Anghara was too full of the joy of her newly regained senses, and Kieran too drained from the damage to his own, they let it go—and the moment faded, was lost. Then al'Tamar was at Kieran's elbow with a cup of steaming *khaf* which had been inexplicably brewed in the midst of all the drama, and ai'Jihaar claimed Anghara's attention.

"You look as if you wrestled with an army of *afrit'in,*" al'Tamar said with a sympathetic grin. "There was an instant when you were gone, completely lost to us; I was not at all sure you would survive the touch of this one of all the Gods. But then—you are no stranger to this, I forget that you carried al'Khur himself through the mountains."

"You told me then that he carried me," said Kieran laconically, keeping his eyes on the steaming mug of *khaf* between his hands.

"Perhaps," said al'Tamar, laughing, "a little of both. If you are sure you are all right . . ."

There were other chores to be done. Courtesy, and more than a little affection, had kept al'Tamar in attendance on Kieran. But the call of other, waiting duties was obvious in the way that al'Tamar crouched lightly on the balls of his feet beside his charge, ready to whirl away as soon as he had satisfied himself as to Kieran's well-being.

Kieran released him. "Go," he said. "I'll live."

And then, even as al'Tamar straightened with a smile still dancing in his eyes, Kieran remembered something. "Wait," he said, stretching out an arm. "What gifts were mine to give in this hour, I gave. But I still carry something you left in my keeping. Perhaps this is the hour in which you, too, can give back something you guarded for her. It is for you, al'Tamar, to do this."

Setting down the *khaf* he fumbled for the *say'yin* with the Royal Seal, drawing it over his head, gathering it between his fingers, holding it out. As al'Tamar bent down to take it, his expression was thoughtful. "I did not even think of this, back at the hai'r," he said. "But it would have gone hard with you if ai'Daileh had found this on you. *Say'yin'en* are a secret of the Way . . . you, *fram'man,* should never even have seen one, let alone worn it. How is it that she missed it? She had you ready for the sacrifice . . ."

Kieran shivered despite himself, recalling many small hands tying the knots on the cords around his wrists, struggling to undo the unfamiliar ones on the laces which held his shirt at his throat. It was that which had saved him—their ignorance, ai'Daileh's impatience, the name of ai'Bre'hinnah thrown into the night like an invocation. It would have taken another second—less—for them to find the *say'yin.* If there was a hand of the Gods anywhere in this whole situation, Kieran saw it in that moment—when they had almost frozen time, allowing him to claim back his life, allowing many secrets better left unsaid to remain so. *"Sen'en dayr,"* Kieran said, quoting a phrase he had picked up from al'Tamar himself.

He'd got the meaning right, but the words were out of context, and al'Tamar smiled again—first with indulgence, then gratitude.

"I thank you," he said quietly. "You cannot know how much being able to do this means to me."

"Oh, but I do," murmured Kieran as al'Tamar turned away, *say'yin* in hand. "More than you know."

As al'Tamar knelt beside Anghara, speaking softly in his own language, Kieran, swallowing the last sip of *khaf* left in his cup, struggled to his feet without being noticed and slipped outside into the moonlight. If anyone had asked why he had chosen to leave the cave in, what was essentially a moment of triumph, he would have found it hard to explain—his reasons were completely irrational. There was a part of him which knew the scene about to be played—knew it with a bitter clarity. He could see it all—the offering, Anghara's tears gleaming in the firelight. There was an entire world they shared, Anghara and her desert paladin, a world which utterly excluded Kieran—and he felt reluctant to witness this exchange, steeped as it was in things completely beyond his comprehension. There were many feelings mixed up in this, but its roots lay in the deepest and the most irrational of them all—jealousy. He'd had the greatness of spirit to offer them the gift which had been in his power to give. That didn't mean he had the strength to watch its consummation, even knowing, as he did, that there could never be anything between al'Tamar and Anghara except shared memories. But those, by all the vanished Gods, were potent enough.

The horse blanket had somehow migrated to Kieran's shoulders, and he was glad of it now as the desert night nipped at him. There was a faint wail in the air, a distant banshee—what was it that Anghara had called this? A song of the spirits . . . *el'lah afrit?* He'd forgotten those half-heard words of explanation, comprehensively submerged in the shock of ai'Jihaar and al'Tamar's subsequent arrival. How the spirits returned, vividly, a lost memory seeking a home. Anghara had said something . . . something about the weather changing. Recalling this, Kieran instinctively glanced up at the sky; but here in the desert clouds were rarely harbingers of change. The recollection of the instant in which he'd first heard of the phenomenon was so potent, that for a long moment Kieran failed to register that the sounds of an approaching ki'thar were real, not conjured from his memory. And finding himself face to face with a veiled golden-eyed rider who stared at him impassively from her high perch atop the ki'thar saddle took his breath away.

A soft command broke the silence. The ki'thar knelt, and its rider slipped off. Beneath a travelling djellaba gleamed gold; a long black-hafted dagger was in the newcomer's hand; but it was not ai'Daileh who stood before him. Another *an'sen'thar,* then.

Kieran regained enough presence of mind to move first. He remembered the desert greeting, brought his hand up to heart, lips, brow, bowed deeply. The dagger dropped a little.

"Knowing of our ways," said the woman, who had still not removed her veil, "makes you no less a *fram'man.* Are you, then, the one they are seeking?"

Kieran straightened, lifting his chin. "I am."

His sword was still in the cave; but even if he had had it

he doubted if he could have raised it. His fingers felt like jelly. But his avowal, instead of bringing the *an'sen'thar's* dagger up and sliding between his ribs, made her drop her hand to her side, "Anghara's, then."

Kieran blinked, surprised, and then assented to this as well, a curt nod.

"These, I presume, belong to ai'Jihaar and her escort," said the woman, reaching up to unfasten the burnouse. "Where are they?"

Kieran's eyes flicked to the cave behind him, back; the *an'sen'thar* smiled, a little sardonically.

"Do not worry. I mean them no harm—ai'Daileh is a bigger fool than I would have believed," she said acerbically. "By rights I should have been the one summoned from the tower to deal with this; we would not have this mess on our hands. But the Gods willed it differently . . ."

Kieran knew he ought to have done something to stop this unexpected visitor barging in unannounced, but he was at a loss to know exactly what that could have been. She gave him little chance, she simply gathered her djellaba up like a cloak and swept into the small cave with a regal air Anghara herself would have not been ashamed to claim. All Kieran could do was follow, swearing that this would be the last time he would allow himself to be taken by surprise. Keeping company with Anghara might explain events constantly catching him unawares, but certainly didn't justify anything. He should have anticipated surprise, been on his guard.

He almost ran her down, the subject of his vehement vows; the *an'sen'thar* had stopped abruptly at the cave's entrance and was staring at the three beside the fire. Kieran could see nothing amiss, but al'Tamar looked stricken, and ai'Jihaar resigned. Anghara alone was smiling, the great amber and silver *say'yin* that had been al'Tamar's gift still lying across her upturned palms.

"How long?" the strange *an'sen'thar* said, her voice oddly

brittle. She was still speaking, as she had done with Kieran outside, in Roisinani. "No, do not tell me. Too long, whatever the answer. He is old enough to have walked in the Way for years. Why? Why did you veil it from me?"

"There are always too many claimants for any place which looks as if it might become vacant," said ai'Jihaar cryptically. "This at least you ought to understand, ai'-Farra—you took steps of your own to make sure the next Keeper in the tower at Al'haria is also Sayyed."

"The mine," ai'Farra said, nodding. "Of course."

Rising to his feet, al'Tamar faced ai'Farra across the fire with no small measure of defiance. She studied him intently, cupping her chin in her hand.

"So," she said, and her voice was deceptively mild. "We have a new *sen'thar.* What shall we do with you now, al'Tamar ma'Hariff?"

"Nothing has changed," said al'Tamar. "Not until I beget an heir to take my place."

"I seem to recall something about a betrothal, yes," ai'-Farra said. "I would have thought that was where you should have been, instead of spending your nights wandering the desert."

"The tower cannot have him," said ai'Jihaar.

"Not the tower," said Anghara unexpectedly. "But he has been too important a part of too many things. There was a time, in the grotto below Gul Khaima, that I promised him *an'sen'thar* gold. I fulfill that tonight." She turned, slipping the *say'yin* she still held over her head, and reached to hold al'Tamar's hands between her own. "I grant you the gold, *an'sen'thar* al'Tamar ma'Hariff—for this night's work, and for all the nights that came before it."

"He is untrained," snapped ai'Farra. "It lies not in your power to do this."

"It does," said Anghara. "You yourself raised me to the gold—and from the moment you did so you gave me the power to grant it to another when I deem it fit. As for being untrained . . . I, too, knew nothing when I accepted gold from ai'Jihaar's hands. It was two years before I came to Al'haria to claim it by right—al'Tamar can be given the same chance."

"And who will train him as you were trained?" ai'Farra demanded. "Out of a tower? And how may an *an'sen'thar* hold secular title? How may he make sacrifice to the Gods when he cannot . . ."

"If you knew about me, then you know everything," Kieran said quietly, standing just behind her. "You must also know that the sacrifice you speak of will never be made again to the Gods you knew."

She turned her head, a small, fierce motion; whatever he had expected it was not this, the glint of tears. The first thing that stirred in him was pity, but it didn't last, killed by the harsh voice so at odds with her face. "All evil comes from across those mountains," she said. "I knew that. I knew when she came that everything I believed in was in danger, I didn't know she would live to be called ai'Bre'hinnah, not here, not in my lifetime. If I had known . . . perhaps it would have been the lesser sin to have destroyed her then."

"You could not have done it, ai'Farra," said ai'Jihaar from within the pool of silence which flowed out of these words and spread around them. "You could not spare those who were doomed. Their hour had come."

"Then is it now mine?"

"I said, no more blood," said Anghara, her voice at once ringing with command and steeped in deepest compassion. After a last lingering look at Kieran's face, ai'Farra turned back toward Anghara, baring her teeth in what could have been a smile.

"You have left me nothing else."

"There are the Records. Would you still leave them to ai'-Daileh? And there is al'Tamar. I look to you."

"What could I teach him?" said ai'Farra, with a brittle laugh. "The world I knew is lost."

"There will come a time," said Anghara, "when he may well come to me." At this al'Tamar drew in his breath with a sharp hiss, but Anghara ignored him, her eyes still locked with those of ai'Farra. "But until then . . . you hold yourself too cheaply, ai'Farra. I do not. I never have."

For a long moment ai'Farra held her gaze, then her golden lashes swept down onto her cheeks. "Why?" she asked, very softly, as though she was merely speaking thoughts aloud. "Why is it that I can never find the words to overcome you—even now, when I see you holding the torch which has left my world in ashes?"

"Because you also see the same torch lighting the dark places which have been lost to you for so long," ai'Jihaar said after a beat.

While ai'Farra hadn't said she would accept anything Anghara offered, not in so many words, she hadn't needed to. She knew all too well that her choices had narrowed down to one. It was too late to destroy, she was left with the option of bending before the wind howling through the land of her birth, or breaking. And ai'Farra, for all her brittleness and rigidity, had not forgotten how to bend.

The change of subject, when it came, was so abrupt that Kieran, despite all his vows to the contrary, was once again caught off guard.

"You cannot go back over the mountains," ai'Farra said.

Nobody had said anything about going back, but Anghara took it in her stride. "Why not?"

You have to ask? Kieran thought with something like appalled astonishment, memories of their brush with the mountain passes rousing to haunt his mind.

But ai'Farra had something far more practical in mind. "There is ai'Daileh in the way, for one. She can be dealt with—but what you do not yet know is that there has been word from Roisinan while you have sought salvation here in the Kadun."

Anghara was shaken. There was a hesitation, so brief as to be almost unnoticeable, but it was there—all who witnessed it knew her well enough to recognize it. "What news?"

"Sif Kir Hama knows where you are," ai'Farra said, her eyes lifting to finally rest once again on Anghara's face. "He has demanded your return, or he will lead an army into Kheldrin."

"He couldn't even lead one into Tath," Kieran said, unable to hold it back.

But for Anghara the news was just the first step of a familiar nightmare. Cascin, Bresse . . . now Kheldrin. Yet again, a place which had sheltered her, protected her, was threatened with Sif's bloody retribution. Kieran saw the memory wake, old wounds, scars long faded standing out livid in her eyes.

He saw it; the rest sensed it in different ways; ai'Farra caught her lower lip in her small teeth as though she were in sudden pain; ai'Jihaar reached out for Anghara's hand; and al'Tamar gently laid his own on her arm.

"Ah, no, child," ai'Jihaar murmured. "It is not the same thing, not at all . . ."

"He gave us a month," ai'Farra said. "But there are men in Shaymir waiting for his command. If you try going back that way, you will be going straight into his arms." She smiled, and the smile was savage. "And I would not have it said that Kheldrin broke its faith."

It could have been an easy way out for her, a way to destroy the viper in Kheldrin's heart without bringing any guilt onto her own head. But ai'Farra knew the Changer was already named, the Change already begun, and such a gesture would have been worse than pointless—it would have been a futile waste.

Kieran, however, was looking beyond the immediate problems and found something almost unbelievable. "He named you," he said slowly. "That means he has finally had to acknowledge you are alive. I told my men to proclaim it on every village green when I left to try and snatch you from Miranei. We left quite a trail when we took you; Sif would have had to come up with something solid to explain Fodrun and Senena's deaths." Something else occurred to him, and he frowned in fierce concentration. "If he comes . . . he brings everything he's got. He has to. He's coming to destroy you. And he leaves it all wide open behind him—Roisinan, Miranei. For Favrin, if he is sharp enough to grab his chance . . . For you. To claim it."

Anghara turned to him, and her eyes were almost accusing. "And this land?" she questioned quietly. "Is Kheldrin to be hostage to my freedom and the price of my crown?"

At this, ai'Jihaar squeezed Anghara's hand lightly in support, and then let go, stepping away. But it was al'Tamar who spoke first, his eyes blazing.

"No hostage," he said proudly, his head high. "Sif Kir Hama will find out the hard way. This prize is beyond him."

"He has an army . . . an army willing to die for him," Anghara whispered.

"They may well be called upon to do that," ai'Jihaar said. "We have been invaded before . . . and none have stayed long enough to leave more than a few lines in the Records. Sif knows nothing about Kheldrin. He may not yet realize he has a foe in this land which could well prove too large a bite even for him to swallow."

"What foe?" said Anghara, her voice still soft—but her eyes had kindled quietly, and now glowed almost silver in the firelight.

"The desert," ai'Jihaar said, then laughed unexpectedly, laughter which fell into the expectant silence like shards of glass. "The desert fights for us."

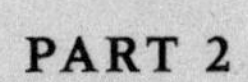

PART 2

Anghara

12

There was little in the lush shore the small Kheldrini sailboat had been hugging for the past week that reminded Kieran of the desert country—but every time he looked across the narrow stretch of water between the boat and the shore Kheldrin rose up to haunt him. The parting words with which Kheldrin's *an'sen'en'thari* had seen them off on Sa'alah's quays, the words which had put an idea in Anghara's mind—an idea which had never occurred to her before.

"I have a message for you from Gul Khaima," ai'Farra had said, "I have been carrying it for months. I knew you were coming back."

"Another long set of incomprehensible triads?" Anghara had asked, rather flippantly. "I've still to find the meaning of parts of the first prophecy."

"No, nothing like that. Something ai'Raisa told me when I was last at the Stone. A single sentence."

"Well, what is it?" Anghara had said after a moment of expectant silence.

"Just this: *Let the lost queen take care in the Crystal City.*"

Kieran had been watching Anghara's face, and it had been completely blank as ai'Farra uttered her words—but it hadn't stayed that way for long. Anghara's eyes became curiously speculative.

"Does it mean anything?" ai'Farra had asked; her tone had been diffident, but Kieran wasn't fooled.

"It might," Anghara had said, keeping her own counsel.

If ai'Farra had hoped Anghara would reveal any meaning before she left Kheldrin's shores, the *an'sen'thar* was disappointed—even Kieran, who should really have guessed right away, had been taken by surprise, yet again and in spite of all his vows. Upon leaving the port of Sa'alah, Anghara had turned the small sailboat's prow more south than east.

The Crystal City. Algira. Tath.

"You're not thinking of walking straight into Duerin Rashin's parlor?" Kieran had demanded incredulously.

"No," said Anghara sweetly. "Not Duerin. For a long time Duerin has reigned in Tath while someone else rules."

"Favrin? You plan to beard *Favrin*?"

"Don't you remember what Feor said in Cascin?" Tears sparkled for a moment in her eyes. "Favrin, he said, was the dangerous one—clever, and strong. When Favrin comes into his own, Roisinan will have to choose: war to the hilt or some sort of treaty." She smiled. "I'm going to offer him a treaty," she said. "Before he realizes what Sif is planning and chooses the war. A war he can win."

"It's madness," Kieran said. "Alone?"

"I have you, don't I?" she said. The words somehow managed to be both a wry barb and a clean avowal of trust and confidence; Kieran could find no response quickly enough for it to be effective. "Besides," Anghara added, "it's not as though this was my own idea. The oracle told me to be careful in the Crystal City long before I thought of going there."

"You don't know anything about the place," Kieran said mutinously.

"I don't need to," said Anghara. "I'm being led; that means I will be shown what I need to know."

There was a sharp brilliance about her, ever since winged ai'Bre'hinnah had restored her power in the red desert of

Kheldrin—the fearless and thoughtless arrogance of an adamant crafted to adorn a royal crown. She had felt reborn; and because she believed nothing foul could touch her again, nothing could. Never had Kieran felt less necessary—she looked as though she would be quite happy to undertake this wild quest by herself. Another moment such as the one they had wasted in the Kadun cavern had not presented itself. Now that all she had lost had been restored to her, it seemed to Kieran as if she was somehow further removed from him. It was as if the closest image he had of her had been snatched away; even the childhood name of Brynna now belonged more to a winged goddess than to the small girl Kieran had found it so easy to love.

He was back to his own self, with senses no more alert than might have been expected of those forged in the fires that had made Kieran what he was. Despite his close acquaintance with Kheldrin's vanished Gods, he was no more capable of understanding what it was that Anghara was doing to help them on their way than any earth-bound man. Somehow she had woven a concealing sea mist around their boat. They could see out, but none could see them within—and it seemed to work. Once, at night, they sat quietly in their little craft and watched the passage of two large Roisinani galleys, part of Sif's force, travelling toward Kheldrin. Anghara's face had been eloquent, and once the ships were past and there was no danger of his being overheard Kieran hastened to chase away the brooding shadows in her eyes.

"As ai'Jihaar said, the desert itself will be Sif's enemy."

"But Sa'alah," Anghara replied with quiet pain, "Sa'alah is not in the desert. And Sa'ila is so easily denied . . ."

That was the hour in which Kieran chose to throw his support behind the Algira venture—it was something that needed Anghara's active participation, leaving her no time to torment herself with dark visions. He pushed her into thinking about what she meant to do, reaching for some sort of plan, despite her expectation of a path waiting to unroll itself at her feet. With that, and the necessities of guiding their small craft on its way, the days drifted by. They passed close enough to Vallen Fen to smell its sweet, rotten corruption in the early morning mists; on their right, a dark smudge on a bright ocean, lay the largest and closest island of the Mabin Archipelago. There was a time when Anghara sat motionless in the midst of the small craft, only her eyes moving, darting from the shore to the island.

"We're too close to two Dances," she told Kieran when he asked if she was all right. "There is something in me that wants to answer the call of both, and is being torn apart . . ."

"I thought the old Gods were gone."

"They hadn't been in Roisinan for a long time," Anghara said. "But the Dances . . . they belong to something else. There will always be power there. I can't help it; the presence of a Standing Stone is like a knife to me. It's like a breath of incense. They . . . remind me of everything."

"Like desert sage," Kieran had murmured.

She didn't ask what he meant, and he didn't elaborate. But soon the island was left behind, and the Dances released Anghara from their thrall. The marshes of Vallen Fen gave way to grasslands, then dark, lush forest sweeping down to the shore. Sometimes they saw small animals swimming in and out of the shadows in the shallows. The raucous noise of a tribe of small monkeys followed them, and once, when they saw a freshwater rill pouring into the sea and stopped to replenish their water supplies, the monkeys came close enough to pelt them with hard-shelled fruit. Anghara sported a blue-green bruise on her arm and Kieran had a walnut-sized lump on his temple, where a larger than average missile had narrowly missed his eye.

"We'll make quite an entry into the palaces of Algira," Kieran grumbled. "When they ask us how we came by these bruises, I just wish we didn't have to say we were beaten up by a troop of monkeys."

Anghara had known the land around Algira was heavily cultivated, but the vineyards and the olive groves took her by surprise—the little Kheldrini boat had made good time. They first saw the silver-leafed vineyards by moonlight, and Anghara leapt up to tack the sail.

"Back," she said. "It was lucky we came here at night. I don't want to sail straight into Algira Harbor. We'll hide the boat in the forest; from here we walk."

They sailed back to a small inlet they had seen earlier, pulling the light craft up onto the sand beneath concealing fronds of lush undergrowth. That night they slept on the beach, in the lee of their craft, and it didn't take them long the following morning to hack their way through the forest and find a road.

The *an'sen'en'thari* had provided them with neutral travelling cloaks, but these were little protection against the curious glances of vineyard and orchard workers, who straightened from their tasks to glance at the two passers-by. Anghara used Sight to blur them both, leaving behind an impression of two nondescript travellers, who merited little attention. They were forgotten as soon as the workers turned back to their labor. Later, as their country road swung north to join a broader artery which eventually led all the way to the banks of the Ronval River and Roisinan, they mingled with other travellers making their way south to Algira. They found anonymity amongst women with large baskets and small unruly children and the occasional cart laden with produce heaving its way into the city. Impatient riders wove through the pedestrians with muttered curses, and old men plodding patiently beside equally ancient donkeys, gray around the muzzles, bearing sacks of olives or sloshing skins of wine.

Anghara had seen paintings of fabled Algira in her childhood. Kieran had not; all he had were elaborate tales, and many of those had been suspect. But the truth was so much beyond even these stories that Kieran stared with something like disbelief. The Crystal City was one of many names with which the chroniclers of history and legend had wreathed Algira. It had other guises; it was also known as the Water City, the Canal City or the Garden City. And all of those were true.

The sun was bright and high when Anghara and Kieran topped a shallow rise and stood looking into the valley sloping down to the blue bay. The ocean sparkled in the sunlight, but was put to shame by the flash and fire of Algira's towers as they broke the southern light like a shattered adamant. The place seemed made of glass, and shimmered before Kieran's eyes; he could see twisting trails of water, sometimes bridged with arching spans of white stone or black obsidian, which wound their way between the glittering buildings. Scattered amongst these, great palms spread enormous emerald fronds, and glimpses of bright creepers upon sheer walls caught Kieran's eye. Above it all, upon a small hill ringed by a broad stretch of water, rose the most magnificent building of all—a delicate edifice which looked as though it had been made from spun sugar. Its gardens were a riot of green and scarlet, well-tended lawns giving way unexpectedly to tangled green masses which reminded Kieran of the forests they had recently passed.

"That's where we're going," said Anghara quietly, having caught him staring. "The White Palace. The home of Favrin Rashin, and his father, the king."

Beauty tempted Kieran into disloyalty. "What in the name of the great God Kerun do they want with our harsh winters and snow-bound crags when they have this?"

"There was a time when the kings of Roisinan had both. The Rashin would have it so again."

"So would you," Kieran said. "Else why would you be here?"

"They would kill for it. I would leave them their world; they would be less kind to me." Anghara allowed her eyes to rest for a long moment upon the White Palace, for so long the summer place of the Kir Hama kings, now home to a pretender to their ancient throne. "Come on."

Kieran, unaware he had stopped, obediently began moving again. His eyes, however, stayed on the White Palace, and once the initial thrill had passed he saw it with a soldier's eye. And he didn't like what it revealed.

"Even assuming you could get into that place—it looks as if it could go hard on you if you tried to leave without your host's consent," he said in a low voice.

Anghara glanced at him, then down to where the white walls caught the sun and flamed with brilliant splendor. "That is not entirely unexpected," she said. "But explain."

Kieran frowned. It was so beautiful and such a deadly trap. "Look at it," he said. "An island, surrounded by water—you, an easy target for an archer upon the walls. And not a scrap of concealment near the waterline—the place might look like it's going wild, but there's a careful plan in the midst of that madness. There isn't anywhere to hide. And, discovered, there isn't anywhere to run."

"I don't plan on running," said Anghara with a curious smile.

She would do it, Kieran thought despairingly. She would walk into this without any thought for the aftermath—trusting to the Gods. Still. But there were no Gods, not any more; there was only Anghara's own bright flame, and the dogged loyalty of a single man. Who would follow her into anything, even this, because for him no other choice existed.

By now they were already in the city, walking beside the first canals coruscating in the southern sunshine. It was more crowded here, people starting to jostle for space on the narrow walkways flanking the canals. One large elbow nearly spun Anghara off into the water; Kieran would have turned to remonstrate, but Anghara's hand on his arm forestalled him. "No, I don't want attention. Follow the greatest crowds; I need a marketplace."

"What for?"

"That's where we'll find a scribe."

Kieran knew this cryptic tone. She had cooked up a plan, but nobody would know a detail of it until she was ready to speak. But Kieran already had an inkling of this plan, and he didn't have to like what he was thinking.

"What would you commit to paper here?" he said. "There is danger enough being courted today without going out of your way to draw it upon you. Don't tell me you mean to challenge Favrin Rashin in his own city?"

"Not challenge," Anghara said demurely. "Merely invite."

"To do what?"

"To issue an invitation in return," Anghara said. "I plan to enter the White Palace as an invited guest-friend."

"Why on the Gods' green earth would he invite you into his palace, and guarantee safety to that which stands between him and his desire?" Kieran asked blankly.

"Out of curiosity. Out of piqued interest in what his sworn enemy might find to talk about while drinking his wine."

"How do you know he's even here, and not chasing Sif's tail in Roisinan?"

Anghara, wise in the way of courts, merely smiled. "You ought to know Favrin's colors by now," she said. "There's a blue and white pennant amongst the banners on the towers. Favrin's. It only flies when he is within." She laughed, then, at Kieran's face. "Duerin might accept the gauntlet, only to try and have me poisoned quietly at his table," she said, her voice light, almost lilting; Kieran's skin crawled at her easy, almost fey, banter on the subject of her own death. "Not Favrin; he's too forthright for poison. Feor was right about that. But he *will* accept my invitation—and he will guarantee my safety, his soldier's honor will see to it."

There was still something she wasn't telling him, but they followed the throngs to a small square. Anghara's attention was drawn to a striped black and white awning, beneath which sat a young man, garbed and turbaned in demure white. Wax tablets, steel styluses, ink bottles and other paraphernalia of his trade were laid out neatly on the ground beside him.

The language of Tath was no more than a variation of Roisinani, a different accent, a few different words. The language of Tath, however, was not what Anghara used. If the young scribe had been surprised to be addressed in high court Roisinani here in the heart of Tath's power, he was too well schooled, to reveal it—and responded in the same language. Anghara was impressed by the young man's self-possession, and so, almost against his will, was Kieran.

"I need a letter written, which will need skill and discretion," Anghara said.

"We may not reveal what we write at another's behest. That is guild law everywhere," the young man said gravely, giving an oblique acknowledgment that he knew she was a stranger in his city. "Your coin buys my silence about whatever you choose to entrust to me."

"What is your fee?"

"Six *sessi*. For matters of import . . ." he coughed delicately, hiding his mouth behind his hand, but his eyes were eloquent enough above it. "For matters of import—a price is negotiable."

"Ten," said Anghara, "if you will also arrange to have it delivered."

"To what address?"

"The White Palace."

The young man coughed again into his palm. "That is a matter of grave import indeed. For this . . . fifteen *sessi*."

"Eleven," Anghara said.

The young man's eyes had kindled. "Thirteen, my lady?"

"Twelve," said Anghara, "and a half."

He considered this for a moment and then bowed to her from the waist without getting up. "Twelve and a half," he acceded. "We can have privacy within my tent, if you so desire."

"Perhaps that would be best," said Anghara.

"Where did you learn to haggle in a manner Borre of Shaymir might have envied?" Kieran hissed at Anghara as she turned to follow the scribe into the black and white striped tent beyond the awning. "And where do you plan to get these twelve and a half *sessi,* whatever they are, from?"

"Kheldrin gave many gifts," said Anghara, smiling at him.

"Khelsies haggle?" Kieran murmured. "By Kerun's Horns, they become more human every time I look. Am I allowed to know what will be in this letter?"

Her eyes were sparkling with the delight of the game. "Come inside and listen."

It was Kieran's role to worry about the young queen who showed no sign of taking a thought for her own safety, and his time as a leader of men had taught him to weigh risks with deliberation. But he was also young enough, and reckless enough, to enjoy putting Anghara's scheme into action. The missive written by the young scribe—who, with admirable self-control, had shown no reaction to what he was being asked to set down—had been sealed with the royal seal hanging from al'Tamar's *say'yin,* and dispatched, with careful instructions, by a street runner summoned by the scribe. Kieran had, of course, been right—Anghara didn't have the coinage to pay for the service she had received. What she did have was Kheldrini silver. While it wasn't legal tender, barter was a matter of course and the scribe quietly and efficiently produced a small set of scales, weighed the offering, and gave her the equivalent in Algiran *sessi*. Made profligate by an odd sense of excitement, Anghara tendered fifteen *sessi* to the scribe rather than the agreed sum; if the man noticed, he made no sign, merely bowing with grace and courtesy as the money vanished into a fold of his garment. They left him then, to find something to eat in the crowded marketplace, and wait for the hour Anghara's letter had appointed.

A wizened old woman, resembling one of the noisy little monkeys of their past painful acquaintance, grabbed at Anghara's hand as she walked past. "Two *sessi?*" she cackled, fawning up at her shamelessly. "Two *sessi,* and I'll tell you your fortune. A kind-faced young lady like you with such a handsome lad by your side—you'll want to know what's in store for you, duckling . . ."

Anghara pulled her hand away, gently. "No, thank you, mother. Perhaps another time."

As Kieran edged past, the crone snatched his hand instead, turning the palm up before he could shake her loose. Irritated, for Anghara had already taken a step or two away and was in danger of being swallowed up by the crowd, Kieran tried to pull his hand back. "Have done," he said. "I don't need . . ."

"I see suffering," the old woman murmured, seemingly tranced, her eyes cast down and wide open, unblinking. "I see partings, pain, a great love almost lost . . . and battles gained . . . and then . . . and then a crown."

Kieran snatched his hand away as if he'd been burned. The old woman, apparently having forgotten this fortune was supposed to be worth two *sessi,* had turned to wander off, muttering about crowns, hurt and hard choices. Kieran stared after her for a long moment, his eyes hard with suspicion and something that was almost fear; and then he started abruptly, turning to rake the crowds in search of Anghara.

"So she did snag you," Anghara said, taking a bite out of a peach she had bought at a nearby stall with her new-gained currency, licking at the juices which ran down her chin. "You didn't even pay her fee. That wasn't very gallant, Kieran. What did she say?"

"Some old rubbish," Kieran said. Too quickly. But the peach was proving to be a successful diversion, and Anghara was looking around, laughing.

"I hope there's a fountain somewhere close by, or else we had better go back to the canals—I won't be able to touch another thing until I've washed my hands."

"Do you know what passes for a han here?" Kieran asked. "Perhaps the best thing would be to find somewhere to hole up until sundown—and you could get cleaned up properly."

"There's got to be an inn somewhere off the canals; I'll have to find somewhere to change," said Anghara, who carried a pack containing all her Kheldrini *an'sen'thar* finery—just as she had done once before on a homecoming. Kieran called to mind the ill-fated King's Inn in Calabra and its consequences, and his notion of finding an inn was roundly and speedily dismissed. He had no wish to have Anghara—or himself—find out what the dungeons of *this* palace looked like from the inside.

"We'll think about that later," he said. "Let's keep moving for now."

It proved to be a long day, heavy with summer. They ate iced cream, a southern concoction neither had tried before, while watching a ship flying the sea-serpent banner of the Mabin Islands dock in the harbor in the long, golden southern afternoon. The galley was bristling with grimly efficient armed men, the sun glancing off lances and body armor.

"Are there pirates in these waters?" Kieran asked, bemused at the sight.

"For that ship there might be," Anghara said. "Its cargo is probably pearls from Mabin, for the king."

"You should have detoured," said Kieran, teasing. "Gone to Mabin, picked up a shipload of pearls in exchange for all that Kheldrini silver and presented yourself at the palace gates. I'm sure you wouldn't have been refused entry."

"They're worth a king's ransom, those pearls," Anghara said. "I might yet have that in common with them before this night is over."

She seemed to be having second thoughts, and, ironically, it was now Kieran who defended her plan. Anghara allowed herself to be persuaded. They left the harbor eventually, finding a quiet inn just off the main wharf, where a handful of coins bought careful silence from the landlord and a jug of cheap but remarkably good wine. They nursed it between them for a while, then Kieran remained at the table while Anghara slipped off to change into garb more appropriate for a royal visit. Anyone glancing at him would have thought him utterly relaxed, his long legs stretched out before him and his eyelids drooping; but beneath those half-closed eyelids he was warily watching the door through which Anghara had left, uneasy at allowing her away by herself. Only when she emerged again, wrapped carefully in her dark cloak, did an unspoken tension leave his shoulders, and he leaned back against the wall.

"Everything all right?" he murmured.

She tossed a bundle on the seat beside him and sat down. "No problems. Is it time?"

"Still early. But sunset is near. We can stay here for a while longer, and then we'd better start making our way to the palace lake." His eyes flickered. "If there's anyone there to meet us."

"There will be," said Anghara, her voice thoughtful but nonetheless ringing with conviction. Her faith might have lapsed for a moment or two, but now, close to the consummation of her plan, it was back, burning stronger than ever.

"I only hope there won't be more than we bargained for."

"He's a soldier, like you," Anghara said. "If he undertakes to do something, knight's honor will ensure he sees it accomplished according to his given word. Isn't that what you would do?"

"I'm not a prince," Kieran said.

A crown, the old crone had said, and the memory broke into his voice, brought a sudden tension into his words. He gazed at Anghara helplessly, caught up in the honeyed trap of his love for a woman who would be queen. *I never wanted this. I wasn't born to claim royalty.*

But he couldn't ask her to lay it aside—not after he had fought and schemed to seize it back for her. He could either stay with her—as simply another of her captains and generals, a leader of her armies—or run, seek his fortune alone in the lands beyond the mountains, of which he knew no more than myth, fable and tangled travellers' tales.

A crown. He could take a third path. He could declare himself, tell her of his feelings . . . ah, had things been different, he would have married her and taken joy in it—but she was royal, would be queen on the oldest throne in their world, and that carried responsibilities of its own. Queens did not—could not—marry for love.

But he pushed those thoughts away. Now was not the time; he needed all his focus and concentration upon the task at hand. Despite Anghara's confidence, there was a great deal of danger; Kieran was far from sure a soldier's honor would prevail over a prince's sense of expediency. Whatever else he might be, Favrin was still Duerin's son—and Kieran knew Anghara would never have contemplated doing what she was about to do with Duerin Rashin.

The light was deep gold outside, the afternoon almost over. Kieran swallowed the last dregs of wine in his cup and rose. "It's time we were moving."

Sunset caught them in the city, with lamplighters passing from lamp to lamp in the main thoroughfares and yellow light from open windows spilling out onto the canals. They sometimes heard music as they passed beneath, or a delicate laugh, a murmur of conversation somewhere above. A woman dressed in scarlet waved in their direction with a feathered fan from a balcony. Kieran froze, waiting for someone to lay a heavy hand on his shoulder—but the footsteps, when they came, were light and joyous, and a young man, wearing an elaborate half-mask beneath a floppy hat adorned with more feathers, pushed past him and hurried toward the balcony. Kieran let out a shaky breath. "Nobody here could possibly know our identity—at least, not yet," he said softly. "Still . . . I wish I could get rid of the feeling that everyone is play-acting and knows exactly who you are."

"What time is it?" Anghara asked doggedly. Kieran realized she hadn't even seen the painted woman wave from above, and the young gentleman hurrying past had left no more impression than a ghost. Anghara had an assignation with destiny that night—other dalliances were invisible in the light of her own.

"We'll be there on the appointed hour," Kieran said, almost laughing. "Don't be so keen to walk into this web; I'm still far from certain you'll be able to walk out of it with impunity."

The scribe had assisted when Anghara planned her assignation—she had wanted to make it on the main quay, to wait for Favrin's boat and escort out in the open, but Kieran hadn't liked the idea and the scribe, unexpectedly, had concurred. There was another quay, he told them, to the west of the palace lake—more discreet. A postern quay, he'd called it, hiding what Kieran was sure had been a smile behind his delicate cough and the concealing gesture of his narrow brown hand. This was the place where Anghara's letter had told Favrin his visitor would be waiting an hour after sunset. Now, as they approached, Anghara in the lead and Kieran a step behind with blade loosened in the scabbard, they could see a boat. Two men waited aboard—a slope-shouldered oarsman, and another, face shadowed beneath a hat similar to that gracing the young nobleman they had encountered outside the bawdyhouse. Favrin's emissary wore a heavily brocaded robe over ruby-colored doublet and hose, and from the shadows cast by the improbable hat, his hair gleamed in long golden curls in the light of a single torch affixed to the boats prow.

"But they dress well, these southerners," Anghara said softly, while she and Kieran were still out of earshot. "I heard they liked peacocks in their gardens; I'm beginning to understand why."

But Kieran had seen past the obvious. "That blade he is wearing is no prop," he said. "The velvets and brocades—it's all show; remember, we've been fighting these men in southern Roisinan since . . . since you and I sat discussing their tactics in Feor's schoolroom. They've taught us many things, not least that they are to be respected. Danger is all the more perilous when you're lulled into believing it doesn't exist. Careful—he's coming ashore; the hood."

Anghara reached out and pulled the hood of her cloak forward over her face. The man had stepped out of the boat and stood waiting as they approached, features shadowed by the brim of his velvet hat.

"I am Moran." He offered first greeting as they came to within a few paces and stopped. "I am Prince Favrin's chamberlain. You are the one seeking him under the royal seal of Roisinan?"

Kieran nodded in silence.

Moran offered them a shallow, courtly bow. "My lord will meet with you," he said. "He has bid me welcome you to the White Palace of Algira, under his own protection. The boat waits to convey you."

Kieran knew Anghara was smiling beneath her concealing hood. He didn't need Sight to sense a delighted *I told you so* in the gray eyes he knew were looking at him. "We come under the protection of your master's word," Kieran replied.

Moran waited until they climbed into the boat and then

followed them, nodding to the oarsman. The other man, having sat patiently through the protocol, now bent over his oars. The boat slid across the still water almost without a sound.

In silence Moran signalled for his lord's mysterious night visitors to follow him when they reached the other side. They were here under Favrin's sworn protection, yet Kieran glanced round warily as they crossed an area of open lawn and plunged into the shadows of an alley of tall bushes bearing sweet-scented white flowers, so pure in color they seemed to almost glow in the dark. It seemed Favrin had a taste for secrecy—which was not entirely unexpected. These guests were to be conveyed into his presence through small and secret gates, not through the bright and guarded main entrance.

"This way," Moran said, speaking softly, opening a narrow door beneath a trellis wreathed with climbing roses.

They entered a tiled corridor, new torches burning in iron sconces set at intervals into the walls. The men's boots woke a soft echo on the tiles; but no one crossed their path as they passed along the corridor and beyond into another, broader and more opulent, where the wall sconces were silver and the echo of their footsteps dulled by soft carpets. Moran glanced up and down the deserted corridor, crossed it, climbed up a flight of stairs with a wooden banister elaborately carved into the shapes of sea-beasts, and turned into another long passageway. Stopping at the third door along, he opened it and motioned them inside.

They found themselves in a small anteroom, panelled in some blond wood, sparsely furnished with a low table and a brace of wooden chairs. The very simplicity of the chamber here in the heart of a prince's apartments pronounced the room to be one of service, not pleasure. A guardroom. It was empty, or seemed to be; but Moran paused.

"I have to ask you to leave your weapons here," he murmured, still flawlessly correct. "They will be quite safe."

It didn't have to be an order. They were in a king's palace, and even mild requests would be backed with force if necessary. Kieran had been expecting something like this, a ritual disarming before entering into the presence of royalty; that still didn't mean he liked the idea. He stripped off his sword belt, the white ki'thar skin of Kheldrin, with reluctance, leaving sword and dagger on the table. Moran, with a curious air of mingled diffidence and implacability, glanced toward Anghara's muffled shape.

"Not armed," Kieran said shortly. Moran hesitated, and then decided to take this at face value. As well he did, Kieran thought, else their ruse would have been blown right here.

And ruse it was, because the letter Anghara had sent, except for the royal seal affixed to whet Favrin's appetite, gave no indication as to the identity of the Prince's visitors—merely that they came with a message from Roisinan, hinting obliquely at the messengers' high birth. As Moran ushered them into the room where Favrin Rashin waited, Kieran had the satisfaction of seeing Favrin's face change when Anghara stepped inside, flinging her cloak back to reveal the piled red-gold hair and the golden Kheldrini robe.

"Your Grace," said Kieran, "I present Anghara Kir Hama, rightful Queen of Roisinan."

Favrin had known the moment Anghara stepped into his chamber—any number of men could have gained admittance to him under that seal, but only one woman. That instant of surprise was gone almost before it came; what was left in its wake was admiration, and genuine astonishment.

Favrin mastered himself, allowed a small smile to play upon his lips, and bowed deeply in the elaborate fashion of the southern court.

"You honor my house," he said. The words could have been facetious. They were not; but those that followed were. Dangerously so. "When Sif Kir Hama ascended the Throne Under the Mountain, we were given to understand it was over the dead bodies of your father, your mother . . . and yourself. I always had my doubts about the truth behind the tomb in the Miranei mausoleum which bears your name; it is gratifying to have them vindicated."

"My father's and my mother's are real enough," Anghara said. Her eyes were hard, gray flint; it had been unwise of Favrin to have mentioned Red Dynan. Anghara's father had, after all, met his death through an arrow fired on Rashin orders.

Favrin shrugged the moment off. "But I am remiss in my duties. May I offer you a glass of wine? It comes from my own vineyards, a vintage of which I am, I think, justly proud."

"Thank you," Anghara said simply.

Favrin turned to Kieran, all southern courtesy. "For you, my lord?"

"No," Kieran said. "Thank you."

The offer had been a fishing expedition, the wine merely bait, but Kieran offered nothing further by way of introduction, leaving Favrin in the dark as to his identity. Favrin, however, took this adroit reflection of his probe smoothly enough; he inclined his head gravely in acknowledgment of Anghara's reply, and turned to pour a measure into her glass. Kieran watched him closely, through narrowed eyes. If poison had been contemplated, now would be the time to introduce it. But Favrin poured from the same decanter into both his glass and Anghara's; unless he was contemplating suicide, there was no poison here.

He was fair to look upon, the Prince of Algira; Favrin Rashin crossed the room to Anghara, bearing two glasses filled with dark red wine, moving with a courtier's elegance, a fighter's grace. His father, Duerin, was a classic southerner—short and swarthy, black-eyed and olive-skinned with curly dark hair. Favrin was different—so different he could almost be taken for a changeling. His mother had been a woman from the north, and he took after her, tall and golden-haired, his eyes as blue as the ocean. Kieran watched him gaze on Anghara as she raised her head slightly to meet those eyes; they made a picture fit for a tapestry depicting the proud and beautiful kings and queens of ancient legend. Favrin knew it, of course—he was playing for effect. But a certain amount of arrogance was allowed a man who almost single-handedly changed the face of warfare in Roisinan.

"There were rumors, of course, that you were very much alive and hidden, waiting to reclaim your inheritance," Favrin continued smoothly, picking up the thread of the conversation. "But it was all too easy to dismiss these, especially as we started many of them ourselves. They worked in our favor, after all."

"As long as Sif feared someone might heed them enough to hold Miranei in my name in his absence, he couldn't venture far from his throne," Anghara said, nodding, twirling her glass between her fingers. "You hobbled the great warrior. The rumors made it safe for you to pursue your war, because you could wait Sif out, and wear him down, knowing you were protected from invasion. You could stop one every time simply by firing up a new round of rumors in Miranei."

"Quite," said Favrin, amused at this succinct summary of his tactics by this unlikely hearth-guest.

"Just how long were you planning to keep up this cat and mouse game?" she asked, sounding genuinely interested.

Favrin shrugged. "Now would seem like a good time to stop." His blue eyes were glinting dangerously through the unexpectedly dark lashes of half-lowered eyelids. "Now that Sif plans to spend his summer chasing wild geese in the Kheldrini desert, I assume the purpose of your . . . visit . . . is to offer me an alternative to sweeping into Roisinan and gathering it into the palm of my hand while he isn't looking?"

He was certainly well informed. But Anghara's eyes were steady.

"How very perceptive, my lord," said Anghara, and there was an acid sting in the compliment. "Do not be deceived—I do not come to bargain for my country. I have one inestimable advantage over my brother. I don't have to lead my own armies; I can hold Miranei while men I trust take this war of yours to the thresholds of Algira."

"But you do not hold Miranei," said Favrin, eyes still hooded.

Anghara lifted her chin, eyes sparkling in challenge. "Neither do you."

Favrin smiled; his teeth were very white, and oddly sharp. It gave his face the cast of a hunting cat scenting prey. "This interests me," he said. "I anticipated this evening would be stimulating when I saw your seal, but this surpasses all expectations. Will you join me on the balcony, my lady? The night is balmy, and the view from this room has always been spectacular."

Anghara assented with a small inclination of the head, briefly catching Kieran's eye as she turned to gather the cloak she'd unfastened and let fall. *This is my game; everything stands or falls by what happens here tonight. Watch; wait. Be ready if I need you.*

Kieran's face remained impassive but his eyes were alert and watchful as they followed Anghara and Favrin through the open doors and onto the broad terrace. Their conversation, resuming after a lull, became a delicate murmur; if he concentrated furiously Kieran could barely make out what they were saying. With an almost equal fury he made himself do the opposite, listening only for a possible change of cadence, for signs of fear or anger from his lady. This, indeed, was her game. Here, in the palace by the sea, far from the seat of her own power, she could reach out and win her land back, whole and complete, finally free of the war that had been eating at its southern borders for years . . . or she could lose it utterly.

Favrin had seated Anghara courteously into a high-backed chair of lacy wickerwork, himself choosing to perch with dangerous abandon upon the stone parapet, seemingly oblivious to the drop on the other side. It was a pose, of course; Anghara felt a stab of what was almost irritation, but it was quickly swamped by something else—a wry amusement, perhaps, that he should feel the need for it. He was cut from a fighter's cloth, easily Sif's match as a leader of men, and had proved himself one of the best soldiers of his generation. But there was something engaging in his need to demonstrate his courage sprang from something much greater—from a right of blood, the courage of princes. Favrin was older than Anghara, by not a few years, but she, younger, untried, felt no need to prove anything. Perhaps it did spring from royalty, the spirit and the courage so rampant in this room. Hers was the older line by far, already proved by the impetuous princelings of its youth and steady in the knowledge of its mature strength and abilities.

For all that, Favrin was worthy of being called prince. It was hardly his fault he had chosen to match wits with a queen.

He raised his glass to his lips now, his back ostentatiously to the view, and took a slow sip. Over the rim of the glass his eyes, bright and steady, remained upon Anghara's face; they had never left it.

"If, as you say, you are not here to bargain for your country," Favrin said, "then to what, exactly, do I owe the pleasure of your company? I can hardly put it down to a burning desire to meet one you doubtless see as an implacable enemy of Roisinan."

"Aren't you?" Anghara murmured into her wine.

"Hardly," said Favrin, and his tone was mocking again. "In fact, I love it so well I would have it all as my own."

Anghara didn't smile at the jest. "This war was of your father's making."

"In the beginning," Favrin admitted. "I wasn't at the battle that felled Red Dynan. But afterward, when my lord father saw fit to give me command of the armies . . . and when I realized what truly was at stake . . . yes, it became my war. There was a time when a Rashin sat on the Throne Under the Mountain. There is a portrait of this ancestor of mine here in the palace. I could show you, if you would care to see. The crown of Miranei sits well on his brow."

"Your crowned ancestor wears borrowed glory," Anghara said, her words more of a verbal lash than any hearth-guest had right to indulge in. "Forgive me, but to my eyes no Rashin would look well wearing this crown. It has belonged to men of my blood for many generations."

"Are you saying it suits Sif Kir Hama?" asked Favrin, with a touch of malice, his eyes glinting.

"That will change," Anghara said, with icy calm.

Favrin raised an eloquent eyebrow. "He took over the armies once before when it was deemed impossible for a woman to lead them," he said.

"A girl," Anghara corrected. "Yes, he took them. I am taking them back. It is time."

"A minor point, but the armies in question are in Kheldrin; you are here, and it still remains for you to convince many you are not your own ghost," Favrin said dryly.

"Red Dynan's royal seal, lost when his daughter vanished, will do much to attest to the solidity of this particular ghost. It worked for you," Anghara tossed out a vivid smile. "As for the rest . . . Sif's armies aren't the only ones in Roisinan. And even they will return to my banner once it is unfurled over Miranei."

"I like your confidence in the future," Favrin remarked conversationally. "I share it—alas, my crystal ball shows quite a different path than the one you have outlined."

Anghara put down her wineglass. "I have said I am not here to bargain for my country. But I am here to bargain. For yours."

She had succeeded in startling him, but, as before, he turned his surprise into sardonic amusement.

"For mine?" he questioned softly, a curious, shadowed smile playing around the corners of his mouth. "You come freely into my land and tell me you come to bargain for my country?"

There was a threat there, however veiled. But Anghara laughed, a brittle laugh which had little to do with merriment. "Yes, I came—I trusted in the given word of a prince and the honor of a soldier. Was I wrong? My friend might be interested to learn his uncertainties are likely to be so richly vindicated."

Favrin's nostrils flared briefly, and there was a spark in his eyes. "I keep my word," he said curtly.

Anghara offered a half-bow from her chair. "I do not doubt it."

There was still a last swallow of wine in Favrin's glass; he drained it, brought it down with a sharp, spasmodic motion. His face was still wearing its mask of gentle amusement, but his eyes had darkened into violet. "You came here to tell me something," he said. "What is it?"

"I claim Roisinan," Anghara said, very softly, sitting very straight, the light wicker chair suddenly a throne. A soft golden light came to play around her head and shoulders; Favrin couldn't see it, but it was hard not to be aware of it on some level—he could sense it, the air around her changed, became charged with royalty. He had to fight against the pull of it, else he would have been on his knees swearing fealty.

"There is still the right of conquest," he said instead, his jaw set.

"There is," Anghara agreed. "Shall I claim Tath, too?"

"You could not," Favrin said.

Her eyes glittered strangely. "Could I not? Would you gamble with your birthright?"

"Others gambled with yours, long ago. The dice rolled against you."

"Then," said Anghara, with light emphasis.

Favrin, prodded into betraying a sudden disquiet, slipped off the parapet where he had been perched and turned away, staring into the distant horizon where the ocean met the sky. He heard a rustle behind him, then a footstep; he sensed rather than saw Anghara come to stand beside him. Surprised, he looked around into a pair of intense gray eyes.

And found himself at once prey to something completely unexpected.

He sought refuge in levity, as usual, but it was a weak and watery smile he dredged up as defense against a wave of sudden desire, a hunger that swept through him and left him acutely open and vulnerable in its backwash.

"In all your designs," he said, "have you considered the inescapable fact that the single most effective way of solving our problems might lie not in sundering our Houses, but in joining them?"

Anghara blinked; for a moment the magnetic gray eyes broke their contact with his own, and Favrin found the strength to look away. "Joining them?" she echoed.

"Marriage," Favrin said, his voice already firmer. His knees still felt suspiciously as though they might give way if he let go of his balcony's balustrade too abruptly, but having gained solid ground after nearly drowning in her eyes his mind worked round the idea and found it curiously pleasant. Which was odd; he had enjoyed his share of bed-mates—women came willingly to one of royal blood—but until this instant he had never contemplated wedlock.

It was Anghara's turn to be startled; this was certainly not the turn of events she had envisaged when, prodded by the cryptic words of the oracle at Gul Khaima, she had first formulated the nebulous idea of coming to the White Palace of Algira. In the short but charged silence following Favrin's single word, she considered the concept. Above the idea towered the shade of Red Dynan—a huge ghost, and one unlikely to ever be laid to rest. Favrin might not physically have Anghara's father's blood on his hands, but they both knew only youth and inexperience had kept him from the battle which had taken Dynan's life. The war had been started by the Rashin clan—the blood guilt would always be there. And yet . . . Anghara was deeply shocked to discover her father's death hadn't been her first concern. Other images had crowded Red Dynan out of her mind. One was a hazy thing, trembling on the edges of comprehension—Favrin was *wrong,* the wrong man. The wrong man for her. It was an instinct that was bone-deep, even if she didn't have time to chase it down and discover exactly why. The other was something far more specific, and far more compelling.

"Clever," she murmured at length, looking down at her interlaced fingers.

"Does that mean you accept?"

"To you, my enterprising lord, would go all the advantages of such a match. Should I agree, it would be no less than a complete surrender—and the battle hasn't even been joined."

"Not so," Favrin said. Too quickly. Anghara braced herself, and looked up; there was an odd, fervid heat in his eyes. She hadn't been afraid until this moment, but now the faintest touch of fear traced an icy path down her spine. "And must there be a battle after all, Anghara?" he added softly, almost as an afterthought.

"You forget what your women accept when they wed," Anghara murmured. "The silken chains that lie behind the Silk Curtain."

"Say rather that they rule their men with a rod of iron from the women's quarters. It is not an ill life."

"I was crowned in Miranei when I was nine years old," said Anghara. "My kingdom is, has always been, my own—I hold what I hold in my own right. If I gain Roisinan and take back my throne, I will not rule my kingdom from behind the veils of the bedchamber, at some man's whim or indulgence. If you are after an easier way to gain the throne of Roisinan, this is not it, my lord."

"It could still be."

"Would you break the traditions of your people and eschew the Silk Curtain? Would you have your barons call you unmanned because your woman would not keep to the confines of the *kaiss*?"

"Do you not think my barons might call me unmanned if they should ever discover what went on here tonight—if they find I stayed to listen to my enemy who is a woman, and then let her go free?" Favrin said.

"Do you measure manhood in this land by how much less worthy a woman is of your attention, except when she is bearing your children?" Anghara said.

"I told you, there is power of a sort in the *kaiss.*"

Anghara shook her head. "Not for me."

"You would not be an average *kaissan,* that is true—but it could still be. It could still be," Favrin said, and something leapt in his eyes at the words.

Anghara forced herself not to shrink from his gaze. "Your word," she reminded him.

He recoiled, swallowed, fought to master his face. Then, again, he laughed. "I think that I find myself in sore need of another glass of wine," he said, with the slow southern drawl she was beginning to recognize. "May I refill your own?"

Her own glass was still half full, but Favrin scooped it up in passing as he turned and made what was almost an escape into the main chamber.

Kieran had been thinking of late that all the trouble and pain of the last few months had been no more than a training ground to provide him with the endless reserves of patience he increasingly seemed to require. He had been sitting quietly by himself in one of Favrin's carved chairs by the cold fireplace. Something on Favrin's face made Kieran leap to his feet, instantly alert; he was not, however, given the chance to find out what it was that had stung him, because this was the moment when everything began to unravel around them.

A tap on the door made Favrin turn with coiled ferocity, betraying a prince's fury at an order disobeyed. It was followed almost instantly by the fair-haired man who had conducted Kieran and Anghara here and had subsequently withdrawn—Kieran supposed he had gone no further than the guardroom. He had shed the coat and the velvet hat, and now showed himself to be an athletic young man. But the face he turned to his lord was drawn and gray, his eyes blazing with pride and pain. Whatever had happened to bring him here in defiance of Favrin's instructions had to have been momentous—and, after a frozen moment, Kieran knew what it was, the only thing it could be. He was a breath ahead of Favrin himself, who suddenly reached blindly for the nearest support. He did it with the hand holding the two wineglasses; the delicate glass, the secret of whose making was something the south guarded as jealously as the honor of its women, shattered. A thin trail of red wine ran from what had been Anghara's glass, like blood from a wound.

"The court doesn't know yet," Moran said breathlessly, ignoring the staring guest by the hearth. "The *kaissar* brought the message to me first, not a minute ago."

"In the *kaiss*?" Favrin asked, his voice oddly hoarse.

"His chambers," Moran said, shaking his head in swift denial. "Delvera. She will stay quiet."

Favrin bowed his head, brought a hand up to cover his eyes. "Oh, my lord father!" he murmured; it was a private imprecation, words hardly meant to be heard by anyone else. The gesture was woven from pure pain, but the voice was Favrin's usual sardonic tone, rich with irony. "You always knew how to live; small wonder you chose to take the God's hand from the arms of a lover . . ."

Behind Favrin's back, Kieran met Anghara's level gray eyes. Alerted through esoteric senses of her own to impending doom, she had entered the chamber almost at the prince's heels. She knew what had happened, as though Moran, opening the door, had let the news in before him and it had come at once to lay at her feet. This changed things. It changed everything. They had come to speak with an heir; they were now in the presence of a king.

Favrin seemed to remember this, and the two of them, at about the same moment. He lifted his head, straightening his back. "Send the *kaissar* back; make sure Delvera says nothing, not before I've had a chance to speak with her. Then come, and wait." Moran, who had dropped to one knee before his new king, bowed his head briefly in acquiescence and departed. Favrin turned, very slowly, to Anghara, and she was astonished at the change a few charged moments had wrought in him.

"I can offer you sympathy, if not condolences," Anghara said, taking the initiative, after a pause which both seemed reluctant to break. "I too lost a father. But you are hardly likely to share my fate—when this old lion died, the lion cub was grown and ready. Whither Tath now, King Favrin?"

The eager fever that had been in his eyes a moment ago had vanished, replaced by something cool, calculating. "It almost seems as though everything about this was planned," he murmured.

Anghara raised an eyebrow. "If you think I had anything to do with this death, you grievously misjudge me—and the last place I would have been found when the deed was discovered would be my victim's son's own chamber."

Favrin found strength somewhere to laugh. "My father would have enjoyed this. Intrigue was his love," he said laconically. "And it seems to be something of a legacy; a plot was not what I was thinking of, but it isn't entirely beyond the bounds of possibility. I should investigate Delvera's links to Roisinan."

"Your father always did have a penchant for the women of the north."

Favrin's eyes flashed dangerously. "Be careful, young queen, for you may yet step on quicksand."

"I came here on a safe-conduct that was the given word of a prince, and trusted in a knight's honor," Anghara said pointedly.

"But you found a king," Favrin said. He seemed to find the concept strange, as if he couldn't imagine holding all that had been his father's—a *kaiss* full of exotic women, a city, one crown held firm in one hand and free, finally, to reach for a far older and nobler royal circlet.

If it hadn't been for the bright-haired girl before him, who now gathered herself with a royal poise he had yet to discover in himself.

"And shall a king's honor be less than the prince's, and both mean less than the sworn word of a true knight?" his strange guest now inquired from the glittering heights of court protocol.

"No, damn you," Favrin said at last, blood rushing to his cheeks. He lifted his hand, only now seeming to realize the glass had cut him as it shattered and bright blood was welling out from a gash across his palm. He stared at this for a long moment, then closed his hand into a fist around the wound and lifted his eyes to Anghara, stepping aside to clear her path. "My word protects you. Leave this place with honor, as you found it. But go, Anghara Kir Hama. Go now, before it is too late. Remember, though, that ere you can become a true queen in Roisinan two men need to step out of your way; and neither your brother nor I will do so lightly." He raised his good hand, palm open toward her, in a gesture of farewell. "We may yet meet again," he said, in a softer voice, "in some green court in Miranei. Very soon."

Anghara gazed at him for a long moment, and then her eyelashes swept down, veiling her eyes. Kieran was already waiting with her cloak, and she allowed him to drape it over her shoulders.

"Moran," she heard the King of Tath say behind her to the chamberlain who had reappeared in the doorway, "make sure they are conducted from the palace in safety. Thereafter," Favrin said, and he was speaking directly to Kieran now, "my writ does not run. I gave you safe-conduct to enter the White Palace, but my obligation ends at the pierhead; I offer you no promises at all if, tomorrow, I find you still in the city."

"You won't," Kieran said.

The expression on the other's face shaded into something oddly like relief; Kieran, who couldn't begin to understand this subtle prince, found nonetheless that it was all too easy to like the man. Once he had seemed larger than life, the subject of his schoolroom lessons, against whose forces he had first bloodied his sword. He offered, at the last, a smile.

"Tend to that hand," Kieran said softly, turning back from the doorway, meeting Favrin's eyes, blue on blue. "Make sure they get any stray slivers out, else it could stiffen."

"We wouldn't want that to happen," Favrin said, unable to resist meeting this unexpected solicitude with a barb.

Kieran parried the jab with relentless honesty. "It would be a pity . . . and a waste."

With that, he turned and was gone, following Moran into the guardroom to claim his sword. The door snicked gently shut behind him, leaving Favrin to sink into the carved chair Kieran had just vacated and stare at the closed portal. The expression on his face was curiously similar to the one with which he greeted Anghara Kir Hama's entrance an hour and a lifetime ago—astonishment, and reluctant respect.

Kieran didn't volunteer where he got the two horses before the young sun cleared the horizon the next morning, and Anghara didn't ask. In fact, they were doing very little talking. She had balked at leaving Algira. *I nearly had him,* were her despondent words; *another hour, and I would have had him.* But Kieran had seen something he could still not completely define on Favrin's face as he came in from the balcony the night before. No—the chance had been and gone. Favrin would have no time and no room for them, not now—certainly not with every baron at court closely monitoring his smallest move. Favrin was a great soldier—but, for all that his had been the unseen hand on Tath's helm for a long time, he was an untried king. There was too much at stake for him to risk a highly visible intrigue with what was, after all, as yet only another pretender to the throne he himself coveted.

But Anghara had been adamant, a stubbornness owing as much to royal self-confidence as to an almost childish frustration at the denial of a cherished wish. In the end Kieran lost his temper and did something he thought he had almost forgotten how to do—he spoke to her from the only height the yawning chasm between their ranks allowed him, that of older foster brother. Perhaps out of sheer astonishment Anghara had stopped arguing and obeyed. That didn't mean she did it willingly. She had taken up the mantle of royalty, with all its prerogatives, and one of those had been a certain incontestable authority it had been all too easy to become used to. Now she found herself resenting the control Kieran had so easily invoked; relations were strained in the early hours of their ride north.

This persisted through a pause for a lunch so stilted and polite they could have been strangers—or, worse, deadly enemies unable to avoid being seated together at a court banquet. They were both relieved when the meal was over and they could divert their frustrations into the physical exertion of hard riding. Eventually monotony began to restore their good humor; when they stopped for the night, Anghara could ask calmly whether Kieran thought Favrin would have them followed.

"Favrin undoubtedly has other things on his mind," said Kieran. "But I think the respite won't last. The man is nothing if not a ferociously good organizer. Sooner or later he will remember you. He may or may not think you pose a serious threat—but, whatever he decides, it would be in his interest if you never reached Roisinan. And he knows you're still in his land, and in his power, should he choose to stretch it forth. This time he gave you no promises."

"You think he'll come after us?"

"Maybe not just yet," Kieran said, feeling absurdly young and innocent; he almost expected the lanky ghost of Feor to emerge at any moment and rap him over the knuckles for an ill-considered analysis. "Right now he's in the same situation Sif was when he swept into Miranei. For all that Favrin inherited lawfully and Sif simply took what had been offered—both are forced to pay attention to home base first, before they can think about striking further afield. Then again, Favrin will never get this chance again—Sif away from Roisinan, and you in no position to offer him serious opposition. What is it?" he said, with a smile, as he saw her watching him with her head tilted thoughtfully on one side, the corners of her lips turned up, but her eyes glittering with what looked suspiciously like tears.

She held out her hands and he stepped closer and took them, searching her eyes.

"I missed you," she said unexpectedly.

It woke an echo in him, a painful one. The words were innocuous enough in themselves but she had said them to him once before—in a bloody dawn on the battlements of Miranei, a day which seemed a lifetime away. They were different people now, their earlier selves so far removed as to almost be creatures of myth. But Kieran shied away from the memory, shutting it away, his smile widening a fraction as he raised a quizzical eyebrow. "Are hostilities over, then?"

She laughed out loud, squeezing his fingers; her mouth opened to say something when, suddenly, the small tin kettle they hung above the fire boiled over with an angry hiss of steam and they both whirled to rescue it. Anghara was more tired than she would admit, and began nodding off over the mug of lais tea, made from supplies eked out all the way from Kheldrin. She was asleep almost before Kieran gently removed the mug from her hand and wrapped her into a blanket beside the dying fire. This, Kieran reflected wryly as he went to check the horses before he too turned in, was getting to be a habit—sabotaged yet again at what might have easily been a critical juncture. Another wasted moment. Kieran was beginning to assemble a library; he would flip through his collection before going to sleep, sparing a moment of regret for all the might-have-beens he held so gently in his memory.

Anghara was quiet at breakfast, almost as if their reconciliation had never taken place. But it was soon apparent to Kieran that this was a new kind of quiet. What had gone before had been a silence of pique, born of brooding frustration. This was different, deeper, with a pain Kieran couldn't initially understand. He sensed a deep foreboding, and recognized the silence of anticipation. And then, mapping out their journey in his mind, he suddenly understood. The Ronval River lay squarely across their path; not so very long ago, its banks had been soaked with the blood of two armies. On this battlefield Anghara's father had been slain, surrendering his crown into the waiting hands of his firstborn son.

Anghara's wanderings had never taken her so close to this spot. Perhaps she would have reacted differently had she not come here from the heart of Algira, from the palace where the Rashin clan's desire for the crown of Roisinan had wrought her father's death in its defense. It was new again in Anghara's breast, and the pain was sharp, the sharper for being an old pain whose true magnitude was being felt only now.

Kieran tried to work out another path, in the first flash of comprehension, but there were no real alternatives but to cross into Roisinan over the haunted ground of the old battlefield. Everything else would take too long. They needed time to escape across the border, time to reach Roisinan and lead Anghara's army to Miranei before Sif returned from Kheldrin with his own. And while Kieran never doubted there would be an army waiting, he was far from sanguine about its size or its abilities compared to the one it would have to face. The stars had turned in this circle, had offered Anghara this chance. If it was wasted, it might never come again.

"I will be with you," Kieran said into Anghara's silence, without touching her, without looking at her. He only turned his head when he felt the almost electric power of her gaze, to meet a pair of gray eyes brimful of memory. For, once again, the words were an echo, the shadow of a Standing Stone upon the moors before Miranei lay across them, across an hour long gone which had been fraught with another hard choice. The memory was no less potent for Anghara than those clinging to the Ronval battlefield.

"Are you sure," Anghara asked gently, "that you don't have the Sight?"

"Quite sure," Kieran said brightly, breaking the mood. "It's time we were moving; the day will not stay for us."

Anghara knew this, and yet she couldn't suppress a sigh that tore itself from her deepest soul. She made no reply in words. She didn't need to.

The Ronval looked deceptively drab and gray. Kieran had steered them west of the fatal fords where Red Dynan's last battle had been fought—the Ronval, after all, was a border between two kingdoms and the fords were constantly patrolled. There had been a ferry, but that had long since been stopped. They would have to swim the river downstream, at a deeper spot. More dangerous, perhaps, on the physical level, but Kieran had learned enough in the past few years to prefer physical peril to exposing himself and his companion to the unpredictable danger of edgy border guards.

"It looks so innocent," Anghara said, putting some of his own thoughts into words.

"I'd prefer it at our backs," Kieran said. He sniffed at the air, already tainted with the fetid odors of Vallen Fen. "As long as we don't cross into Roisinan branded with the same perfume that led our army to the Rashin men when they tried to cross the Ronval."

Anghara smiled, remembering the story. She allowed herself one regretful backward glance for all the opportunities lost in Algira, and then dug her heels into her horse's flanks.

Kieran took a moment to watch her lead the way into the kingdom she meant to win back, and found himself wrestling with a moment of bittersweet ambivalence. In Roisinan she would be royal again. It was what he wanted her to be, what he had fought and planned for, risked other men's lives, and his own, for; and yet—by the very act of becoming what he had dreamed, she was removing herself from his ambit, a queen to his knight. With every step she took toward the borders of her own land Anghara was taking away choices. In the end there could be only one, and Kieran felt the blade of it against his heart.

His own choices were few. There was little he could do other than urge his horse forward in Anghara's wake.

She had no wish to linger on the other shore, waiting only long enough for Kieran's horse to struggle up the uneven muddy bank before she urged her mare into motion. She kept her face resolutely turned to the north, with only her eyes, wide and bright, betraying her by occasionally straying toward the east and her father's last battlefield. Kieran caught up with her in silence, and they rode for a while without speaking. The plain that spilled out flat and meadow-green from the riverbank was empty of movement; it was easy to imagine themselves alone in the world. But for all that none were in sight, it wasn't as though the people of the place hadn't left traces. Near an isolated copse Anghara drew rein and contemplated with interest what seemed to be a small shrine—but it was a shrine to no God she'd ever known. A broad, carved wooden pole had been set into the ground; its crown was rounded, buffed and polished into a semicircular sphere, and a crest, or a halo, of plaited golden straw had been fixed onto this. Below, at the foot of the pole, lay a number of wreaths. A few had fruit twisted into them, sweet-smelling apples or a wilting peach, but most were of flowers—some dry and already crumbling, others fresh, as though they had only just been left there. The one thing they all had in common was that every one had a trace of yellow—a yellow flower, or a weaving of golden straw, and in at least one Anghara saw a thread of what looked like a thin strand of gold.

"Curious," she said. "What do you make of it?"

"From the flowers, I'd say it was Nual's," said Kieran, leaning forward from his saddle to get a closer look. "But the nearest water is the Ronval, and that's too far away to build a shrine to Nual. Besides, there's gold. That's Kerun's."

"And the fruit of the harvest is Avanna's," murmured Anghara thoughtfully.

"Too many questions," said Kieran after another moment, kneeing his mount into a turn. "We won't learn the answers here."

After another long look, Anghara turned to follow. "Where to now?"

"The Tanassa Hills. If Adamo or Charo aren't there, they'll have left a message. They had no way of knowing which way we might come back; they will have left a message in every stronghold."

"We've been away a long time," Anghara said, her voice oddly flat.

Kieran snatched a look; she was very white, her teeth worrying at her lower lip. "Faith has been bred into them," he said quietly. "The last time you disappeared, they believed for years."

Anghara glanced at him from beneath lowered eyelashes, betrayed into a smile; and then her expression changed, into something more subtle, more sad. "After Sif destroyed Bresse . . . this is where it all began, in the Tanassa Dance," she said. "It's where I first met ai'Jihaar."

Kieran had pieced the tale together from scraps that had come his way, but only now did the story begin to assume its true shape. He tried to imagine the Kheldrini woman, old and blind and yet wrapped in a cocoon of power, away from her desert home, and almost failed. Almost, because in the final reckoning he would have found it hard to believe anything was impossible for ai'Jihaar ma'Hariff. It would not be entirely beyond the bounds of possibility, Kieran thought wryly, if they were to find the old *an'sen'thar* waiting for them in the Tanassa Hills.

It was not, however, ai'Jihaar who met them when they finally slid off their mounts. They stood before the same cavern from which Kieran's men had issued forth to ride after a captured princess on her way to the dungeons of Miranei. They entered carefully, Kieran in the lead, one hand lightly on his horse's bridle. The horse snorted as it stepped inside, alarmingly loud in the dark, echoing silence of the empty cave.

What they thought was an empty cave.

Another horse suddenly answered from the shadows, and Kieran froze, peering into the gloom, halfway through the swift motion toward his horse's muzzle. "Who's there?"

"You took your time," said a familiar voice.

Kieran closed his eyes for a moment, his fingers knotting in the horse's mane. The silently eloquent relief of his gesture was transmuted into radiant joy as his eyes opened and sought eagerly for a man-shaped shadow. "I thought you were lost," Kieran said, very softly.

"You left me with the honor of dealing with Sif Kir Hama's entire army, with the victorious king-general himself at its head. Why in the world should you think me lost?"

"Stop crowing in the dark, young cock-a-hoop, come out and let me see you!" Kieran said, laughing.

A piece of darkness peeled off a cavern wall and flung back a concealing cloak the color of winter twilight, to reveal itself as a stocky young man with an enormous grin splitting his broad face.

"Rochen!" Kieran said, stepping forward to clasp the other's arm. "You've no idea how glad it makes me to see you in one piece! I thought Sif had done for you. We found the camping place, it looked to tell a grim tale."

"Grim indeed," Rochen's voice changed in the space of a heartbeat, from teasing banter to harsh pain. "I had lookouts posted, so at least Sif didn't take us totally by surprise. But there was surprise enough, in the end. Only a handful lived, and most have souvenirs of the encounter. Mine was a sword across the back of my legs from a man I thought dead. I was lucky he didn't hamstring me."

"The others?"

"We gave a good account of ourselves. We fought as best we could. And in that hour we didn't know if you had succeeded, or if you had already failed, and our stand was in vain." His eyes strayed at last to where Anghara waited in silence, a hand rubbing her restive mare's nose. To her he was still half shadow, but there was no mistaking the expression on his face—the pride and exultation as he glanced back at Kieran, the glow of joy as his eyes returned to her and then dropped as he went down on one knee. "It was not vain; those who died there would regret nothing in this hour. I give you welcome, my lady. I wish it could be in a place more fitting . . ."

Anghara took the few steps that divided them and raised him with her own hand. "I saw that campsite. I saw Sif's Army. It would have been a brave band who dared to challenge that. I would have liked to have known them all."

"They knew you," said Rochen gravely. "They all knew you. So do those who now follow in their wake."

"What news, then?" said Kieran briskly. "Where are the twins?"

"Adamo is in the woods below Cascin, where most of the men are gathered."

"Charo?"

Rochen grinned wolfishly. "In Miranei."

"What?" Kieran said sharply.

But Anghara, after the first moment of surprise, laughed quietly, and both men turned at the sound. "His words at our parting by the Hal were that he would be there to open the gates for me. I didn't think he meant literally. What is he doing in Miranei?"

"He's with Melsyr," Kieran's lieutenant said. "He . . ."

"Charo joined Sif's *Guard*?" Kieran demanded incredulously, his eyes wide with disbelief.

"In a way," Rochen said. "To hear him talk you'd swear he and Melsyr were a private army. Even so, they've been making converts for us inside the walls; plenty of the Guard lost stomach for all too many things after your stunt, Kieran, and were ripe for the taking."

"Then we can take the keep?" Kieran said. "If we have men inside, and Adamo is waiting at Cascin with more . . . how many did you manage to gather? Melsyr could let us in through the western postern, and we could be in before anyone was any the wiser."

"Not that easy," Rochen said.

Kieran's eyes clouded for a moment. "How many have we got?" he asked quietly.

Rochen shook his head. "No, you don't understand. The numbers are not the problem. We have plenty. This time there are enough to present a formidable barrier even to Sif's main army—for all that our men are lamentably untrained—let alone a handful of half-won keep guards."

"What, then?"

"Charo swore he wouldn't have it."

Anghara smiled again. "Wouldn't have me enter Miranei?"

"Not until he could throw open the main gates and invite you inside with acclamation," Rochen said, managing to keep a straight face.

"Ever the grand gesture," Kieran said, but without rancor. "Sometimes it's hard to believe he and Adamo are brothers, let alone twins. Ansen was much more . . ."

There was a moment of brittle silence as Kieran abruptly bit off his words. Ansen's ghost hadn't been raised for a long time; the Ansen Kieran invoked had been his close companion at Cascin, not the youth who had grown up to envy, hatred, and betrayal. And yet it was the latter who would always overshadow the more innocent days. The young Ansen might be what triggered a pleasant memory—but it wouldn't be long before it was swamped by the recollection of a long-past midsummer's eve, and a sharp dagger in Ansen's hand.

Rochen didn't know the whole story, but was sensitive to the atmosphere Ansen's name had conjured up. He back-tracked, fast. It's probably best to join Adamo at Cascin as soon as we can. I've been here for a while; maybe there's fresh news."

"Are the men all at Cascin?"

"Not at the house itself. There's a camp hidden in the forest. But Adamo himself is at the manor, with a few lieutenants. Sif's men give the place a wide berth; there are rumors at the han that the manor is haunted."

"Somebody must have seen the new inhabitants prowling around, and it's been deserted for such a long time . . ." Kieran began, but Anghara shook her head.

"It's more than that. There's the Stone."

"What Stone?"

Anghara turned with a smile. "Gul Khaima wasn't the only Standing Stone I raised. There's a Standing Stone at Cascin . . . of a sort. And those things always haunt a place."

Their eyes met briefly, slid apart. Neither said it—that Cascin was also haunted by Ansen's brooding spirit. Cascin's heir had inherited the manor in his own strange, dark way; it would never be free of him. Kieran found a moment to wonder how Adamo was dealing with the shade of his dead brother.

"Well," said Anghara quietly into the moment of silence. "This has proved a true homecoming. The path from Miranei to Kheldrin led through Cascin . . . and it is just as well that Adamo has chosen it for his headquarters. Cascin would have had to lie on my road back; there are things I left there I need to bring with me to Miranei."

"We could stay here tonight, rest your horses . . ." Rochen began.

Anghara shook her head. "There will be time for rest. We rode them hard yet there is life and spirit left in them. We can rest soon enough, in the woods."

"She's right," Kieran said. "Too many things are riding at our back. We need every hour we can snatch."

Rochen wasted no more time, turning to reach for his riding gear. "On our way, then."

Anghara withdrew into solitude during their ride, leaving her two companions to reestablish severed bonds and catch up with one another's doings. Rochen plied his friend with questions and, while there were some he was reluctant to answer, Kieran still found himself doing most of the talking. Later, when they made camp, Anghara sat a little apart beside the fire. Kieran, although keeping a constant and wary eye on her, was content to respect her mood, choosing instead to turn questioner himself and get the full story of what had transpired on the moors before Miranei. Anghara didn't seem to be listening. She sat with her legs drawn into the circle of her arms and her chin resting on her knees, staring into the flames. When she suddenly laughed quietly into the night Rochen physically jumped as if the laughter had ambushed him.

"What is it?" Kieran, more used to Anghara's ways, asked almost casually.

Anghara lifted her eyes and there was a glow in them that wasn't firelight. "He'll be coming home soon," she said slowly. "Many will be back before him; he will be following his army, not leading it. And still he will find enough power to make a stand at Miranei." She laughed again, more sharply, with an edge. "A winter campaign," she said. "That's what it might come to in the end. And by tradition, the one who loses a winter campaign is branded as being of the true Kir Hama line."

"You lost," Kieran pointed out, "last year."

"Not a campaign," Anghara said, tossing her head. "Just my freedom. On that, there is no season."

"Sif is coming?" said Rochen hesitatingly, looking from the one to the other. "How in the God's name does she know his hour?"

"Which God?" Anghara asked sharply, before Kieran had a chance to reply. There had been something, a strange inflexion in his voice . . .

Rochen's reply was intriguing. "Well, it hasn't exactly been forbidden, although it isn't liked by Kerun's lot," he said, a shade defensively. "It's Bran that many swear by now."

"Bran?" Kieran said, mystified. "Who is Bran? Where did all this come from? We haven't been away that long . . ."

"I don't know," Rochen said. "Someone had a revelation. The word went out, and it took. There are no temples, but there are already men who are holy to him, men who serve the new God, and they raise shrines in Bran's name, in their own fashion. It is said that Bran of the Dawning is the new guardian of the bridge into Glas Coil."

New shrines. Kieran suddenly remembered the flower-wreathed pole on the plain. A new God would inherit the name of Gheat Freicadan; a new guardian for an ancient gate. "Where does that leave Kerun?" asked Kieran, curiously bereft at this obliteration of something immortal which had formed a cornerstone to his entire life. And only then did he make a connection. Bran. In Kheldrin it had been a winged goddess called ai'Bre'hinnah. And the prototype for both had been a name he had released into the night, a name which had once disguised an exiled princess.

His eyes sought Anghara's, and in them he read equal comprehension. He remembered ai'Jihaar's voice in the desert night: *You might well become a Changer for your own land.*

Glas Coil had survived; but a new God had come to guard its gates. Bran of the Dawning, Rochen had called him. And a new Goddess stood in the portals of the Land of Twilight across the sea. Brother and sister; husband and wife—a making whole of two separate halves.

"You must tell me more of this new God," Anghara said very quietly. Her eyes strayed for a moment into the fire, passed over the flames, and then flicked back as though riveted there by something. "There's a ship coming in," she said quietly, her voice making even Kieran's hackles rise. "Men will step ashore in Calabra tonight, and find their native land stranger by far than the strange country their king led them forth to suffer in."

Even though it was no longer possible for him to see it with his physical eyes, Kieran's mind could easily supply the gleam of golden soul fire which must have wreathed Anghara in this moment—and yet another thing fell into place. The straw halo on the carved pole raised to Bran was a crude attempt to depict that golden glow. They had been wrong when they tried to analyze the shrine in terms of Roisinan's ancient Triad. There was nothing there of Nual, Kerun or Avanna. It was all Anghara's. Brynna's. Bran's.

Rochen stared at Anghara, his feelings plainly written on his face—something between horror-struck awe and adoration. This would be a thing that would follow her wherever she walked amongst her people. Kieran had to admit defeat on one point and agree with his queen that in this, at the very least, she had been right when she said she was no longer human. She was already beyond herself. She was becoming the incarnation of a legend before his very eyes.

As if being queen was not enough.

He stood quietly and went to rummage in their packs for the last remnants of the lais. In the aftermath of vision, Anghara would need rest; tonight, at least, he could provide it. After that, she was on her own.

They crossed into the straggling edges of Bodmer Forest by the sunset of the next day, and were deep into its secret paths by the following day. Anghara watched with interest as Rochen and Kieran navigated by signals invisible to anyone else—they'd ride a narrow path through the underbrush and emerge into campground clearings, or veer from a broad and well-defined way into what appeared to be no more than a wilderness of fern and scrub, only to find a hidden path. They moved surprisingly quickly for all that they were hindered by the terrain, and it was with a start that Anghara reined in her mare at Kieran's signal. She saw a man wearing a forest-green cloak and carrying a long woodsman's bow step into their path from amongst the trees.

"Ho, Mical," said Rochen calmly, as though he had parted with the forest guard a matter of hours before. "I bring guests."

Mical, eyes shining, glanced from Rochen to his companions. "Guests?" he all but whooped, protocol forgotten as his eyes met Kieran's. "Friends, rather, unlooked for! Welcome back, Kieran!" And then, recollecting himself, he dropped onto one knee and lifted his face to Anghara. "Welcome, my lady!"

"Yes," said another, more familiar voice; Adamo, wrapped in a cloak the mate of Mical's, stepped from behind his man. "Welcome home."

Rochen rode in the van, leading the small procession into the camp in the woods beyond Cascin. Kieran followed just behind, his head bare, smiling gently to himself. Mical had remained at his guard post, and thus it was that Anghara and Adamo brought up the rear in the deep, companionable silence she had always associated with her cousin and foster brother. Some instinct made her keep her hood pulled well forward, and she rode shadowed, a slight, anonymous figure who was by this small ruse given an instant where she could be the observer and not the observed. Word had gone ahead in some mysterious manner, but had obviously not included all the details. It was Kieran's name that greeted them as they rode into the camp. It was the first time Anghara had seen him with a larger body of his men, and she was both touched and strangely shaken to see the affection and deep respect that brought them pouring out of their tents and cabins to welcome him. His horse was ringed ten-deep with grinning, whooping men; Kieran had a name and word for most, and a warm smile for those he had yet to meet.

"They love him," Anghara murmured.

"If you were the candle he held out to them, his was the hand that bore the light," said Adamo, oddly eloquent for once. "Yes, they love him."

Anghara glanced at her companion, and wasn't surprised

to see his expression bearing no less pride and fierce affection than the men around them. To Adamo and Charo their brother Ansen had often been condescending and overbearing. Kieran hadn't always been a perfect older brother, but for all his occasional impatience he had been closer to them than Ansen ever managed. The two younger Cascin sons had hero-worshipped Kieran since earliest childhood, shadowing him since they had been old enough to walk. The Taurin twins had been amongst the first of his band; they were still the youngest holding positions of authority—although Kieran sometimes entertained doubts, despite his indisputable flashes of brilliance and courage, as to Charo's suitability as a leader and a role model.

But Anghara was out of time to muse and ponder. There were those in the crowd who, if they didn't know precisely where Kieran had been, knew well with whom he had left. Curious eyes turned to the slight, shrouded rider. And then Kieran turned, catching Adamo's eye, and Adamo slipped from his horse and came to Anghara's mount to help her down. His action focused hundreds of pairs of eyes on her. She allowed herself a small sigh as Adamo helped her alight, throwing back her hood with a toss of her head; this was how it would always be, from now on. This was the reason Sif craved the crown. It must have been a heady feeling for the youth whose semi-royal status as the king's bastard meant he had never been a true prince in his own right, to see men bending their knee before him. Perhaps he would have known what to say in this moment, some powerful, exhorting speech, girding his men's hearts with that insane courage with which they seemed to follow him. But Anghara had no such speeches. The moment held her spellbound; she struggled to find words, completely unaware of how eloquently the expression on her face and in her eyes spoke to the men gathered in her name. In the end, she didn't need to say anything, because they said it for her. One man in the front ranks had risen, and stepped forward to bow over her hand. She recognized him: Bron, who had been with her foster brothers and herself on that wild ride from Miranei, with Sif's army treading on their heels.

"Tomorrow, my lady," he said, "in Miranei."

They might have rehearsed it, so flawlessly did the rest follow. There was a beat of silence as men looked at one another, met each other's eyes in recognition of a war cry. And then it was raised, in perfect unison, as they lifted clenched fists into the air—hundreds of voices, a vow of thunder. *"Tomorrow, in Miranei!"*

Anghara found the words she needed, only two. She had clung to Bron's hand, her vision swimming in sudden tears, and now she freed her hand gently, bringing it up to clasp it with the other on her breast, a gesture of gratitude as old as time. Her voice was a whisper in the wind, but every man heard her. "Thank you."

It was Adamo who allowed this scene to run precisely long enough to maximize its impact, before leading up Anghara's horse and advising the young queen to continue on to the manor and rest from her journey. Anghara, who had spent more than she knew on this instant of rapport, suddenly felt drained of every ounce of strength and energy she had ever possessed, and was all too happy to take his advice.

But Kieran was the camp's for the moment, until all his men could have the chance to talk, to ask, to welcome him back. It was an oddly wrenching experience for them to take different paths—it was as hard for Kieran not to watch until Anghara's horse passed out of sight as it was for Anghara not to ride with her head turned back toward the camp. She felt strangely cold and exposed, as though a shield had been torn away; she had grown used to having him around every moment of every day, waking and sleeping, hers, a different Kieran to the one who had just vanished into the throng of excited men.

"He'll be back," Adamo said unexpectedly, showing a startling ability to read the situation. "I'll be surprised if he stays away an hour before he rides into Cascin to find out if we've tucked you in properly."

Anghara swung round to glare at him, but he looked so serenely complacent it was difficult to do anything but admit a direct hit with a smile. "He has taken good care of me," she said.

"Feor made you his Responsibility," Adamo said, and Anghara could hear the capital. "Kieran has never been aught but responsible."

You are the hawk I will send to seek for her . . . Yes, there was that; Feor had begun Kieran's quest. But there was something in Anghara that flinched at the logic. She sought refuge in memory—it had begun long before the responsibility was passed. Anghara recalled a rainy day in Cascin, and a cloak a young boy had flung over her shoulders. And then, on a midsummer's eve some years after, a night when she had been the one to have taken Responsibility—and precipitated so many tragedies . . .

Anghara felt her breath catch painfully as she saw the manor appear through the trees. Other memories crowded in—of cold exile, bewildered hurt and incomprehension at what was happening to her, and then of what she had found in this place.

Welcome home.

Anghara had never thought of it as such until Adamo had said it, back in the woods with Mical. That word had always conjured up Miranei—the Miranei whose perfect image she had carried in her heart ever since she had left it at the age of nine, running from the whirlwind. But now she discovered it was all too easy to think of Cascin of the Wells as home. For all the upheavals and the searing memories tied to this place, it had also been the setting for so many gentler things. Anghara's parents had always been distant—her father doted on her, but had little time to share with a young girl-child; her mother, capable of fighting like a tigress for her child's life and inheritance, loved her dearly—but was, nevertheless, queen first and mother second. Anghara had forfeited a world when she fled to Cascin—but she had gained a family.

And lost them all, she realized in the next moment—all but the child Drya who had been too young for anything enduring to have grown between them, and the youth who rode beside her and his brittle, brilliant twin. There were other things in Cascin besides intangible memories and dreams. There were graves.

She turned to Adamo. "I'll come to the house a little later," she said quietly. "I would go first to the vaults."

"The dead will stay for you," Adamo said, his eyes soft. "It would be better . . ."

"I wouldn't rest," she said. "Not until I have gone to them."

"All right," Adamo said after a pause. "I'll take you."

"Adamo . . . I'd like to go alone."

He was silent for a moment, and then smiled, reaching to touch her cheek. "I understand," he said. "I'll wait for you by the Well."

"I know the way home," said Anghara, dimpling at him. "You don't have to ride guard on me; I'm sure these woods are crawling with your men."

"If you were our Brynna," Adamo said, "I'd leave you your solitude. But you are no longer Brynna; you are Anghara Kir Hama, and you will never be alone again."

Hama dan ar'i'id. The saying flashed briefly across her mind, bringing a breath of hot desert wind into this misty land of moss, bracken and laughing streams. *You are never alone in the desert . . . you will never be alone again.*

Anghara bowed her head, acknowledging the inevitable.

Adamo shifted in his saddle. "No one will intrude. Go, give them greeting. I'll be waiting for you."

She didn't stay long; for her the place was haunted in more ways than if she'd been an ordinary mourner. She had the Sight, and knew how Chella had died; and Chella's was a restless and pervasive ghost, for all that she would never hold the manner of her death against her niece, whose turbulent life had inevitably shaped her own. Lyme was in the crypt beside his lady, but the other restless ghost haunting this burial ground was one whose power lay in the very absence of his bones. Ansen lay buried far from his family—yet his angry, brooding spirit was as much a part of this place as any whose moldering remains lay beneath the gray stone slabs. It was an unquiet burial ground, and its unease was mirrored in Anghara's eyes as she rode back to where Adamo had dismounted and now sat on a storm-felled tree trunk. On the face of it he was totally relaxed and at ease, his eyes closed, leaning against another tree trunk growing close behind him. But his head turned fractionally at the sound of her approach, and when his eyes opened a moment later they were full of understanding.

"I should have warned you."

Anghara laughed dryly. "Rochen said the place was haunted."

"Not the house," Adamo said firmly, getting to his feet. "But here . . . I always feel him, and he's stronger than any buried here, for all that he lies far away in an unmarked grave."

She could cry for Ansen—for the anger, the resentment, the waste. Adamo saw her gray eyes film with tears, and looked away, busying himself with his horse. Charo, more alike to Ansen than he ever knew, had recoiled from their brother when he had learned the full truth of what Ansen had done, disowning even his memory. Charo had never wept for him. With the same capacity for deep passion Ansen had possessed, albeit tempered in his case with a lightness of spirit, Charo was aware at some deep level just how close he was to the chasms that had swallowed his brother. He had chosen to turn away, clinging instead to his loyalty to Kieran and Anghara with the same fervor that Ansen had devoted to the pursuit of his own darker goals. But Adamo had wept quietly for his older brother—not for his death, but for his life. He had Ansen's intensity, but not his arrogance; he had a measure of real understanding for what had led to Ansen's fall. And, unlike Charo, he had embraced the knowledge, not buried it. Ansen couldn't touch Charo, for whom he had ceased to exist. But Cascin's flawed heir could reach and shake his other brother through the very bridge of his empathy—and now, Adamo saw Ansen had the same power over the cousin and foster sister he had once done his utmost to destroy.

Adamo urged his horse forward, brushing Anghara's arm in a comforting caress. "Come," he said. "There *is* peace to be had here. Come to the manor."

They returned to the great house, and Anghara was shown into her old room. All the memories of this particular sanctuary were good ones, and they gave her rest, and healing. She slept for hours, the sleep of the exhausted and the innocent; when she woke, rested and alert, it was to realize she had slept away the afternoon and right through the night; the light filtering through her window was the pearly light of morning. Somewhere in the trees beyond the house she could hear a weave of birdsong, and smiled as she recognized the same sound she had woken to for years in this room. The memory of her morning routine washed back, so strong it was almost more than she could do not to braid her hair and run for Feor's schoolroom before she was late for the morning lesson.

The pull of the schoolroom proved entirely too much to

resist when she finally got up and made herself presentable. She could have been forgiven for the sharp intake of breath when she pushed the door ajar and was greeted by a familiar scene. It looked as though the same fire burned in the grate, with the chairs arranged around the hearth just as they had been when Anghara had sat here with Ansen and Kieran, analyzing her father's battles and nursing her secret identity. The chairs were occupied, and Anghara jumped when one creaked, and Kieran's face popped around to look at the door.

"About time," he remarked equably. "We were about to start without you."

There was no need to ask what they had been about to start—the room was piled with maps and letters, and in one corner, incongruous in this place of learning, rested a stack of naked swords, with three long spears leaning against the wall. The men in this room were a war council, beginning to plan for tomorrow—that tomorrow they had sworn to see in Miranei.

This interlude in Cascin, time to rest and plan, was the last step in a long journey. The three children who had grown up in this house began to appreciate Feor's true legacy, as the qualities and abilities he had fostered in them quietly came into their own in the planning of the taking of Miranei. It was here, as much as anywhere, that Kieran had become a leader of men, that Anghara had unobtrusively changed into a young queen. The small select circle—Kieran, Anghara, Adamo, Rochen, and two more of Kieran's lieutenants—sat and planned, aware that every hour slipping past was one hour less they had to put those plans into action before Sif returned. They had to work fast, and they knew it—and yet they had to resist the temptation to work too fast. A sloppy plan could fail—and there would be no second chance.

It took them several days to hammer out the beginnings of a plot, and at the end of that time Anghara paid another visit to the family graves, this time accompanied by an unexpected ghost. Beside the stone-sealed niche which held the remains of Rima's mother, Anghara's grandmother whom she had never met, Anghara vividly recalled her first visit to this place. It was only days after her arrival at Cascin as a bewildered nine-year-old. March had accompanied her then, guiding her hand toward a specific carving on the frieze adorning the stone covering her Grandmother's grave. He showed how a piece of the stone could slide out and reveal a long, narrow, dusty hiding place. They'd pulled out a handful of childhood treasures—relics of Rima's childhood, and for a moment Anghara had been distracted by the sudden insight into her mother's past. But soon the niche was empty, waiting for the next treasure it would to be called upon to guard—the document weighed with the Council Lords' seals. Anghara held it in both hands as if it were too heavy to support with just one. In some ways, it was—this was the proof and bond of her inheritance, bearing witness to her crowning. March had taken it and laid it with gentle reverence into the narrow space; they had replaced the stone, sealing the document into its secret chamber. Nobody would have thought anything was amiss; the graves would need to be taken apart stone by stone for the document to be discovered by anyone who didn't know precisely where and how to look.

Now, returning to claim it, Anghara heard March's voice float down to her through the years. "One day, Princess, this will take you home."

And now that day was here. Even Kieran hadn't known about this—half his work was already accomplished by the simple existence of this paper, wrought years before he began striving toward the very goal it embodied. For a moment, when Anghara had told the little council of war about it, he vividly recalled his earlier sense of betrayal, when he had first learned that Anghara wasn't the innocent foster sister he thought her to be, and hadn't trusted him with her secret identity. And then, as he had done before, he grew ashamed of holding her responsible for secrets others had thrust upon her. He stopped thinking of the document as yet another thing she had kept hidden, and started to build it constructively into their plans.

It was Rochen who was charged with taking the document to the Keep Under the Mountain, and with making sure it became common knowledge before Anghara herself swept into Miranei. He left within the hour, alone, with the precious paper wrapped in a cocoon of yellow jin'aaz silk from Kheldrin. The rest made preparations for their own departure, set for twelve days hence—striking the forest camp at Cascin, and organizing the fighting force into the arrow of a new God, ready to be loosed—to find their mark, or perish in the attempt.

Adamo, Kieran and Anghara, the son of Cascin and the two who had fostered there, found they had little time to themselves. They managed to snatch an hour or two in the evenings to sit by the fire and talk of old times, of things other than the battles looming before them—but the battles were all-pervasive and it proved difficult to keep their mind off them. All too soon the time had sped, and Cascin was ready to let them go. On the eve of their departure Anghara rode up to the family vaults, perhaps for the last time, to say goodbye. Alone, in defiance of Adamo's words of prophecy—or so she thought.

It was with an odd sense of history that Kieran climbed after her to the family graveyard when she had been there too long for his peace of mind—to find her crying quietly as she leaned on her grandmother's tomb and gazed in the direction of Miranei.

"What is it?" he said, stung by a pang of sudden fear.

"It's begun," Anghara whispered, almost too softly for him to hear, her voice drowned beneath the muffling of her tears. "I felt them die . . ."

"Who?" Kieran asked, a cold shiver running down his spine as he thought of all the friends who were in Miranei in this hour of reckoning.

"I don't know them. Some of them . . . were Sif's. But Rochen . . ."

Kieran clutched her shoulder. It never occurred to him to doubt her words. "What of Rochen? Is he . . . dead?"

"No . . . I cannot tell if it has happened, or is yet to come—but I saw him laid out, very white, a bloody bandage around his left shoulder . . . not dead!" She cried out, as his fingers tightened painfully. "Wounded—but there is blood—there is so much blood . . ."

She swayed toward him and he caught her, holding her close, burying his face in her hair as she clung to him with both hands twisted into the material of his tunic. Here, in the charmed circle where their childhood yet clung to them, Kieran was still the rampart against which all terrors crumbled—he still had the power to protect her against anything, even the nightmares flung at her by Sight. She quietened in his arms, relaxing her grip, smoothing his tunic with a strangled sob.

"It's just as well I won't be leading the men into battle," she said, her tone filled with self-reproach. "These fits take me when they choose . . ." She sniffed, wiped tears off her cheek with the back of her hand and lifted her head, with a smile that looked like sunshine breaking through rain. Strands of her hair curled around her face; her eyes were red, her cheeks smudged with traces of tears—but she had never been as beautiful. Kieran's arms tightened around her instinctively, but here, in the haven where she was strong, she was oblivious to the source of that strength. Her thoughts had already ranged wide, to the army of men waiting under the eaves of Cascin's woods for a signal to depart. "Are they ready?"

"We leave in the morning," Kieran said quietly, releasing her. "They will be ready. Will you be all right?"

"Riding out under my own banner, with you at my side and an army at my back? How could I not be all right?"

It was simple faith. But now wasn't the time to ask or expect more of her—and Kieran had been sustained in his faith for years. But that had been before he knew he loved her. Before he knew faith was not enough.

The army raised the ancient Kir Hama banner and rode out at dawn the next day. Halas Han lay in their path, the only road north out of Cascin led through it; they found the place packed with the usual crowd of traders, river-men, journeymen singers, and an assortment of travellers breaking their journey at the han. It was also tenanted by a small *cheta* of Sif's men. There was no skirmish to speak of—Sif's handful of soldiers were far too experienced to make a pointless stand against an army. Once they understood who rode beneath the banner they had thought of as their master's, many joined Anghara's forces, while those who didn't were too demoralized to put up a fight. And the acclamations which almost raised the roof of the han once the common people learned who led the forces before them were all that Charo could have wished.

It would have been too much to ask for them to proceed unremarked; they found every place on their road waiting for them. In places where Sif was strong they were met with a show of force; in others they were greeted with joyous shouts by the local populace, who had already dealt with Sif's men themselves. Time and again they marched away with their numbers swelled by those who had followed Sif only for the Kir Hama name, who came forward in increasing numbers to pledge their faith to Anghara. It didn't escape Kieran that many worshipped the new God, Bran.

It was inevitable that Miranei knew of their coming long before they were near. The keep was poised on a knife-edge, with men loyal to both Kir Hama scions trapped within its walls. There had been no word since Rochen had departed, not unless Anghara's vision was counted; and there were men in Miranei with longbows, and far-reaching arrows. Kieran took Anghara no closer than necessary, and the army made camp within sight but well out of bowshot.

A tent was raised for her in the encampment, with its own guard. At her campfire, one of the dozens that had been lit, Anghara stood with her elbows cupped into her palms and stared dry-eyed at the castle. The image she had taken away as a child hadn't changed, except for the different pennants flying from the high towers. She couldn't tell what she felt at the sight. She seethed with a strange mixture of elation, fierce pride, and abject terror—the last time she had seen Miranei it had not been as a returning queen or an avenger. She remembered the dungeons of Miranei, and trembled. They were the most recent memory, not the hall where she had been crowned when she was nine.

Kieran, watchful and waiting, didn't rest. He paced the camp, exchanging a few words at every campfire, passing a moment with the men at the picket lines, with the surgeons who were grimly preparing for the inevitable on the morrow. He was a shadow that passed like hope through the ranks, and where he went men turned away with a sigh of release and tried to grab a few precious hours of sleep. At length he came to Anghara's own tent; the guards, recognizing him, retreated a few paces, giving their queen and her commander a shell of privacy.

"Tomorrow, in Miranei," Kieran said softly.

She had been wrapped in her own thoughts, and started at the sound of his voice; he grinned with an almost childish sense of triumph at having caught her out.

She tried to offer a smile in return, but suddenly, as though triggered by his arrival, the tears she had held at bay in her solitary vigil glinted in the firelight. "I'm afraid to think about it," she murmured.

"You're going home," he said. "That's all you need to think about."

"I dare not look into the fire," Anghara said, as her eyes slid past his into the flames and then hurriedly out again into the darkness. "Being afraid of an unknown future is in all of us . . . but it would be infinitely worse . . . I don't think I could face tomorrow if I knew what it really held."

"We have not come so far to fail," Kieran said.

The smile she couldn't find a moment ago now came as she looked up at him from underneath her lashes. "You keep me sane," she said softly. "Tomorrow . . ."

"Everything according to our plans," he said. "You will wait here, until I come back for you." He anticipated her next sentence, reaching out to tuck away a stray tendril of bright hair. "I will be back," he repeated. "Don't doubt that."

She looked at him for a long moment, and then nodded slowly. "I know."

He melted away into the shadows, sketching her a low, graceful Kheldrini bow. She smiled at the place he had been, and turned away from the black bulk of Miranei. Once more, Kieran left rest and faith in his wake. Anghara retired into her tent and discovered she could sleep, only a few hours before the confrontation that would decide her fate.

They were gone, Kieran and a few dozen men, when Anghara woke into the pale light of sunrise seeping through her tent flaps. He'd said he would be back for her, to escort her into her city; she donned the gold robes of the desert and hung the *say'yin* with her father's Great Seal around her neck. And then she waited for Kieran's return.

It seemed as though the sun was hurtling through the sky. No sooner did it rise than it seemed to be noon, and the sun hung hot and still above the encampment.

"What is happening out there?" Anghara, flushed with tension and fear, asked Adamo, whom Kieran had left in command of the camp. "Surely they've been gone too long . . . was that fighting I could hear on the battlements?"

"Wait," he said, in his usual sparing manner. He had his orders; and the hour in which he was to act was not yet upon them.

It was almost four hours past noon before sentries hurried over to report movement at Miranei's gates. A group of armored men on horseback had broken away from the keep, one of them bearing Anghara's banner. Which was also Sif's. Adamo and Anghara waited by her tent; her men stood with swords loose in their scabbards, and archers stood by with arrows poised on bowstrings, ready to let fly.

Another sentry came back toward the tent, pausing to offer a sketchy bow to Anghara before blurting that the riders had been recognized. But it wasn't until she saw Kieran riding bareheaded, with Melsyr at his side bearing her banner with a triumphant smile, that Anghara could allow herself to breathe again. She caught at Adamo's arm for support, and he stepped forward flawlessly, as though the gesture had been a command to conduct her to the riders from Miranei.

In the first instant Anghara had eyes only for Kieran, reaching for him with one hand as if to make sure he was really there. He leaned down from the saddle to take it. There was weariness in his face, and blood on his armor. None of it was his—but it was the first thing Anghara saw, and she clung to him for a moment, eyes wide with the sudden shocking thought that she could so easily have lost him.

"Are you all right?"

"In one piece," he said, with an economy of words almost on a par with Adamo. And then his eyes slid from her face, up to the gray battlements of Miranei, and down again. "It is yours," he said simply.

It was still Miranei the impregnable—for they had been let into the keep by the postern gate by Melsyr, Charo and their men. Kieran, although he knew that there had been no other way, had brooded upon the necessity of this treachery, for it had never been in him to fight his battles from the rear; but a frontal assault on Miranei was suicide. As it was, they had been in before the startled garrison had really known what was happening, with all their attention fixed on the army encampment down below. There had been just as many who raised arms for Anghara in Sif's Guard as there had been opposing her; Charo and Melsyr had done their work well. What resistance there had been was fierce—but in the end it had been no great task to overwhelm the defenders.

And now the great gates stood open, waiting. Adamo had signalled for Anghara's horse and it was brought, turned out in royal style in silk and silver. With Kieran on one side and Melsyr with the banner on the other, Anghara rode out to claim Miranei.

Charo, as he had once promised, was waiting at the gate to greet her, mail hood thrown back to allow the breeze to play with his pale hair. In an unconscious echo of his brother, he rode up to bow over her hand and then raised his head, beaming. "Welcome home."

But it felt less like home. The path left open for them to ride through was lined with the people of Miranei—quiet, watchful, even anxious. Anghara's return had been on everyone's lips for weeks—but now she was here, in the wake of the skirmishes in the keep, they could see the shaping of another war in which they could very easily be ground between two armies. It was hard for some of the ordinary folk of Miranei, despite all the evidence they had heard, to fully accept her return from the dead. There was a murmur in the crowd, like wind stirring fallen leaves, and underneath that a wary silence as Anghara's horse passed through the gate and into the city.

And then it was shattered by a single cry, a woman's voice cracking with passion, "My lady!"

Anghara's head snapped around. "Catlin?" she whispered.

And Catlin, for it was she, fought past a couple of gawking apprentices standing in her way and ran to Anghara's horse, tears streaming down her face. For a moment she couldn't speak for sobbing. "The Gods be praised," she managed at last, gulping it out as she clung to Anghara's skirts. "The Gods be praised for sending you back to us!"

Anghara was finding it hard to speak past a lump that had lodged in her throat—this had been the first companion of her exile, one of two friends who had been with her from the start. The only one still there at the end. "Come up," she said after a moment in which she fought to keep her composure. She turned her head a fraction, catching Adamo's eye. "Can you . . ."

"Lady Catlin, with your permission, I will take you in," he said courteously, taking his cue and leaning down from his horse.

With a last lingering glance at her mistress, Catlin turned away only long enough to accept the proffered hand, and Adamo hoisted her into the saddle before him amidst envious looks from the crowd. Catlin sat shaking as though with ague, unable to tear her gaze from Anghara's face.

The incident had cracked the crowd, and the murmurs were louder, with people turning and nodding sagely at one another. This was confirmation indeed. But still there was a deep stillness at the root of the whispers, a holding back—almost unwilling, ashamed of its own existence, but there, impossible to bypass.

Until Kieran's sword sang free of its scabbard and swung in an arc that made the closest in the crowd shy away with a gasp of fear. He reached with the sword over their heads to lift one of the topmost garlands from a shrine to Bran which stood in an alcove a few paces to the side of the street. As it slid down the blade he caught it, sheathed the sword in one smooth movement, and lifted the purloined garland above his head with both hands.

"Today," he said, his voice intense enough to be heard by the gasping throng, changing the war cry of the young queen's army. "Today, in Miranei—Roisinan's own queen!"

With the polished grace of the accomplished horseman, he stood in his stirrups and held the garland for a breathless moment over Anghara's bare head before lowering it gently like a crown.

It might have cut both ways; there could have been devout worshippers of the new God in the crowd who might have taken this gesture amiss. But as Kieran had gambled, Anghara completed the moment of power by responding in a manner beyond conscious control—the flame of her soul fire blazed forth, and even those without sight saw the garland shine like a crown of true gold. Those with the Sight—there weren't many left in Miranei, but enough with eyes to See—gasped and stared at the golden glow. Perhaps it was such a one, unable to hold in her wonder, who cried out Anghara's name in a passionate avowal of fidelity and belief. It was taken up, slowly at first but gathering momentum until it rolled in the crowd like a wave and shook the old walls of Miranei. The cry followed them into the keep, and Charo, riding beside his brother, wore a smile of smug triumph, as if he had arranged the whole thing himself. This was the way he had wanted it to happen, for Anghara to ride into her city on the wings of her people's love and acclamation. Adamo forbore to comment that it had been Catlin's spontaneous affirmation and Kieran's potent crowning of his queen with a garland of flowers that had precipitated the cheers. Charo was still reliving the glory as they retreated into the royal chambers of the King's Tower. There they collapsed gratefully into chairs beside the fire burning brightly in the great hearth, each claiming a glass of wine to replenish all they had spent on this day.

Despite the core of exhilaration which burned quietly in them all, they felt too exhausted and wearied to contemplate any further celebration. Only Charo was unquenchable, bubbling with excitement, filled with it like a glass of sparkling wine, blazing with a great light.

"We did it," he said, lifting his goblet in a salute. "We really did it!"

Kieran looked up, met the eyes first of Melsyr, then of Anghara. He glanced back at Charo and his expression was curious, but he kept his counsel. It was left to Anghara to answer her youngest foster brother as she cradled her own goblet in her hands.

"There is still one thing left to do," she said, "the hardest."

"What?" Charo said with his usual swift impatience. "What is there left that we haven't already accomplished?"

Anghara had looked away, into the flames, and her voice was slow and distant, like the resonant echo of a great bell. Her reply shaped an eternity into a single word.

"Wait," she said simply.

The days remained balmy, but a distinct nip was beginning to be felt in the evening air, and the morning mists flowing down from the mountains began to curl with the promise of winter chill. The leaves in the enclosed garden beyond the Royal Tower had turned, and some branches were already bare; inside the keep, the fires had been lit. The old stone stored up the cold, and breathed it out—and nowhere was it colder, to one as sensitive to atmosphere as Anghara, than the royal apartments in the tower. This was the room where Anghara had been conceived, where Rima had died, where the tragic Senena had carried Sif's unborn heir. Sitting beside the fire, wrapped in a robe of gray wolf-fur, Anghara shivered. There were too many ghosts sharing the room.

The ghosts of the dead—and of the living. Days ago the fire had given her the vision of Sif stepping off his swan-prowed ship in Calabra, grim-faced and set. The flames were showing her he was on his way to Miranei even now. The news of her claiming of Miranei would have met him on the wharf, although it would have been a brave man who dared to tell it. Sif had wasted no time in gathering his men—he still had enough to form the core of a formidable army—and leading them north. And the men he led would see him as a rightful king seeking to restore his reign. After an initial guarded wariness, the land had risen wholeheartedly for the young queen it had once mourned as dead, but Sif still saw himself as the only true King Under the Mountain. And because he did, his men could do no other. A human king, over a human people, who had tried to scour the gift of vision from his people's soul—and who, if he could not reclaim his throne and restore his edicts, was even now faced with the utter confusion and failure of all his schemes. Not only had the "witch-queen," whom he had thought safely buried, returned to Miranei, she had become part of a new faith—and a new God that was partially of her making had greeted his return to Roisinan.

Sif had always been a powerful distraction. Anghara was so absorbed that Kieran had to knock twice before she called on him to enter. She looked up with a whimsical grin; they held the keep ready for action at any time, and Kieran was never parted from his sword, not even when entering his queen's chambers. The sight of the white ki'thar skin girding his waist had drawn her smile—for a man of Shaymir, his sword belt was the ultimate irony. "Khelsie!" any Shaymiri worth his salt would spit at the sight of it. But like Anghara, Kieran had been touched and changed by Kheldrin's potent power. He hadn't uttered the word Khelsie in months. He no longer thought of them in those terms.

"Have you eaten?" Kieran said, slipping easily into his old protective mode as he saw her alone, curled in her armchair by the fireside. "Sitting out here and pulling Sight out of the fire won't make Sif come any faster. And at this rate you'll be a wraith by the time he arrives. A fine queen you'll make to greet him."

"I'll greet him, and he'll know who I am," Anghara said, her smile full of subtly barbed innocence. There had been times of soul-searching when she was far from sure she could be the queen Roisinan needed—but she had come to terms with that. "And he will be here sooner than we think."

"Well, all the posterns are guarded by loyal men," Kieran

said equably. "He won't find it as easy to take Miranei a second time." He hesitated—there was an edge between the two of them these days, which both were dancing around gingerly—and then subsided gracefully at Anghara's feet. She gazed at the shadows the dancing flames cast on his features.

"You look tired," she said unexpectedly. "Are you doing it all yourself, as usual?"

Kieran looked up, reaching to rake his fingers through his dark hair. "No," he said. "There are plenty of good men to help. Adamo and Charo make a great team; with twins on your side you can literally have a man in two places at once, and I learned to appreciate that gift a long time ago. Rochen isn't always in the sweetest of tempers—it's the frustration of his wound, and the knowledge that the begetting of it was his own fault. By the Gods, for breaking cover so impetuously, I'd have almost taken him for Charo! But when he has been himself, he has been a rock. And Melsyr . . . Melsyr has his eye on becoming First General."

"I thought that was you."

"Am I?" Kieran said, with genuine surprise. The question of formal titles had never arisen.

"You've been one in all but name for years," Anghara said. "Are you telling me you don't want the job?"

"I don't know," Kieran said. He was something . . . different. He had been both friend and guardian. He had been the one to guard the path to her throne; he had been the one to crown her in the sight of the people, even if it had only been with a wreath of flowers. He was less than a general—and so much more. Most of the men under his command had been his companions during his outlaw years, and were his through friendship rather than set command structures. Kieran found himself curiously reluctant to formalize that relationship now. But he looked up with a lopsided grin. "Are you appointing me?"

"I might need to appoint someone," Anghara said. "Sooner than I know."

Kieran glanced into the fire. "It's better any day to have one Sighted guardian by the fire than a hundred spies in the field," he said, with just the faintest touch of irony. "I don't doubt you will tell me the exact hour in which Sif Kir Hama will appear below Miranei. Do your visions also show what happens then?"

It had been a largely rhetorical question, but Anghara's monosyllabic reply brought Kieran's head up sharply, his eyes wide with shock.

"No," she said.

A dozen thoughts exploded in Kieran's mind at once like a flock of startled pigeons. Not least was a sudden appalling fear that Kheldrin had not, after all, completed its work and that parts of Anghara remained permanently lost. He could find no words at all, and then Anghara smiled into the silence, softening the blow.

"No. Everything is closed and misty. I've been trying to move past that for hours, but it seems there are some things it isn't good for a mortal to know ahead of time."

"You once said you weren't," Kieran blurted, forgetting he had taken her to task at the time.

"That is still true, up to a point," Anghara said. "But much of that part of me has become a winged spirit of Kheldrin."

"And Kerun's successor here in Roisinan," Kieran said thoughtfully. "That's a lot of yourself to lose."

"I threw down an ancient oracle, and raised a new one," said Anghara, more thinking out loud than making conversation. "I spoke with the old Gods, only to see them vanish at my touch; and yet . . . all of that is gone, past, and all I have left is Sight—the homely vision of the humblest Roisinan village hut where the spaewife reads the fire. And, somehow, it is enough." She raised luminous eyes to Kieran. "I'm not sure I want to know what happens next."

Kieran knew these moods. She was getting fey again, less dangerously so than she had been when madness had taken her on the Shaymir plains all that time ago, but it was the same frame of mind. It needed the same selfless faith to serve as the antidote.

He reached out for her hand where it lay upon the fur coverlet. "I don't need the Sight. I know what's coming. The stars are turning your way; you are where you are meant to be, and nothing can stand in your way."

"Not even Sif and his army?"

"We'll deal with Sif and his army," he said confidently.

"Well, then, you'd better make ready," Anghara said. "You should be able to see the dust of his army before the moon turns full in three days' time."

"We'll be ready," he said, not missing a beat.

"And are you ready to deal with Favrin Rashin as well?"

Kieran stared at her in blank incomprehension. "*Favrin?* What has he got to do with this?"

"I have seen him at Miranei," Anghara said with a calmness which was almost terrifying. "The flames show me very little now, but I have seen Favrin in the Great Hall of Miranei, and I have no idea of how he came or what he seeks. And I suspect that he is coming hard at Sif's heels."

"Kerun and Avanna!" Kieran breathed, taking refuge in the old familiar Gods although he knew full well they were too far away to heed his prayers. "I suppose we could always hope the two of them tear each other apart."

"That would make Favrin my ally," Anghara said, "and I am far from sure he is that."

"I'm not sure it isn't beyond him to aid Sif, and then turn on him when they've dealt with us," Kieran said helplessly. And then, after a moment of thought, shook his head. "No. That would be Duerin's ploy. Whatever else one can say about Favrin, he doesn't stab in the back. He's direct to a fault."

"Perhaps a deeper immersion in his father's plot-soaked court has whetted his appetite for intrigue," said Anghara. "That might not have been too difficult to achieve. He is his father's son." She shivered involuntarily as she recalled the last intrigue Favrin had proposed. Had she accepted, she could have been incarcerated in his *kaiss* these long weeks she had spent gaining Miranei and then waiting within for Sif to reclaim it in blood and thunder. It could have been so much more pleasant, waiting instead in silk-draped dalliance with a husband who would have taken over the plotting and planning and who would have raised his own strong arm on her behalf.

And his own.

The mental picture of Favrin Rashin on her father's throne with herself as the veiled and modest consort at his side was enough to shatter that particular reverie. But she had thrown Favrin into the melting pot, and now he was Kieran's problem. And Kieran was by now far away in his thoughts, organizing and reorganizing his plans in the light of two armies, not one. It wasn't long before he withdrew to meet with his lieutenants. Anghara had once told Favrin that being a woman had its advantages in a war—she could leave the fighting to her generals. Now, in the hour when that remark was taking physical shape around her, she recognized its truth with bitter clarity. When a queen's generals were also her friends, wars were a lonely time for the woman who stayed behind on the throne. Feor had done his job all too well—he had made no distinctions between his pupils, and she was just as well versed in strategy as Kieran and the twins. Hers had been an important contribution back in Cascin, when they planned the taking of Miranei. But there was little for her to do in the present situation except wait. Things were being handled as well as they could be by those she had entrusted with the keep's defense; part of knowing how to rule wisely was knowing when to leave a job to those best equipped to deal with it. There was nothing for her but the fire, and the obstinate veil hiding the future from her Sight.

She had been out by a day in her estimate of Sif's time of arrival; it was on the fourth day after her conversation with Kieran that his approaching army was sighted. Adamo had come to tell her, and she climbed onto the battlements with him and Kieran. It was a gray and overcast day, promising autumn rain, cold and constant, and Anghara shivered as she hugged a fur-lined cloak against the wind. Perhaps it was the wind that stung tears into her eyes as she watched the approach of her father's firstborn son—her brother, her enemy.

"It looks a sizeable army," said Adamo quietly.

"We've already spotted a few outriders," Kieran said, turning to Anghara. "Some rode almost to within arrow range before turning back. I'm not entirely sure what Sif had in mind. It's not as if he were riding to conquer an unknown place that needed scouting."

"He's just letting you know he's coming," Anghara said.

"As if I needed reminding," Kieran muttered.

"We can withstand an indefinite siege," Adamo said, also turning to face Anghara. "All we need do is sit it out."

"If it weren't for Favrin," Kieran said darkly.

"And if it weren't for those who aren't within the keep," Anghara said. "I could not sit safe in Miranei if I knew Sif was taking his frustrations out on those less able to defend themselves."

"What do you mean?"

"The city below us is much more vulnerable than the keep; and then there are the villages beyond. We must have a way out of here, if we need to go out to him."

Kieran exchanged a swift glance with Adamo over Anghara's head. "Somehow I knew you'd say that," he said. "We've already thought of it. There are men posted in the woods beyond the western postern. Sif won't get into the mountains behind us, and we have an exit. But our strength is this keep. If we give Sif a chance to orchestrate a battle in the open, I'm far from sure we could get the better of him. Especially if . . ." He bit off the sentence with a savage sharpness as he turned away to gaze at Sif's approaching army again. Anghara raised her eyes to the profile he presented to her.

"Especially if Favrin plays a wild card," she finished his thought softly. "I'm sorry, Kieran. I have no comforting promises for you. What will be on this field, will be. It is beyond me to know."

She reached out to lay a gentle hand on his arm, and after a moment he turned, covering it with his own. "Well," he said philosophically, "we've beaten the odds before. Nothing much has changed, after all."

Something in his voice made Adamo glance at him keenly but he kept his counsel. He thought it better not to interrupt the moment; had he been his brother, he would probably have made a quip, and then quite possibly instantly regretted breaking into the way his royal cousin and his foster brother and friend were looking at one another. It could have easily been another addition to Kieran's book of Lost Opportunities. Instead, Anghara simply smiled, looking into the blue eyes which held her own.

"If anyone can, you can," she said. "I always believed in you."

Kieran's mouth quirked at this. "I thought that was my line."

Adamo chose his moment. "Charo should be back from the city, and Rochen and Melsyr will be waiting. Will you come, Anghara? Sight or no Sight, you are still the one who best knows this place from the inside . . . and the only one who has ever been close enough to Sif to know his mind."

"You might as well ask Kieran, who spent years skirmishing with him," Anghara said. "I only know he is angry, and frustrated. Anyone could have told you that much. But I will come." She hesitated. "Can you give me a moment?"

"We'll be in the Little Hall," Adamo said. He bowed his head briefly in token of farewell and turned to leave. "Kieran?"

"Yes, coming," Kieran said. He closed his fingers around the small hand he still held, brought it up to brush with his lips in a simple, natural gesture which had been completely unpremeditated. "Don't stay too long," he said softly. He could have been talking about the physical aspect—the cold wind and imminent rain; but they both knew he spoke about the deeper folly, of staying overlong to stare at what was coming and darkening her spirit with black premonitions. He said no more; he didn't need to. The two of them were already far too attuned to need to spell things out in words. After another moment, he dropped her hand and followed Adamo down the uneven stone steps leading from the battlements.

Left alone, Anghara leaned forward on the parapet and pillowed her chin in her folded hands, staring into the distance in the direction from which Sif was approaching.

"Oh, Father," she whispered, bringing up a ghostly image of Red Dynan in her mind's eye. "What you have done here . . . I know you loved this land, but you planted an evil seed for its future. Only one of us can hold the Throne Under the Mountains; Sif will not give it up, and I—I cannot, not now, not in the face of the faith and sacrifice which have brought me here. So it has come to this—your blood warring against your blood. And all I have . . . all I have are the words of an oracle. I never sought his death. But what choice can I have, when he is forcing me to choose between his death or my life?"

The oracle. The first words of Gul Khaima by the sea. It was something Anghara couldn't forget, and much of the prophecy had already come true. It was almost done with

Anghara, except for a few revelations still defying comprehension. *A hunter shall be snared by the prey he baits.* But which was the hunter and which the prey? And what of the last cryptic pair of unsolved lines? *A broken spirit shall opened lie, a bitter secret to learn.* Whose the broken spirit, and what the bitter secret? It was all coming to a head, and Sight was closed to her, the future murky.

She sighed deeply, wondering whether Sif spent half as much time agonizing over this as she did, and turned away, back toward the keep where her friends waited.

Had she but known it, Sif was resigned to yet another sleepless night when the army made camp that evening. There had been all too many, beginning long before the decision to fly against his instincts and chase into Kheldrin after the prey snatched from his own keep while he had been on a wild goose chase to punish those who attacked his mother's manor. He had analyzed the events over and over again, and counted that foray as his first mistake—giving in to the hot thirst for revenge, to the burning urge to find the Rashin scion, and teach him a lesson he would never forget. Of course Favrin had long since vanished by the time he arrived, and Sif had to be content with raids into the hills. They had found one small group of men stupid enough to fall into his clutches—but it had been a singularly futile campaign, and the desire for revenge had lost its bite after he cooled sufficiently to think things through.

So he had headed back for Miranei, only to be greeted with chaos on his return—his chancellor and his queen dead, his heir lost, and both his prisoner and the secret of her identity free of his dungeons. Again taken by white heat of fury, he had led his army out again after the fugitives. And he had almost got them, frustrated only at the last moment when they had gained the River Hal and somehow vanished into the country beyond. Sif paid a number of savage visits to the nearest villages, ransacking the places for his quarry; he found nothing, but left smoldering ruins filled with wild-eyed victims in his wake.

Upon his return to Miranei, he immediately had the escaped prisoner declared an impostor, and went to pay very public respects to the vault which purported to hold the remains of Red Dynan and his family. And then his hand had been forced in no uncertain way—he would not soon forget the morning when they came to tell him Anghara's tomb had been broken open, and anyone who cared to look could see the grave was empty.

The state funerals he had organized for Fodrun and Senena turned into a grim shadowplay as Sif fought an elusive and yet persistent rumor that the real Anghara was very much alive. Whispers told of the deaths of Fodrun and Senena, and the loss of her child, being no more than punishment for Sif's stealing the throne. Many recalled the way Sif had claimed his kingship, and the role Fodrun had played. There was even a murmur about a document bearing witness to Anghara's crowning in the presence of her father's Council before Sif had ever set foot in Miranei, making his claim even more tenuous. Sif thought he knew who had started that particular piece of gossip, but, although he had taken steps to try and find her, the woman named Deira, who had once been his means of extracting truth from a dying queen, seemed to have vanished completely.

So had Anghara and her companions. As once before, when she had been a nine-year-old child, Sif sent out patrols to search for her, and met with as little success. He cursed himself for a soft fool, swore that this time, when he had Anghara once again in his hands, he'd finish the job properly and be done with her.

In the meantime, back home in Miranei, he was beleaguered by sharp tongues which he knew could turn into knives soon enough. It was hard to keep denying what seemed more and more like an obvious truth, not when he was devoting such huge resources to hunting for the escaped prisoner—and not hunting her was inconceivable.

And then word had come from Shaymir. Sif had long had a network of spies in Kieran's native land—the land to which the outlaw might well return. It was this net which now caught a bigger fish. Hearsay, a rumor, a mere breath, but it had to do with Anghara, and Sif had sent orders to trace it. It didn't take his men long—a small village on the edge of the desert was located, and a camel trader found who remembered bartering three camels to a lad and a bright-haired girl in exchange for three tired horses out of Roisinan. The proprietor of the only inn in the village remembered having these two young travellers under his roof, together with a couple of singers who had really been too good for his establishment. The musicians acquired names—Shev and Keda. The thing was clinched for Sif when he discovered Keda came from the same village which had been Kieran's birthplace, and that before her marriage she had borne the outlaw's own name. Word was sent out for their capture.

Whether through timely warning or her husband's selfless sacrifice, Keda escaped. But Shev was taken, and perhaps his own guilt accounted for the ease of his capture—for it had been his tongue which had loosed the secret of Anghara's passage. There had been true power in Anghara's departure into Kheldrin; Shev had been a part of that, and was enough of a singer not to be able to resist the lure of the song he'd seen taking shape that day. In Sif's hands, Shev had initially tried to deny any knowledge of Anghara, but Sif needed to find her whereabouts, and fast; his men had orders not to be overly nice about extracting that information. The musician cracked when they systematically broke every finger on his left hand, and threatened to start on his right. Sif learned of the trip into the Shaymir desert, of the singing rock, and of the semi-mythical passage through the mountains. He learned, at last, of Kheldrin, solving more than one mystery—for Anghara must have been there before to head for it again. Kheldrin, by repute a land where witches reigned and magic was loose, even if they didn't call it Sight; it made sense for Anghara to seek sanctuary there. Thwarted yet again by that which he had sworn to destroy, Sif made his third mistake—he sent a message into Kheldrin demanding they surrender Anghara, or face war.

In doing so, he sent more than one message, to more than one place. There could be only one reason he would go to such lengths to destroy the girl—she could hardly be the impostor he claimed. It was only the inescapable fact that he too was descended from the Kir Hama kings that kept a rising from flaming there and then. But Miranei was a city steeped in royal intrigue and politics, and knew that without Anghara there to take the throne if they overthrew Sif, true queen or not, they would surely face an invasion from Tath. That was unthinkable; what saved Sif was the simple fact that Miranei preferred a descendant of the ancient Kir Hama line, whatever his credentials, over a Rashin pretender. Besides, the army was still Sif's, and it would have taken a rash leader to risk a rising then, with the army itching to turn on someone to protect their besieged leader. When Sif proposed invasion, the men jumped at the chance to channel their frustrations against an identifiable enemy—and instantly forgot everything they had ever been told about Kheldrin.

They had taken Sa'alah easily enough—it was a trade city, enjoying all the privileges of that status, and had never been fortified against massive assault. It had also been surprisingly empty, almost as if it had been sacrificed, bait to draw the Roisinan king deeper. If that had been the plan, it succeeded magnificently, for Sif roared through and took the road to the mountain pass whose name, had he taken the trouble to discover it, should have given him pause. By the time he emerged into the yellow sands on the far side of the Ar'i'id Sam'mara it was too late for second thoughts, the press of men behind him forcing him forward.

There had been no attack while they were threading their way through the mountain, although there had been ample opportunity—a single orchestrated rock fall would have decimated the winding line of men packed tightly into the narrow pass. But there had been no need. There was nothing to meet the invader on the other side of the pass except desert, and Sif's inexperience soon proved more than enough to begin, slowly and pitilessly, to destroy him.

There were men in his army who came from the desert country in northern Shaymir; with presence of mind Sif moved these into positions of command, and some semblance of order returned. Their horses were useless as a means of transport; men were sent back to Sa'alah to procure camels to support the baggage and supply train, as well as mounts for the army leaders. But that in itself necessitated learning new riding techniques; in the meantime, the men who were to cross the desert on foot had still not found an enemy to vent their anger and frustration on, and were rapidly running out of water.

An advance guard found and "captured" a hai'r, although no resistance had been encountered. This solved the immediate problems. But no map had ever been made of Kheldrin. None of them had any idea in which direction to turn, and mistakes could prove costly in this inhospitable country. Sif tried to clear his head and think logically—he knew of dun'en, the desert horses, and knew they had to be reared somewhere relatively accessible to Sa'alah Harbor, from which they could be shipped out of Kheldrin. Only Sa'alah itself lay beyond the mountains at his back; the horizon stretched away for a great distance to the south and west before it met the blazing desert sky. There seemed to be a suspicion of high ground to the north, though, and Sif turned his army that way.

There were no paths in this desert wilderness, and it was hardly Sif's fault that he missed the caravan trail to Kharg'in'dun'an. The first he knew of his blunder was when he felt the air change into something oppressive with an almost living heat which offered no respite, and the yellow sand gradually gave way to black rock. Ten men died on that first day, six from heat and exhaustion and four from deadly encounters with diamondskin lizards, before Sif could extricate himself from the Khar'i'id—and this was long before any enemy had been sighted. Another twenty crossed to Glas Coil the next day; and after that, not even Sif's charisma was quite enough. Every day that followed saw fewer men stumbling at Sif's heels, even though the army, on retracing its steps, sometimes came across mortal remains, proving that those who fled Sif's ranks stood little chance of making it out on their own. But perhaps they found the odds acceptable, for the desert proved to be an eminently worthy adversary. As Anghara had before him, Sif saw the deadly beauty that drew and enchanted, and then reached out to kill with the careless ease of true power. By the time the right path out of the Arad had been found the fight had been knocked out of his men. It was doubtful if they would have managed a successful sortie had a phalanx of enemy soldiers suddenly risen to bar their way. In any case, when they did encounter their first Kheldrini it had not been an army—but, rather, a veiled woman whose golden eyes were twin embers of cool fire over the blue burnouse concealing the lower half of her face.

"There is nothing that belongs to you in this realm, King of Sheriha'drin, and nothing here to which you belong," the apparition informed the stunned army leaders in flawless if accented Roisinani. "Leave now, and the spirit of this land will be merciful."

Sif had urged his mount forward, a few steps ahead of his captains, his eyes narrowed at the desert vision. "You do hold something . . . someone . . . that I seek," he said, refusing to allow himself to be intimidated. "I will have what I came for."

"You will have a waterless summer in the desert of Arad Khajir'i'id," said the woman, her voice lilting with the evocative syllables of her own tongue. "You have already looked into one face of death—and here, in Kheldrin, death has a thousand faces."

Sif loosened his sword in its scabbard. "Who are you?" he demanded. "Do you speak for your king?"

"We have none," the woman said. She thrust aside her black cloak, shrugging it back over her shoulders, revealing golden robes and several ropes of amber and silver *say'y-in'en.* Her slender arms, full of silver bracelets, lifted toward the sky. "We are the People of the Desert, following the Way. Our lords do not reign by right of birth alone, they are chosen to lead the caravans of their folks' lives. And we of the *an'sen'en'thari* stand between the People and the Gods to whom all in this land is sacred. Leave us, Sif Kir Hama. Kheldrin is not a prize for you."

"I do not seek it," Sif said darkly. "But I will have . . . what . . . I . . . came . . . for." He spoke slowly, emphasizing each word. There was a flash of sun on metal as his sword began to leave its scabbard. At once there were a dozen loose all around him, leaving his captains' scabbards in a concerted hiss of metal against leather. The woman's eyes glowed even more gold than before.

"Al'ar'i'id akhar'a, rah'i'ma'arah na'i smail'len," she said, her voice soft but carrying. There was a texture to the foreign words, a feeling of the brooding power of an ancient land, and it was mixed with a dose of something much more down-to-earth—contempt. The phrase was not a curse, but to those who could not comprehend its meaning it might as

well have been. It was an incantation, a thing of witchcraft born of a witch-country. Many made surreptitious signs against evil; and one, who had perhaps discerned the contempt and been enraged, unwittingly perpetuated the legend—with an outraged roar he threw his spear, only to see it pin no more than an empty black cloak to the hot sand. The woman seemed to have vanished into thin air.

The people of the desert country did, finally, meet Sif on the winding trail which led up to the Kharg'in'dun'an plateau. The terrain was of their choosing, and theirs were all the advantages of the encounter. That Sif did not lose this battle was a tribute to his abilities, and the spirit his presence still imparted to his suffering army. They held their ground. But it was hard to fight an enemy who had a knack of disappearing, vanishing into the land as though they had been water poured into the thirsty desert sand. The skirmish was brief, bloody and inconclusive. Ahead, it seemed, there was nothing but more empty country, sand and stone, and a powerful people who inhabited a twilight realm and were able to reach out in absolute mastery. Sif was nothing if not headstrong, but still lucid enough to know when to draw the line, to give up a prize in order to reclaim it another day. The sight of his suffering and dispirited army was enough to tell him he had reached the end of this particular road. Mere days after his first and last battle in Kheldrin, Sif announced they were returning to Roisinan.

"We will be back," he had said grimly. The summer campaign had been a mistake, even if it had been undertaken in the fires of frustrated rage, and the light of the Kir Hama tradition of the invincible summer kings. But admitting failure came hard; harder still was the chilling certainty, deep in Sif's heart, that she whom he sought had already left Kheldrin and was somewhere behind him, filling a place he had left empty. Upon his return to Roisinan, he had greeted the news of Anghara's entry into Miranei with a weary resignation that stunned the hapless captain detailed to tell him. He did the only thing he could: gathered the remnants of his army and led them out to reconquer that which his anger, and his vulnerability to Anghara's legitimate claims, had allowed him to lose.

Now, within the shadow of the keep that had been home to both Red Dynan's children, Sif remembered the last time he had seen Anghara—locked safely away in the depths of Miranei's dungeons. Thin, drawn, and, when she wasn't curled up in a lethargy that was half sleep and half numbness, staring with empty eyes at the shadow-filled darkness, wild with the loss of something Sif could never comprehend. If someone had told him then that the creature in front of him would hold his fate in her hand not a year hence, he would have laughed. But the truth was, she had always held his fate. And only now, at the last, was he finding enough strength—or desperation—to end it. One way or another.

He remembered the damning record of her coronation, and blocked it out with the memory of his own—the night Red Dynan had died by the Ronval, and the face of Second General Fodrun as he had knelt at his feet, offering him a crown. And it had been sweet to accept, to come to his father's castle no longer as an illegitimate son but as its lord, its crowned king. Against that bright memory was set a shadow Sif obstinately refused to face—a black premonition that time was running out, and the price of the bite he had taken from the apple of temptation was about to be demanded. He could feel the cold breath of something riding behind him, and, perhaps for the first time, he was afraid.

The siege of Miranei did not, in the end, last long, and for the very reason Anghara had foreseen. It was over the minute a band of Sif's men gained entrance to the terrified town below the keep, and tried to cut a swathe through to the postern gates of the castle. The walls of Miranei were thick stones but Anghara didn't have to hear the cries of those who found themselves in the way of Sif's swordsmen in order to sense them. When Kieran and Charo came to her with the news, she lifted burning eyes and stopped them with a single look in the doorway of her chambers.

"Go," she said, without their having to say a word. "It is in the God's hand now. Go, for what is fated will be, and that which awaits us will find us, in the keep or without these walls. Go out to him."

After a moment of silence Charo had simply nodded, and turned to stride away. Kieran lingered for an instant longer, exchanging an eloquent look with the woman who was all queen in that hour, and then turned away without a word. There was too much to be said, and not enough; it was a simple choice—take refuge in silence, or stay a lifetime, talking of everything left unspoken for so long.

They had gone, then, all of Anghara's knights; even Rochen, who had bound up his shoulder and ridden out with the shaft of a Kir Hama banner tucked into the space between his body and the sling supporting his left arm. The army they rode out to face would fight under the same banner.

Anghara cleared her chambers of attendants, huddling alone by the fire, hoping that this time, her Sight would clear and allow her a glimpse of what was shaping at the foot of Miranei's walls. The flames were bright this day—bright with a burnished coppery glow. So bright it hurt her eyes—she kept having to turn away and blink back tears. Within, she could see nothing but billowing mist and smoke. In the end, Anghara fled the suffocating atmosphere of her chambers and made her way to the heights of the battlements, to see for herself that which her recalcitrant Sight refused to reveal. The copper blaze from her hearth seemed to follow, a bright pain beating behind her temples. The views with which she was presented were confused; at least one building in the city was aflame, and out on the moors a deadly dance was shaping, although it was difficult to make out its form. The crisp cool air brought Anghara remote, almost mocking, snatches of sound—a ringing clash of swords, an inarticulate shout, the distant thunder of horses. She couldn't make out individual figures, but tried to harness her Sight at the very least to seek out Kieran amongst the tangled ranks below. She found him, at last, his mind tightly focused on the burly soldier swinging a heavy two-handed sword toward him with an ease that made the weapon look as though it had been made of willow-withies and not tempered steel. One blow, and it would all be over; Anghara remembered with extraordinary clarity a vision she had seen once before of a naked sword descending upon Kieran. Then . . . was it in Bresse . . . it seemed a thousand years ago . . . the vision had resolved into his knighting on a distant battlefield. Now there would be no such reprieve, Anghara heard a voice cry out, and knew it only a moment later as her own. But Kieran seemed to hear something too, for the barest instant. He hesitated, perhaps for too long. The great sword came down; Kieran's flashed up to meet it. There was hardly enough power in Kieran's counterblow to deflect the deadly blade, flung out defensively an instant too late; iron rang against iron, and sparks flew as the two blades slid against one another with a metallic scream. But the strength which should have carried through the blow never seemed to materialize. A moment later it became clear why as the soldier's hands fumbled and dropped his great sword from a suddenly nerveless grip. He toppled sideways from his horse with the barest handspan of a short, hand-hewn ash spear protruding from his back. Kieran glanced up in the direction from which this had flown, and Charo waved jauntily before turning his horse with his knees and plunging the screaming beast into the thick of another fray. Up on the battlements Anghara made a queer sound, somewhere between a laugh and a sob, and leaned heavily against the battlements as her legs began to give way. She sensed rather than heard an attendant hurry toward her, and made a swift warding gesture with her hand without turning around. "I have no need of assistance."

"My lady . . ."

"Clear this area," Anghara said, softly but emphatically. "I will be alone."

"Yes, my lady," the attendant said, after a moment of eloquently grim silence. She might not have been ceremonially crowned yet, but the young queen's instructions were obeyed. Anghara found herself alone on the battlements, as she had commanded; but in that instant of distraction she had lost her focus, and the battle was once again a churning chaos. And, obstinate and enduring, the copper blaze she had taken from her hearth still danced and shimmered in her mind, an ache that wouldn't go away. Anghara caught herself rubbing her temples, seeking the knot of a headache, but this was no physical pain, just a persistent hot glow which gave everything an odd cast, as if she were seeing things simultaneously through . . .

Through a different pair of eyes.

There was a moment of sudden stillness. Even the wind died down in that instant, as though the world itself grew hushed in the split second of comprehension, a moment in which the words of the oracle of Gul Khaima abruptly took shape and form.

Through a different pair of eyes. Through a different Sight.

A broken spirit shall opened lie, a bitter secret to learn. Yes, Rima had been Sighted, and Sif had hated her for it. But Feor, at the last, had been vindicated, for he had been right when he had surmised that Anghara's own precocious gifts had not been the legacy of her mother alone. Dynan, too, had carried the gift of Sight. And Dynan had sired another child besides Rima's daughter.

Sif, Sight's implacable enemy, had a soul fire that burned with the glow of burnished copper in the darkness of the battle frenzy below. A soul fire every bit as bright as the gold of his half-sister who watched from the castle they both called home. A soul fire of pure and powerful Sight.

Anghara, suddenly aware she'd held her breath in the instant of revelation, drew in a ragged gasp. There were so many images in her head she experienced a brief sensation of vertigo, and had to clutch once again at Miranei's solid and comforting stone.

It all made sense. Sif's uncanny power as a leader of men had more in it than charisma; his vicious campaign against the Sighted of Roisinan had roots in an unconscious wish to exorcise something he sensed deep within himself but had been unable to pinpoint. Anghara had probably owed her life more than once to his ignorance and inability to channel his gifts, and his consequent reliance on others to seek for her. If only he had known how to use it. With the power he had, rooted at least partly in the same foundation from which her own had sprung, he would have found it all too easy to have accomplished himself what his minions had spent fruitless years trying to do. It would have been over for Anghara before it had truly begun. Instead Sif had renounced and denied his heritage, and that repudiation had brought him, at the last, to his final battle. Even now he fought in the shadow of the castle which had seen the kindling of his own soul's fire, the place which had seen his early humiliations, and the triumph of wearing the crown which was the only legacy of his father he had chosen to acknowledge.

Anghara's first instinct had been to call for her horse and ride into the melee below, seeking her brother. But he would be in the thick of things, and if she charged in bearing these tidings he would likely sheathe his sword in her body. She checked the suicidal impulse, a quizzical half-smile playing around her mouth. Going to Sif in the flesh would not, in the end, prove necessary—not when she had his mind before her, bright and strong. She would have liked to have been beside him when she touched him in the higher senses he had striven so hard to cleanse from his people's soul, to see his face in that instant of realization. There was something entirely too calculating and cold for Anghara's liking in hailing him thus, from a distance, pinning him down with savage shock and opening him up to the God alone knew what, while she waited here, safely away from the consequences. But there were other voices in her mind, voices that would cry out in mortal pain and then be silenced with an abrupt finality which froze her marrow. There was too much death. It was time to stop it, stop it now, and it lay within her hands to do so.

Now that she recognized it for what it was, the fiery copper glow of Sif's soul fire marked him amongst the combatants as clearly as though he had been branded. Anghara found the source of the copper flame and arrowed in toward it, her own soul fire flaring in a bright gold aura around her head and shoulders in a manner any worshipper of Bran of the Dawning would have instantly recognized.

* * *

Sif had deliberately forced this battle. Time was against him, and he couldn't afford a slow or leisurely resolution. He knew Miranei too well; many of the improvements of its defenses had been his own work, and he knew them to be impregnable. He realized his only chance lay in luring the defenders out into the open where he could deal with them swiftly without Miranei's formidable battlements between them.

Perhaps because he was still ridden by the demons of his dark premonitions, he fought like a man possessed when Anghara's men came pouring out to meet his army. His sword seemed to have a life of its own as it danced and weaved, sowing death where it fell. It was soon red to the hilt with other men's blood. Sif, although he seemed to court self-destruction, remained untouched. It was as though death rode at his back, lending strength to his arm, keeping others from closing with him. He'd sought the leaders, the best in the army that faced him; but circumstances had sent Kieran and the twins in the other direction. Sif never wore distinguishing insignia into battle, wearing the same scarred armor as most of his men, and it was hard to pick the king from the press of his army. He'd had to be content with lesser lights.

Until Kerun sent a familiar face his way.

The other had lost his helmet, and already bore a long gash seeping red across his right temple. But his loss, and the wound, didn't seem to have hampered him; his weapon was fully as gory as Sif's own as the tides of battle swept them to face each other. Sif, who had the disconcerting ability to remember the face and name of any of his men, found both swimming out of his memory to name the man who stood against him.

"Melsyr."

The other's eyes narrowed at the voice, and his grip tightened on the hilt of his sword, itself slippery with blood beneath his gauntlet. Impulsively, Sif reached up to unfasten the straps that held his own helmet in place and threw it aside, releasing bright hair so much like Anghara's own.

"You turned your coat, I see," Sif said softly. In the noise of battle, his words should have been inaudible to anyone but himself, but Melsyr heard, and his cheeks flushed beneath the bloody streaks running across his face.

"I was never unfaithful to my true allegiance."

Sif laughed, a harsh sound with little mirth. "Kalas' son. I should have known. I remember Kalas all too well. I should have recognized that rigid backbone of idealism the moment I laid eyes on you, I suppose you engineered the escape which killed my queen?"

Melsyr flinched, but didn't look away. "I would never wish harm upon a woman, especially not one in Queen Senena's condition—not in payment for things I could hold against her husband. She wasn't responsible for your doings. But no, you are wrong. I didn't plan the escape. I merely lent my aid when they came to take the young queen from your dungeons."

"You knew where she was all along, didn't you?" Sif said savagely. "Afterward, while I sought the breadth of the country for her—you knew all along . . ."

Melsyr smiled, his teeth unexpectedly white underneath the grime and blood on his face. "For what it is worth, King Under the Mountain, I did not. My part ended when he took her from Miranei. Where he was taking her, I didn't ask. The last thing I wanted to do was risk betrayal of her secret. But even had I known . . . I would have died before you had it of me."

"So you would," Sif said. "You are one of the fanatics, and your honor is Kalas' high twisted version, damn his hide. I'd expect no less from his son." He paused for a moment, and then met the other smile for smile. "And you can stop shielding Kieran Cullen. I know full well only he would have had the nerve to try."

"Twisted?" Melsyr asked, passing over the late admonition and returning to the slur upon his father. The grim smile was still painted upon his face. "Better that, than some of the paths along which your honor has led you."

Sif hefted his sword. "We all do what we must," he said levelly, and swung, without further warning.

Melsyr's smile vanished in an instant as he raised his blade to parry, and then parry again, and again. Sif channeled all his fury, and the grief—for, unexpectedly and surprisingly, there had been bitter grief when he had learned of the death of the little queen he had taken for granted—and his sword sang as he beat Melsyr back. Melsyr found himself hopelessly outclassed, fighting for his life against a master. He got a blow or two in, managed to blood his adversary, which seemed to be more than anyone else had achieved before him—but even as he stole a moment to revel in that accomplishment he knew this was all he would be able to do. His Gods had thrown him into a fight he couldn't hope to win; he would meet the new Guardian of the Gate, and walk with his father in Glas Coil, before this day was over.

Even as the thought came to him Sif broke through his guard. The edge of Sif's sword bit into the side of his neck, and blood fountained out, spraying Sif's face and armor. Melsyr swayed in the saddle, his own blade slipping from his grasp, slicing at his horse's shoulder as it fell. Maddened already by the smell of blood and the clamor of battle, it screamed and reared, throwing its rider, and bolted across the battlefield with trailing reins and an empty saddle bright with blood. Melsyr was dead before he hit the ground.

Sif spared a moment to gaze upon his erstwhile opponent with something like grudging respect. "Faithful to the last," he muttered. Even as he straightened, raising his hand to finger the trivial wounds Melsyr had managed to inflict and looking around for his next opponent, Sif reeled from an assault which came from a completely unexpected quarter.

Sif! Stop! It is time to stop. You swore to destroy the Sighted, but in whose name do you fight us? You are yourself one of those whom you seek to destroy!

This was unthinkable. Impossible. Unbelievable. It was the black flower of his premonition opening to engulf him. His mind was a cauldron of confusion, fury, fear. *What . . . Who . . .*

It is Anghara. You and I shared the same father. He bequeathed the same power to us both. I am Sighted . . . and so are you. So are you, my brother.

There was a moment of frozen silence in the heart of the copper gleam, and then it flared into even greater luminescence; a cold fire like a bronze sword cut back across the empty space between them and lodged in Anghara's mind like a dagger. There was grim acceptance in it, and understanding, anger and bitter defeat. *I should have killed you when I had the chance.*

Anghara gasped at the cold brutality, bereft of words. And Sif, coming into his own in the midst of desperate battle, untrained, raw, reached into her mind across the channel she herself had made and took the knowledge he needed to shape his own message, his own mind-voice strong and clear. *I knew it was coming,* he said, and he was bleak. *Before this battle began I knew it was coming. I am everything I have ever loathed and feared . . . I am the cancer I sought to cut out! Defeat is bitter; I have rarely known it in the field, but I know this to be true. Well, so you have it all at last, little sister. It was a long wait, but as it was written, so it must be in the end. And I . . . I shall be no more than a falling star in the firmament of history.*

She caught his intent, and screamed his name out loud on the battlements of Miranei, little caring who heard or what interpretation might be put upon it by those who did. But she was high and far, and down on the moors Sif was master of his own destiny. In the end, he was oddly gentle.

Do not take it to heart, little sister. I may have wished you dead, but what I do now, I do not do to hurt you. But we cannot both live in this Roisinan we have made between us; it is your vision that prevails, and I cannot, will not, live by it. I always knew I would recognize the end, and I see it before me. Farewell, Queen of Roisinan. I can only wish you more good fortune than fell to me. There was a beat of silence and then, fading, his final words—an uncanny echo, had he but known it, of those which crossed Melsyr's mind mere moments ago: *May my father's spirit have mercy on my soul when we meet in the shadows of Glas Coil . . .*

When she could see again through the haze of hot tears that came to blur her vision, the chaos below seemed to have changed, acquired a different cast. This time, heedless of consequences, Anghara whirled and called for her horse. This was no time to cling to the safety of bolted doors and high walls. Down in the field of battle the destiny of a nation was being decided, and if she couldn't find the strength and the courage to meet it she didn't deserve her father's crown.

They balked at her orders in the stables; it was Sight, more than the power of royalty, which finally gained her a mount and a clear path out of the keep. She had chosen the fastest steed, unconscious of the irony of its being a pure-blooded Kheldrini dun, and she rode like fury, streaking through the gate of the keep when it had been opened barely wide enough for her to pass. It had started to rain, but she hardly noticed—the cloak she wore, streaming out like a flag behind her, was little protection against the elements. She exploded onto what had been the battlefield, scattering confused, milling men like so many sheep before the flying hooves of her horse, aiming unerringly to where the bright copper soul fire now flickered at the edges of existence. The loose knot of men formed around its source opened at her approach, and she tore through, bringing her mount to a skidding halt inches from the booted feet of an armored figure lying on the ground. One of the three men who had been kneeling beside it in the churned mud of the battlefield rose at her approach. He reached out to grab the reins of the plunging dun with one hand and steady Anghara with the other, as she slid off.

"We all felt him do it," Kieran said, retaining his hold on Anghara's elbow and releasing the dun's reins to another willing pair of hands. "I felt it as it happened—it was as if the earth shuddered . . ." He sounded bemused. If anything, the feeling had been similar to parts of the journey to Kheldrin, a time he would prefer to forget.

"Sight makes you a part of the land, and he was its anointed . . ." Anghara said. But then, trembling beneath his hand, she looked past Kieran and stepped swiftly forward to sink to one knee beside the body of her half-brother, heedless of the bloody mud in which her gown and the edges of her cloak trailed. "He's still alive," she whispered, reaching to take one of Sif's gauntleted hands. Beneath her fingers, as she fumbled for the glove's unfastening, an insubstantial pulse still beat at the base of his palm. He feebly resisted her attempt to free his other hand from the pommel of the kingly sword thrust beneath his ribs. The bloodied end protruded from his back and even Anghara knew the wound was mortal. His eyes opened slowly and tried to focus, but they were already filming over, and it was beyond his power to speak. But the copper-colored soul fire shimmered still, a ghost of itself and as their eyes locked there was no need for words.

I loved this land, he said directly into her mind, his words already distant, as if spoken from another world.

I know, she said, her eyes brimming with tears even as the last vestige of the copper flame flickered and died.

Sight, the word went sighing through the gathered men. *He was Sighted. Sif too was Sighted . . .*

But that was not the least of the surprises.

"You weep for him," said one of Kieran's captains standing close by, surprised into irreverence.

Anghara closed her eyes for a moment, as though she were praying, and then gently laid Sif's hand back on his chest. Kieran assisted her to her feet and she looked around almost blindly for a moment. The men nearby her respected her silence, until a bloodied and dishevelled warrior suddenly moved forward to kneel at her feet, offering her his sword hilt first.

"My lady," he said, his voice hoarse with battlefield dust and raw emotion, "we lay down our arms, and give ourselves into your hands."

Anghara reached for the proffered weapon and lifted it two-handed from the warrior's palms. "It ends here," she said, very softly, but her voice carried into the sudden hush that had fallen across the moors. She stabbed the sword she held into the churned ground at her feet. "It is over. The world is changed; tomorrow, we begin again." She turned, gazing for a long moment into Sif's face. Someone had closed his eyes, and the rain had slicked his hair back from his face; all of a sudden, he looked very young. "Bring him into the keep; tonight we will keep vigil for him, and light his passage to the Gate. Tomorrow we will lay him to rest in the royal vault."

"He was a tyrant," someone said in barely more than a whisper.

Anghara's head came up at the words. She didn't turn to see who had spoken them, but her words were cool with rebuke. "He was a son of kings, and he was King Under the Mountain in his turn," she said. "He was Kir Hama, and royal. That, we will remember, of all the other things he was." She glanced up at Kieran, standing mute and solid at her side, and what he saw in her eyes was suddenly for him alone, a complete reversal of the queenly poise and level voice which had just uttered these words. He felt her shudder beneath his hand. "Kieran," she said, soft and low. "Take me home."

He knew what she was asking—take her back to the keep, without revealing how much of an illusion she was in this hour. From this battlefield which had split a nation, anointed with sudden tragedy, those who had fought must take a message of hope and strength. Anghara couldn't afford to reveal how shattered she was by what had transpired. She needed his strength, a staff to lean upon, and, as always, he rose to her need.

"Adamo," he said quietly, without turning toward the foster brother who stood at his back. "My horse, and her dun. And get Rochen, with that standard. I'll help her mount, and Rochen and I will ride in with her. You and Charo take over here. Has anyone seen Melsyr?"

Anghara turned her head a fraction and Kieran instinctively followed her gaze—and found his question answered. His jaw clenched at sudden recognition of the blood-soaked, crumpled shape lying a few steps away from Sif's body, a figure that had once been a man . . . and a friend.

"Bring him, too," Anghara said, softly. "There will be those who will keep a king's vigil tonight. But Melsyr's, we will keep ourselves."

Her dun was brought, its eyes still rolling at the memory of its wild ride. Kieran lifted her into the saddle, turned to vault into his own as his horse was led up, and nodded briefly to Rochen who had come up behind carrying the brave Kir Hama pennant he had taken into battle. It was somewhat the worse for wear, but still in one piece. The cold autumn wind had freshened again, driving the rain at an angle, and lifting the limp, soaked flag into a snap and flutter. Kieran dug his heels into the flanks of his horse. "Anghara," he murmured, directing her to move.

She obeyed, urging her own mount forward, a step ahead of her escort. With her hair wet and heavy on her shoulders and across her face in long clinging strands; her hands mired with Sif's blood and the trampled earth of the field she had won; her cloak and gown torn and muddied, she slowly rode away from the battlefield. But there would be few later who would remember. Instead, the stories would tell of the glow of power that mantled the young queen, and the depth of the wholly unexpected mourning she had shown for one who had been her kin, and her enemy. Her right to Roisinan had been sealed. The gesture of a state funeral had not been looked for; it had been a surprise, and while it would form part of her legend, there were those who could not let it pass unremarked.

Rochen muttered something under his breath, riding at her side, his face faintly rebellious as his fingers curled with latent ferocity around the slick shaft of the noble banner he carried.

Anghara turned at the murmur. "What was that?"

"I said," Rochen repeated, "that it was more than he would have done for you."

"You forget that he had already done it for me, when I was much younger," she said, with a grim humor. "He buried me in the family vault with all possible royal honors years ago."

"Then he was trying to bury his mistakes," Rochen said obstinately.

Anghara lifted a hand that trembled only slightly to push a strand of wet hair back from her eyes, and offered him a sad smile that never quite managed to reach her eyes. "So am I," she said softly.

The day after the battle dawned suitably somber. The rain held off but the sky was a mourning shade of dark purple, heavy on the white-crowned mountains above Miranei as Roisinan's dead king was laid to rest in his family's vault, interred with savage irony next to a broken and empty tomb which bore his successor's name.

Anghara, garbed in purple, stood throughout the ceremony, silent, bareheaded except for a token circlet of beaten gold around her brow. They had taken the sword from Sif's heart, and, with his hands clasped around its hilt and his wounds concealed by his robes, he looked asleep. His hair had been combed back, bare of any sign of kingly glory; this had been the priests' decision, that he should be buried thus humbled. They had even wanted to do away with the sword, but Anghara had been quietly adamant—it might be her father's sword as well as Sif's, but it was a significant part of what Sif had tried to be. By laying claim to it he had effectively severed its links to Dynan, and its symbolism for the crown. For all the memory of his tyranny, there was an odd nobility about him this day, marked by the hush that followed him to his tomb. Watching from a respectable distance enforced by the occasional poker-faced palace guard, the crowd could just as easily have jeered as they sent their oppressor on his way to meet Gheat Freicadan, at the shadowy gates of Glas Coil.

And even this was a mystery, for there seemed to be ambivalence as to which God Sif would encounter there. Two sets of priests were at hand, Kerun's trio glowering at the simply dressed pair who served Bran. Anghara had allowed it; it seemed like a royal sanction to the new God, and Kerun's priesthood was seriously alarmed. They struggled to maintain the appearance of dignity and decorum as they went through the ancient rites of burial sacred to their God; as for the other two, they seemed serene, and unconcerned. Their rites were few, and, compared to those that had gone before, startlingly plain; a few whispered words, a strange sign over the body by the long, white-fingered hand of the younger, and then they had laid one of Bran's ubiquitous yellow-marked garlands on Sif's chest, before offering one last bow as they backed away from the bier.

The four knights whose duty it was to lift the bier into the niche of the tomb now stepped up to perform their task, but a sudden gesture from the young queen stopped them. "Wait," said Anghara. "It isn't right."

"My lady . . ." One of the priests of Kerun, standing a few paces to Anghara's left, turned sharply. "All the necessary rites have been performed, as the God directed; is there something . . ."

"Anghara," said Kieran, much closer to her, softly enough for only her to hear. "Don't give him too much glory. It will make for an unquiet ghost."

"As mine was," Anghara said, with a sharp-edged smile. But the few extra seconds gave her time to think, and to abandon her original plan, arguably reckless—she had been ready to lay her own golden circlet into the tomb with Sif, a token of his royalty. Perhaps, on reflection, that had not been such a good idea. But Bran's priests as well as Kerun's were watching her now, and she owed them something.

The nearest knights around Sif's bier stepped away as she approached and stood for a moment looking down on Sif with a strange and inscrutable expression. Then she sighed, and glanced at the mountains of Miranei as if for inspiration before she laid her hand gently on Sif's brow. "Sleep a king," she said softly, yet all heard her words.

A golden glow kindled beneath her palm, seeping out between her fingers as it intensified; slowly she withdrew her hand and stepped away, to a gasp that was torn out of a thousand throats as the crowds saw what she had wrought. It was illusion, and would last only as long as it took to raise the stone that would seal Sif in his tomb—but now, still in the sight of his people, he wore a living crown of golden flame.

Kieran's expression was almost comically at war with itself. "I'm not sure if it wouldn't have been better to leave him with a crown more of this world," he whispered as Anghara returned to her place. "This kind of thing lives on for a long time in people's minds; you've just branded the tyrant a saint. Look at those two priests of Bran!"

Anghara took in the priests' beatific smiles, and then glanced back to where Sif's bier was being raised into the niche of his tomb. "They will remember he was buried with it, but they are unlikely to forget who gave it to him."

Kieran decided to ignore the Kir Hama arrogance, for it was, in this instance, no more than a dressing on the truth. She was right—the crowd would remember. He sighed as he looked again at the priestly contingent and saw the black frowns that, for all their efforts to hide them, still wreathed the faces of Kerun's anointed—many more would flock to Bran of the Dawning after this demonstration. Kieran spared a brief moment to wonder if even Glas Coil the eternal could be the same after grim Kerun had given way to this bright new God, and then shook it off. These were morbid thoughts, borne by the somber atmosphere of the funeral; he, Kieran, was a long way from Glas Coil.

The gravestone was raised into position; as the last of the golden glow was cut off, the crowd, who seemed to have been holding their collective breath, let it out in a massive sigh—and then someone raised a solitary cheer for the queen. In an almost eerie replay of her entry into Miranei the cry was quickly caught up, until the multitude was calling out Anghara's name. As she turned to leave, Kerun's priests made her the silent obeisance her rank required, but the young priest of Bran held his palm over Anghara's brow and looked up, ignoring all the rules, straight into the young queen's eyes. There was a hiss of indrawn breath from her entourage—priesthood gave one some prerogatives, but hardly this—but the expression on his face was so serious and rapt that it stayed the consequences.

"You are Bran's," the young priest said, in a voice of awe. "You are Bran's own blessed one. The gold that is his . . . it is yours, it flows through your hands . . . Bran's blessing on your days, royal lady, now and always. Bran's blessing."

He fell to his knees then, but it was not obeisance—it was as if he had been poleaxed, and he would have sprawled had his friend not anticipated him and gone down on one knee beside him, supporting him. He too now lifted his face. "He has always had vision, my lady . . . the Sight. He doesn't mean any impropriety, but when Sight comes to him he never knows what he does. I ask your pardon for his transgressions."

"No offense was taken," Anghara said softly, looking down at the stricken priest with something like compassion. "He but blessed me, after all . . . and I have walked in his shoes. You are far from your brethren; if there is any assistance I or mine can render in their stead, call on us."

"My lady," stammered the other priest in confusion, bowing his head. These new priests had taken to tonsuring their hair, and his meticulously shaven pate gleamed as she stood for an instant longer looking down at the kneeling pair. Then she passed on.

Not far away, a cloaked figure seemed to smile at the

scene, and, as she moved away, followed at a decorous distance, flanked by a closely following shadow of its own. It slipped into the gates of the keep at the heels of the royal procession without being challenged, and then, glancing down an arched opening to its right, stepped through this into a quiet courtyard shadowed by a gnarled old pine. Its companion, after receiving something wrapped in white silk, left the courtyard to hurry toward the Royal Tower.

This time, the way was barred—the guards at the gate lowered crossed spears to cut the messenger off. "Your business within?"

"I bear a message," the man said. He shed the cowl of his cloak, and threw back the cloak itself to show he wore no sword belt—indeed, bore no weapon except for a small dagger tucked into his boot which he now bent to retrieve and offer hilt first to the nearest guard. The man took it, balancing it in his left hand. "And your message?"

"This," the man said, producing the silk parcel from a pouch at his waist.

"What of it?"

"To be taken to the queen."

One of the guards raised a quizzical eyebrow. "Indeed. And then?"

"Then, safe conduct for my master, who would meet with her."

"And who might your master be?"

"I am not at liberty to say," the messenger said with cool dignity.

The guard measured him through narrowed eyes. "Southerner, by your accent," he said. "And your coloring. What is your business this far north?"

"My master's business is his own," said the other. "Please. The message."

"Well, I don't know," said one of the guards, glancing at the other. "I'm not sure I hold with some cloak-and-dagger fellow who won't even give his name strolling into the Tower."

"It's not your call," snapped the other, still hefting the dagger. "Inside, you; into the guardroom," he told the messenger, indicating the way with a toss of his head, and then turned back to his companion. "Who's on duty upstairs today?"

"Adamo Taurin, I think."

"Get this to him, see what he says. With your permission, m'lord?" This with gentle sarcasm as he reached for the silk, and its bearer, for the barest instant, showed every intention of being ready to lay down his life to hang on to it. But it was surrendered, with a graceful bow, and the guard inclined his head in return, with a grin. "I'll keep an eye on our guest."

The guard bearing the package vanished into the shadows. The messenger walked inside in the man's wake as the spears were lifted, and sat quietly, hands on knees, on one of the chairs beside the arrow-slit window in the small guardroom. The guard who had stayed behind hovered for a moment at the guardroom door, and then offered a grudging smile.

"Damned if I don't like your style," he said. "I don't know who your master is but it can't be someone we'll like very much, else he wouldn't have had to resort to you and yon secret package to gain entry. And there you are, sitting pretty, with not a blunt food knife between you and the palace guard."

"As to that," said the other, smiling with the grave arrogance born of generations of aristocratic ancestry, "I have no need of knives; where I come from, we make weapons of our hands and feet."

The guard's smile slipped, as his eyes went to the slim brown hands resting relaxed and innocent on the man's lap; the other's widened a fraction. "But you don't need to worry," the visitor said, his obsidian eyes gleaming with amusement. "My master sent me here under instruction not to use my art." He paused, just long enough to be sure of his impact. "Unless," he qualified gravely, "in defense of my freedom—or my life."

The guard had an instant to regain his aplomb—and took refuge in bluster, in stark contrast with the calm and poised bearing of his guest. Uncomfortably aware of this, the guard became all the more incensed, and in the end could only trust himself to return to his post by the door. He had managed a bluff, "What kind of talk is that . . ." before his eloquence deserted him. His companion's face hadn't changed, but that only made it worse—the guard hadn't needed to observe his calm amusement in order to be aware of it, and be mortified. He was a Royal Tower guard, and it galled him to realize he had been drawn onto thin ice with consummate ease and allowed to fall through and flounder. He should have taken it all in his stride. Out at the gate, fuming, he found himself wishing Adamo would come down and throw the cocky foreigner out on his ear—feeling even more ashamed that he should have been brought to this pass.

When the second guard returned, he brought a companion. The messanger received back the square of white silk and its contents with a formal bow, and then straightened to meet a pair of piercing blue eyes. "And if you got your safe passage?" the blue-eyed man asked softly.

"My master waits, my lord, to be conducted within. At the queen's word of protection."

"As once he gave his own," said Kieran with a strange smile.

The emissary, eyes hooded, bowed again in acquiescence. "That is so," he said.

"He has that word," Kieran said briskly, after a small hesitation. "If you will take me to him, or conduct him here, I will escort him to the queen myself."

"I will bear your message," said the other. "If you will wait, he will not be long."

Kieran's features lit up with a swift, appreciative smile. "He's here, in the keep? Well, I guess I'd expect no less. My compliments to your master; I will be expecting him."

The messenger tucked the silk package back into his pouch and asked with an eloquent glance for the return of his dagger. This was given him, at a signal from Kieran, and he slipped out into the gray day, pulling up the hood of his cloak. Kieran remained in the doorway, framed by the two guards who were doing their level best to stifle irresistible but, they suspected, entirely unhealthy curiosity. Presently two shapes, as muffled in dark cloaks as the first messenger had been, were seen to make their way slowly across the courtyard. As they approached, one of them drew off a glove made of white kidskin and presented a hand bearing a heavy golden signet.

Kieran offered a small bow. "Admit them," he said to the guards, who raised their spears to clear the way inside and tried hard to keep looking straight ahead. "This way, my lord," Kieran said neutrally to the man with the ring. The visitor entered, drawing off the other glove as he did so. His hands were long-fingered, strong, brown from a hot southern sun; as the right hand closed over the pair of gloves, slapping them lightly against the man's thigh, Kieran nodded slowly. "Your surgeons did a good job," he said.

There was a chuckle from inside the hood. "I must admit to having been astonished at that particular piece of advice, especially when I found out who had offered it. In some ways you were my enemy's enemy, Kieran Cullen, which should, according to folk wisdom, have made you my friend; but then, you have been no less of a thorn to me than you ever were to Sif. I never knew what you looked like—else I should not have been taken by surprise when your young queen turned up on my doorstep."

"Thank you," Kieran said, as though he had just been offered a compliment—which he had, although it took some finding in the elaborate wrapping in which it had been presented. The three of them, the two visitors still cloaked against prying eyes, had climbed a narrow side stair before gaining a broad carpeted corridor, and Kieran glanced back briefly. "My apologies for the back stairs," he said, "but from your manner of entry I take it you did not wish to be announced at the front door. If you will step in here, I'll have to ask you to do the same thing you once asked of me. Your weapons will be quite safe."

"I carry only these," his guest said, flinging back his cloak and presenting Kieran with a pair of slim daggers. Kieran bowed, accepting them, and then glanced beyond their owner at the second cowled figure, none other than the obsidian-eyed messenger who had delivered the signet.

"Your friend all but declared himself as a weapon in the guardroom."

"He is," Favrin Rashin said composedly. "But he is one loosed at my word, and I will not give that word, seeing as I come here under safe conduct. Still, if you will feel more comfortable, Qi'Dah can remain in here. With the other blades."

Kieran hesitated for a moment, remembering vividly his search for a secret weapon in Favrin's own chambers—the way he had looked at the wine flagon, expecting green fumes of poison to curl from its lip. His own analysis of Favrin: *He plays straight.* He squared his shoulders, reaching for trust. "That will not be necessary," he said at length. "But if he tries anything . . . by all the Gods, I can be faster than any death he deals, and I will be watching him."

Favrin crossed gazes with him as though they had been swords. "I know," he said softly.

After a moment Kieran disengaged, turning to open the inner door of the guardroom. "His Royal Highness, Favrin Rashin, King of Tath."

Inside the inner chamber, Anghara turned with a rustle of bruise-colored silk; it was a shade both subdued and oddly violent, appropriate for the funeral of a brother toward whom she was, even now, so dangerously ambivalent. She hadn't had time to change before receiving this unforeseen visitor.

But she *had* seen him coming, in the flames; and there was not, in the end, that much surprise at his presence. Merely his timing.

"I was waiting for you," she said calmly by way of greeting. "Though not in this guise. I didn't expect you to walk into Miranei on your own."

Favrin, momentarily glancing down to disengage the clasp of his cloak, looked up with a smile. "You walked into my palace. Our ancestors both wore the same crown; would you expect a prince, a king, to dare less?"

"Ah, but I had the goad of prophecy, and thought I could stop a war. What is your motivation? Simply to show me you dare even more, strolling in by day where I crept in twilight?"

"You wrong me," he exclaimed, and his voice would have been saccharine had it not been leavened with his usual irony. "Could I not have come here simply to see you again?"

"No, Favrin," Anghara said, looking him straight in the eye.

For a moment the eyes held, and then Favrin seemed to step out of a costume, changing from frivolity to a still and steady gravity, turning from jester prince to king before Kieran's eyes.

He turned to Kieran now. "With your permission," he said gravely, "I would speak with the queen alone."

They had done so before, after all, in Algira. It had been much more dangerous there. This was Anghara's own territory, loyal men were within earshot . . . Still, there was a twinge of something. Something that wasn't entirely concerned with safety . . .

Kieran swept his eyelashes down, veiling his eyes for a moment until he had them under control. Then he looked up, at Anghara. She nodded, once.

"I will be in the antechamber if you require anything," he said. "My lord." He swept the obeisance due a king, and retired, followed by the silent dark man Favrin had called Qi'-Dah . . . to wait, as he had waited so many times.

Inside the royal chambers, Anghara, now the hostess as Favrin had once been host, turned toward a small rosewood table. "Wine?" she asked, reaching for a decanter. "I regret I do not have that subtle southern vintage you offered me; our northern wines are much more . . . robust."

Favrin came over to inspect the offering. "Thank you," he said. "I'm sure I'll find it . . . invigorating."

"Will you sit?" she said, gesturing gracefully once he had relieved her of his wine goblet.

Favrin subsided into the nearest chair. He had yet to take his eyes from her face; it was as though he were steeling himself to do it at any moment, and couldn't quite gather enough courage. He did, at length, glancing abruptly and deeply down into the wine as if he were searching for something at the bottom of the goblet.

"I was expecting you to come with an army," Anghara said softly, breaking the silence.

"And if I had . . ."

"You might well be sitting on my throne," Anghara said, brutally honest. "There was little chance we could have stood against you."

"You defeated Sif, and his reputation was just as formidable as my own."

"We didn't defeat Sif," Anghara said bleakly. "*Sif* defeated Sif. He learned something he couldn't live with, and he died. That was the end of it."

"I was at the burial," Favrin said, an odd light in his eyes. "That was quite a gift, for a defeated enemy."

"He was Kir Hama. He had been king," Anghara said in swift response. "He was my brother," she added after a pause, looking away, into the flames. "And also . . . I did what I did partly because of Senena."

"The little queen?" Favrin said, honestly surprised. "She was reputed to be such a fey, shy thing . . . like a mountain fawn."

"What do you know of Senena?" Anghara countered, her turn to be surprised.

Favrin offered a lopsided grin. "Enough," he said. "Did you think my father had no spies inside the court at Miranei?"

"Do you?" Anghara said, giving him a strange look.

Favrin laughed. "If I had, it would hardly be politic to tell you, now, would it. In any event, I don't deal in gossip. I have ears, not spies. I know Sif had ears in Algira. It was a game we were playing, his House and mine. If I had been asked, perhaps I would have changed the rules—but it was my father's game. But then he died, and you happened. And that changed everything."

Anghara put her wine goblet down. "Favrin, what are you doing here?"

"What would you say if I told you I came to ask you once again to marry me?" He grinned at her expression. "I wouldn't believe it either. Too glib, even for me. And besides . . ."

His eyes strayed for an instant toward the door to the anteroom, and Anghara found herself blushing at nothing at all—at the things he hadn't said. It was a moment of silence more eloquent than any speech, so solid and enveloping they found themselves struggling with a compulsion not to break it, to leave the balloon unpacked and its contents safely sequestered away. But then Favrin, who had never lacked courage, took control—resorting once again to his favorite subterfuge.

"Would it break your heart, young queen, to hear I am about to wed another?" he said, his voice vivid with hidden laughter.

But Anghara too had recovered. "With all those women in the royal *kaiss* . . ."

"They were my father's," Favrin said, dismissing a dozen exotic women with a languid hand. "Besides, they were too old—some were old enough to be my mother. One of them *was* my mother." He grinned. "I retired them all. I'm starting fresh. There will be time to collect, later. I need an heir, and to get an heir I need a wedded queen. And there are women who do not scorn the prospect of ruling a royal *kaiss*."

"Congratulations," Anghara said dryly. But she couldn't help a wide grin, and in another moment they were both laughing.

"So I got over my broken heart and found myself a lady fair . . . and even as we speak the succession to the throne of Tath appears to be concluded," Favrin said lightly. "If it proves to be a boy she carries, I will wed her; and she becomes queen. If a girl—well, she will always be senior in the *kaiss*. Whatever happens, she will be the mother of my first-born. And there is time enough for sons, to inherit."

Entirely unintentionally, Favrin had loosed a barb he had never meant to wound with. The matter of succession hadn't crossed Anghara's mind, but now it reared suddenly like a cobra, and just as poisonous. Sif had died without an heir, and her own kingdom needed a promise of tomorrow; she was the last Kir Hama.

Favrin saw the gray eyes cloud over, and pulled back. "But I didn't come to speak of that," he said. "I came to speak of kingdoms."

Anghara folded her hands in her lap. "So. Your errand seems much the same as mine to you."

"Indeed," he said. His blue eyes met hers, squarely, steady and earnest. "I want peace between us."

"It was never a war of Roisinan's making," she said, choosing her words carefully.

He rose from his chair, somewhat violently. "I didn't come here to surrender!" he said, and his voice was sharp.

"No, not with an heir on the way." She came to stand beside him by the hearth, where he stared at the leaping flames. "What, then?" she asked, and her voice was quiet and steady. "Believe me, I would have liked this to be at less cost to royal pride."

"I know," he said. They were standing very close; their eyes met and locked once again. Favrin almost reached out to cup her cheek in his palm; he had forgotten, by all the Gods, the effect this chit's eyes had on him.

"But however you phrase it, if you give up what you covet and I hold, then it is surrender. And there is nothing I can do to soften it," Anghara said, her voice low and intense. "I cannot offer you a title, because you already hold one almost as high as my own; I cannot offer you land, because you already hold what was part of Roisinan. I cannot offer you a sop by way of royal marriage, because . . ."

"Because there is only you to offer, and we have been down that road." He found the strength somewhere for his old devil-may-care grin. "But what a pair we would have made, you and I! And yet—if I ride into your court and waive my claim to the Throne Under the Mountain, I would be vilified in my own country for yielding at a woman's feet that which could not be won from me on the battlefield." He paused to drag a hand through his hair in a gesture of unguarded and utter weariness. "I am so tired of wars . . . Even though my claim to Miranei's throne is twice that of any of my ancestors, I am tired of trying to catch this questing beast . . ."

"Twice?" Anghara said.

Favrin glanced at her sharply, and then gave her a longer, more speculative look. "You really don't know?"

"Know what?"

"Sit down," he said, his eyes snapping with what was at once humor mixed with an odd touch of spite. "There's a gap in your knowledge of your family's history I am about to remedy."

Anghara was hardly minded to obey such a peremptory command but somehow found herself seated nonetheless, with her wine goblet in her hand and Favrin leaning over her in a fashion that would have made Kieran instantly reach for his sword.

"You may remember my father took a northern woman to wife," Favrin said. "Do you know where she came from? Who she was?"

"I know her name—Isel Valdarian," Anghara said. "So much was written. What has this got to do with . . ."

Favrin was shaking his head. "Then it was *written* wrong. When Father came to Miranei to wed her, she might have been raised as the natural daughter of Ras Valdarian, one-time councillor and court lord—but that was only to save Ras Valdarian's wife from scandal. He had accepted the child and retired from court, trying to salvage what he could—for Isel's mother had aspired to much greater heights than Ras could ever hope to gain."

Anghara was flooded with sudden shocked comprehension. Favrin saw her blanch and nodded. "I see you've made the connection. You and I are cousins, Anghara, Queen of Roisinan. My mother was half-sister to Red Dynan himself."

"But then . . . if I were gone . . . you are the rightful heir to Roisinan," Anghara said slowly. "You're the closest thing to a Kir Hama king a Rashin could ever aspire to be!"

Favrin couldn't help a shout of laughter. "That was a backhanded compliment if ever I heard one," he said. "I should apologize; I never meant to use my mother as a weapon. I merely wished . . ."

"But with this . . . the whole war . . . you could have dangled your mother's identity in Roisinan, and your father might have gained more than he ever did by . . ."

"My father never knew the truth," Favrin said. "He picked the one woman who could bring him what he wanted—and never knew what he had. He married Ras Valdarian's daughter, not King Connach Kir Hama's. If he had known, don't you think he would have used that knowledge ruthlessly?"

"But you know."

Favrin shrugged. "My mother had a wooden box she had brought from home as a new bride," he said. "After Father's death, when she was moving to new quarters, a porter allowed a load to slip from his grasp and tumble down a flight of stairs. It smashed apart at my feet, and when I bent to pick it up I saw the coat of arms emblazoned beneath the shattered inlay. What would my mother be doing with a concealed Kir Hama trinket? And so I sent a man, and he found the truth. I have known of this only a few weeks longer than you."

"And armed with this truth, you come to Miranei alone, and offer it to me freely?"

He hesitated, far from certain of his own motives. Hers had been an eminently reasonable question, and he found he had no answer. "I only . . ."

"But don't you see?" Anghara interrupted. "You've just given us a way out of an impossible situation!"

"I have?" Favrin turned to look at her, his face blank.

"You've given yourself an honorable way to end the war," Anghara said, clutching at his arm.

"Easy," he murmured, covering the small hand with one of his own. "What are you thinking, witchling?"

She grinned at him. "If Dynan was Sighted, then Isel probably was—and that means you're probably a latent witchling yourself. And watch that heir of yours." Favrin grimaced, acknowledging a hit. "I am to be crowned soon. What if I announce by royal proclaimation, that while I remain childless, you are my appointed heir?"

His blank stare turned to complete stupefaction. "What?"

"Don't you want to be heir to Roisinan?"

"I've been an heir for too long," Favrin answered, with unaccustomed savagery. "Besides, there will be those who advocate that, as Heir Apparent, all I have to do is get rid of you and have it all."

"Are you content with Tath?"

"Yes, damn it!" It was wrenched from him, an admission he found hard to make—at least to her, who held by birthright a realm so much richer and greater than his own.

"Then take it. Hold it."

"And when you get yourself another heir?"

"You're still king in Algira," Anghara said. Her voice was level, but she was blushing furiously. "And you remain second in line."

Favrin grinned, a dangerous grin completely at odds with the mirth dancing in his eyes. "More people to clear away," he quipped.

Anghara did a double take, and then laughed. "You don't mean that—you're strong enough to control your barons. When you sneaked into Miranei . . . I don't suppose you thought to bring a robe worthy of a queen's heir?"

"Sif was supposed to have had a coronation to outshine all coronations," Anghara said conversationally. "Check."

"He had to," Favrin said. He bent over the game board, frowning. "He had to reinforce the idea of Dynan's son as the conquering hero, to erase the memories of his entry into Miranei, your supposed death, and Queen Rima's bloody end. There was a lot for people to forget. He had to provide a spectacle." Favrin grinned wolfishly, and swept Anghara's attacking piece off the board with a languidly graceful hand. "And check," he said. "I believe I win again."

Anghara scowled. "Your southern games," she said. "They're so devious . . . and it takes too long."

"For a people so used to decisive action, you northerners certainly run in tighter circles than a cat chasing its own tail. We lazy southerners might take longer to get to somewhere, but at least we know where we're going."

Anghara looked about to leap to the defense of her folk and her realm, but after a moment had the grace to laugh. Sif's funeral was ten days gone, and this evening with Favrin was her first chance to escape the endless rounds of coronation plans. It seemed to take up all her time; she was constantly enmeshed in endless meetings. Those in charge of organizing the ceremony couldn't agree on the smallest of things. The representatives of Roisinan's various Gods had each presented a different version of the most auspicious date, and everyone had their own ideas on the guest list. It all seemed to need Anghara's input and approval; and she had already complained that she didn't see why she had to be measured four times for the creation of a single set of coronation robes. Favrin had waited in seclusion, with commendable patience, but eventually had Kieran ask the young queen if she could spare another hour or two for him. Anghara came, expecting almost anything except this—a quiet evening by the fire, playing a southern board game called *sheh.* She lost every game, but the purpose of the meeting had been achieved—she had relaxed and unwound, and was able to talk about the goings-on at court with a modicum of good humor.

Favrin now began putting the game pieces away into their box. "Are things anywhere near a conclusion?"

"The Gods seem to have put their heads together and come up with a mutually acceptable date," Anghara said.

"Being?"

She grimaced. "My birthday."

"That's still a good few weeks from now," Favrin said, glancing up. "I hadn't anticipated being away from home quite that long."

"I'm a little relieved," Anghara admitted after a short pause, reaching for a cup half-full of cooling mulled wine.

"Leave that, here's a fresh cup," Favrin said, playing host to her here in his quarters. "Relieved? Why?"

"It gives me a little extra time," she said enigmatically, accepting the cup from his hand. He cocked an eloquent eyebrow at her, and she smiled over the rim as she took a sip. "They want a spectacle to outdo Sif's. The delay gives them time to think about gracing the occasion with royalty . . ."

Favrin bowed elaborately from the waist, and Anghara laughed.

"No, they don't even know about you yet. They wish to invite Aise Aymerin of Shaymir."

"And what do you think of that scheme?"

"I should have proposed it myself," Anghara said. "I've never met him, but he holds a realm only a mountain pass from Miranei. He knew better than to go to war about it, but he didn't come to Sif's coronation, and as far as I know he has shunned both travel and trade with Roisinan for most of Sif's reign; inviting him now, and seeing what his response will be, might be instructive."

"But you've got your own guest list," Favrin said, raising his glass in a toast, "one you haven't told anyone about."

She shot him a startled look. "How did you know about that?"

Favrin looked equally startled. "I meant myself," he said. "Why, who else did you have in mind?"

"Nobody knows of this yet . . . nobody but Kieran," she said. "But guests whom no one will expect to see are already on their way."

Favrih knew nothing of the friends Anghara had left in Kheldrin; he frowned as he tried to recollect someone who might fit Anghara's mysterious description—anyone. Finally he had to confess himself beaten. "All right, what have you done?" he asked.

"They're going to remember this coronation," was all she would say.

Favrin returned to an earlier topic. "If this new date is agreed, I might return to Algira. I can easily get back in time for the ceremony, and I think I ought to see to a few things in Tath."

"And check up on your lady?" Anghara asked slyly.

"That too," Favrin said with a grin. "She will be nowhere near her time, but I should like to know how the babe is doing. I would be more useful at home than staying in these rooms, opulent as they are, until your birthday." He looked at her thoughtfully for a moment. "You'll still only be eighteen," he said. "I keep forgetting how young you really are."

Anghara reached out to tug at a lock of his hair. "I see no gray in this," she said.

"The difference is I have been leading armies since I was a boy."

"There are many ways of growing up," Anghara said gravely.

He bowed his head, hiding a smile. "I meant no slight," he said. "Well, then, if that is agreed—Qi'Dah and I will leave in the morning. I will be back in plenty of time for the coronation . . . if you are still of a mind to make your pronouncement."

"Aye, Heir of Roisinan," Anghara said.

Favrin looked away with a snort of laughter, and Anghara rose gracefully to her feet. "Tomorrow will be another heavy day. Thank you for tonight; I will look forward to your safe return."

"Your other guests should be arriving shortly to fill the gap I shall be leaving," said Favrin, almost too carelessly, a glint in his eye.

But Anghara wasn't taking the bait. "They should," she agreed blithely.

And they did. They were simply there one day, Anghara's folk out of Kheldrin, as though they had materialized in the keep out of the thin mountain air. They came prepared for the cold winter winds of Miranei in unaccustomed robes of *shevah* fur and cloaks of tanned *haval'la* hides. They remained almost invisible, for all that—Anghara all but ran one old friend down in the corridor without even glancing at him. He stood unobtrusively to one side, removing himself from her path, and addressed her retreating back. One name, enough to stop her in her tracks, for it was spoken in a language—and a voice—which brought a hot breath of the desert into the cold stone walls of the keep.

"Greetings, ai'Bre'hinnah," al'Tamar said quietly.

Anghara turned, very slowly, her eyes stinging with unexpected tears. "Welcome," she said, holding out her hands to him. "Oh, be welcome here!"

"I thought that you would be different here in Sheriha'drin," al'Tamar said after a pause. "But I should have known—it is the nature of the Changer to remain constant."

"Oh, but I have changed," Anghara said, smiling gently.

While at first al'Tamar looked as though he might disagree, he veiled his eyes beneath golden lashes and offered a deep desert bow in acknowledgment.

"Where are the others?" Anghara said eagerly.

"They are waiting. Come, I will take you to them."

Fewer had come than Anghara had anticipated. A bare handful. First to greet her was al'Jezraal, himself changeless, his hair perhaps a shade more gold but otherwise looking exactly the same as he had when she had gone to him one morning, a lifetime ago, with a dream of vision. He greeted her with the same grave courtesy.

"Much has happened since you walked in Harim Khajir'i'id," he said. "It gladdens my heart to see you well, and coming into your own. Gul Khaima has told us this would be so. But I bear sad tidings as well. One whom you would have wished to see is feeling her age at last, and is no longer fit to travel. I fear she will not leave her hai'r again."

ai'Jihaar . . .

From somewhere far away an echo of an answer came to the name Anghara's mind had flung into the distance.

There are some things even a Changer cannot do twice. I received my life at your hands when you faced al'Khur in the Khar'i'id, but al'Khur is gone. You are all that is left, and you cannot fight yourself. I have had a good life—and it is my hour at last. Be well, be happy, child of my heart . . .

"I would have wished her to see . . ." Anghara murmured.

"She does not have to be present to see," said another familiar voice, and there was a flash of gold as ai'Farra ma'Sayyed stepped forward to greet Anghara. The priestess's eyes were softer than her usual wont, mirroring an odd compassion. She wore the full regalia of her rank, eschewing the comfort of a warm cloak; she was resplendent in gold robes and a mass of *say'yin'en,* with the black dagger of her office still hanging in its sheath at her waist. She gave a crooked smile as she saw Anghara glance at it.

"They are really gone, the Old Gods," she said, "but there are still times when I try and speak to them in the old ways. They never answer . . . but perhaps, one day, they will return. But we are no longer in Kheldrin, and there are other Gods here. I will not invoke any unwelcome presence in this land."

"They are not gone, *an'sen'thar,*" al'Tamar said unexpectedly. "They are within us, as all things are that pass away. Nothing is ever gone completely. The Old Gods sleep, until their time comes round again."

He had gained the gold, by Anghara's own hand; now he was equal to the priestess from whose notice his family had once schemed and plotted to hide him. He met her eyes squarely, and it was ai'Farra who looked away—al'Tamar was no longer a boy.

News of the Kheldrini party's arrival spread quickly—Anghara's guests were shown to their chambers by wide-eyed servants who wasted no time in passing on the gossip. The Kheldrini had been given the freedom of the keep, but the naked curiosity of the court played its part in limiting that freedom. For too long Miranei's experience of Kheldrini had run to no more than the occasional trader bearing silk and dun'en and the grooms who remained behind to care for the desert horses. While it was immediately obvious that Anghara's guests belonged to neither class, there were those in the court who thought of all "Khelsies" as nothing more than servants. However, it was impossible to reduce al'-Jezraal's calm dignity and ai'Farra's high pride to that estate. It was hard to say which did the more damage—those who came to fawn and to stare, or those who preferred to keep their distance, knowing that their high-handed approach would antagonize both the Kheldrini and the queen. A few tried genuine overtures, but by and large the visitors found it was better to keep to themselves, giving the court at Miranei time to adjust to their presence.

Anghara was aware of the situation, and knew the Kheldrini preferred to avoid close encounters with the locals. She fully realized some of this had perhaps been unavoidable, given the ancient gulf that had existed between the two lands. But bridging that gap was part of the reason why the Kheldrini had been invited. She had been given the chance to become part of their world; she wanted them to be part of her own. She made a deliberate effort to extricate herself from some of her more onerous duties and spend more time with them. When al'Jezraal declined an offer to tour the battlements of the keep on the grounds that the cold air irritated his lungs, ai'Farra elected to stay with the *Sa'id.* But al'Tamar said he would go, and found himself alone with Anghara on the ramparts, leaning on the embrasures and looking up into tier upon tier of snow-clad mountains.

"On the night we first met, you spoke of a lake somewhere in the mountains, close to your castle, a lake fed by a hot spring."

"I remember," said Anghara slowly. She recalled the incredulous joy she felt when the palm trees of Fihra Hai'r, the First Oasis of Kadun Khajir'i'id, swam into sight against the desert sunset after the living, brooding heat of the Black Desert; the sensuous feeling of precious water running down her parched skin. And the memory, in that arid place, of Miranei's mountain lake—the place where she had bathed in summers past in pools warmed by hot springs. And then there had been three riders in the night . . .

"I should like to see it," al'Tamar said, breaking into her reverie.

"Now?" Anghara said, taken aback. "It's winter; even if the passage was not already made difficult by the first snows, there would be little to see in this season."

"Water is holy in any season."

"But in winter," Anghara repeated, perplexed.

"I should like to see it," he repeated. "I still cannot believe I am in Sheriha'drin—but you have brought me here, as you promised. And now, in this strange country . . . it is the Way, it is that which you term Sight, that spurs me to see this lake. There is something there that is important, but which I still cannot wholly see . . ."

Anghara stared at him for a moment, and then nodded. "All right, I'll see what can be done. If I arrange a party . . ."

"As few as possible," al'Tamar said, quietly but with a steady purpose. "I would prefer us to go alone, but if that is not practical . . ."

"It is not," said Anghara with an affectionate smile. "The court would be scandalized at the very thought. And then, in an emergency, you wouldn't have the first idea what to do in the snow." She paused, giving al'Tamar a long, measuring glance. "Very well," she acquiesced. "I'm curious. Besides, if my life has taught me anything at all it is never to stand in the way of Sight. We will take one with us, and he is a friend."

"Your Kieran?"

She had been about to deny possession, her mood flippant, but something in al'Tamar's voice made her swallow the impulse. Instead, she simply nodded.

"That will do," al'Tamar said, very seriously. "You have seen very little of him recently."

"Not much," she said grudgingly. "I never seem to have a moment to myself—I'm cornered by someone as soon as I set foot outside my chambers, and it all seems important . . ."

"He is not with you at these times?"

She shook her head miserably. She had come to depend heavily on Kieran and the Taurin twins; Kieran had responsibilities of his own, largely as a result of her own expectations. Their paths didn't cross nearly as often as Anghara would have liked; it wasn't as though he had been avoiding her, but he seemed to be on duty more often than not, and even when he wasn't, there was always something else needing his attention.

"Then it is good that he is to come," said al'Tamar. "How far to this lake?"

"In summer, perhaps just over an hour—an easy ride. Now . . . I don't know. And we must keep an eye on the weather. I don't want to be caught on the mountain with a storm front moving in."

"I leave it with you, who knows this land," he said. "When you give the word, I will be ready."

Kieran, who had long since learned never to be surprised by anything to do with Anghara, took the news of the trip with commendable equanimity. Anghara would be the guide of this little expedition, but Kieran would be the leader, and he made preparations.

The mountains above Miranei were in Anghara's blood, and she knew their moods; but it was Kieran who finally called a time for their departure, taking advantage of a break in the weather. For winter, it was warm; but nights were icy in the mountains, and there was a bite of that in the air as they left the keep in torchlight, in the pearly half-light of dawn. Somewhat ludicrously, al'Tamar wore a desert veil drawn across the lower half of his face. The cold air which hurt his throat when he breathed was likely to be even harsher the higher they climbed. Kieran and Anghara's unfettered breath curled in visible plumes before their faces.

"This is crazy," Kieran kept muttering, well into the first hour of their ride. The sun had risen and was glinting on the broad white expanses glimpsed through the trees above them. "The snow must be waist deep in places—al'Tamar, are you sure you wouldn't rather come back after snowmelt? This place is not a transient hai'r that might vanish; this water would be here for you to see in the spring."

"Spring would be too late."

"Too late for what?" Kieran asked.

"For you," al'Tamar replied, turning an inscrutable face on him, golden eyes glinting beneath a hood of white fox fur.

Kieran gave him a long, troubled look. This sounded like Sight, and Kieran knew well his measure against things that were of Sight; besides, the comment cut rather close to the bone. The choices before him had come to the point of painful decisions, and al'Tamar sounded as though he knew all about the thoughts that kept Kieran awake during the long winter nights.

The path was difficult but not impassable for the horses, and once he had satisfied himself that the venture lay within the realms of safe possibility Kieran relaxed and started enjoying the crisp winter day. The sky was an intense blue, and stretches of virgin snow marked only by deer tracks glittered in the bright sunshine. The air was still chilled, but the day had warmed a little, and al'Tamar had dropped his veil. They rode single file and Anghara, riding in the van, smiled occasionally as she sometimes turned around to glance at the deeply fascinated expression on al'Tamar's face. It reminded her vividly of what her own must have looked like when al'-Jezraal's little caravan had started out for the place which was to become Gul Khaima. For Anghara the desert had been unimaginable; for al'Tamar, it was these endless expanses of shimmering white mountainside, threaded with the deep green of the pines beneath their loads of snow. Once they surprised a snow-hare fastidiously cleaning its long ears by their path; it gave a frightened snort and darted behind a tree.

"A snow *shevah,*" al'Tamar chuckled. "Our worlds are not so different."

They made good time, given the season, reaching their goal by mid-morning. Most of the lake was frozen, except for one small area free of ice, where still water mirrored the winter-blue sky.

"There," Anghara said, pointing at the pool when they had approached to within a few paces of it. "That's the hot pool. We used to . . ."

"Wait," al'Tamar lifted a hand for silence. "Listen. It is coming."

The other two glanced at one another, then up at the wooded slope above the lake. The woods seemed silent, and quite deserted. "I can't hear . . ." Anghara began, in a whisper, but Kieran suddenly reached over to touch her wrist and then pointed into the trees.

"It's a white hind," he murmured.

It was hard to believe al'Tamar could have heard this beast. She moved with a delicate grace, silently, placing her feet with careful precision in the hock-deep snow. Ignoring the three riders only a few feet away, the hind made her way to the edge of the open water and bent her head to drink. Then she looked up, tilted her head slightly in their direction as if in greeting, gave them a slow and measuring regal glance, then turned to go.

Kieran suddenly tensed as the white silence was broken by a low growl from amongst the trees. He saw the hind pause, uncertain, dainty ears flickering, trying to place the danger . . . but it was too late even as she turned. A huge wolf with great glowing golden eyes and a pelt matted with heavy whiter fur was already springing at the transfixed white hind, open jaws reaching for the throat . . . *"No!"*

In the same instant, Anghara saw the white hind walking away, her head bowed as if in pain—and as she did, she began to slowly fade. She could glimpse the trees of the woods beyond through the hind's body as if through a fine curtain. Fading to a pale wraith . . . *"No!"*

It was a cry torn from both throats in the same instant. Kieran was already reaching for his sword as his horse leaped forward under the pressure of his knees. The weapon stuck, and Kieran, knowing every second counted, let it go and drew his dagger, leaping recklessly off the horse to intercept the wolf. He saw its red jaws coming closer, and raised an instinctive hand to ward it off.

Anghara was already off her own horse, running toward the ghost deer on foot with her hands stretched out before her.

She was expecting to feel soft white fur; he was braced for the impact of teeth and bone. Instead, reaching hands met one another, palm against palm, fingers instinctively interlacing, and the images they had tried to touch shivered and melted away. The great wolf was gone, but beneath the bridge of two joined hands the white hind lifted a head which was no longer gentle and delicate but great and proud, bearing a set of mighty antlers which gleamed dull gold and looked much like a crown. The stag turned its royal head to gaze for a long moment first at Anghara, then at Kieran. Then it walked away, very slowly, toward the woods. Kieran thought he glimpsed a gray shadow which might have been all that remained of his wolf slink into the trees.

They watched the stag go, dazed, and then, slowly, met each other's eyes over the interlaced fingers of their linked hands.

"You wish to leave Miranei," a voice said suddenly, seeming to come from a great distance. Kieran looked up sharply at al'Tamar.

"You wish to leave, Kieran," al'Tamar repeated, "and what you each saw was what would happen to the other if you do. Without you, Anghara would face the wolves alone—and there would be wolves, for she would be eighteen, a crowned queen, and in need of an heir to consolidate her throne. There are always men eager to make of their seed a royal dynasty. And if Kieran left you now, Anghara, and sought his fortune in places distant and strange, the memory of Miranei and the woman who remained would eat at him until he faded away, like the white hind. But together . . ."

"Leave?" Anghara said, gray eyes wide. "Why?"

His fingers tightened on hers a fraction, and then he dropped her hand. "How can I stay?"

"I thought it was over now. I thought the separations were over, that we could stay together," she whispered.

He turned to face her at last, his pain clear in his eyes. "Anghara," he said desperately, "I love you. It might have started when we were children together, and I cared for you as a sister—but I have long known that it wasn't a sister for whom I searched all those years. And now—now you are queen, about to be crowned, and I cannot claim you."

"But you were the one who helped put me here," she said.

"I know," he said. "But that is where you belong."

"And where do you belong?"

He looked away. "I don't know," he said bleakly. "I am a miner's son, a soldier, a knight; by force of circumstance I led a band of men to fight against a tyrant. I wasn't born to a crown, like you. And that crown has narrowed your choices. Queens don't . . ."

"*This* queen does," she said, reaching to lightly trace the line of his jaw.

His hand had leapt to hers, with what intention it was not immediately clear—even he didn't know whether he wanted to take her fingers from his face or hold them there. Her eyes, as she looked into his own, were full of tears.

"You have always been there for me, with me," she whispered. "When Sif stole my soul, you carried it for me. Where were my eyes, that I didn't see? Kieran . . . how could I possibly go on without you?"

He had known her in many guises. There had been young

Brynna, who had won his affection; there had been the winged goddess, ai' Bre'hinnah, he himself had helped create. There had been a royal heiress, the last in the Kir Hama line. But in between, always and ever, she had been Anghara, part of his heart, part of his soul. Now, here, in the white winter morning in the mountains of Miranei, she was nobody's but his own.

You are the hawk I will send to search for her . . .

Are you her qu'mar?

I see a great love almost lost . . . and battles gained . . . and then . . . and then a crown.

Ask what you will of me, for it has always been yours . . .

She will need a friend . . .

So be it.

He looked down into her eyes, and smiled.

Glossary

Some names and concepts originating from different parts of the world have been annotated for ease of placement, i.e., Kheldrin (K); Roisinan (R); Shaymir (S); Tath (T).

Adamo Taurin: twin to Charo Taurin (q.v.), Chella's younger sons, later important to Anghara's cause

afrit (fem. afritah; pl. afrit'in) (K): evil desert spirit

-ah (K): feminine suffix added to words to indicate feminine gender; sometimes occurs within a word (as in havallah), implying an inherent grace, beauty, or feminine quality in the concept the word describes

ai'Bre'hinnah (K): secret name of the Kheldrini Goddess known as the Changer of Days, the Ender of Ages; the goddess has had male incarnations before (al'Bre'hin); each incarnation, when it appears in the world, has broken the world in some way and remade it in his or her own image

ai'Dhya (K): Kheldrini Goddess, Lady of the Winds

ai'Farra ma'Sayyed: Keeper of Records in Al'haria, chief an'sen'thar of the Al'haria Tower

ai'Jihaar ma'Hariff: blind Kheldrini priestess (see an'sen'thar); Anghara's friend and teacher

ai'Lan (K): the Sun Goddess; similar to Roisinan's Avanna except that her worship is more bloodthirsty—can offer great power and protection in return for the right sacrifice

ai'Raisa: young gray-robed sen'thar who remains as the voice of the oracle of Gul Khaima (q.v.)
ai'Ramia: bride of al'Tamar
Aise Aymerin: Prince of Shaymir
ai'Shahn, often known as ai'Shahn al'Sheriha (K): messenger of the Gods, Water Spirit; a holy entity
Akka! (K): ki'thar command: Go!
Algira (T): a beautiful canal city in Tath, once pride of Roisinan; a training center for the Sighted, similar to Castle Bresse, lies nearby
Al'haria: red city of Kheldrin, place where the Records are kept, city of scholars, priestesses and craftsmen
al'Jezraal ma'Hariff: Lord of Al'haria, brother of ai'Jihaar
al'Khur (K): Lord of Death and also of dreams that come in the Little Death that is sleep, he manifests as half-man, half-desert vulture
al'Shehyr ma'Hariff: son of al'Jezraal
al'Tamar ma Hariff: nephew of al'Jezraal, son of his brother; sen'thar-gifted, but untrained because he is heir to an important Hariff silver mine
al'Zaan, Sa'id-ma'sihai (K): al'Zaan the One-Eyed, Lord of the Empty Places, Kheldrin's chief God, cannot be worshipped in any confined place, only in the open
Anghara Kir Hama (ma'Hariff): Princess of Roisinan and an'sen'thar of Kheldrin, heiress of Red Dynan whose crown was usurped by her half-brother Sif when their rather died in the battle at Ronval River, powerfully Sighted, events turn around her
Ansen Taurin: Anghara's oldest foster brother and cousin, son of her aunt, Chella
an'sen'thar (pl. an'sen'en'thari)(K): wearer of the gold robe in the sen'thar priesdy caste of Kheldrin; high priestess, used both as noun and form of address
arad (K): south

Arad Khajir'i'id: the Southern Desert, sometimes also known as Mal'ghaim Khajir'i'id (q.v.)

ari'i'd (K): desert

Ar'i'id Sam'mara: Desert Gate, name given to the canyon which forms the passage between Kheldrin's coastal plain and Arad Khajir'i'd

Avanna of the Towers (R): Lady of the Lights, Roisinan's harvest goddess, patron of all that is bright, glowing and growing; she created the sun, the moon, and the stars, and blesses everything grown under them; Roisinani infants are presented to the Gods within her towers

Aymer: capital of Shaymir, semi-desert independent principality to the north of Roisinan, origin of the Aymer Harp (q.v.)

Aymer harp: a difficult Shaymiri musical instrument.

Beit el'Sihaya (K): the Empty Quarter, from beit (geographic quarter) + sihaya (empty)

Beku: city of Kheldrin

Bodmer Forest: large forest in the heart of Roisinan

Bran: new god in Roisinan, born in the fires of Anghara's metamorphosis into the Changer, after her return to Roisinan to claim her crown

Brandar Pass: mountain passage from Roisinan into Shaymir through the range behind Miranei

Bresse: see Castle Bresse

Brynna Kelen: Anghara Kir Hama's alter ego, the name by which she was known at Cascin

burnouse (K): a head covering and desert veil against sand and heat

Calabra: main port city or Roisinan, at the mouth of the River Tanassa

Cascin (Cascin of the Wells): the ancestral manor of Anghara's mother Rima, Anghara's sanctuary in the first years of her exile, held by Lord Lyme, married to Rima's sister, Chella

Castle Bresse (R): training school for the Sighted, where Anghara first learns a measure of control over her gifts; levelled by Sif in the first stroke of his vicious campaign against Sight

Cerdiad (R): Midsummer Harvest Feast with connotations of ancient fertility rites when harvested fields and the harvest are blessed on midsummer's eve by a priestess of Avanna of the Towers, patron goddess of the feast and the rest of the night given over to celebrations; romantic superstitions practiced by girls wanting to know who they will marry are commonly associated with this night

Chanoch (R): The Festival of New Fire; on the night of the first full moon of winter all hearth fires are extinguished and every hearth scraped clean and the head of the family goes to the temple of Kerun to obtain a handful of blessed Temple Embers with which to kindle a new fire on the old hearth; very holy festival, under the auspices of Kerun the Horned One

Charo Taurin: twin to Adamo Taurin, Chella's younger sons, Anghara's foster-brother

cheta (R): a military company in the Roisinani army

chud! (K): a Kheldrini exclamation of frustration

colhot (S): a cross between a lion and a coyote—a lazy but dangerous predator of the Shaymir desert

Colwen: Sif's first queen, put aside because she could not give him an heir

dan (fem: dan'ah) (K): alone

Dances (R): circles of huge hewn stones with an ancient and often feared power; there are four in Roisinan: in the hills by the river Tanassa, in the middle of the central plain in Shaymir, on the edge of the Vallen Fen in

Tath, and in the Mabin Islands (now largely ruined); the three mainland Dances are more or less intact, their original purpose or ancient builders unknown; there may once have been more, as there are solitary stones in other places, which exude something of the power of the Dances, known as Standing Stones (q.v.); both Dances and Standing Stones are avoided at night, and especially during the high festivals as they are believed to be the haunt of spirits

desert sage (S): a herb with a sharp, bittersweet scent which grows in the Shaymir desert

diamondskin (K): lethally poisonous lizard found in the Khari'i'd; no antidote to its poison, which is almost instantly fatal; gray with black diamond-shaped markings on the skin

djellaba (K): desert cloak

Duerin Rashin: King of Tath; scion of the Rashin Clan who once wrested the Throne under the Mountain (q.v.) from the legitimate Kir Hama incumbent—Duerin's ancestor failed, but Duerin still wants Roisinan, and went to war over it

dun (pl. dun'en) (K): desert horses, exported to Roisinan, Tath and Shaymir from Kheldrin but affordable only to the very rich; beautiful, graceful animals, faster than the wind, dun breeding is largely the province of the Sayyed clan

Dynan ("Red Dynan") Kir Hama: Anghara's father, King of Roisinan, killed in battle against Duerin Rashin of Tath

el'lah afrit (K): the Song of the Spirits; sometimes the desert sands sing in the evening, when the air cools rapidly; often this warns of an advancing storm, or heralds a change in the weather; this often brings a feeling of discomfort, hence the laying of blame on evil spirits

Empty Quarter, the: see Beit el'Sihaya

Favrin Rashin: Prince of Algira, son of Duerin Rashin of Tath
Feor: ex-priest of both Kerun and Nual, Sighted tutor in the household of Cascin who grooms Anghara Kir Hama for queenship
Fihra Hai'r (K): literally, The First Oasis; the name given to the first water-bearing oasis a traveller encounters upon emerging from the Khar'i'id—depending on which direction the voyager is travelling in, the same oasis can also be known as Shod Hai'r (q.v.)
Fodrun: Dynan's Second General, on whom leadership devolves during the Battle of Ronval when Dynan is killed and Kalas, the First General, so badly wounded as to be permanently disabled; seeing the conflict ahead, he chooses to support Sif Kir Hama, Dynah's grown son, in preference to his legitimate heiress, the nine-year-old Anghara, but not without some misgiving; also known as Fodrun Kingmaker
fram'man (pl. fram'man'en) (K): stranger

Gheat Freicadan(R): The Guardian of the Gates (see Kerun, Glas Coil)
Glas Coil (R): Grey Wood, something along the lines of the Celtic Tir'na'n'Og, land of youth—Roisinani believe in it as an afterlife
Gul Khaima (K): Oracle Anghara raises in Kheldrin, on a stone pillar by the sea; human oracle
Gul Qara (K): the ancient oracle in the Empty Quarter, which gives Anghara the name of its successor

had'das (K): species of fish caught off the coast of Kheldrin
Hai! Hai haddari! (K): an expression of amazement or admiration
hai'r (pi. hai'r'en) (K): oasis
Hama dan ar'i'id (K): Kheldrini adage: "You're never alone in the desert"

han (R): inn, as in Halas Han (Inn on the river Hal)
hari: red (Kadun Khajir'i'id is sometimes known as Harim Khaijir'i'id)
Hariff: Powerful Kheldrini clan or family involved with silver mining; root hari, red, may indicate they originated in the Red Desert
Harim Khajir'i'id: the Red Desert (see Kadun Khajir'i'id)
haval'la or ha'vallah (pl. haval'len) (K): desert gazelle

iman'et (K): enter; response to sa'hari
iri'sah (K): hot desert wind
Isel Valdarian: mother of Favrin Rashin

jin'aaz spiders (K): large desert spiders who cocoon their larvae in a chrysalis of silk; Kheldrini use silkseekers (q.v.) to find jin'aaz spider lairs and extract this silk; much prized and very expensive—one of the main Kheldrini exports

kadun (K): north
Kadun Khajir'i'id: the Northern Desert; sometimes also known as Harim Khajir'i'id (q.v.)
kaiss (T): (pron. kish; the ss sound is like the English sh): a broad concept covering the women's quarters in Tath culture, a semi-purdah to which married women withdraw and from the confines of which high-born women are married, from father's kaiss to husband's (q.v. Silk Curtain)
kaissan (T): (pl. kaissen; pron. kishan, kishen) (T): a woman living in a kaiss
kaissar (T) (pron. kishar): castrates who rule the kaiss
Kalas: Dynan's First General, badly wounded at the Battle of Ronval
Keda Cullen: sister to Kieran Cullen, gifted musician from Shaymir

Kerun (R): Roisinani god, also known as The Horned One; he is the Guardian of the Gates to Glas Coil (q.v.). He is the avatar responsible for death and life through death. He is the God of War, of Destruction, of Catastrophe; he must be propitiated at the beginning of every new venture, lest he claim it for his own; his sacrifices often involve gold, and he has his own incense, manufactured specially by the priesthood

khaf (K): strong brewed desert beverage, similar to coffee

khai'san (K): hot storm wind of the desert

khajir (K): sand

khar (K): stone

Khar'i'id: black stone desert of Kheldrin; deadly, hot and poisonous, but also strange and generous with occasional obscure and hermetic gifts; sometimes known as Rah'honim Ar'i'id, the Black Desert

kharkhajir (K): coarse sand, rock-sand

Kheldrin: Land of Twilight, from khel (dark, twilight) + drin (land, country); desert country to the west of Roisinan, for many ages closed to outsiders, except for a tiny cultivated strip in the lee of the coastal mountains, where Roisinani visit the trade port of Sa'alah to bargain for silk, esoteric drugs or dun'en

khi'tai (K): medicinal plant; reduces fevers, acts as a painkiller for minor aches; can be used as an anesthetic in conjunction with lais (q.v.)

Kieran Cullen: a Shaymiri boy, Anghara's foster-brother, already fostering at Cascin manor when she is sent there; later knighted in battle

ki'thar (pl. ki'thar'en) (K): camels, desert animal of Kheldrin

lais (K): squat, ill-favored small bush found largely in Kadun Khajir'i'id; lais tea, soporific, slightly opiate and possibly addictive, can be made either from the whole leaf or from dried leaf powder; sometimes exported from Kheldrin into Roisinan and Tath; well known in Shaymir, where the plant is named selba

mal'gha (K): yellow (Arad Khajir'i'id is sometimes known as Mal'ghaim Khajir'i'id)

Melsyr: son of First General Kalas, whose wounding at the battle of Ronval where Red Dynan fell gave command of his armies to Second General Fodrun

Miranei: Roisinan's capital and the King's Keep, a powerful fortress never taken by force—and only a few times by treachery

Morgan of Bresse: the head of the Sisterhood of Bresse, she chose death by martyrdom at Sif's hand in the knowledge that this would hasten the return of Sight to Roisinan's persecuted people

Nual (R): Roisinani God of the Waters; not as powerful as Kerun and Avanna, but noteworthy because his temples are sanctuaries which cannot be breached; as some stay a lifetime Nual is sometimes also known as the God of Exile; his temples are always found near water, and anything found on or near the water has always been his; every shipwreck is salvaged by his priests; usually content with light offerings, a garland of flowers thrown into a river is pleasing to him; his priests are as simple as Kerun's are devious and plot-ridden, and dress in blue in honor of his element

omankhajir (K): soft sand

pa'ha (K): fermented juice of the pahria fruit

pahria palms (K): desert palm bearing large, hard-shelled fruit, soft inside, juicy but tart—an acquired taste; sometimes cultivated, but usually grows wild in desert hai'r'en (q.v.)

qu'mar (fem. qu'mar'ah; pl. qu'mar'en) (K): spouse, mate
Qi'Dah: Favrin Rashin's bodyguard

Rab'bat Rah'honim (K): the Black Drums, sometimes used by sen'en'thari to promote a trance-like state facilitating communications with the Gods
rah'hon (K): black
Rah'honim Ar'i'id (K): see Khar'i'id
Rashin: Tath clan of pretenders to the Roisinan throne
Rima of the Wells: Red Dynan's queen, Anghara's mother; dies during Sif's takeover, but is instrumental in saving Anghara from his avenging arm
Rochen: Kieran Cullen's friend and lieutenant in the rebel band fighting Sif in Anghara's name
Roisinan: Ancient land, lush with wood and field ruled by the Kir Hama dynasty until the Rashin clan from south Roisinan rose in revolt and took the throne in blood and rebellion, when the Kir Hama king, Connach Kir Hama, was killed in battle. His son Garen went first into a Nual Sanctuary and then took himself into the mountains, living as an outlaw while he gathered together his father's shattered army. He took his kingdom back two and half years later, in a successful summer campaign. The Rashin usurper was killed, but his son fled south into what had once been a province of Roisinan and declared it to be the independent kingdom of Tath with its capital at Algira, one of the jewels of Roisinan. Shaymir in the north, once also a part of Roisinan, chose to break away as well, but remained a vassal principality, with Garen Kir Hama as High King in Miranei. Tath was not rooted out, but subdued, and forced to pay tribute. The border, marked by the River Ronval, lies ever uneasy. Garen was succeeded by his son Connach II, and he by his son Dynan, known as the Red for his fiery hair, who in his turn would meet his death at Tath hands like his great-grandsire

Saa! (K): ki'thar command: Stop!
Sa'alah: main Kheldrini port and trade city on the coastal plain
Sabrah: Kheldrini clan or family
sa'hari (K): Are you there? (Equivalent to knocking on a door requesting permission to enter)
Sa'id (K): Lord
Sa'ila: stream close to Sa'alah, only running water in Kheldrin
saliha (K): thank you
salih'al'dayan (K): ritual of giving thanks to the gods
sarghat (K): a desert root, distinguished on the surface only by a pair of insignificant-looking leaves, easily overlooked by an inexpert traveller, it can sustain life for a long time
Say'ar'dun: Kheldrini city, stronghold of the Sayyed clan, capital of dun'en breeding country
Sayyed: Kheldrini clan or family
say'yin (pl. say'in'en) (K): necklace of rank, usually of sea amber and silver
sea amber: soft yellow globes found in the sea off Kheidrin—deep sea amber is much prized, but smaller and less regular pieces are often found washed up on the shoreline. Exported to Roisinani and Shaymir
se'i'din (K): Khar'i'id plant. A swift-acting poison, no known antidote (Roisinani name: rosebane)
Sen'en Dayr (K): gods willing
Senena Shailan: Sif's second queen
sen'thar (pl. sen'en'thari) (K): Kheldrini priestly caste, usually female, but sometimes also has male acolytes, none are devoted to a single god—all belong to all gods, and must know all their rituals; there are four levels: novice, white robe (first circle), gray robe (second circle) and gold robe (an'sen'en'thari, q.v.) (Linguistic roots: sen, or

sen'en, meaning God or deity, and thar, thari—meaning serve, server, service)

sessar (pl sessi; pron. seshar, seshi) (T): Tath coinage

Shadir: Kheldrini clan or family

Sheriha'drin (K): Kheldrini name for Roisinan, Land of Running Water

shevah (pl. shevah'en) (K): desert hare

Shod Hai'r (K): literally, the Last Oasis—the last place to find water before stepping into Khar'i'id; there are two, one in the Kadun and one in the Arad, depending from which direction the traveller is coming, both also known as Fihra Hai'r (q.v.)

Sif Kir Hama: Anghara's half brother, Red Dynan's son by a Clera; Sif seizes the throne when it is offered to him at the battle which saw the death of his father; he hates and fears Sight—seeing his own bastard birth due solely to the fact that Dynan chose to marry Rima (who was Sighted) instead of Clera (who was not); this plays a large role in his later violent campaign against Sight.

Sight (R): a power with roots in Second Sight, or prescience, granted to those born with it—usually but not exclusively women; current usage covers a multitude of gifts, some rare; a Sighted person may exhibit an ability to "eavesdrop" on conversations many miles away, move objects without touching them, dream true, establish when truth is being spoken (and, more importantly, when not), and sometimes the ability to control their immediate environment (invoke a rainstorm, for example); some of these gifts are taught to aspirant Sighted initiates at Castle Bresse and a similar establishment near Algira in Tath, run by a Sisterhood of Sighted women who have devoted their lives to teaching; largely accepted as a fact of life in individuals—many women are Sighted in Roisinan—but often feared in large numbers

Silk Curtain (T): a euphemism for the Tath custom of kaiss (q.v.), symbolic of a border beyond which women rule their own kingdoms; strange men entering another's kaiss and passing the Silk Curtain are living dangerously; while Tathi men like to believe they own a kaiss, it is not unknown for the kingdom to be ruled by a mind sequestered behind the Silk Curtain, with the so-called king no more than a mouthpiece

silkseeker: golden-yellow and white bird often used in Kheldrin to seek out nests of jin'aaz spiders (q.v.), on whose larvae it feeds; the larger adult jin'aaz, in turn, has been known to devour unwary silkseekers; wild silkseekers are seen as Gods' birds, and are protected

soul fire: aura around Sighted people, which is visible to others with Sight; of a shade specific and unique to every individual (Anghara's is gold, ai'Jihaar's is white, ai'-Farra's is crimson)

Standing Stones (R): huge, hewn, solitary stones, often but not always upright, scattered across Roisinan; thought to have been part of an ancient Dance; sometimes used as a focus for sacrifice by underground worshippers of the Old Gods and practitioners of black magic, but even without this connotation they possess power and are avoided at night, especially on major festivals like Cerdiad

tamman (R): originally a medicinal herbal concoction, but used ruthlessly by Sif in his anti-Sight pogroms when its concentrated form was shown to inhibit or suppress Sight; at this concentration, and at the dosage required to maintain this suppression, tamman has both serious side-effects and a potential for addiction

Tath: ancient province of Roisinan, now an independent kingdom ruled by the Rashin Clan, pretenders to the Throne Under the Mountain